# PERFECT TOAST

By

# Bob Bryant

# DEDICATION

*To the 50s.*

# CONTENTS

# ACKNOWLEDGMENTS

Thank you to my wife for her patience, my family for their encouragement, and to Steve Brown for his advice.

# PROLOGUE

If there is one thing for which the 1950s can be held responsible, it is the invention of the 'teenager' as we know him (and her) today. Forget all the horrors pondered at the time, the teenager was a phenomenon far more lethal and enduring than Reds under the bed, flying saucers or the Common Market put together. No longer just spotty imitations of the previous generation, these scallywags created their own sub-culture, adopting musical and sartorial preferences so far removed from the norms of the day that their parents must have believed Martians had, indeed, colonised the Earth. In less time than it takes to pull on a pair of drainpipe trousers, and with the connivance of a voracious and burgeoning media, a New Order was establishing itself before the bemused eyes of an adult generation still reeling from World War 2.

So let us step back in time to those post-war days of innocence when 'PC' was a village copper who would clip your ear if you were cheeky; 'gay' was upper-class folk having a jolly time; and the 'web' was something your mother removed from the toilet window with a feather duster.

It is June 1959, less than six months since the Grim Reaper ended the brief life of Buddy Holly and, as this astonishing decade draws to a close with the advent of its final summer, Colin 'Brillo' Paddick and his pubescent peers contemplate a future of independence, rockin' round the clock, and endless sexual opportunity in the shimmering, mysterious world that beckons to them from the other side of their imminent GCE examinations.

But first, Brillo must navigate the turbulent waters of another summer season in his home town of Fayling, a jaded Victorian resort mouldering somewhere in the west country. A matter of weeks separate our hero from the freedom he so earnestly craves and, as he teeters on the very brink of his sixteenth birthday, the future lifts its skirt a little higher every day, teasing him recklessly. It's all out there for grabs.

Or so it would seem.


PERFECT TOAST BY BOB BRYANT

# CHAPTER 1

## *'Here Comes Summer' (Jerry Keller…1959)*

There is now no room for doubt. I am convinced that my mother is up to no good. No good at all. The stale smell of hanky-panky is in the air. Or is it my socks? Anyway, this is the third time this week that I've got in from a hard day's slog at school, sweating over revision for my imminent GCEs, only to be catapulted out the door again on a shopping errand. Yesterday it was:

"Colin, I need sausages for tea. Not those silly little chipolatas, mind, get the fat, pork ones."

Today it's:

"Right, young man, don't take off your shoes. I want you to pick up my groceries from the Co-op. And bring home the correct change this time."

When, I ask, was slavery abolished? Eighteen o-ruddy seven, by my reckoning. But here we are in nineteen fifty-nine and it's still flourishing in Fayling Bay.

I mean, what in the name of Satan has my mother been doing all day that prevents her pursuing her domestic duties? Sitting out on the back lawn smoking a fag and reading the 'Woman's Realm' most likely. Well I wish I could do the same instead of spending the entire day gawping at text-books and having a nervous breakdown worrying about how I'm going to bluff my way through the next two weeks of exams. And does anyone give a tinker's toss? Certainly not my mother who, for all I know, could be having an affair with the milk-man. Now there's a thought, and it might explain her extra special irrational behaviour of late. (I'd have to rule out the milk-man though because she was ranting on yesterday about the poor quality of his cream.)

So here I am struggling out of the Co-op with a hundredweight of assorted victuals in a cardboard box the size of Hampshire. I'm barely through the exit when that psychopath masquerading as the under-manager almost skewers me to death with the door bolt. OK, it's early closing day and he had to open up to let me collect the box, but you don't expect to be impaled for your trouble do you? I give him one of my sardonic Elvis lip-curling sneers through the plate-glass and he gives me the V-sign. I call that evens.

Oh, one thousand turds! There's that Wendy Matthews from 4B standing over at the bus stop. What a pair of utterly sumptuous breasts she is in possession of (or should that be: 'of which she is in possession'? Who cares? I won't pass English language anyway). The real point is, what sort of a prat do I look tottering about with this box of shopping? Hardly the height of 'hip' and 'cool', as Bill Haley might say. I toy briefly with the idea of dumping it in a waste bin as though it was some litter I had found. How would that appear? Yes... stupid! OK, I'll just place it down, light up a Senior Service, and lean back against the Co-op window trying to look like James Dean. Oh yeah, dressed in my Fayling Grammar School blazer?

Of all the inconvenient moments to see her and try to create a rakish impression! I bet Tommy Steele never has this problem. But, joy of joys, all is not dung, she gives me the eye and then backs it up with a saucy little smile. A green double-decker bus shudders to a halt, obliterating her from view until I catch sight of her again as she drops into a rear seat. Once more she glances my way and, to my intense gratification, she flexes her fingers in a very provocative bye-bye wave. Air-brakes hiss and the bus rumbles off, whisking her back to the bosom of her family at the West Cliffs Hotel. Oh, what transports of delight! I never would have believed the back end of a Leyland bus could look so desirable. I sweep up the box as though it was filled with goose down and make my way along the High Street, a spring in my step and a twitch in my trousers.

Fortunately, being a half-closing day and early in the season, my progress is unimpeded by dozy holidaymakers wandering the streets like the living dead and generally getting under your bloody feet. This is, of course, the calm before the storm; give it another month and it will be hell on Earth along here. A familiar voice hails me.

"Brillo!" I turn to see my mate Tulip trotting towards me.

Let me enlarge: Tulip is as close as you can get to being a best mate. Don't get me wrong, we really are close friends but, like all human beings (and I use the term cautiously in his case) we have our differences. For example, he tends to be a twat at all times whereas I save my finest twattery for the likes of Taff Davis, our sports master, and other walnut brains. Tulip's mother is Belgian and his dad is Dutch, which, I suppose, makes Tulip 'Belch'. And he does, frequently and with continental creativity. Christ only knows how his parents came to be living in Fayling but some very strange things happened during the war. Ask my mother!

"Wanna fag?" he calls, waving a packet of Weights.

I hold up my lighted ciggy. "No, I've got one 'ere."

"So's Van Gogh," he retorts.

See what I mean?

He grabs one side of the grocery box and we proceed into Balaclava Road and down the hill towards the sea-front. This is actually the opposite direction to my house but we fancy a quick recce for any incoming holiday crumpet. A little early I suppose but you never know. One thing you learn growing up in a coastal town is, even if you keep a steady girl stashed away on the back-burner for winter usage, you always keep your options open for the summer season.

"Done any physics revision?" asks Tulip.

"Yep. A bit."

"Understand any of it?"

"Nope."

"Me neither."

A period of deep silence follows during which we both contemplate our academic Armageddon, beginning with English Literature tomorrow. 'A merrier hour was never wasted there,' as old Puck might say. As for physics on Monday... forget it.

At this point in our doom-laden progress we notice that the town

Salvation Army Band (and so they should be) is currently occupying the hideously decorated bandstand, a decrepit circular podium with a wonky roof and looking much like a battered cupcake. From their elevated position they are kicking out the most unholy din. If God really had any mercy he'd send a thunderbolt down and fuse all their instruments.

Rows of dangerous deck-chairs are marshalled before the podium to accommodate the throngs of eager supporters naively expected to come and sing along to their ghastly efforts. The band plays on with a complete disregard for the musical score or the public's eardrums and this afternoon's performance has understandably tempted but a smattering of fans: a couple with two bored kids, one reading the Beano the other picking his nose; three old biddies with electric-blue hair and glossy Sunday-best hats all eating chips from one bag; and a seedy, bearded bloke who looks dead. Will Jesus save them today?

We flop into deckchairs and puff on our fags. Why, we wonder, would anyone want to listen to this junk now that Rock 'n' Roll has been invented? Where's the beat? Does it inspire us to leap up and jive with those blue-rinsed old dears over there? No, it does not. We endure a few more minutes of it then tap our fag-ash contemptuously into adjacent deckchairs and slink away.

"Got any loot?" enquires Tulip. I nervously fondle my mother's three and sixpence change in my pocket.

"Why?"

Tulip steers me in the direction of 'Christie's Cavern', Fayling's gaudiest and loudest amusement arcade. Elvis is belting out 'Jailhouse Rock' as we swing in through the entrance, blinking at the riot of flashing lightbulbs. The place is empty but for a lone figure pumping a one-armed bandit over against the rear wall.

"Bugger!" mutters Tulip as he lowers his side of the grocery box to the floor. "That's the very machine I need. We'll have to wait until porky has finished."

"Pourquoi?" I ask, surprising myself on my spontaneous use of oral French. Tulip draws thoughtfully on his Senior Service.

"Because I've spent all winter priming that little beauty."

He glances around anxiously in case wee Jock Christie is within earshot. Jock is the proprietor and rules his fiefdom like a robber-baron. One whiff of skulduggery on the part of a punter, local, or holidaymaker, and you are out the door forever. Never mind the fact that Jock is barely four feet eleven and has a club-foot with one of those half-ton boots at the end of it; you upset him and the wrath of Glasgow will descend upon you. There are bruised bums the length and breadth of Britain who will testify to that. (Incidentally, quite why anyone would want to belong to a 'club' for deformed feet escapes me.)

We draw near to the rotund bloke playing the fruit machine of Tulip's desire. He's a big, ruddy-faced sod sporting a very expensive beer belly and a very cheap undersize flannel suit that lends him a likeness to Oliver Hardy. He's shovelling shillings into the slot and mumbling in a strange dialect each time the cherries cascade past the window making him a poorer man. Tulip, by contrast, is glowing with joy and audibly whispering, "Yeah," at the sight of each lost game. Ollie glowers at him constantly and finally his patience snaps.

"Cut it out, tha little booger!" he barks.

Tulip fixes him with a blank stare, something for which he has a marvellous talent. Ask anyone, especially our wondrous headmaster, the Count. 'De Groot' he often says, 'There are moments when I wonder if you will ever make your mark in the world, and for the remainder of the time, I am convinced you will not.' Nobody has quite worked out what he means but Tulip is adamant that it's a compliment.

"Tek a hike down t'beach or summat," continues Ollie, pressing yet another bob into the slot.

As Tulip and I have no idea what he's talking about we both now gaze at him blankly. This seems to irritate him even more and he suddenly jerks a large, nicotine-stained thumb over his shoulder.

"Bloody scram!" he growls.

That's more like it, we got the gist of that. At least he's reverted to passable English and not that gibberish he was using previously. I think he's from the North which explains a lot. I doubt he's quite got used to things down here, like inside lavatories and kids not wearing clogs. The ever-adaptable Tulip turns on his Belch charm.

"Forgive us," he beams inanely. "Ve are foreigners and do not understand your customs."

He then clicks his heels and gives a shallow bow, much in the manner of an SS officer.

Oliver squints at the badges on our blazers and snorts scornfully. He seems a trifle unnerved by Tulip's rather mad grin. He frowns and brings his florid features closer to Tulip.

"'Aven't I seen your face somewhere else?" he enquires, as though some distasteful past encounter with a teenager has sprung to mind.

"No," smiles my idiotic friend. "It has always been here at ze front of my head."

Oliver's lips move but nothing emerges. I believe he has met his match in this verbal joust. He finally mouths some obscure Northern oath, pockets his remaining shillings, and waddles across to the next row of fruit-machines.

Tulip now swoops on the vacated one-armed bandit like a man possessed. He removes his blazer and drops it to the floor, rolls up his shirt sleeves and links his fingers, bending and plying them in a most business-like way. Next he turns his attention to the machine's outer casing. He runs his fingertips down its contours with the most sensual intimacy and then, gripping the chrome lever, begins to caress it in a way which can only be described as suggestive. (Watching his performance here, I have every confidence that the Count's sneering predictions for his future will be proved wrong. Far from ending up at the end of a dole queue or a rope, I see him making it to the very pinnacle of safe-cracking.) He tightens his fist and slides it down the lever, giving it just the vaguest hint of a pull. A faint click is detected from inside, followed by the merest whisper of a turning cog. He lowers his ear to the belly of the machine and places a finger slowly to his lips. To our right Oliver has been reduced to silent awe as he observes the master at work. The lever is eased down to about thirty degrees from the vertical and more eerie metallic pings and clunks tell him that all is going to plan. He nods ponderously and his knuckles turn white as he puts maximum pressure on the handle. I sense a moment of impending glory. BANG! Tulip brings the lever forward with one almighty jerk, almost giving me and old Ollie a heart attack. The machine appears to be having one too. It shudders wildly as its whole mechanism is thrown into a fit of activity. The little oblong window becomes a blur as the fruits spin at incredible speed, slowing gradually until they pass before our eyes as individual frames, teasing us with each revolution. I glance at Tulip and he's standing back with his hands in his pockets, grinning like a chimp. All of a sudden he leans forward, gives the bandit a good slap on the side and, Jesus on a Vespa, all the cherries click to a halt in a neat row! With one final reluctant convulsion, the machine spews out an avalanche of shillings, filling the tray within seconds until the coins spill into our welcoming palms. Laughing like drains, we throw handfuls of coins into the grocery box for safekeeping.

The effect on Ollie of this dastardly Southern knavery is electric! He storms across the gum-speckled floor like a pillaging Viking and stares with popping eyeballs at our glittering hoard of loot settling in among the Heinz bean tins and cornflake packets.

"Bloody little towrags!" he explodes. "Tha's tekken all me brass."

Being unfamiliar with the Norse tongue, Tulip and I merely nod and beam merrily. We gather up the stray currency from around Ollie's feet as though he were of no more significance than a tree or a phone-box. Over the speakers and drowning our giggling, Elvis begins singing 'I Got Stung'.

Our jubilant commotion has roused the attention of Jock Christie and he leaves his smoke-filled kiosk to hobble over to investigate. He stands over us (well, just!) as we scramble about on our hands and knees retrieving wayward shillings.

"What's to do here then, boys?" he growls. But Ollie is on a mission and his dander is well and truly up.

"I'll tell thee what's up," he roars. "These boogers 'ave stolen me 'ard earned 'oliday cash."

Jock peers up at Ollie, down at the Co-op treasure box, and lastly at the fruit machine. He's shrewd enough to guess that our little windfall is not entirely due to good fortune, but we are local lads and he relies on our patronage during the 'bookend' weeks each side of the peak season. He shifts the weight off his clumpy foot and stands slightly off the vertical, much in the manner of the leaning tower of Pisa.

"So who won this money?" he enquires.

"I did," says Tulip, deftly prising a silver coin from beneath the toe of Jock's grisly boot. "I won it fair and square after he left the machine."

"Fair and square ma bloody ass!" exclaims Ollie, his face turning a curious shade of purple and his piggy eyes burning bright with fury. He pulls out the lining of his pockets, leaving them waving like a pair of elephant ears. "See what they've left me... bloody nowt!"

We expect, from past experience, that Jock will simply ignore Ollie's theatrical tantrum, give us the thumb to leave, turn on his one good heel and head for his office. But not today. Events are beginning to spiral out of control. Ollie, in a display of wrath and Northern petulance, gives our grocery box a penalty kick. An ominous crunch is heard. He accompanies this provocative outrage with a torrent of oaths and insults directed at all teenagers living south of Worksop and all club-footed Glaswegians.

Well, frankly, Tulip and I care not a two-penny toss what he thinks of us as we've already secured the bulk of our ill-gotten gains and retired quietly to the fringes of the action to gloat. Jock, by contrast, has taken much of Ollie's abuse personally. Hardly surprising, as it was aimed directly at him, in particular phrases such as 'one-legged haggis-munching dwarf' and 'clump-footed Celtic freak'.

From our vantage point beside the little crane machine that always drops your prize just when you think you've secured it, we are privileged to witness what seems to be a paranormal event. Jock's head, just visible to us from our observation point, slowly rises in the air as if he is being raised on a hydraulic lift. His entire little body appears and hovers momentarily before dropping onto the top of a pinball machine. The glass surface shatters and lights flash on and off, illuminating the wee man like Piccadilly Circus. We bend our necks to get a better view and see Ollie's hands gripping Jock's shirt collar. Very dangerous. Ollie then releases his grip and stands back a pace, hands on hips, and probably about to give the naughty Caledonian a bloody good lecture on hospitality and fair business practice. But I am afraid Jock is not playing ball. Scottish pride and geometry are in the ascendant and, even with my very limited grasp of arcs, diameters, and isosceles triangles, I can calculate that Ollie's groin is within range of Jock's fearful club-foot. And the speed with which the great boot travels is a marvel of science and cobblery.

Spectacular, too, is the shriek of agony which issues from Ollie's gob as his testicles are crushed.

To our annoyance, a small band of nosey holidaymakers has gathered and, like a flock of vultures, they crane their scraggy necks, heads dipping and weaving to get a better gawp on the proceedings. One of 'em even slides in front of me completely blocking my view at the very moment when Jock locks his powerful little legs around the neck of the kneeling Ollie, so all I get is the gurgling sound coming from his throat.

All of a sudden, the crowd is disturbed by some officious prat who breast-strokes his way through to the edge of the action, followed by his mouse of a wife and ghastly little brat. He's a pale, skinny bloke with enough hair poking out of his nose to make a wig for his bald head. He clearly had a fit whilst dressing this morning because he's garbed out in a tweed jacket over a bright blue pullover and massive khaki shorts big enough to conceal Monty and the Eighth Army. Beige knee-high socks and Jesus sandals serve to complete the image of an utter pillock.

"What's going on here?" he calls imperiously.

The crowd shrugs. "It's a fight," says Tulip.

"To the death," I add for effect.

The Nutter's face turns the colour of his socks. "Well, we have to stop them!" he cries.

At this point, Ollie suddenly rises from his kneeling position and struggles upright... or as upright as is humanly possible with a deranged Scotsman sitting on your shoulders desperately trying to garrotte you with his wee leggies.

The throng gasps and, incredibly, one of the blue-rinse biddies begins to clap and, before you can say 'Death in the Afternoon', they're all applauding. Do they think this is a cabaret or something? I can assure you Ollie thinks otherwise because his chubby cheeks are turning blue since Jock inserted two fingers into the Yorkshire nose and is attempting to rip it off.

The spectators shout with excitement and roar their approval as Ollie and Jock twirl and lurch about bringing down fluorescent light fittings and tipping over pin-tables. Fortunately, I now have a clear view of the mayhem as the Nutter seems to have left the scene. But, no, to my bitter disappointment, here he is again at the head of a troop of Salvation Army bandsmen.

He marches towards us, his band of bewildered Soldiers of Jesus trailing behind him. Some of the silly buggers still have their instruments with them. Maybe they could provide a musical accompaniment to the carnage. And, as she steps back to make way for them, the old dear leading the applause seems to think so, too.

"Can you do 'The Old Rugged Cross' first?" she enquires of Bert Rumson, butcher of this parish and lousy sousaphonist.

Elbowing his way through the throng, the Nutter steps recklessly into the debris-strewn danger zone surrounding the two protagonists.

"Alright," he bawls. "Let's stop this before someone gets hurt!"

Understandably, Ollie and Jock are so preoccupied with trying to kill each other that they completely ignore his demand. In fact, his very presence seems to inflame their passions even more. Ollie is definitely trying to edge toward him and the look in his bloodshot eye would give anyone with half a brain the hint to retreat. But, of course, the Nutter does nothing of the sort and is immediately pole-axed by the protruding boot of Jock as he completes another revolution squatting rodeo-style on Ollie's shoulders.

As the Nutter hits the floor like a sack of spuds, Bert Rumson and his cohorts clearly have a quick decision to make: withdraw to regroup on the bandstand and continue playing as though nothing has happened, or pile in to break up the fight before the Nutter is mashed to mincemeat. Naturally, being good Christian souls, they make the wrong decision and enter the fray.

Things could hardly get better and Tulip and I climb onto an overturned pin-table to enjoy the spectacle. This is when we hear the unmistakable clamour of an approaching police car and, without exchanging a word, we gather up the battered box of groceries and high-tail it through the rear exit. Loath as we are to leave a front-row seat during such a once-in-a-lifetime extravaganza, there's no sense in risking being hauled in to explain our part in it all. Discretion, as some smarty-pants once observed, is the better part of valour.

We make our way up Arnhem Road and into the High Street, pausing in the doorway of Timothy White's to light up before tackling the steep incline of Tobruk Avenue. Quite why they had to build Fayling on the side of a bloody mountain has always puzzled me.

At the summit we turn right into Bannockburn Grove and enter the bus shelter for a breather. It's cool in here and the old wooden bench is good to stretch out on and reminisce on the thrilling spectacle just encountered at Christie's Cavern.

"The best bit, I reckon," reflects Tulip, "was when Jock booted Ollie in the nuts."

I ponder awhile, rewinding events in my head like a movie projector reel. "Dunno really. That bit was great, but how about when all those light fittings came down on the Nutter?" We both chuckle and agree that the whole performance was a classic.

Tulip climbs onto the bench and begins to stroke one of the roof beams. Maybe he's finally flipped his lid. I have no way of telling.

"There's a load of old carving up here," he announces. Is this supposed to rouse my interest? "From the war I'd say," he rambles on. "You know, G.I.s' stuff." I yawn loudly and light another Senior Service, offering him one on the chance that it will distract him from his historical investigations. He takes the ciggy but continues his waffling. "Listen to this. 'Elsie G does it for ten smokes'. Wow, I wonder where she lives."

"Probably at the local cemetery or an Old Folks' Home," I suggest.

"What about this, then? 'Staff Sergeant Capaldi is a faggot!'"

He erupts into laughter and slumps back to sit on the bench where he giggles uncontrollably for some time. Eventually he shuts up and gets to his feet to lean against the entrance. He blows a smoke ring out into the still air. "So what do you reckon a 'faggot' is, Brillo?"

"For Christ's sake," I snort, "you've been laughing about it for ten minutes!"

"Yeah, well I thought you knew what it meant."

"Well I don't," I admit grudgingly.

I have nothing further to add to this futile conversation so I turn my attention to retrieving Tulip's share of our winnings from the brown swamp which has formed at the bottom of my mother's grocery box. The bottle of HP sauce is in pieces and the contents have combined with the broken eggs and self-raising flour to form a very interesting burnt-umber coloured paste. I have serious doubts that my mother will appreciate it though, in spite of her delusions of being an artist. (I should mention here that I am obliged to live under the same roof as a number of her paintings, mostly scenes of Fayling Bay and the harbour. My god, they're hideous beyond belief! I almost puke when I see them. I do my best to avert my eyes as I pass down the hall but some ghastly fascination always draws my attention to them. I swear there's a kind of black magic or voodoo going on. They once burnt a witch up on Fayling Knoll and strange things go on up there at certain times of the year. Ask my mother.)

"Three pounds twelve and a French coin," I declare as I wipe egg yolk from the last shilling I can find in the box.

Tulip whistles. "Bloody hell! Plus we got to watch the show."

"Less my mother's three bob change," I add.

Before we get to divide the spoils, Tulip suddenly throws his ciggy to the floor and grinds it with his size eight. "Buggeration," he growls, "here comes that poncey actor bloke in his MG."

I am surprised and annoyed at Tulip's readiness to destroy a perfectly good Senior Service, particularly as I gave it to him.

"What poncey actor bloke?" I enquire.

"You know, the one that runs the Fayling Light Operatic thing. Quentin Lamont, that's his name. Big mate of the Count's."

Hearing this, I too grind out my fag. Although we are within a cat's whisker of escaping the clutches of our all-powerful headmaster, he still casts a dark shadow across our world. Underage smoking is a heinous crime in his book and almost carries the death penalty. Persistent offenders walk the streets with flailed arses.

I peer inquisitively around the entrance to get a glimpse of this Quentin Lamont. A bright red MGA Coupe is approaching driven by a scrawny-looking bloke with a large quiff of ginger hair darkened by nicotine. Both he and his female passenger are wearing sunglasses.

We withdraw into the shadows as they pass and my heart receives a tremendous jolt as I recognise my mother in the passenger seat! Dear God, all my worst fears have been realised… she's having an affair as I suspected. And with a weirdo like Quentin Lamont, a failed actor with nothing better to do than mince around directing the bloody 'Mikado' and getting his skinny ginger leg over married women. I am appalled at their brazen promiscuity. Haven't they had enough hanky-panky in their long lives already? God, my mother is pushing forty. How can she still enjoy all that groping and panting at her age?

A vision of the two of them swims into my turbulent imagination and I see them fumbling in the confined space of Lamont's car. His hand is sliding into the forbidden area of bare skin at the top of my mother's stocking and his slavering lips are wetting her cleavage as he attempts to undo her blouse with his teeth. What a disgusting bastard he is! And why doesn't she pull his tobacco-stained fingers from twanging at the elastic of her Marks and Sparks knickers? Has she no shame?

I'm now so angry I feel sick. I mean, what about Dad? Has he not been out all day sanding down architraves and undercoating window-sills to keep my mother in the lap of luxury? Does he deserve this betrayal of trust? Doesn't he take her every August without fail to visit her daft aunt in Minehead, even though he hates every minute of it? And how does she repay him? By rolling around half naked in some hidden glade with Basil bloody Rathbone!

Fortunately, Tulip is hiding in the darkest recess of the bus shelter as the car burbles past and thus has no idea of my mother's depravity... and I'm in no mind to tell him. I can just imagine the fun he'd have with that little gem of information.

Curiously, my black mood begins to wend a different path in my feverish brain. My fury is suddenly focussed almost solely on Lamont. After all, in the eyes of society, he is the seducer. It's always the bloke. I resolve, there and then, to kill Lamont at the earliest opportunity, following the completion of my GCE exams. Yes, that is clearly the answer. With Lamont the Seducer dead, maybe my mother will come to her senses. But how to do it? There's the rub. (Christ, I've been swotting too much Shakespeare.) Tamper with his MG's brakes? No, he could lose control and kill a pedestrian. Wendy even! Where would I be then? My mother, an unforgivable tart, Dad having a nervous breakdown, and my own sweet love lying under Lamont's front wheels. What a mess! I rack my brain for a better idea but, as expected, nothing comes up. You can never rely on your brain in an emergency, I've found this time and time again. When the chips are down and your back is up against the wall, don't expect any help from your frontal lobes. The only suggestions you'll get are 'Run away,' or, 'Poo your pants.'

Tulip brings me out of my dark reverie with the announcement that he's missed a romantic tryst with his latest flame, Anthea Tucker, who may still be waiting for him outside the Post Office as arranged.

"How you getting on with her?" I ask.

"Big tits," he replies with a grin. "Big teeth too, though," he adds.

I assume, then, that her overall score is about evens and, as she is still on his available list, the tits are holding their own against the teeth. Very much like Lamont's outrages with my mother.

"She's been helping me with my physics revision," he sighs. "Her being a genius and everything. She seems to enjoy it." I nod knowingly. Yes, I've heard that Anthea is a bit of a swot. In fact, she seems to be a regular know-it-all. I find such people hard to bear, especially when they're in the year below me and female.

"Nice legs," adds Tulip, as if reading my mind and attempting to boost Anthea's other attributes.

"Yeah," I nod. "Big teeth though." I can't allow her to get away scot-free.

We part company and go our separate ways: Tulip to his goofy girlfriend, and me to an uncertain future.

Deep in thought, I turn into Bannockburn Grove and head for the narrow, unsurfaced track that services the rear of Number Three where I am almost run down by a red MG emerging at breakneck speed. I am bowled to the ground as the wing-mirror whacks the grocery box, sending it spinning from my grasp into the road. I sit rubbing my bruised knee and muttering revengeful thoughts to myself. But as I rise and walk to retrieve the much-abused groceries, my brain quite surprisingly decides to side with me for a change. *Colin*, it whispers to me, *every cloud has a silver lining.*

*Yes,* I agree. *So what?*

*Well,* it continues, rather patronisingly, *you can use this near calamity to your advantage. You can now present Mama with her mangled vitals with a conscience as clear as crystal.*

Bingo! How true this is. Not only that, but with a bit of method acting thrown in, I can adopt the role of the injured party and, thus, kill two birds with one stone. I feel better already and, as I limp confidently through the back gate, my spirits are soaring, happy in the knowledge that Lamont will take the blame for everything. Oddly, now that he has inadvertently got me off the hook, I feel less disposed to kill him. Perhaps maiming him will do. I wonder if he would be such a reckless driver in a wheelchair?

Dad is removing his white overalls in the downstairs bog as I push open the back door. He's forbidden to enter the kitchen after work until he has discarded all evidence of his activities as a painter and decorator. I don't know why he puts up with it.

"Hello, Col," he says as I hobble past. "Hurt your leg?"

I grimace and nod, over-acting to just the required degree. You can't exceed the limit otherwise all your finest bullshitting becomes transparent and you lose the game. No, believe me, there's a fine line between an award-winning performance and total ham-acting. Fortunately, I think I have perfected the art. And let us not forget, to fool your old man you have to be flawless because he's been there himself!

I drop the soggy box onto the draining board and slump into a chair. To my dismay my mother is standing at the stove holding a spitting frying pan and has completely missed my dramatic entrance. Worse still, the sausages she is frying are kicking out such a noise that she will be unable to hear the account of my near-death experience at the hand of her boyfriend. She glances round and frowns at me.

"Where on earth have you been, Colin?" she squawks. "I've had to cook up these frozen sausages. Just listen to them." Right on cue the sausages enter a heightened phase of activity and one of them explodes noisily, speckling the wall with pink meat. My mother drops the pan to the stove and steps back with a cry.

"Oh, for heaven's sake!" she cries and Dad saunters over to dab at the wall with a dishcloth.

"Oh, leave it, Donald," she brays. "Just pass me another two eggs from the groceries."

Joy of joys, this is the instant I've been waiting for. The dreadful truth is about to erupt from the depths of the box and I will be immune from the fallout. These golden moments in life are to be savoured. They don't come round often.

Dad leans across and peers into the box, then straightens up and tweaks the bridge of his nose like he does when his eyes are tired. He looks in again and turns his head to me, his face a picture of amused bewilderment. I stand to state my cast-iron case but I am forced to raise my voice to out-do the sausages and this tends to give my voice a quality of barely controlled hysteria. I dig deep and call up my most outstanding acting talents.

"Yes, I'm sorry to report that the groceries were the victim of a hit-and-run driver in a red MG."

My mother has either failed to hear my plea of 'not guilty' or, perish the thought, she is an even better actor than me. She casually breaks an egg into the pan as though no reference whatsoever has been made to her sordid double life. This is a setback but I must push on before the initiative is lost. I roll up my trouser-leg to expose the bruised knee as Exhibit A.

"A red MG knocked me down right outside our house," I call above the frying-pan uproar. Dad tilts the box to enable my mother to view the loathsome slop within. She clasps her hand to her mouth with a stifled cry as though the box contained the severed head of John the Baptist. Dad asks if she heard my tale of woe, and shouldn't she take a look at my injured leg?

"Not now," she mumbles into her palm. Then, as if as an afterthought, "Does it hurt, Colin?"

"Only when I walk," I reply stoically.

I can't be sure whether I've scored a tactical victory or not. Certainly the destruction of her groceries has not prompted the expected tantrum. I have not been threatened with exile to my bedroom nor have there been menacing references to deductions from my meagre pocket money. However, as I watch her preparing our tea with her customary indifference to nutrition and presentation, I sense an air of defeat in her demeanour. I believe that I am, indeed, the victor.

Pulling my chair to the table, I tuck into charred sausage, rubberised egg, and lukewarm baked beans, all sitting reluctantly on a slice of under-done toast. Why is she incapable of making proper toast? Surely at her school it must have been Part One of Lesson One at Domestic Science class? Any girl failing it would, I imagine, have been dispatched to carpentry lessons.

Dad pours tea into my cup and gives me a wry grin. "You'll never guess what a hullabaloo I witnessed just now down the sea-front."

My stomach does a somersault and I choke on sausage. My god, has he twigged that Tulip and I were involved? That we started the whole thing going? He's a fairly lenient sort of bloke and always gives me the benefit of the doubt, but if my mother got wind of it, all hell would break loose!

Dad saws gallantly at one of his eggs, awaiting a response to his revelation, whilst my mother leans against the sink sipping a cup of tea, the trace of a frown lingering on her face.

"Well, what was it you saw, Don?"

Although she has clearly calmed down, I am aware of furtive little glances in my direction. Has she got hidden ammunition up her sleeve? Anxiety begins to gnaw at my bowels. Or is it these sausages? Either way I'm not the cocky little bugger I was a moment ago.

"Yes," says Dad, "I was driving past that amusement arcade, the one with the loud music. What's it called, Col?" This time I'm swallowing a mouthful of tea and, only with masterful self-control and creative plumbing, do I manage to avoid squirting the whole lot over the table.

"Uhhh... Christie's Cavern?"

"That's the one," nods Dad and starts to chuckle. "There were two police cars, an ambulance and a fire engine outside and..." he drops his knife and fork to the plate and begins to shake with laughter.

"Oh, for goodness sake, Donald, what was going on?" asks my mother irritably. He holds out his palms like he's checking for rain.

"I don't know, but there was a queue of Salvation Army bandsmen being bundled into the back of a Black Maria and a bloke with enormous shorts on a stretcher and..."

He is unable to continue for laughing. I make appropriate sounds of astonishment and regret at not having seen it for myself. For a brief moment, I swear Dad's tear-filled eyes lock onto me with one of those million-year-old looks, but he says nothing.

"Don't you have an exam tomorrow, Colin?" asks my mother as she turns to load dishes into the sink. I grunt ambiguously (a skill I have established over the past few months) and, scraping back my chair, I limp theatrically from the kitchen.

Ah, the sanctuary of the bedroom! A place where a young gentleman can get away from it all, become himself, abuse himself, and generally give the world two fingers. Within these four walls I have done my most accomplished thinking. In my head I have written chart-topping songs, trod a clear path into a brilliant future, and undressed certain young ladies on countless occasions. Not a bad record, I think you might agree, for a young stud of fifteen and eleven twelfths.

Strewth, it's hot in here! I unlatch the window and swing it open, but the air is as stale as a British Railways doughnut. I lean out and gaze idly round the back garden; it's so humid even the sparrows can't be bothered to squabble in the old apple tree. The only one enjoying it all is that perverted little bastard of a gnome forever dangling his fishing line in the pathetic garden pond my mother forced Dad to build. One of these days I'm going to drill a hole between the cheeks of his chubby terracotta ass and ram his fishing rod up it. That should take the smirk off his face.

I drop onto my bed and decide there's no point in putting it off any longer. I have to do some English Lit revision. Firstly, though, I must check on Wee William's progress. I lock the door and strip off completely, which, to be honest, is the most comfortable way to get anything done in this heat. Raising Wee William to full erection is but a momentary thing: I have only to imagine Wendy lying on the bed and he is up in a trice! Sadly, an inspection of both right and left profiles in the full-length wardrobe mirror reveals no significant improvement in his extent and a cursory measurement with my maths ruler bears this out. In the longitude stakes he remains a very modest player. Mind you, I'm no expert, so who's to say he couldn't hold his own in a competition? And I've never had any complaints from Caroline Dunn who is familiar with his every inch.

Reluctantly, I spill the text books from my duffel bag and flip through the grubby pages of 'A Midsummer Night's Dream'. Why, I ponder, am I being asked to study this play? Is it suitable material for a young man at the threshold of adulthood? As far as I can deduce, it's full to the brim with sex, drugs, and some very seedy goings on between fairies, transvestites, and people called Bottom. As for this character called 'Puck', well, I leave you to draw your own conclusions from his name alone! Yes, I think old Will was sailing very close to the wind when he penned this hotchpotch. Don't get me wrong, I enjoy a bit of smut as much as the next bloke. All I'm saying is, if I went around tipping old dears off their stools and frightening the maidens of the villagery, I'm bloody sure I'd get more than a slap on the back for being a knavish sprite.

Oh, sod it! I can't stand another minute of this. Swotting up has never been my cup of tea. I prefer a last-minute scan through the relevant points in my exercise books and hope to God some of it sinks in. It's not a guaranteed strategy but it's got me this far. Only time will tell if it gets me through the rest of my life.

I slide off my bed and grab my guitar, a semi-acoustic Framus in cherry red. Jet Harris plays the bass version in the Shadows. It cost me a whole summer holiday working for Dad plus birthday and Christmas money.

This is more like fun. I strum the chords to 'Teenager in Love', singing along in a high-pitched whisper in case older ears detect that I'm enjoying myself. I stand before the mirror with the guitar slung round my neck and attempt a few Elvis gyrations, curling up my top lip in the sexiest snarl I can muster and spreading my legs. I have to admit, it's not half bad and I resolve to try it out when our Rock group begins the summer season at the Half Moon Hotel. Naturally I won't be appearing stark naked as I am at present.

I lie back on the bed and sigh. It's been a long day and, in many ways, an eventful one. The highlight was seeing Wendy and getting the come-on. Surely that's what it meant, that cute little wave at the bus stop? I begin to have doubts. Suppose she was just flicking a fly from her face or, worse still, what if she was waving to that cretin in the Co-op! My god, that's it… she's got a crush on an older man. But how could she fancy that dim bugger? No, no, this is the work of the Devil, he's been out to get me for years, I'm convinced of it. Hold on, why the hell am I thinking like this? Is this what they call 'paranoia'? Get a grip on reality, Paddick, this has nothing to do with

Satan. It's just this infernal heat! Christ, I'm turning into Saunders of the River.

My eyelids have curiously turned to iron so I allow them to close and I am drawn into the shallows of a mellow slumber. Finally, I sink into deeper waters and the day's ingredients start to produce a broth of weird dreams. I am sitting in a deckchair watching helplessly as Lamont and Puck ravish my mother on the bandstand whilst the Salvation Army band, conducted by Jock Christie, accompany the outrage with an out-of-tune rendition of 'I Belong To Glasgow'. In a flash, I am standing on Fayling beach watching the Count leading a scantily clad Wendy away by the hand. She turns her head and blows me a kiss. I blink and she has transformed into Bottom, complete with ass's head. What does it all mean? Only old Freud could tell me that, I suppose. Maybe all these references to bottoms and asses have some connection to my lust for Wendy. The unconscious mind is a mysterious world. Ask Tulip.

# CHAPTER 2

## *'A Fool Such As I' (Elvis Presley...1959)*

As we file out from the gym with the other survivors of our English Lit exam, 'Clanger' Bell and I duck into the boys' shower room and escape out the side door into the bright mid-morning furnace of another June day. It's time for a well-earned fag in the privacy of the alley between the gym and the boiler room. Clanger opens his Shag baccy tin and offers me one of his finest roll-ups. We light up, inhale, and lean back against the wall to contemplate the past two hours of our valuable time on Earth spent trying to convey our thoughts on various chunks of England's rich literary heritage to some distant, whiskey-soaked academic who will probably strike our papers through with his quill and give us a 'D' Fail. Ah, sweet mystery of life, etcetera.

All of a sudden, we are horrified to see the boiler room door fly open and the gruesome figure of the Count appears on the top step. Quick as a flash, Clanger whips the cigarette from my lips and, as the Count turns to lock the door, he drops our smokes into his baccy tin and slides it into his blazer pocket. This is composure and dexterity beyond the call of duty.

The Count approaches and stands towering over us, his wolfish eyebrows lifted in mild surprise.

"Paddick and Bell," he says. "Well, well, well."

We pull away from the wall and clasp our hands behind our backs like a couple of deserters about to be shot. The Count addresses me first.

"So, Paddick, how do you think you did today?"

I shrug. "Not my strongest subject, sir," I mumble. What a bloody understatement that is; but I add a sweetener, as much for my own benefit as his. "I did attempt all the questions though."

His menacing smirk grows wider. "Quality is what we seek, Paddick, not quantity."

Strangely, I feel less intimidated by his presence than normal and, to my surprise, I lift my gaze to look him straight in the eye. Either I have summoned up undiscovered reservoirs of courage or, more likely, my subversive brain is on the rampage again and has decided we both need to commit suicide. Nevertheless, I hold my stare and notice that the ebony pupils of his eyes no longer carry the gliding bat shapes I usually see there. He seems a trifle taken aback by my boldness and the dark slash of his grimace contracts to its customary tight slit. His gaze turns to Clanger.

"And you, Bell. As an enthusiast, so I am told, of the written word, how did you fare?"

Clanger's response has since entered the folklore of our band of teenage heroes.

"I fink I done good, sir," he smiles amiably.

The Count stares at him, his brow suddenly etched by deep furrows. He seems temporarily muted by Clanger's grammatical atrocity. And I believe this to be our first triumph in our five long years of tyranny at his hands… because he says nothing. Instead, his right hand disappears inside his breast pocket and re-emerges clutching a folded sheet of A4 paper. He flicks it open and glances at it.

"Right, you two," he snaps, "I've got both of you down for the school-leavers eleven. Mr. Davis tells me you scrape into the team by the skin of your teeth."

The cunning swine! He's roasting us alive over the very dying embers of our school life. This is his final swipe at the few of us who have decided to take our chances in the big world and leave school. He views our premature escape as a personal affront to his vast ego and a failure by his lickspittle underlings to convince us of the merits of the sixth form. So, in order to squeeze the last drop of misery from such as we, he annually organises a staff versus school-leavers cricket match for our final day. To ensure complete annihilation of our team he will ship in ex sports teachers, cronies from Fayling Cricket Club, and his nephew who has apparently turned out for Somerset. Never in the history of the Final Day Match has the 'leavers' team been anywhere close to a draw, let alone a win. The whole idea is that we leave the school premises with our tails between our legs.

"Get yourselves up to the nets," he leers, "and join Mr. Davis and the others."

I gesture forlornly towards the gym where we have just spent two hours at the coal-face. My brain, of course, deserts me in my time of need, leaving me speechless. Even Clanger seems devoid of rebellion. The Count merely smiles and shakes his head. "To the nets," he instructs, then turns on his heel and sweeps away, his black gown billowing behind him in true vampire fashion. Strange, too, how he deliberately keeps to the shadows.

We head off towards the cricket nets, cursing everyone from Satan down the evolutionary tree to Taff Davis. Can this really be happening? Here we are, still reeling from the mental athletics of a GCE English Literature exam, and now forced to suffer the slings and arrows of outrageous bloody fortune at the hands of a partisan Welsh sports master! Surely there are laws against it? Did we fight the Second World War for nothing? Is this a land fit for heroes?

We hear his high-pitched Celtic piping from a hundred yards away.

"De-fend, boy, de-fend your wick-et!"

I mean, what gives a Welshman the right to teach us how to play cricket? Who invented the game, Dylan Bloody Thomas? No, we English did, along with football and rugby. What game was ever invented by a Welshman? Tossing the leek? Throwing the Welsh rare-bit? Throwing it up, more likely.

"Come on you two, get over yeuuh," trills Taff. "Yeuuh, catch this," he yells and tosses a compo practice ball our way. I wait until the last split-second before whipping out my right hand to catch it neatly. That will cheese him off. He's always trying to trick us like that.

Jeff Atyeo is in the nets doing his best to survive Billy Rice's demon bowling. Billy lives on a farm and hurls cricket balls like he throws stones at crows... to kill. They're usually full-tosses and aimed at the head. Billy has rendered most of the cricket-playing fifth-form unconscious in his time, a record he has much pride in (or should that be 'in which he has much pride'? Oh, for Christ's sake, English Lang is days away!). Sadly, Billy is no longer allowed to bowl for the First Eleven as all the other local school teams have blacklisted him as a menace to life and limb. This is a pity because the only match Fayling Grammar lost last season was one in which the umpire allowed the entire opposition's batting order to wear motorcycle helmets. Even then, Billy managed to break our own wicket-keeper's nose, so it wasn't a complete waste of time for him.

Clanger and I approach and Taff hails us. "Paddick, I want you in the nets when Atyeo has finished being a girl in there." He turns to Clanger. "And Bell."

"Sir?"

"Your pocket's on fire, boy."

Clanger shrieks, tears off his blazer, and stamps on the smouldering pocket. Taff makes no further comment. Nor should he, as he gets through thirty fags a day himself.

I notice that Jeff has been permitted to use Taff's own, personal, made-from-Welsh-willow cricket bat. A deep honour indeed, as Taff cares more for his bat than he does for his wife. (Mind you, if you saw his wife you'd understand. The bat is far more attractive.)

"Atyeo," bawls Taff. "You're like a three-legged wai-tress! Yeeuh, give me the bat, boy, and ob-serve." Jeff happily relinquishes the treasured bat and joins us as we sprawl about on the grass bank to 'ob-serve'. "Alright, Rice, send one down on the wick-et," calls Taff. And to our amazement, that's exactly what Billy delivers: a perfectly acceptable ball that hits the concrete about two yards before the stumps and which is blocked by Taff in text-book manner. This remarkable behaviour continues until Taff becomes bored with demonstrating his skills and summons Jeff back to the crease. But, as soon as Jeff takes up position, Billy turns into Attila the Hun again and sends down a rocket-propelled ball designed to take your head off. Poor old Jeff can only defend himself as best he can and, in doing so, takes the ball on his bare elbow. I never heard such a yell! He lets go of Taff's pride and joy in mid-swing and the sacred bat sails out of the roofless nets on a flight of unknown destination. In fact, it lands out in Jutland Grove, immediately in front of Tom Berry's coal lorry as it turns into the school with a ton of anthracite for the boiler. No doubt startled to see a bat flying in daylight, Tom brakes hard but the old Bedford skids on and reduces the Welsh artefact to firewood. Taff scampers to the fence and grips the wire netting, staring with disbelief at the pile of splintered willow. I walk over to him and address his trembling back.

"I think Atyeo may have a broken arm, Mr. Davis." There is no reply, just the faintest trace of mumbling. "We'd better get him down to the hospital," I say. Still no response, so I lean in a little closer. Taff is singing to himself as he gapes out into the road; a mournful whispered dirge. He's chanting the Welsh National Anthem. I draw away quietly and return to the crowd gathered around the writhing Jeff. He's swearing like a trooper so it can't be life-threatening. I turn my head to look back at Taff, a forlorn figure, still singing softly in his native tongue. In all fairness, it must be hard to lose your best friend, your mind, and to be Welsh, all on the same day.

Jeff whinges and complains all the way down the road towards Fayling Cottage Hospital and all through the time we await a response to our bell-pushing and general clamour at the reception desk. He finally shuts up when a nurse materialises and attempts to straighten his arm. Actually, that's about when he passes out, relieving us of his pitiful moaning and verbal tripe. The nurse gives us a supercilious sniff and tells us to bugger off.

We head on down into town and make for the 'Tarantella' coffee-bar. This is our favourite haunt and the only place in town whose juke-box carries every Buddy Holly record we know. As we enter, Momma Bonetti has her ample back towards us as she builds a pyramid of ice cream dishes against the wall-long mirror behind the counter. We have to shout our order above the racket of the Gaggia coffee machine. Why anyone would want to own such a thing is beyond me. Only Italians would cheerfully work alongside a steam-bomb. It's no surprise to me that they all bellow at each other and wave their arms about, it's the only way to be heard. They should've come at us with Gaggias in the war instead of tanks with four reverse gears.

"'Ello boys," beams Momma, "whatt-a you want today?"

We yell for two Cokes and I leave Clanger to settle the bill while I plug a couple of bob in the Rock-ola. The room fills with the splendid sound of Eddie Cochran's 'C'mon Everybody' and the world belongs to us again.

Clanger spots some reporter he knows from the Fayling Gazette sitting on his own. He says he's on a mission to join the local rag as a 'cub' reporter so he'll sit with him for a chat and see me tomorrow.

I thread my way between the tightly packed tables towards the rear of the café where the light is dim. In one of the alcove seats right at the back by the bogs, I spot Tulip with two others. He's laughing so he's either with someone we know or, just as likely, he's gone off his head. I stop dead in my tracks and my stomach does a somersault when I see that he's with Anthea and... yes, you've guessed, Wendy.

I am thrown into a state of complete disarray. I know I'm blushing and, oh no, my upper lip is beginning to perform an involuntary Elvis twitch. Please, dear, kind Jesus, don't do this to me! I know I'm not one of your most reverent disciples. I confess to numerous sins, but you know I'm just a simple rustic lad. I admit I swear too much and, yes, I smoke, tell disgusting jokes, and spend too much time in the company of Wee William but, after all, it was your own father who fashioned me from a lump of clay or something so it's not entirely my fault. All I crave is a moment's lip control.

Wendy looks up as I slide in next to her. Oh, dear God our heavenly father, our shoulders and thighs are actually touching! I swear there's electricity passing between us and now I wish I'd paid more attention during Arthur H. Wishart's physics lessons.

"Is there something the matter with your lip, Colin?" enquires Anthea, the Witch of Fayling.

What a cow she is! I'm tempted to ask if she'd like me to straighten up her goofy teeth with a slap around the chops, but that would not go down well in the present company. Instead, I stuff the frosty neck of my Coke bottle in my mouth and take a long swig. That's better and, thankfully, the twitch has moved from my lip and down to Wee William who is, of course, free to writhe and jerk to his heart's content in the unseen confines of his evil nest. Meanwhile, I am preoccupied with returning Wendy's gentle leg contact. It's a delicate but definite rubbing movement and it's set my pulse racing. A grin is spreading throughout my whole body. My liver is laughing, my tonsils are tittering, and my bowels are beaming. I am suddenly aware of Wendy's eyes on me and the caress of her breath on my cheeks as she speaks.

"How did your exam go, Colin?"

I can't speak! Can you believe it? I can't utter a word. Well, thank you so much, brain; just at the one critical moment in my life when I need you most, you have the bloody audacity to close down. Who the hell do you think you are, British Railways? I turn to gaze deep into the azure pools of my beloved's eyes, but can only wonder what a complete toss-pot I must appear to her: speechless, witless, and now afflicted by an excruciating pain in my foot! Some sod is standing on it with a stiletto-heel. I yelp with agony and look up to see the familiar features of Caroline Dunn. Ah, yes, the Devil is at work here once more. Does he never have a day off?

"Oh, sorry, Colin," smiles Caroline, "was that your foot?"

She wiggles across to a seat where she can observe me and sits, running her fingers up and down the neck of her Coke bottle in a very suggestive way. I must admit, she does look very tasty today, decked out in her trainee hairdresser's overall, crossing her shapely legs and letting one high-heeled shoe just dangle from her toe like that.

Anthea leans forward. "She's that Dunn girl from the council estate," she sneers, a little too loudly for my liking. "I bet she's a tart!"

"That's not fair, Anthea," retorts my gracious and generous love, springing to Caroline's defence. "You can't judge people just by where they live."

"That's absolutely true," pipes up Tulip. "I live over a fish and chip shop and I don't even like cod."

Maybe Anthea has a point after all.

One good thing to come out of all this distraction is that my brain has grudgingly agreed to resume normal service. I find I am able to speak once more so I spend a few minutes describing the afternoon's fracas at the cricket-nets. I also have the satisfaction of breaking the news to Tulip that he has been volunteered by Clanger and myself to join our school-leavers team for the ignominy awaiting us on our final school day. To my dismay, he greets the news with enthusiasm, a sure sign of Belch lunacy.

Turning my attention back to Wendy, we begin to discuss the world as we find it. To my delight we seem to share many likes and dislikes and touch on a variety of topics: our futures, our families, Cliff Richard's shirts… and why is that girl making faces at me?

Yes, what's got into Caroline? She knows perfectly well that our relationship is, well, a casual one at best. She just happens to have the available equipment I need to help me on my journey of exploration. You could describe her as a pit-stop rather than the complete road race. After all (and I disclose this in the strictest confidence) Colin 'Brillo' Paddick is still a virgin. Whether or not Caroline also retains her cherry is open to debate and remains her secret.

Anthea, having grown weary of Tulip's attempts to fondle her in full view of the British public and Momma Bonetti, announces that she has to leave and, girls being girls, Wendy insists on joining her. Happily, we have all made an arrangement to meet in the dunes on Saturday afternoon when the girls promise to help us with some physics revision. What a shame it's not a biology exam on Monday.

To my wonderment and joy Wendy pecks me on the cheek as she brushes past me to go. Oh, thank you Jesus, and you too Satan. I forgive you both for all the trouble you've caused me lately. I do understand that it can't be easy being the Most Good and the Most Evil. Why don't you both strike a balance somewhere in the middle like the rest of us? You could go out for a beer together.

Tulip stays for a few minutes until he's confident that Anthea is well into her long walk home on her own and then says he has to leave to peel potatoes for his dad's chip shop. So, it looks like I have no choice but to join Caroline.

"Oh, so you still remember me, then," she says sarcastically as I drop into the seat beside her.

To be frank, I'm not entirely sure why Caroline still pursues me as she does. After all, even though she's six months my junior, she's been working since April and, let's face it, she could pass for eighteen easily. Most birds her age have got boyfriends with cars or motorbikes. There must be something that keeps her hanging on. What the hell could it be? I'm not exactly a good catch financially… Being the owner of a used Framus guitar and a selection of fluorescent socks hardly catapults me into the millionaire bracket.

OK, I'll probably inherit a semi-detached house and a set of decorator's ladders one day, but would any female wait around for that? I think not. And as for Wee William's attributes, she's told me on more than one occasion that he could do better.

I explain to her that it's been a very trying day, what with a GCE exam and administering to Jeff's injured elbow, etcetera, and the last thing I need is a lecture. Besides, I reason, Anthea is Tulip's girlfriend and Wendy is Anthea's best friend so what's the problem?

"Toffee-nosed little bitches," she grumbles.

I swig the last dregs of my Coke and stand up. I have no intention of wasting my time listening to this feline twaddle so I tell her I'll see her around when she's in a kinder mood. The Gaggia fires a parting shot of steam as I pass the counter and Momma Bonetti waves 'ciao' with her tea-towel before returning to her ice cream dish mountain. What a strange world exists here beneath the roof of the 'Tarantella' coffee-bar.

My mind is a whirlpool of Wendy-thoughts as I climb up through the town towards home. The aroma of her lingers in my nostrils and I still feel the touch of her leg against mine, a sort of tingling sensation like a softly fading nettle sting. Is it biology, chemistry, or physics? How would I know? I'll probably fail all three. But the prospect of a Saturday afternoon in her company, scantily clad in the dunes, brings on a surge of adrenaline, most of it bound for Wee William for some reason. He really is a greedy little bugger. I shall be obliged to take him in hand shortly.

As I turn into our back lane I am once again appalled to see Lamont's MG parked jauntily against the grass verge. Is there no stopping the man? He's like a rutting stag. As for my mother, words fail me. One thing is now clear… Lamont must be dealt with.

Do you believe in fate and all that stuff? I never did, but I think I may have just been converted because, as I make my way past our woodshed, my eyes are drawn to what can only be described as a sign from King Arthur himself. Dad's wood-axe is embedded in the top of the chopping block, looking for all the world like Excalibur in the stone. This is very weird, but who am I to ignore destiny? If I have been chosen to rid the world of evildoers, rapists, and Lamont, then so be it. I seize the axe handle and, with one mighty pull, I release

Excalibur (Made in Sheffield) from his imprisonment and set forth to do the will of the gods.

But am I justified in actually killing Lamont? Is it, perhaps, a trifle harsh? Also, I'm not too sure how a jury would view the situation. Would they sympathise with a dutiful son who, on returning home to find his mother being ravished by a deranged ginger actor, smites him down? Or would the same twelve just men decide that a Rock 'n' Roll crazed teenage delinquent planting an axe in the head of a respectable thespian deserves nothing less than the death penalty. Well, what else could I expect from a bunch of twerps from a generation who thinks the Common Market will be a good thing!

But right now, I am a warrior; I am Hiawatha, stealthily entering the house with the axe in my right hand, removing my shoes at the kitchen door and progressing down the hall, one silent footfall following another. I hear voices coming from the front room. So here they are, caught in the act, the libertine and the floozy. Pressing my ear to the door panel, I immediately recoil at the conversation I am privy to (or should that be 'to which I am privy'? Oh, for God's sake, Brillo, give it a rest!). Lamont speaks.

"Oh, come now, Marjorie, it's not that long. Just open your mouth and take a deep breath."

"I don't know, Quentin," replies my mother, "I'm not sure I can get my tongue around it all."

I can scarcely believe my ears. If I'm not mistaken, there is an act of gross indecency taking place on the other side of this door. (Does the word 'fellatio' mean anything to you? Well, my cousin Phil, the National Service soldier, described it to me on his last leave from Germany and I can tell you, it's not something you'd describe to your granny. And to find that your own mother is indulging in it in your own front room is enough to turn a young man to seek counsel from the priesthood.) No, this is an insult too far. Honour is at stake and justice must be served; this is no time for the fainthearted. Seizing the door-handle I burst into the room to the simultaneous accompaniment of the opening piano chords to 'The Major-General's' song from 'The Pirates of Penzance'. My mother terminates her piano playing on a ghastly discord and Lamont leaps back in terror, scattering his music sheets across the floor. They stare at me in stunned silence as I stand riveted to the spot with bewilderment. There isn't a phallus in sight. Not the merest hint of hanky, let alone panky.

"What on earth are you doing with that dreadful chopper?" asks my mother flintily from her position on the piano-stool. What an incredible coincidence... that's exactly what I was going to ask *her*! Lamont has turned as white as a ginger person can and side-steps to position himself behind my mother, placing his trembling hands on her shoulders in a pathetic gesture of protection.

"Steady on, old chap," he quavers, eyeing the axe nervously.

"There's some ham in the fridge, Colin," continues my mother, as though being confronted by a barefooted, axe-wielding lunatic is an everyday occurrence. "Did your exam go well?"

I grunt, nod, and grunt again and, as I exit and slowly draw the door shut, I glimpse her eyeballs rising in despair.

For a good while, I stare gormlessly at the door panel, inches from my nose. My brain is grappling with the enormity of my humiliation and, true to form when faced with enormities and grapplings, the old grey matter turns to porridge. Eventually, even my brain grows bored with white gloss paint and I make my way aimlessly back down the hall, pausing beneath the accursed oil paintings just long enough to threaten them with the axe. But, unlike Lamont, they retain their colour.

With little idea how I got here, I find myself once more outside the woodshed and, stepping inside, find that its woody warmth gives me some comfort. I feel strength returning and the desire for vengeance oozing back. Yes, that's it, I need to take out my frustration on something. Normally it might be Tulip or Wee William who would bear the brunt of my wrath, but in view of this recent rout in the front room, an extra degree of violence is called for. OK, I may have just chickened out on actually murdering Lamont but nobody can prevent me performing a symbolic execution. And while I'm at it, I may as well finish off a couple of other pain in the asses (or should that be 'pains in the ass'? Oh, who cares?)

It doesn't take long for me to select three suitably shaped victims from Dad's neatly stacked logs. One is thin with a streak of yellowish bark; he shall be Lamont. Another is long and gnarled and will play the part of our revered headmaster, Septimus T. Darke, alias the

'Count'. Finally, a squat, knobbly little bastard is a perfect substitute for Taff Davis.

Lamont, being the prime object of my wrath and disgust, will die first. How he grovels and pleads forgiveness for his repulsive extravagances and liberties with my mother. He promises to change his ways but I know it's all an act, and a ham one at that. No, the curtain must fall on his final performance. The axe falls and splits him in two. Boy, it sends a thrill through me to be able to silence him forever! (I wonder if this charade is bringing out some dark side of my character that was previously hidden. Let's hope so.)

Next to be dragged whimpering to the block is the Count, infamous persecutor of boys, suspected vampire, and all-round bad egg. He immediately tries to trick me into clemency by offering to lose the forthcoming cricket match. I always knew he was corrupt at heart but this kind of wickedness is beyond the pale. Without further ado, I drive the blade down and end his terrible reign. It feels good.

Last, and of course least, is Taff. Although he's not in the same bestial league as the other two, I feel it's my duty to rid the world of him. After all, he is merely occupying a space that could better be filled by... well, let's not beat about the bush... an Englishman. In other words, his very existence can only be described as pointless, particularly as he can no longer even contribute a cricket bat to the common good. No, I'm sorry Taff, I know you've had a bad week but your whining is more than I can stand, and calling me a brainless English cretin is merely hastening your departure to the Land of your Fathers. I bring Excalibur down with a mighty swoop and he thuds sickeningly into Taff's chunky bulk. But, give the Welshman his due, he's made of sturdy stuff and the blade lodges in his bonce. I am now forced to take a two-hand grip on the handle to lift both him and the axe into a concluding chop. And that's when it happens. The log parts company with the axe at the top of my swing, hits the corrugated roof like a howitzer shell, and ricochets down scoring a direct hit on my forehead.

After an unknown period of time, I come to and discover myself on my knees with my chin resting on the chopping block, much in the manner of Charles the First. Sitting back onto my heels, I raise a hand gingerly to inspect my brow and find that I appear to have grown an extra head; a bump the size of Fayling Knoll has sprouted forth from my forehead and is throbbing like a power station. On attempting to pull myself to my feet, a violent earth tremor throws me back on my bum where I sit and watch the shed roof swaying in a great arc above me. If I didn't feel so sick, I might find the whole thing fascinating.

The heat in the shed combined with my banging headache is causing me to feel faint. Best thing to do is to crawl outside, find a shady corner of the garden, and die quietly. No, no, I'm forgetting my date with… what was her name? Wendy, you daft bugger. I must recover for that if nothing else. Maybe I could die in her arms. But why would she want to cradle a bloke with two heads? This is a catastrophe; no sooner have I made it to first base with the love of my life, than all the demons in hell conspire to thwart me. What hope has a young man just setting out on the great journey of life, and the possibility of a snog in the dunes, when the entire malevolent forces of the universe are massed against him?

On my slow, crawling traverse of the back lawn in search of a patch of shade beneath the plum tree, I am obliged to pass at close quarters to that pervert, the gnome. How loathsome he appears when you are down at his eye level and staring into his repugnant, florid little face. If only I could vomit right now, what a triumph that would be! Instead, my brain decides to perform one of its innumerable acts of subversion and I topple into the pond.

For the life of me, I cannot understand why my mother insisted on this pond being so deep. It takes me two attempts to drag my aching body from its depths and, as I lie there like a beached whale with fronds of pondweed hanging across my face, I am overcome with an urge to let the world know my feelings. I let rip with every swear-word I know plus a couple I've never heard before and, in spite of my sopping wet clothes and a thumping headache, I do now feel that I will live. However, as I struggle to a sitting position, I find to my dismay that I am being observed from the back door by my mother and Lamont.

"Colin," she trills, "I don't think I've ever heard such language!" Take note that she's not entirely sure.

"Yes, put a lid on it, old boy," adds Lamont.

I'll put a lid on you one day, old boy, and I'll nail it down. Who the hell do you think you are, coming round here to fondle my mother and then giving me a lecture on garden etiquette?

"What's that on your head?" asks my mother, approaching me across the tiny lawn with Lamont in hot pursuit. "It looks like a nasty red lump." Yes, and there's another one just behind you, mother. "Where did you get it?" she enquires. Well, I didn't buy it down the Co-op, nor did it turn up in the post. Anyhow, I can't be bothered to explain how a harmless log managed to cause all this carnage so I give her one of my stock grunts and wave vaguely in the direction of the wood-shed. Lamont bends to squint at my forehead and strokes his long ginger locks.

"I really think we should get him down to the hospital, Marjorie," he says, much to my surprise.

"Oh, it doesn't look that bad," she warbles, "I'll get some TCP and a plaster."

TCP and a plaster! Have you no maternal instincts, Mother? What about possible concussion and brain damage, not to mention splinters and dry-rot? But, please, don't put yourself out in any way. After all, it must almost be time for 'Mrs. Dale's Diary', so why not put the kettle on and have a nice cup of tea while I just get on and die?

"No, Marjorie," insists Lamont, "I'll run the young fellow down to the Cottage Hospital. Heads are unpredictable things."

He's right, look at me, I've got two.

Between them they haul me to my feet and walk me like a string puppet to the downstairs toilet where my mother instructs me to remove my wet outer clothing. Were it not for my extreme wooziness I would refuse such an indignity, but, in no time at all, I am kitted out in one of Dad's freshly laundered white decorating overalls. The sleeves flap ludicrously beyond my fingers but I'm past caring now as a wad of stinking TCP is applied to my forehead and I am frog-marched out to Lamont's MGA.

Grudgingly, I have to admit that Lamont has shown more compassion for my injury than my own mother. But, being of a suspicious nature when it comes to adult behaviour, I begin to wonder what his little game is. And shining like a beacon through the fug of my half-consciousness glows the answer... 'get into the son's good books, ergo, get into the mother's underwear'! It's a trick as old as the human race itself. The brighter Lamont's halo shines, the quicker he'll get her into the back seat of his car. I turn with difficulty and inspect the MG's tiny rear seat. Not a chance. He'll have to get her back to his flat. Hang on, what the hell am I doing, planning his depraved manoeuvres for him?

"Are you alright, old boy?" enquires Lamont, straining a false smile. I expect he's concerned that I might throw up over his red leather. Maybe I will, just for the hell of it.

We squeak to a halt as the traffic lights at the Balaclava Road junction turn red and, to my horror, I see Wendy and Anthea on the zebra crossing smack in front of us. If she sees me now in this state and in the company of a washed-up actor with ginger hair and a cravat, what are my chances of ever unclipping her Debenham's bra on some golden day in the future? I attempt to slide myself down into the foot-well but, can you believe it, my oversized sleeve slips neatly over the gear lever and I am trapped. At this precise moment, the lights change to green and Lamont is searching frantically for the gear lever. A taxi driver behind us leans on his horn and the noise seems to transform Lamont into a raving maniac.

"What have you done with the gear lever, you spiteful little bastard!" he bawls, sweat beads breaking out on his freckled brow. I wonder what my mother would think of him now? He doesn't seem quite so suave and genteel in this state of hysteria. "Come on, come on, you worthless piece of excrement!" he rants, running his hand desperately up and down my sleeve. "Give it to me right now." With that he yanks my shoulder back and my arm flies out of its overalled imprisonment. Shrieking with mad triumphant laughter, he rams the sleeve-draped lever into first gear and we catapult forward at full revs just as the lights wink back again to red. Lamont's crazed laughter ascends the scale into a howl of terror.

From my limited aspect, slumped as I am almost in a lying position and with a large wad of cotton-wool impinging on my vision, I see very little of the impact as we torpedo broadsides into Jack Peale's milk-float. To be truthful, all I catch is the sight of the MG's bonnet pivoting upwards into the vertical and a cloud of steam and smoke issuing from the engine. All very entertaining, but I do regret missing seeing the milk-float toppling onto its side as Jack and his son Mike dive out in the nick of time.

A crowd has gathered, of course, to watch the fun, so I clamber from my seat and lean on the roof to observe the continuing drama. I keep a sharp eye out for Wendy and mentally map out an escape route should she reappear.

Meanwhile, Lamont has lost all semblance of self-control and erupts from the car cursing me, the non-thespian world at large, and bloody idiots driving milk-floats in particular. With little more than a glance at his wrecked MG, he crunches across the carpet of milk-bottle fragments to where Jack stands, rubbing a bruised shin and probably contemplating early retirement from the dairy trade.

"What in the name of God do you think you were doing, dawdling along at five miles an hour like that?" raves Lamont, recklessly jabbing Jack in the shoulder with a ginger finger. "I had absolutely no alternative but to hit you, you oaf!"

Jack straightens up and pulls his grubby old woollen hat tighter down over his ears. I sense impending peril for Lamont and this feeling is reinforced when I notice Mike stepping discreetly to one side.

"Oh, in that case," says Jack evenly, "I have absolutely no alternative but to do the same," and he slams his gnarled, ex-paratrooper's fist into Lamont's nose. The faded artiste emits a sort of gargling noise, staggers back a few feet and disappears into the steam billowing from his MG's radiator. I hear a cry and a metallic clang so perhaps he's collapsed into the engine compartment. I have no way of telling.

Mike sees me, sticks his thumb up, and picks his way towards me. "Hiya, Brillo," he grins. "Waddya make of all this then?" He looks me up and down and chuckles. "What's with the overall? And what the hell is that sticking out of your head?"

I recount, as briefly as possible, my misfortunes with the wayward axe, the unnecessarily deep garden pond, and my journey into Hell with the kamikaze actor.

"Fantastic!" glows Mike admiringly. "I'd better go help my old man," and he turns to thread his way through the glass. "Don't forget tomorrow night," he calls, "we need to practice those new numbers."

Not that I needed reminding at this precise moment. But, yes, our summer season begins in early July at the 'Half Moon Hotel', Fayling's slickest holiday trap with twenty-five refurbished bedrooms, a brand-new dancefloor, and a real Italian chef from Manchester. Our 'man on the inside', Glyn the bar-waiter, has negotiated a deal for our Rock group in which we play three times a week as support to the resident dance band, 'Maurice Witts and the Half Moons' (known affectionately by us as Maurice Moon and the Half Wits). We will be receiving two pounds ten shillings per week each and, unofficially, all the lager and lime we can drink in return for two twenty-minute sessions whilst the Half Wits get tanked up in the public bar during their break. All in all, an excellent arrangement for everyone concerned, in particular the younger holiday residents who get to hear some Rock 'n' Roll instead of all that fuddy-duddy rubbish that Maurice churns out.

But all this is irrelevant as I stand marooned within the chaos seething around me. I gaze with wonder at the sight of two policemen pulling Jack Peale's muscular hands from Lamont's throat; I turn to observe the ambulance crew changing a punctured tyre on their vehicle; and I watch, dumbfounded, as the fire-brigade fill Lamont's MG with water for no apparent reason. But I am awakened from my reverie by a gentle tugging at my sleeve.

"Colin," purrs the voice of an angel, "are you hurt?"

Have you ever been in Heaven and Hell in the same instant? I am now convinced that such a state exists. 'Heaven' is turning to see my love standing before me, her beautiful blue eyes filled with concern, and her hand sliding down my arm to link fondly with mine. 'Hell' will be her reaction when she claps eyes on the throbbing protuberance springing from my forehead and the subsequent end of my dreams. But...

"Oh, your poor head!" she croons, placing cool hands to my face and drawing me nearer until our lips are inches apart. There's nothing left now but to go for broke and, as I cancel out the space between us, she offers no resistance as our lips touch. To my utter shame, Wee William uncoils like a steel spring and his unbridled lust knows no bounds as we press our bodies together in our embrace. But, to my relief, my beloved shows no sign of distress. Maybe she thinks it's a paint-scraper in my pocket. All I know is that sweet music is wafting up the High Street, rose petals are cascading down upon us, and my heart is adrift and floating out to sea. On the other hand, I might be overdosing on TCP.

"Let me walk you round to the hospital," she coos. "We'll get that bump looked at and then I'll walk you home."

I attempt to protest but she silences me with a finger to my lips. Who am I to object?

A brief visit to the cottage hospital, where the same ogress who attended to Jeff dabs and pokes at my forehead and resentfully applies a plaster, and we are hand in hand climbing Tobruk Avenue towards home. A quick snog in the bus shelter seals our new bond. Bidding her farewell at my garden gate, I stand to watch her as she turns to wave before disappearing. I am knee-deep in honey, the world is a great big juicy peach and Wendy has the cutest bottom I ever saw.

*

There never was a brighter June morning as I pause in the front porch to make yet another check on the contents of my duffle bag: Physics text-book, ham sandwiches, bottle of Tizer, packet of Senior Service, old Zippo lighter, large towel. Yep, that seems about right for an afternoon in the dunes with my heart's desire. I run my fingers across my forehead to measure the extent of the lump. Thankfully, it is much reduced and a jauntily positioned plaster gives me, I feel, a certain rugged John Wayne image.

I step into the sun and almost collide with Lamont who appears from the side of the house like a burglar. What perverted prank is he up to now, I wonder? Skulking around hoping to catch a glimpse of my mother in her underwear I shouldn't wonder. Ah, let 'em get on with it. Perhaps they deserve each other.

He forces a grimace as he squeezes past me and, I have to admit, he looks a whole lot better with that broken nose. Not quite so poofy; and the swollen black eye definitely lends him a harder look.

Soon I am out on the edge of the abandoned pre-war golf-links and scrambling up onto the American road that skirts the dunes, separating them from the downs that rise behind Fayling sands. Making my way carefully, and jumping the pot-holes that pepper the surface, I find myself wondering about the Yanks who laid down this road to give access to the beach. Suddenly, I can hear the metallic rumble of tank-tracks and the throaty whine of Jeeps. Out in the surf, I visualise landing craft practicing an approach, spewing out marines into the shallows. Now I am confronted by a ghostly platoon of young GIs marching towards me. One of them even grins and offers me a stick of gum as they file past. I refuse with a smile and they are gone. God, they're not much older than me! I blink and run a hand across my still-aching brow. Hallucinating now, are we, Paddick?

The irritating cackle of Tulip's laugh brings me back to the present and I peer over the dusty bushes to see the three of them down in our secret dune hollow. I creep through the marram grass and leap out, giving them all a heart attack.

Tulip is lying with his head in Anthea's lap while she tests him on his physics knowledge. That should be a short exercise. My own true love lies on her tummy on a tartan blanket, her one-piece swimming suit clinging to every delicious curve. I drop down beside her and she stretches her beautiful neck to give me a kiss. Ah, what bliss is in my sweetheart's kiss? Christ, I'm turning into Lord Byron.

"I've had enough of this rubbish!" announces Tulip, and he flings the text-book into the adjacent bushes. Anthea scrambles to her feet and retrieves it, her face a picture of outrage.

"This is school property, Andrew," she chastises, "do you treat your own books this way?"

"No."

"Well, there you are then," she says, settling his head back into her lap. "What books have you got anyway?"

"The complete works of 'Health and Efficiency'," grins Tulip.

To my astonishment, Wendy rolls over onto her stomach and wriggles out of the top of her swimsuit. "Would you rub some suntan oil on my back, Colin?" she asks. Yes bloody please! I pour a small pool of oil onto her shoulders and begin a slow, circular massage allowing myself the occasional liberty of running my fingertips down to the very edges of her breasts. She makes no protest but, as someone once said, slowly, slowly catchee monkey, so I'm not pushing my luck. Wee William, by contrast, is behaving in very poor taste and keeps trying to peep over the top of my bathing trunks as though he's missing something.

Thus passes the afternoon, with a short snog here, a nibble of the ear there, and whispered intimacies interrupted only by the squawking of herring-gulls attracted by our sandwiches.

Anthea, who is stoically ploughing through the physics text-book, requests Tulip to outline the basic principles of Newton's Law of Motion.

"Oh, up its bum!" he declares inaccurately. Anthea responds by slamming shut the book in exasperation.

"OK, that's it. You're completely hopeless and vulgar," she sighs, which sums him up to a tee. In fact, were there a qualification available in Hopeless Vulgarity, Tulip would get an 'honours'. He gets to his feet and climbs up onto a tussock where he stands, one hand shielding his eyes, seemingly staring out to sea. Perhaps he's contemplating drowning himself. I have no way of telling.

"What's going on down on the beach?" he calls. "That's Danny Zawadzki on his Norton."

The reaction from the girls to this piece of information is electric. You'd think Tulip had announced that Bobby Vee was running naked along the sand. They both leap to their feet to join him. Sure enough, it's Danny alright, all six foot of him; leather jacket, jet-black Tony Curtis hairstyle, perfect white teeth... the needlessly handsome town rogue. He's powering his big motorbike along the water's edge, a miniature rainbow formed from the spray of his wake following him like he's some kind of supernatural being. Bathers and strolling couples scatter in all directions as he weaves among them. But there's more to this than meets the eye. In pursuit is Papa Bonetti at the wheel of his veteran Austin ice cream van, flat-out but ever so slowly losing control as the little vehicle bounces and jerks over the wet sand. Finally, he comes to a shuddering halt in one of those treacherous puddles that pock-mark Fayling beach. All the stock from the rear of the van joins Papa in an avalanche of pop bottles, cones, and drinking straws. We hear his shrieks of fury all the way up here and watch in fascination as he leaps from the van to perform some kind of Italian war dance in the shallow water. It really is very entertaining. He runs around the Austin cursing everyone from the Pope to Mario Lanza. Colourful phrases float to us on the shimmering air, like 'Polish bastardo' and (my favourite) 'son of a bloody damn-a bitch'!

Curiously, a queue is forming at Papa's service window. Now, call me a young cynic if you wish, but what sort of bone-head expects to be able to buy a ninety nine from an ice cream van that is lurching at thirty degrees in a deep pool and whose proprietor is banging his head on the bonnet and screaming Neapolitan obscenities?

Meanwhile, Desperate Danny continues his dash along the beach. Reaching an outcrop of granite rock, he goes into a classic slide with one leg jutting out to steady the Norton and, making a faultless ninety-degree turn, accelerates towards us with the front wheel in the air. Just ahead of him, Hettie Trimble and her brood of Brownies out on a nature trail with a marine theme, fling themselves onto the rocks as Danny thunders through their ranks. Enraged into uncharacteristic violence, Hettie swings a jam jar above her head, biblical sling style, and lets it fly in Danny's direction. But it's a futile gesture of defiance and, to hoots of laughter from the Brownies, she loses her footing and totters backwards to sit in a rockpool.

To my dismay, Danny has spotted our girls jumping up and down and waving their towels. He powers the bike into the soft sand below us and switches off the engine.

"Hi girls," he calls and kicks out the bike-stand as he lights up a fag.

"Hi Danny," they both warble in unison. For God's sake, what's got into the pair of 'em?

They've turned to goo! I can scarcely believe my eyes. Is this really what you can do to birds when you look like Ricky Nelson? Catastrophe is brewing, I fear, for my embryonic love affair. I detect the faint aroma of decomposing bliss in the air. (Or is it Danny's exhaust fumes?) Whatever it is, life is about to knee me in the groin again.

Ignoring the presence of Tulip and myself, Danny climbs the sandy slope and sits between the kneeling girls.

"Why was Mr. Bonetti chasing you?" enquires a drooling but ever-inquisitive Anthea.

Danny eases his lips into that dazzling grin of his and pulls a Coke bottle from his leather jacket. He removes the cap with a sinister-looking knife produced from his motorcycle boot.

"Oh, he got it into his head that I'd nicked a bottle of his Coke," he chuckles, taking a swig. "He's such a suspicious old sod."

The girls gasp and giggle at his audacity, completely out of their minds with adulation. But why? Their parents would have a blue fit if they caught their daughters consorting with the likes of Danny Zawadski. I wonder if it's that hint of danger that makes him so irresistible to the fairer sex? After all, things I only dream about doing, he would go right ahead and do. Whatever it is, it's about to pour cold water on the flickering flames of my new romance.

"Oh, my gosh," squeals Wendy. "Look at the time. I'm on duty in fifteen minutes!"

Danny's lustrous leer expands to unprecedented widths. He points to his Norton.

"Well, your carriage awaits, my lady."

"Oh, Danny," mewls Wendy, "that'd be great. Are you sure?"

Of course he's bloody sure, he's been undressing you with his eyes since he arrived! Now he's got the chance to whisk her away and do it for real. I give up on women, they're unfathomable, treacherous, and totally fickle. If they weren't so good to look at I'd pack 'em in permanently.

Within seconds Wendy has swept up her bits and pieces and is sitting astride Danny's pillion seat, her arms around his waist and a rapturous smile on her lips. Ah well, c'est la vie, etcetera; the end of my current hopes and dreams. Off you go, then, you selfish, cruel... gorgeous girl. I hear the Devil's mocking laughter. Or is it a herring-gull? What's the difference? They both crap on you.

Anthea seems to be in a worse state of shock than me as she stares after the speeding Norton. She barely utters a sound as we watch Danny waving to the apoplectic Papa Bonetti who is stomping on the roof of his ice cream van, having taken refuge from the rising tide. She makes no comment whatsoever at the sight of her uncle, Mad Farmer Wilkes, trundling out towards the water aboard his grey Ferguson tractor in an attempt to rescue the sinking Italian. Has she, too, seen another side to her best friend? Or is she just jealous that it's not her tight little buttocks bumping up and down behind Danny?

"We may as well bugger off, too," says a despondent Tulip, gathering his belongings and stuffing them haphazardly into Anthea's beach-bag. She snatches it from him, empties everything onto the sand and repacks it, folding and placing each item neatly. Then, in complete silence she strides off across the dunes with Tulip trailing her, much in the manner of a naughty dog.

Letting forth a huge sigh, I fall on my back and, with the back of my head cradled in my hands, I contemplate the sky and my immediate future. The sky seems much the brighter of the two. "What is left?" I cry out aloud to the cosmos. Not a word of encouragement is returned; no booming voice giving me succour; no bush bursting into flame. Sod all. All I can see in the cotton-ball clouds scudding across the big sky is Wendy's face. No, I tell a lie, that one there looks more like her bum. Oh, for Christ's sake, what's the point in prolonging the agony? She's probably down some alley with Danny's hands all over her.

"Colin... what are you doing here?" rings a familiar voice. I almost jump out of my bathing trunks! Caroline is gazing down at me through a pair of massive sunglasses. For an awful moment I thought Martians had landed.

"Swotting up for an exam," I answer, moving swiftly to one side as she flaps a beach towel beside me. She dumps her gear and slips out of her blouse and skirt. All she's wearing is a brief bikini and a very suggestive smile. She lies on her side facing me and begins tracing idle patterns on my navel with her finger. Wee William, always one step of the game, has registered his interest and has enlisted the support of my pulse to keep him primed.

"What's that on your forehead?" she frowns, reaching to prod it.

"Don't touch, it's throbbing!"

She grins lewdly. "Is it now?"

We lie silently for a few moments, each in our own dream. "I think I passed your friends in the dunes," she murmurs eventually.

"Yeah?"

"Umm. They were arguing I think."

"Ah, that'd be Tulip and Anthea."

To my amazement and huge delight, she suddenly sits up and flips off her bikini top.

"Want to mess around?" she asks.

What a silly question to put to a red-blooded youth who has just been cruelly jilted. I am in dire need of diversion and get to work at once on the job in hand. There's plenty to occupy me as Caroline is pretty well-endowed. To add to the fun, she has deftly released Wee William from his nest and is giving him what for. He's very excited.

These are the moments when I feel on a par with the great British explorers. I looked up 'explorer' in the Oxford Dictionary and it perfectly describes my activities with Caroline: 'a traveller into un-investigated territory'. Yes, old Livingstone and Captain Cook would recognise a fellow adventurer if they could see me now, wandering the hills and valleys of Caroline's torso. And I know that Mason and Dixon would forgive my failure to draw the line at her navel, so on I plunge, into the Matto Grosso and the Great Divide. My daring knows no bounds today.

Have you ever had that creepy feeling at the back of your neck when you suspect you're being watched? It's most likely some kind of throw-back to our primitive past when you might well have expected to be consumed by a sabre-toothed tiger or some other monstrosity. Anyhow, I'm getting that uncomfortable sensation right this minute and, to be blunt, it's interfering with my interfering. Slowly I turn my head and, lo and behold, my primal instincts have come up trumps. We are being observed by two pint-sized Brownies! Who do they think they are, Burgess and Maclean? But worse still, before Caroline and I can remove all offending equipment from their eager little eyes, the dreadful figure of Hettie Trimble rises behind them like a Griffon vulture, her outstretched arms enfolding the two miniature spies, turning them away from our display of raw nature.

"Brown-owl," pipes the little red-haired one, "are they making a baby?"

Hettie guides them away, turning to glower at us before she disappears from view.

"No, dear, they're just being disgusting. Now let's go and catch some crabs."

I do hope *I* don't, Hettie!

# CHAPTER 3

# 'Bird Dog' (The Everly Brothers...1959)

I've just survived the worst week of my life. The combination of half a dozen GCE exams, a broken love affair, and missing the 'Goon Show' due to my radio melting, has left me in a state of mental and physical exhaustion. The only spark of joy illuminating my black mood is the knowledge that I have all but finished my school days. Just a few drab formalities remain, including the sickening farewell ceremonies organised by the Count, followed by our inevitable defeat at the hands of his superior forces on the cricket pitch.

I lie on my bed and stare aimlessly at the wardrobe door. It's a stifling hot Friday afternoon and the only sound coming in through my open window is the bored cooing of a lone pigeon. 'Ya baas-tard, ya baas-tard,' he calls. You too, mate.

I study the cracks in the ceiling. One of them seems to outline the shape of a woman's bottom, sadly connected only to one leg. Could she remain standing, I muse, bending over like that? Hallo, now it's all turning into Italy and part of Switzerland and I can't get it to revert to the one-legged woman. Strange how your brain swans around like that with absolutely no respect for your preferences. Who does it think it is, the Government?

Downstairs I detect the click of an electric wall-socket and my worst fears are realised. My mother is about to commence hoovering the carpets. That's the end of peace and tranquillity for half an hour. Why the hell Hoover had to invent the thing in the beginning is a mystery. What's wrong with a brush and pan? Why create a machine that drowns all other sound, chips the skirting-board paint, and runs out of cable before you reach the end of the hall? The words of our esteemed physics master, Arthur Harold Wishart, ring true: 'Nature abhors a vacuum.' How right he is.

The horrendous din gets louder as my mother reverses herself up the stairs, humping the bloody awful appliance from step to step. Finally, my bedroom door is flung open and all hell is let loose. To make matters worse, my mother leaves the damn thing roaring away as she bustles around the room, dusting anything that doesn't move. Handfuls of my clothes, which were carefully dropped so that I know precisely where they are, are scooped up and thrown out the door destined for the weekly wash. The 'Reveille' I was reading yesterday, featuring some scantily-clad totty, is screwed into a ball and rammed into a waste-basket. I reach for the wad of cotton wool left over from my head-wound dressing and jam two plugs in my ears, more as a gesture of protest than anything else. To my surprise, my mother places a gentle hand on my forehead and gazes down at me with a look bordering on affection.

"Have you still got a headache, dear?" she bawls above the din of the Hoover. I have now. "Good to see the bump has gone down," she continues at the top of her voice. "TCP, you see. Mother knows best." She moves away and flaps the duster through the open window like a distress signal and I notice the pigeon propel himself from the window-sill to escape the dust cloud. 'Ya baas-tard,' he coos as a parting shot.

My mother switches off the Hoover and begins to move around the room, picking up objects at random and polishing them furiously with her duster. This is a sign that she's building up a head of steam and, at any given moment, will launch into a tirade against my idleness and total absence of ambition. I don't have to wait long.

"Have you thought any more about applying for a job, young man?" Aha, how rapidly I've been downgraded from 'dear' to 'young man'. In a minute it'll be 'lazy little tike'.

The truth is, I haven't done a thing about it. Not only that, I don't have a clue where to start because I can't decide what career would hold my interest for more than a week. At this stage in my life, all I'm interested in is chasing crumpet, strumming a few chords on my guitar, and drinking illegally purchased cider. Sadly, none of these agreeable activities can actually provide you with a good living, unless you're a Rock n' Roll star. I'm well aware, of course, that my mother sees her only son as a world-renowned brain surgeon or fifth in line for the throne or something but, the sad truth is, I don't have any major talents. Dad? Well, he's a bit more realistic and would be perfectly happy if I entered the Civil Service or joined the Royal Navy. Right now though, I need to come up with an acceptable response to my mother's inquisition. Grunting inanely will not get me out of this one. I need a plan.

"Yes, I intend to start doing something about it on Monday," I say. This is not necessarily a lie as I have neither specified which Monday or what exactly 'start' might mean.

"I see," she says tersely, "and what was it again that Mr Darke said during your Careers interview?"

I dare not repeat the Count's precise words so I resort to poetic licence or what I believe is called tweaking the truth.

"Oh, him. He said something like, 'If you set your mind on it, Paddick, you'll make it stick in the end'." His actual words were: 'If you don't make up your mind, Paddick, you'll come to a sticky end.'

Her face brightens somewhat. "So he has some faith in your ability then?" That's not the same interpretation I put on it.

She turns to face me, leaning against the window-sill and bringing up a high polish on a pebble I brought home when I was ten. "It's a pity you're not more like your cousin, Adrian. He's already been offered a job at Barclay's Bank and he's doing ever so well in the Scouts."

I twist my head just sufficiently to give her a look of disbelief.

"Mother, Adrian is a raving homosexual!"

She ceases polishing the agate and glares at me. "Whatever do you mean, Colin?"

"I mean Adrian isn't interested in girls." Strewth, do I have to elaborate? Didn't they have poofs in England before the war? Or did we send 'em all to Germany to get 'em gassed?

"I don't know what your Aunty Gwen would say if she heard

you," says my mother, gathering the Hoover cable and blustering towards the door. "Adrian loves the Scouts."

"Yeah, at every opportunity!" I remark rather coarsely.

"You really are the giddy limit at times, Colin," she snaps. "Mark my words, you'll eat humble pie one day when you have to get on your knees to Adrian for a bank loan."

Humble pie? What the buggering hell is that, some delicacy only served up in banks? As for getting on my knees anywhere near that brown-hatter Adrian, forget it!

"Where is he today, anyway?" I call. "He usually minces round here on a Friday to borrow something or other."

"He's camping," comes the acid reply.

I rest my case.

But all is not poo. My verbal tussle with my mother has spawned an idea. I, too, fancy a night under canvas; a few hours of reckless abandon with my good friends Tulip and Mike. I spring into action as I am gripped by the prospect of a whole night's debauchery under the guise of 'getting some good fresh air and fending for myself for a change'.

My first port of call is the back of our garage where I know Dad has stored an old U.S. Army tent his uncle 'acquired' when the Yanks left Fayling in 1944. It's one of those enormous bell-tent efforts with a ground sheet and everything. I pull it from its webbing container and sprawl it out on the floor. My god, it's heavy. I'll need some help with this.

Tulip's dad, Rudi, answers the phone. "Yes," he says in his Dutch brogue, "Andrew can shleep out under the shtars tonight as long as he gets the shpuds peeled and chipped first." An hour's work? Bugger, I'll have to belt round there and give him a hand. "OK, just as long as it's done," says Rudi.

Right, that's that organised. Next, Mike; he'll be at the milk-depot with his old man sorting out tomorrow's delivery in their brand-new milk-float. I'll drop in and see him on the way to Tulip's. Mike's got his old pick-up truck to transport the tent. This is looking good. Hang on, you twerp… where are we pitching the tent? I've got it, Mad Farmer Wilkes's bottom meadow. He allows a couple of tents in their every summer and, as he also fancies my mother for some unknown reason, I'll get her to ask him. Are you nuts? You just upset her so why would she do you a favour? Bugger! No, it's OK, I've solved it yet again… I'll write out a phoney job application and show her. She'll be so shocked, she'll be a pushover!

Wow, I'm impressed with my own brilliant organisational skills. Clearly I should be running the United Nations or the Mafia. All that remains now is a quick visit to the 'Three Sheets' and a quiet word with mine host, Ivan Zawadski, where the customary greasing of palms will guarantee the laying down of (mildly) alcoholic supplies for the expedition. Ivan is a co-operative sort of bloke and doesn't pay much heed to the British laws of hostelry. I can see where his son, Danny, gets his cavalier ways from. Of course, this particular part of my enterprise will have to be done with caution as the local constabulary take a dim view of underage adventurers cruising the streets, laden with illegally purchased bottles of Manns Brown Ale. Quite why the authorities get so wound up about it beats me when you consider that next month I can legally start smoking myself to death; the following year I can lawfully drive a car into a tree at seventy miles an hour; and the year after that I'm old enough to be shot dead in the service of Her Majesty. I can't wait.

I scribble two mock job applications in my jotter as rough proofs to present to my mother. She will be impressed. One is to the Provincial Bank, the other to Tottering and Tripp, quantity surveyors. Why either of them would consider employing me is for her to ponder. It may, or may not, occur to her that I have never shown the vaguest interest in figures or quantities, other than female ones.

One thing I almost overlook during my sudden rush of administrative zeal, is grub. The mere thought of it brings on hunger pangs. Time to inspect the contents of the fridge, which I suspect will be a contradiction in terms. Sure enough, on opening the door I am greeted by a sight which would cause any self-respecting mouse to cry out in anguish: a jar of mayonnaise; a half empty bottle of milk; two grease-encrusted sausages, clinging together for comfort; and, ah yes, a chicken carcass. Hardly a cornucopia of culinary delicacies. Well, there's always some meat to be wrenched from the carcass of a chicken, so I set about dismantling the corpse on the kitchen table, much in the manner of an autopsy. I discover that I have a flair for dissection and, in no time at all, not only have I satisfied my immediate hunger by stuffing my face with large amounts of pink meat, but have assembled a pile of overweight sandwiches (bread edging towards stale). Wrapping them in greaseproof paper, I drop them into a carrier bag and set forth.

Mike is up for a night of carousing under a khaki roof and also agrees to bring round his Morris Minor pick-up van to collect the tent. I hasten on towards the 'Cod Almighty' fish and chip shop and my appointment with a grubby vegetable. Yes, Tulip will be wondering where I am!

Forty-five minutes into our finger-numbing chore and we have dropped the last naked spud into the water-filled drum just as Rudi comes in to turn on the chipper. "OK, clear off you two," he grins. We're already gone.

Jogging whilst attempting to puff on a Senior Service is not recommended, but all haste must be made to meet Mike at my house to load the tent into his van. As we trot through the back alleys of Fayling, Tulip quizzes me about Wendy.

"To be honest," I wheeze, "what with the exams all week, I haven't thought too much about her."

"I haven't seen her all week," says Tulip. "Anthea says she wasn't at school."

Sounds like Danny has been working his magic. Oh, I can't be blowed to start fretting over it again. Like old Rudi, I've got other fish to fry. We pound on and meet up with Mike as he pulls into our rear lane. With three of us on the job, the tent is secured in the back of the van in no time. Next stop, the 'Three Sheets'.

We open the pub rear yard gate, drive through, and park the Morris against the skittle-alley wall. Ivan is washing glasses behind the bar as we enter. Just visible in the gloom of the snug-bar sits 'Flash' Moule with his fearsome one-eyed mongrel lying menacingly at his feet. Flash is the town pervert and is reputed to have done a stretch in Exeter Prison for indecent exposure. He's a short, sleazy bag-of-bones, permanently wrapped up in an old army greatcoat, and a damp roll-up always hanging from the corner of his mouth. Flash has a unique, mangled grasp of the English language in which he chops words in half or dispenses with them altogether. Evidently he never bothered to give his dog a name but the evil little bugger is known to us as the 'King Liddle Basta' because that's how Flash addresses him. You can easily work out what it translates as! We nod to him and wish him good afternoon. "'Noon," he grunts. The mutt snarls and bares its teeth at us. "...Tup," rasps Flash, "...king liddle basta!"

Ivan pulls three halves of lager and slides them towards us with his giant Polish hands. He considers the Licensing Laws to be an encumbrance to trade so he will always serve us on slow days. He's alright, is Ivan, despite begetting that miscreant, Danny. He's yet another left over from the war, escaping Poland when the Krauts invaded and making his way to England to fly with the R.A.F. Sometimes, when he's had a few himself on a winter's Saturday evening, he recounts some of his wartime experiences. I tell you this much, I wouldn't want to be the German holidaymaker who eventually walks into this bar! Ivan hates 'em with a passion. "I kill one in Warszawa," he whispered to us one wet evening last December. "I strangle with these," and held up those sodding great hands for us to marvel at. "I chuck in Vistula," he elaborated further, meaning I think, that he threw the body in Warsaw's river and not, as Tulip insisted, that he'd been sick in the toilet. "Then I run and come to England." His English is still a bit patchy but we usually get the gist of it.

We adjourn to the tiny beer garden at the rear of the pub where we can quaff our ale, smoke, and generally ass about in complete privacy. The local constabulary never bother us. I think Ivan is a Freemason and, as he also supplies the booze for the annual Police Ball at rock-bottom prices, I guess he's immune from harassment. It's a bit like the Cosa Nostra, only without the bloodshed.

Ivan appears with a notepad to discuss our victualling requirements for the expedition. We order half a dozen bottles of brown ale, a quantity of salt and vinegar crisps, and a quart of scrumpy cider to be supplied in a large ex-vinegar jar which Ivan assures us has been thoroughly washed, not that it would make much difference to the flavour of the cider. He asks if we need French-letters (another little sideline of his) but we lean back in our seats, puff on our fags, and tell him we're OK in that department. My guess is that, of the three of us, only Mike has probably used one in earnest. Perhaps I should rephrase that in case Ernest is reading this!

Whilst we are absorbed in negotiations with Ivan, who should come ambling into the beer garden with his wife and dozy kid in tow, but the Nutter! He has clearly been released from custody following the amusement arcade fracas and is sporting a very fetching eye patch with matching Elastoplast across the bridge of his nose. Sadly, the police have failed to caution him about his shorts. Surely they contravene some bye-law?

Inspecting each table for flaws and health hazards, he finally settles for one which meets his stringent standards. He stands with his hands on his hips, much in the manner of Heinrich Himmler, whilst his family make themselves comfortable. The mouse-wife orders a Babycham and the brat asks for a ginger beer. The Nutter then turns smartly on his heels, gestures to Ivan with a raised forefinger and disappears into the pub.

As it happens, along with Germans, Ivan doesn't have much time for holidaymakers so he ignores him and continues with our requirements. Would we be interested in some saucy magazines he's recently acquired from the Continent? Possibly, we nod... at the right price. OK, he'll show us a couple of pages to whet our appetites.

But, alas and alack, we are thwarted once more. Before Ivan has barely taken a step in the right direction, there issues from the interior of the pub an horrendous shriek accompanied by the crashing of tumbling chairs and a snarl from the King Liddle Basta. Almost simultaneously, the Nutter materialises once more. He explodes from the back door, a blur of lily-white legs and khaki shorts, and a split second ahead of the largest rat you ever clapped eyes on. In hot pursuit of the pair of them, yelping and slavering with unrestrained joy, is the Basta, his one functioning eye wide with bloodlust. We cheer and whistle as they do a circuit of the yard. The Nutter's wife claps a hand to her mouth and begins to rock with laughter, whilst the kid bursts into tears.

On their second lap, the rat shows its superior intelligence by suddenly veering off on the Basta's blindside and escaping among a pile of mouldy barrels in a corner of the yard. The crazed dog, however, maintains a straight course and seems oblivious to the falling numbers in the chase. As long as there is something in his limited sights, I suppose he's perfectly happy. The Nutter, by contrast, is far from cheerful and, watching his flight through the yard gates and out into Quay Street, I fear for his sanity and his shorts. His screams echo up to us as he pounds unseen down towards the harbour. I hope the tide is in because, with only two good eyes between the pair of 'em, the chances of careering off the edge of the harbour wall are high. And, once in the water, would they swim in endless circles? I have no way of telling.

We fall back chuckling into our seats. The Nutter's wife raises her hand and asks Ivan if she can have a Gin and Tonic, and make it a double. The kid scampers off across the yard and stares pitifully down Quay Street. "Daddy," he bawls, "where's my ginger beer?"

*

Our arrival at Mad Farmer Wilkes's bottom meadow is slightly marred by the sight of another tent occupying our favourite pitch on the bank of the stream. Is nothing sacred? Have we no rights during the summer months? Would these holidaymakers be amused if we drove to Wolver-bloody-Hampton, camped on their postage-stamp sized lawn, peed on their begonias, and stuffed chip-paper in their letterbox?

Anyhow, it's nine-thirty and the light is failing so we park the van upstream and dump all the gear on the grass. I'm very glad we've got Mike with us because Tulip and I would never figure out this tent. It's as heavy as hell, too. And, as if this wasn't enough, my stomach is beginning to churn around in great heaving, gas-accompanied waves. I'm sure the culprit is that swine of a chicken!

We manage to make some sense of the general shape of the tent and we are soon whacking pegs into Farmer Wilkes's sun-baked earth. Tulip's pointless announcement that this is his biggest ever erection coincides with a colossal upheaval in my downstairs plumbing and, grabbing Mike's edition of 'Tit-bits', I hasten away in the fading light towards the stream. I'm sure you will agree that trying to walk briskly whilst, at the same time, clenching the cheeks of your ass is one of life's sternest tests. Add to this the gathering darkness, a treacherous river-bank, and a vicious swine of a chicken doing its utmost to escape through your sphincter, and nothing bodes well.

I make it to the stream with what I estimate is seconds to spare and scramble down the bank to duck under the little timber foot-bridge. Foolishly, in a moment of foolhardy inventiveness (for which

I blame by brain entirely), I have managed to drop my jeans and free one leg whilst on the move. A clever piece of forward planning, I hear you murmur. Well, maybe… but not when the trailing jean-leg decides to hook itself around a rogue spar poking out of the bridge woodwork. Before I realise what's happening, I'm standing with one leg in the stream and the other leg high in the air like a dancer at the 'Folies Bergere'. Ever tried removing your underwear in this position? Don't bother. Only a supreme example of one-legged, Olympic-standard hopping allows me to distort my y-fronts sufficiently to extrude the foul fowl into the stream. My god, what a relief! My guts rumble and hiss with gratitude.

Gripping the remaining pages of 'Tit-bits', I struggle back up the bank, removing my jeans en route only to suffer another near bowel movement as I pass beneath the hazel-bush hedge when one of Farmer Wilkes's heifers thrusts its head forward from the gloom and tries to lick my face. "Bugger off!" I yell, and clap my hands a few times, driving them off up the meadow. For God's sake, has the entire animal kingdom turned upon me? What next, a band of pillaging badgers? My jeans are so wet and muddy I decide to leave them off and attempt to dry them out back at camp. So, feeling much refreshed, I head off to rejoin the lads. But the Devil has clearly not quite had his fill of fun at my expense tonight. I take no more than a dozen paces when something metallic is poked into the small of my back and a vaguely familiar voice instructs me to "Hold it right there, son!"

"Now turn round… slowly," says the husky voice. I do as requested and am confronted by the dimly discernible figure of Mad Farmer Wilkes himself, brandishing a shotgun. His appearance is bizarre, something between Davey Crockett and a Commando. His face is blackened and he's wearing a hat constructed from two very elongated grey squirrels whose heads meet to form a gruesome emblem on his forehead. Dangling from a webbing belt around his camouflaged jacket I can faintly discern a number of recently assassinated rabbits.

He squints at me and speaks, weaving the shotgun barrel as though spelling out the words in mid-air. "What are you up to, son?" he asks. Then he sniffs the air and peers around into the semi-darkness. "Can you smell shit?" he enquires. Farmer Wilkes is not one to mince his words and has a reputation for, well, earthiness. I suppose if you spend your days wading through manure, wringing the necks of poultry, and assisting bulls to serve cows, you end up with a pretty basic view of the world. "I'd better check that damn sewage pipe again tomorrow," he mumbles.

Curiously, either that poisonous chicken has impaired my eyesight or I have just seen three spectral forms swimming into view behind Wilkes. No, I'm not hallucinating, we have definitely been joined by three mysterious figures, and Wilkes is aware of their presence because he calls to them over his shoulder. "Is this him?" he asks. They move closer and I can now see that they are three girls. I position my jeans over my groin to retain my modesty.

"Dunno," says one, "it wasn't his face we saw."

I distinctly hear the other two giggling, but I get the feeling this is no laughing matter for me personally. Suddenly I am bathed in the fierce glare of Wilkes's hunting torch as he runs the beam up and down my cringing half-nakedness. He takes a step closer and scrutinises my face. "Hang on… it's young Paddick, isn't it?" I nod and wonder how this catastrophe will be detailed when relayed to my mother. I sense impending ruin. But, to my surprise, Wilkes's black-streaked cheeks pull apart displaying a wide grin. "Give your mother my warmest regards," he says. "Tell her I'll see her at rehearsals on Wednesday." My god, I finally have something to thank my mother for! Quite why every old bloke in Fayling wants to get her behind the bike shed is beyond me but, on this occasion, I welcome all elderly horniness. But my confidence is immediately shattered as Wilkes leans forward to whisper to me. I am obliged to remove one of the rabbit cadavers from across my ear in order to catch what he is saying. "Thing is, young Paddick, these three little fillies are camping just down-stream," he jerks a blood-stained thumb over his shoulder, "and they're making a serious charge." He stares at me with his face slightly askance as though waiting for me to confess to some gross misdemeanour. All I can muster is a bewildered shrug.

"Righto then, picture this," he continues briskly. "Three young wenches in their tent. All of a sudden, a bloke in the doorway exposing the member." He raises his eyebrows and nods, still with that knowing look in his eye. Well, he's completely lost me now. Member of what? The Parish Council? The AA? But before I can request further details, he's off on another tack. "Try this then," he continues, gesturing between his legs with a fluttering hand. "Tent flap opens and there's the 'old gentleman' on display." OK, I give up. As far as I can gather, these three girls have been startled by an old gentleman and a member of some society. What does it mean? Wilkes gives me the once over again with the torch. "You can see my problem, young Paddick," he sighs. "I've got you here with your trousers off and three broody hens pointing the finger at one cock... if you get my drift."

At last he's speaking everyday English and I now understand the misunderstanding. I also smell a rat here or, more likely, a bloke with a one-eyed dog.

"Oi!" shouts one of the wenches. "Who are you calling a broody hen?"

"Yeah," joins in another. "You're not exactly Adam Faith yourself."

"And anyway," calls the tallest one, "it wasn't this boy... it was some dirty old bugger showing us his todger." This announcement is accompanied by stifled guffaws of mirth from the other two. "I mean, look at him, he's not up to it," she adds sarcastically.

This is a twist in the tale, but I am cut to the quick by her insinuation. For a dangerous moment I toy with the idea of dropping my Y-fronts and demanding a reappraisal, but a brief glance at the dead rabbits reminds me how close I might be to joining them!

Wilkes seems to be losing his patience with the whole thing and, swinging the shotgun recklessly over his shoulder, he turns to leave. "Right then," he snaps. "Nothing more to be said. Vermin to kill," and he melts away into the half-darkness leaving me in the company of the three harridans. They whisper amongst themselves as I struggle to pull on my damp jeans. This is not my finest hour, but dignity must somehow be maintained. So, bidding them farewell and wishing them a phallus-free night, I jog off towards the safety of my own encampment. In the distance, floating on the still night air, comes the unmistakable yap of the King Liddle Basta. As I suspected, Flash is abroad tonight and lurking nearby.

"Ah-ha, the wanderer returns," hoots Tulip as I rejoin them. I must say they have been busy since I set off on my adventures. The Primus-stove is burbling happily and the aroma of frying sausages sets my taste buds all a-quiver. My bowels appear to have swiftly forgotten their recent trauma at the stream.

I give the lads a potted version of my escapade with Wilkes and the distressed damsels.

"What? You've been chatting up three birds," brays Tulip, "and you come back empty handed!"

I explain, once more, my trouser-less condition and the fact that I was the prime suspect in an exposure incident but he remains unsympathetic. We all agree, however, that Flash must have been responsible for such a carnal outrage. Mike also registers his apprehension about the Basta being in the same field as a herd of young cows.

When we have consumed the sausages, Mike fetches his old acoustic guitar from the pick-up and, as the moon slides out from behind a cotton-ball cloud, Tulip and I lie back in the cool grass, swigging on our brown ales and vocalising to Buddy Holly's 'Think It Over'. We do a pretty good job on the harmonies and Mike gives a brilliant accompaniment on the beat-up old Hohner six-string. Across the shallow, moonlit valley, no more than a hundred yards away, harmony has also descended on Wilke's top meadow where a motionless ocean of silvery tent-tops stretches away to the far hedgerow. Only the rickety foot-bridge separates us from this throng of snoring campers, but they have no place in our world tonight. This could be one of the sweetest moments in our lives. But, of course, I have no way of telling.

Tulip raises himself onto his elbow and expels a thin stream of blue tobacco smoke towards the sky.

"Brillo, did I mention that Wendy was asking about you yesterday?" he mentions casually. I almost choke on my ale. My solar plexus goes into overdrive together with my imagination. My god, is the old magic still there, even after two weeks? Does she want to start again where we left off, I wonder? Has she discovered that raunchy old Danny isn't quite her cup of tea after all and wants to beg my forgiveness? Am I living in cloud cuckoo land? That sounds more like it.

"Oh, yeah?" I reply, trying hard to sound no more curious than if he had declared a passing interest in flower arranging. "So why didn't you mention it earlier?"

"Forgot," he shrugs.

There is a short interval of stony silence.

"And so?" says Mike. "What did she say about Brillo, numbskull?"

"Dunno really," he retorts uselessly. "Anthea ran out of money in the phone box."

Let me announce something. If the Good Lord should ever call to me one day, say, from a burning bush on Fayling Knoll saying, 'Brillo, I'm off sick this week and I need someone to go forth into the baking hot wilderness for forty days and forty nights with no water, no compass or even a bloody hat. Got any suggestions?' I would unhesitatingly volunteer Tulip.

"Sounds promising, anyway, Brillo," consoles Mike. Maybe, but who can read the mind of a woman? Look at the way they behave, there's no reasonableness to 'em. Did you ever hear of a woman philosopher? I reckon that as soon as God had created man he thought to himself, *That seems to work reasonably well, but let's try it another way then I'll have a choice.* So he made another mould, overdid the curvy bits in his enthusiasm and consequently had to cut back on the logic department in the brain. Trouble was, Man caught sight of it and said 'Never mind about the brain, the rest looks great. I'll keep it for Friday nights after the pub!' The rest is history.

Mike delves into his old haversack and pulls out one of those enormous alarm clocks, the type you see in cartoons with a massive bell on top. He winds it up, checks his wristwatch, and sets the clock alarm.

"Hell's bells, Mike, the whole town's gonna wake up when that bugger goes off!" laughs Tulip.

"Can't be late for the milk-round, mate," says Mike. "Half past five I'm off. You two dismantle the tent and I'll meet you here with the van about twelve." We nod and I throw them both a ciggy. Tulip drains his brown-ale bottle, belches like a moose, and lies back with the fag between his teeth.

"What about changing the name of the group this summer?" he suggests. "I'm fed up with being introduced as the 'Cosmonauts'. That was our skiffle-group name. We're playing all rock now."

He has a point and we all agree that times have moved on. For a start, we all have electric guitars now, even our fourth member, Jeff

Atyeo on bass; and the speakers we bought last year can really belt it out.

"How about something like the 'Crickets' then?" offers Mike. "You know, something on an insect theme."

"What, like the 'Blowflies' or the 'Woodlice'?" smirks Tulip. "Come off it, Mike, they're the Chirping Crickets and that sounds bloody good." He leaps to his feet and spreads his arms. "And now, folks, straight from their sell-out appearance on a pile of horse-shit… the fantastic 'Dung Beetles'!" We all chuckle.

"OK, point taken," nods Mike. "So how about just… the 'Beetles'?"

We throw empty bottles at him and he ducks and grins. He squints at his watch. "Well, anyway, I'm hitting the sack. It's one-fifteen."

Mike being our natural leader at seventeen years and working, Tulip and I take the hint and follow on. In no time, we're all cocooned in our sleeping bags. Tulip insists on smoking one more fag as he claims it helps him sleep. This may be true, but it does nothing to sedate me and Mike because the silly sod keeps up a constant stream of drivel. Subjects range from, 'how do you know when Stilton cheese has gone off?' through, 'why don't males have just one large testicle?' to, 'what is the point of Max Bygraves?' Finally, Mike threatens to strangle him and he promises to shut up just as soon as he's had what he calls his 'goodnight pee'. Naturally, his sleeping bag has the world's noisiest and slowest zip and, when he eventually struggles out of it, he trips over the alarm clock and literally falls out through the tent flap. We may as well get up and start cooking breakfast for all the sleep we're going to get. As a finale, Tulip manages to find the only hard baked patch of earth in Wilkes's meadow to urinate on which, in the still night air, sounds like thunder-rain on a tin roof.

He returns to the fold by tumbling back into the tent and whispering excitedly that there is something odd and not quite right outside.

"No there isn't," calls Mike curtly from the depths of his sleeping bag. "It just entered the tent!"

"I'm telling you, there's a prowler out there," he claims.

"Doing what?" I enquire, wondering if perhaps Flash is preparing for another incursion.

"Prowling, of course," he replies. Why did I ask? But as we prattle there comes a sound from outside.

"Anyone in?" calls a female voice. Mike's head emerges from his bag and he trains his regulation milkman's flashlight on the tent entrance. To our amazement, a mousey-haired girl pokes her head in and beams at us, and two blonde heads appear, one above and one below. Christ, it's the Beverley Sisters! No it isn't, it's those three idiots who almost finished me off down by the stream.

"What do you want?" asks Mike, rather testily. He reaches for the storm lantern and fires it up.

"Who cares!" murmurs Tulip, licking his lips in a very lascivious manner. The girls step boldly into the tent and link arms. They gaze around as the lantern illuminates the vast interior of our war-time relic. "Blimey," coos the short dumpy one, "i'nt it a whopper!"

"Thank you," says Tulip, grinning like a savage. The two blondes titter at his bawdiness. I wonder if Anthea would be just as amused?

"We think that there pervert is still hanging about," says the tall one, "so we thought we'd be safer with you... if you don't object, so to speak."

I've now got my suspicions about their story of Flash and his liberal member. This tall one looks like she could take care of herself. In fact, she wouldn't be out of place in the front row of our rugby first team. The other two might be a bit vulnerable, I suppose, especially the pretty one in the red jeans; the dumpy one with the daft grin might well be capable of administering a slap across the chops, but that's probably about all.

My misgivings about their phoney motives are strengthened when, almost as though rehearsed, they drift apart and home in on us individually. This is a bit creepy. What if they are three witches? We could all be turned to toads by sun-up. Or suppose they're aliens from some far-away galaxy. I've read about such stuff. They might be able to transform us into some kind of molecular soup, whisk us off to their planet, and reconstitute us to be their slaves or, even worse, lunch!

Sure as eggs is eggs, I get the podgy one. It's always the same. Mike, just because he bears a likeness to Tab Hunter, always attracts the best-looking crumpet. I don't hold a grudge about it, it's simply irritating that the others are never up to scratch and Tulip and I end up with the dregs. There should be a law prohibiting tasty totty from knocking about with plain ones. That way, you'd get three cracking birds together, so no problem, or three ugly ones who might at least buy you a coffee for a few minutes of your time. Either way, you win.

The plump blonde squats down next to me. "My name's Violet," she says, running a hand through her hair like Marilyn Monroe. "You can call me Vi, if you like."

"Can I call you Vile?" I ask, rather unfairly. She cocks her head to one side and stares at me.

"No, I don't like that much." Small wonder. To make minor amends, I offer her a Senior Service. "No thanks," she says. "It's a dirty habit." In that case, I fear this relationship may be doomed from the outset.

She begins to rabbit on, telling me that she, her sister Susan, and friend Brenda are down here camping for the week from Bristol. They are with a band of happy Christian brethren from one of those loopy fringe churches, but she doesn't really believe in any of it so don't worry, she won't try to convert me and, anyway, crucifixes give her the creeps and a skin rash.

I peer across the gloom within the tent trying to establish how the other two are progressing. Mike and the gorgeous Susan seem to have disappeared but I catch some movement inside his sleeping-bag and assume that all is well. Tulip, by contrast, is maintaining a lively rapport with the lanky Brenda. I tune in to a snippet of their conversation and it goes thus:

Brenda: "Yeah, I've got two brothers at home in Fishponds and a half-sister what lives in Gloucester."

Tulip: "A half-sister in Gloucester?"

Brenda: "Yep."

Tulip: "So, where does the rest of her live?"

Total silence from Brenda.

Meanwhile, Vile has embarked on a different conversational tack and is trying flattery to gain my attention. "You've got nice legs," she remarks, "I saw them earlier… in the field. So what were you really doing there?"

I see no reason to lie to her. Maybe she'll clear off if I disclose that, two minutes prior to our moonlit rendezvous, I was discharging sewage into the stream. However, taking a leaf out of Tulip's book of inanity and insanity, I decide to introduce a hint of eccentricity into my reply.

"Getting rid of a dead chicken," I answer truthfully though enigmatically. She's obviously puzzled but continues to decorate her face with that stupid, half-baked grin and presumably decides to ignore my strangeness.

"That farmer, Wilkes, he's a bit odd isn't he?" she says.

Time for a full-blooded assault on her sensitivity. I elect to wheel out some Hillbilly weirdness.

"Well, it's hardly surprising when you've got four wives," I smile.

She claps a hand to her mouth. "My god," she gasps. "That's not legal!"

"It is down here," I nod, widening my eyes and my smile. I'm enjoying this no end so I tweak up the eccentricity. "And you know that unfortunate little surprise you all had in your tent?" She nods nervously and I lean forward to stare into her pupils. "That was our local vicar." She pulls back and cradles her face with her chubby hands, her mouth dropping open in horror. I'm in fourth gear now, there's no stopping me. "Actually, you should feel honoured… he usually prefers sheep!" At this juncture, to add to the general flavour of rustic insanity, I give her one of my finest Elvis sneers. She pulls herself to her feet, glancing swiftly at the open tent flap.

"Where are you going, my dear?" I drool, sounding just a little too much like Long John Silver "The night is young." She crouches and scuttles over into Tulip and Brenda's territory where the two of them are having a lively exchange.

"No I will NOT," I hear Brenda protest. "It's staying on." Perhaps she's referring to the storm-lantern. I have no way of telling. I pick up some muttering from Tulip. He's complaining about a waste of bloody time and he might just as well be with Anthea. "And who's she when she's at home?" hisses Brenda. Tulip's response is a magnificent belch, a fitting end, I feel, to their brief romance.

Having failed completely to gain Brenda's attention, Vile slithers across to plead with her sister but finds only a pile of clothes. Mike's double sleeping bag has fulfilled its purpose. "Susan," whines Vile, "we have to go. They're all sex-maniacs around here!" Oddly, Susan is ignoring her sister's good advice, but she persists. "Susan, come up for air, you're panting." It's nice to see a young girl showing so much concern for her sister.

Quite suddenly, Mike scrambles from the sleeping bag and begins to hop about, pulling on his jeans.

"Get out of here!" he cries. "Everybody, grab your clothes and get out quick!"

We don't have a clue what the hell is going on but, when Mike is this serious, something is afoot, so we all run about like headless turkeys (I prefer not to mention 'chickens').

"What is it?" I shout as Mike literally throws us one by one into the cool night air.

"Wilkes's bullocks are stampeding," he yells. "Just run for the foot-bridge."

I can scarcely believe my ears. Has Mike been drinking too much Gold-top? Did Susan drive him insane with desire? Did I just step in a cow-pat? I mean, this isn't the prairies of Kansas… we don't have cattle stampedes in Fayling. This is ridiculous, for the second time this evening, I am abroad without my trousers. If Wilkes catches me this time, I swear he'll shoot me!

Imagine then, if you can, speeding barefoot through the night, a bundle of assorted clothing under your arm, and ten stone of sobbing Somerset dumpling hanging on for grim death to the waistband of your underpants. Add to this image, if you wish, a forest of knee-high thistles, a sea of cow dung, and the knowledge that twenty-five excited Devon Reds are heading your way, and you may get the picture. All I know is, when the soles of my feet hit the rough timbers of that rickety old foot-bridge, I've never felt happier, and a wild whoop of triumph escapes my lips.

We make it en masse to the other side of the bridge and collapse in a tumbling tangle of sweaty limbs and pieces of luggage. Incredibly, Mike has managed to escape carrying his guitar and his alarm clock. The rest of us have most of our clothes with us, except Susan who seems to be minus her jeans.

As soon as we have all regained our breath and Tulip has stopped laughing, we get to our feet and peer upstream into the gathering morning light. Our tent, although just visible, is but a shadow of its former glory. In fact, it looks like a wreck; the herd must have bulldozed straight through it. Downstream, standing in a steaming throng beside a pollarded willow and chewing the cud as though guiltless, the cattle gaze at us.

"What d'you think frightened them into stampeding?" asks Susan, cuddling up to Mike. He slowly raises his hand and points across the bridge at a small, demonic being that has crept into view. It sits studying us with his one serviceable eye… the King Liddle Basta. His lips curl back and a low, unholy growl rattles from his throat.

"Oh, no," whispers Tulip. "Now *he's* going to kill us!"

Unbelievably, Violet steps forward and approaches the hound from Hell.

"Don't be daft," she purrs. "He's lovely."

"Don't go near him!" I warn, but she walks on to what must surely be a grisly end. In my mind's eye I see the police searching the field for her gnawed limbs and shovelling her blood-soaked remains into a sack. God, it's gruesome! But, to our utter amazement, she crouches down beside him and tickles him playfully under his slavering chin. Instead of taking off her hand with one snap of his formidable jaws, he rolls onto his back and allows her to scratch his foul belly. The other girls join her and within seconds they've got him wriggling around with his paws padding the air and moaning like a new bride! We three lads can scarcely believe our eyes. Flash would be flabbergasted to know that his canine killing machine is secretly a sucker for the ladies.

At that moment, Mike's alarm clock bursts randomly into life, nearly giving us all a heart attack. In his surprise, he drops the damn thing and it wobbles away down the bank of the stream ringing like a fire engine. In the adjoining field, lights glow inside tents and voices are raised in agitation throughout the canvas settlement as the slumbering campers are rudely awakened at this early hour. Time to make ourselves scarce, we decide. Mike decides to call it a night and heads off on foot for his milk round. He instructs us to return to the campsite, survey the damage, and load what remains into his pick-up ready for evacuation at mid-day. We wave farewell to the girls and they skip away into the new-born morning with the Basta yapping excitedly at their heels. It is, indeed, a bloody peculiar world.

"You know," observes Tulip, exhibiting a rare burst of insight as we wend our way uphill, "I reckon old Flash has trained the Basta to flush out crumpet." An intriguing thought so, please, my Belch companion, expand your theory. "Well, he must have seen the girls come to our tent." Yes, I agree, so what? "So he uses the Basta to create a stampede and force the females back to their own quarters." Yes, I nod once more, so?

"Well, then he can repeat his indecent exposure act, hoping for more luck." Sadly for him, I pooh-pooh the idea on the grounds that Brenda would be far more inclined to attack him with a saucepan the second time around. I am then subjected to a stupid joke about a 'flash in the pan' but he finally shuts up.

The campsite is a bit of a mess but, thankfully, the tent remains fairly intact. The charging cows snapped a few guy-ropes and the tent has skewed to one side, but it escaped any major trampling. Dad need never know.

On our journey back into town, we stop at the newly installed 'ice-cold milk' dispensing machine at the bus station and slake our thirst. One of the early shift bus drivers gives us a suspicious look as he climbs into his cab and fires up the diesel bus so we move on down the sea-front.

A seaside town at this hour, even in summer, is a desolate place. It's getting light but the streets are deserted and the shops locked tight. We could commit some heinous crime right here and nobody would be aware of it for hours. It's the 'Mary Celeste' on dry land.

"You know what?" announces Tulip again. Oh, no, not another ground-breaking hypothesis for God's sake. "I've figured out what breed Flash's dog is… he's a bird-dog!"

We both break into song at the tops of our voices:

*Johnny kissed the teacher*

*He tip-toed up to reach her*

*He's the teacher's pet now*

*Gets what he can get now*

*Johnny made the teacher let him sit next to my baby… he's a bird-dog.*

# CHAPTER 4

## 'Stagger Lee' (Lloyd Price...1959)

The 'Fayling Gazette' lies open on the kitchen table where Dad left it when he went to work. I expect he was checking the position in the league of his skittle team and a quick glance confirms their usual place on the bottom. Dad just laughs and says, so what, he only goes for the beer, the banter, and the decorating work he gets to hear about from his mates.

A note from my mother, casually propped against the tomato ketchup bottle (the note, not my mother) informs me that she has 'gone shopping, your breakfast is under the grill, and don't you dare forget that you are helping your father this morning'. Bugger, I'd completely forgotten that I'd promised to rub down Mrs. Lee's soffits and window-sills ready for Dad to drop by and undercoat them. But a deal is a deal and the money will come in handy. I've got my eye on a really great striped shirt I've seen in Newman's window. Cliff wore an identical one on TV the other evening.

Breakfast turns out to be down to expectations: a wizened egg, a twisted slice of burnt bacon, a congealed clump of baked beans, and a piece of blackened toast so misshapen that if you threw it across the room it would probably return to you. Where did my mother learn to cook, Hiroshima? I slide the whole lot into the waste bin and prepare myself a couple of rounds of bread, butter, and honey. To hell with the cost, a man has to eat!

Flipping idly through the Gazette, my attention is captured by the following, under the heading 'Judge raps writer':

*Historian and author, Selwyn Boarhunt, was fined twenty pounds and bound over to keep the peace at Fayling Magistrates Court on Tuesday following an affray at Christie's Cavern amusement arcade. District Judge Theodore Felch, presiding, also imposed fines on the arcade proprietor, Alistair Iain Christie and holidaymaker, Albert Tyrone Wigginshaw. Several members of Fayling Salvation Army Brass Band were also taken into custody at the time of the disturbance but were released with cautions from the police. Mr Boarhunt, who is staying in the area with his family whilst doing research for a book on local family connections to the seventeenth century Pilgrim Fathers, was also warned by Judge Felch with regard to racing recklessly through Fayling's narrow quayside streets in the company of a dog and jumping fully-clothed into the harbour in a non-swimming area.*

So, the Nutter is an historical writer. Well, he's certainly written himself into Fayling's history.

There is, to my chagrin (don't you just love that word?), a PS to my mother's note instructing me to pop next-door to the Lucas sisters and ask if they have baked the cake as promised. Apparently the cake is a donation towards the annual jumble sale (or 'rubbish redistribution' as I call it) organised by the Fayling Light Opera and Pantomime Society (FLOPS). I hate going round to the two Lucas spinsters, Moira and Mavis. They always insist on dragging me through to look at their back garden. It's a freakish wonderland designed to attract every known species of garden bird in England. Trees are festooned with nut-filled feeders and lumps of stinking cooking fat; crap-encrusted bird tables rise at jaunty angles from the feeble lawn and the whole place has the aura of a bombsite.

"Oh, hello, Colin," beams Moira, stepping to one side to allow me to enter.

"It's OK," I smile wanly, "I'm not staying. I'm just here to collect the cake."

Mavis's ruddy-cheeked face appears on her sister's shoulder like some mad parrot.

"Would you like to see our tits, dear?" she trills.

"We've got twelve," declares Moira proudly.

I fall into a fake fit of coughing in order to cover the hysterical shriek of laughter which is welling up inside. The outlandish image pops into my head of the sisters lying naked in the back yard, each suckling a row of six piglets.

Before I am able to recover my composure, I am manhandled down the sepia-painted hall, pausing briefly to gawp at the fruitcake (how appropriate) they have made, and out into the garden. It's mayhem out here with every sparrow, blue-tit, and chaffinch in Fayling squabbling and chirping over the bounty on offer. Even that idle bastard of a pigeon is down amidst it, strutting around like Adolf Hitler.

Suddenly, to my delight, the entire circus rises in the air with a strumming of beating wings and seeks refuge amongst the bushes. At the same time, our cat, Archie, appears from next-door and seats himself smugly on a fence post. Mavis loses her cool.

"Oh, you naughty, naughty puss," she howls and, grabbing a nearby rake, she makes for Archie with malice aforethought. But Archie isn't eight and a half years old for nothing. He waits until Mavis has swung the rake behind her and, as the weapon arcs round to take his head off, he drops effortlessly back into our garden. The rake head connects with the post with a fearful crack and Mavis releases it, bawling with pain. The birds exit the garden with a flurry of wings, leaving Mavis kneeling in a flower-bed gripping her wrist and gasping terrible threats to Archie. I'm not sure he'll make it to nine. Moira scurries across to administer to her and attend to the quivering wrist. She glances darkly in my direction.

"Colin," she calls, "your mother's pussy is causing a lot of trouble lately."

Well, I'm with you on that one, Moira.

The fruitcake and I leave discreetly.

*

The trouble with Mrs. Lee, charming and generous though she may be, is her weird sense of domestic hygiene. She opens the door to me holding a sink plunger in one rubber-gloved hand whilst her free hand is covered to the elbow in flour. To me, the two don't quite gel somehow.

"Oh, hello dear," she chirps, adding a streak of flour to her brow with her wrist. "You must be your father's son." This is undeniable so I nod. She swings the plunger around gaily, sprinkling us both with what I hope is tap water. "Come on in, dear, you'll need to go round the house and open the windows for your undercoating. The loo window is already open." She brandishes the plunger again. "I'm trying to clear a bit of a pan blockage." Yeah, but, saucepan or toilet pan? I feign a sneeze in order to wipe the droplets from my chin. "Whoops-a-daisy," she laughs. "Dust, I expect. The hoover bag burst in the lounge earlier." She closes the front door behind me and ushers me down the hall. "I'm making scones so I expect you'd like one later." I turn to decline her offer but she's vanished into the kitchen, singing along at full throttle with the radio.

I make my way from room to room releasing corroded window catches. The whole place is in a state of benign chaos. To reach a window I have to climb over furniture or make enormous, exaggerated strides to step over piles of clothes, magazines, or boxes filled with God knows what. A musty aroma hangs in the air, sort of a cross between putrefying vegetables and a ferret's hutch. Maybe it's a putrefying ferret.

The third bedroom door is shut so, just in case Mrs. Lee's son, Ronny, is still in bed, I knock. Ronny is a classmate of mine, but not what you'd call a close friend. Personally, I like him, even though he tends to be a bit of a loner. Having said that, on the occasions I've been in his company, he strikes me as being a witty bloke, in an offbeat sort of way. There's no doubt about one thing though, Ronny is a bloody genius at science, mainly chemistry. He consistently comes way ahead at the top in all three science subjects; in fact, there was talk of him taking 'A' Levels simultaneously with his 'O's. He knows one helluva lot more about Chemistry than 'Jacko' Jackman, our so-called teaching expert. Let's face it, if Jacko is so qualified, how come half his hair is missing after a classroom explosion at his previous school? He's a danger to the school population. I always make sure I sit at the back during his classes, which is where I made Ronny's acquaintance as it happens. Well, when I say 'made his acquaintance', I sit next to him but Ronny is usually fast asleep. And that, of course, gets right up Jacko's nose so he repeatedly reports him to the Count. Trouble is, Ronny falls asleep in physics and biology too so he's constantly in the shite. His defence is that the lessons are so basic that he can't stay awake during them. Naturally, that gets the Count mad as hell and, once, hoping to humiliate him into changing his attitude, the Count arranged for Ronny to visit a psychiatrist. Ronny said he really enjoyed the interview and spent a pleasant hour discussing frontal lobe function and pituitary-gland chemistry. The shrink told him he was a bright kid and maybe it was the Count who needed treatment.

"Thanks, Mum," calls Ronny from inside his room. "Leave it on the floor. I'll grab it in a mo."

He thinks I'm his old lady calling with the toxic scones so I open the door and peer in.

"Stone me, Brillo," he grins, "what the hell are you doing here, daddyo?"

"I've come to rub down your soffits, mate."

"Perish the thought. Come in and shut the door."

It's only because I know Ronny to be eccentric that I'm not totally dumbfounded at what he appears to be engaged in. He's standing at the window holding a hamster which he is clearly about to inject with a vicious-looking hypodermic needle. I squeeze through the narrow space between his bed and a row of metal filing cabinets and get to his side just as the hamster receives the jab with a muffled squeal.

"Hells bells, Ronald, what are you doing to it?" I ask anxiously. I don't normally enjoy watching pain being inflicted on dumb animals, although I do make an exception where Tulip is concerned.

"It's OK. He'll be fine, man," assures Ronny, popping the terrified rodent into a cardboard-box. "It's an accelerated growth experiment I'm working on."

"So what d'you expect to happen?" I enquire, trying to disguise my scepticism.

"That," he says, nodding towards a dimly lit alcove. I step closer and lift a grubby sheet draped over a large, odorous cage.

"Christ al-bloody-mighty!" I cry, dropping the sheet and falling back onto the bed. Glaring at me through the mesh, pink eyes wild with hate, and teeth gnawing menacingly at thin air, is a hamster the size of a fully-grown cat! I'm not kidding, this is the godfather of all hamsters, a rodent to marvel at and I swear he'd have your fingers off in a trice if you gave him half a chance. Every freak-show should have one. Never mind about lettuce and carrot tops, this boy is a meat eater, I just know it.

"My god, Ronny, what d'you call that?" I murmur.

"Well, I call him Mr. Hyde," chuckles Ronny, snapping off his rubber gloves.

All of a sudden, I am overcome with a strong desire to get out of Ronny's bedroom/laboratory. There are things that are not quite right in here and I'm beginning to believe one of 'em is Ronald himself. An air of menace pervades the room. There's also an air of reeking hamster. Let's face it, how does Ronny ever get to clean out that cage with that savage bugger in it? No, I've had enough of this and, besides, needles make me queasy. I make valid excuses to leave, explaining that I have to get busy with sandpaper and paint scraper.

Boy, am I glad to breathe fresh air... well, as fresh as it gets in Mrs. Lee's back yard with the sewer manhole open. Dad has left all the necessary gear including his brand new electric sander, and soon I'm beavering away in a cloud of dust. To relieve the boredom I'm singing my way up through the hit parade, leaving out the ones I don't like. By the time I reach 'Dream Lover' all the sills along the yard are stripped down to bare timber, so I move across to the detached, two-storey garage and prop the ladder against the wall in order to climb up and attend to the small window in the gable-end.

It's a long climb up this ladder, and a long climb back down again when I realise that the sander cable is too short to reach the apex of the gable. I clamber back up again with a handful of assorted sandpapers, a Senior Service drooping from my mouth. Dad won't say much if he catches me smoking. He knows I'm virtually sixteen, although he might be surprised at how many I smoke.

The window up here is a small, four-paned affair with peeling paintwork and, being a nosey bugger at the best of times, I find myself polishing a circle in the thick layer of grime in order to take a peek. To my surprise, the interior of the garage is illuminated by a single fluorescent tube and, at the far end by the closed door, I can just make out the figure of Ronny seated in a lopsided armchair. He appears to be sipping some kind of clear liquid from a wine glass.

"Strewth," I murmur to myself, he's finally flipped and is drinking his own concoctions. My imagination whirls into overdrive and I see Ronny leaping from his chair, hurling the glass against the wall, and grasping his throat as long black hairs begin to sprout from his skin. Yes, it looks as though Fayling has its own Dr. Jekyll. But, wait... would this necessarily be a bad thing? I wonder, because what else has Fayling got to offer the visitor? A beach polluted with raw sewage or tar, take your pick; a pier which is so rickety people have been sea-sick walking along it; and a decrepit little museum where the oldest exhibit is Horace Bale, the curator. Take last summer. The highlight of the season was when a couple pleasuring each other in the back of a delivery van rocked it out of gear and it rolled over a cliff, killing 'em both. (I do not believe the lurid rumour that they were found with smiles on their faces.)

I carefully squeak out a larger hole on the dusty pane and press my eye to the glass. Yes, there he is, and now he's leaning forward to fill his glass again from... well, I can't make out what the hell it is. It looks like the tail-end of some giant chemistry set. My god, it *is* a giant chemistry set... it's a liquor-still! I have to steady myself on the ladder as the enormity of my discovery sends a thrill down my spine. Ronny has shot to new heights in my estimation. My earlier doubts about his sanity over the hamster experiments melt away like frost in sunlight. Here is a genius, a bootlegger, and a bloke to foster closer relationships with (or should that be 'with which to foster'? Oh, shut it, Paddick.) How many other mates do I have who actually distil their own spirituous liquors? Nary a one.

Foolishly, in my eagerness to gain a clearer view of the still, I jerk the ladder and it rattles against the window pane. Ronny instantly catches sight of my face, but, instead of rushing to switch off the light, he grins and beckons me in, tilting his wine glass temptingly as he does so.

As the garage door scrapes shut behind me, I enter the world of Al Capone and twenties American prohibition. It's a big thrill. I glance around half expecting to see a couple of trilby-hatted heavies chewing on cigars and cleaning their Tommy-guns. But what I do see is just as impressive: a monstrous, gurgling liquor-still stretching the entire length of the garage.

"Do you take it with orange juice, lime juice, or as it comes?"

enquires mine host, blowing dust from another wine glass. As I have no idea what the liquid is, I opt for orange juice and Ronny turns the little tap at the business end of the apparatus and half fills my glass. He hands it to me together with a bottle of orange cordial and then drags a sack of something from a corner. "Take a seat, man." I sit and sniff the clear spirit, then take a tentative sip. Strong fumes invade my nasal passage and my nose feels like someone just grabbed it and gave it a bloody good tweak. The front of my head momentarily separates from the rest of my skull and my eyes melt in their sockets. Well, that's what it feels like for a second or two. But it is immediately followed by an overwhelming feeling of wellbeing and, as I lean back against the wall, contentment floods my body and the world is my dearest friend.

Three glasses later, Ronny sits in his armchair smiling at me. Nothing is said but much is being considered, I believe. One thing that does occur to me is why he appears to be stone-cold sober and yet I am most assuredly half-pissed. Unless… yes, unless he is permanently drunk, in which case I'd never know the difference. Yes, of course, that's it, that accounts for his constant sleepiness in class. He's always half-cut! I am suddenly overcome with the marvellous knowledge that I am in the company, not only of a master chemist and moonshine manufacturer, but a genuine alcoholic. It's a great privilege.

If you put plenty of orange juice in this stuff it slips down like honey. And that's the problem… it's far too easy to drink. But we are soon past caring. We begin to open up to each other and, in no time at all, I've told him all about Wendy, my adventures with Caroline, and my struggle with Lamont. Ronny says he knows nothing about girls but, if I want, he could let me have a mixture which, if administered clandestinely, would render Lamont harmless in the 'mother seducing' area. I thank him but decline. The thought of a gigantic, rampaging, tooth-gnashing (even if impotent) Lamont is too much to contemplate.

Ronny goes on to discuss his musical and literary preferences. It's all a bit way-out for my liking. He says he 'digs' Modern Jazz and why don't I borrow some of his MJQ and Dave Brubeck records and a book he's got hold of by some bloke called Jack Kerouac. I've never even heard of 'em, but I envy Ronny's knowledge and the way he speaks. I suppose he's what you'd call a 'beatnik'. He also tells me he's got some real good 'stuff' growing in 'a certain location', but my attention wanders a bit as I'm not much interested in horticulture. He calls it 'grass', which you have to admit, is about as boring as gardening gets.

Now I'm squinting at my trusty Timex and grappling briefly with the thought that I should actually be doing something with window-sills but I can't remember what. There is a knock at the garage-door and Mrs. Lee's voice calls to us.

"Ronald, tell your friend his father rang to say he won't be coming over today, and to bring Sandra home." (I translate the female mentioned as 'sander'.)

"OK, Ma," bawls Ronny, slumping further down into the distressed armchair.

"I've left some scones here by the door, dear," comes the muffled voice from outside.

"That's cool, Ma," shouts Ronny.

"No, they're still warm, dear."

How different are the worlds of the young and the aged.

I struggle to my feet only to discover that my brain is having another of its bolshie moments and point-blank refuses to transmit any instructions worth a tinker's toss to my legs. In fact, this current rebellion is so severe that it seems unlikely that walking, as it is general accepted, is even possible. I make a trial shuffle around the garage, deliberately leaning to starboard to avoid tilting over into Ronny's burbling moonshine equipment, but it's a difficult passage involving much wall bumping. Not a good omen for any lengthy journeys, but I'm determined to at least exit the garage. Yes, that'll be objective number one: opening the garage door.

"Leaving already?" Ronny asks, refilling his glass for the umpteenth time.

"Yep, godda go, mate," I reply.

The door seems to be in league with my brain and will not open no matter how hard I pull it. Ronny suggests I turn the handle and push it as that's how it opens, ya twerp, and immediately I find myself outside in the glaring sunlight. Something gives way beneath my foot and I peer down to see that I've stepped on the scones and broken the plate. I stick my head back into the garage. "I prob'ly just saved you from food pois'ning," I leer. Ronny salutes me with his empty glass.

"Cheers, man," he smirks, and sinks back into his chair.

I stand gawping mindlessly around the yard, desperately trying to bring my head back into line so that I can make a decision of some sort. I mean, what is the point of owning a brain if it continually deserts you in your hour of need? I can't go through life with an incompetent cerebrum. It's going to have to shape up. Maybe there are exercises I can do. I'll look into it when I'm sober.

But all is not lost. My wibbly-wobbly gaze settles upon a bike leaning conveniently against a dustbin. This fact alone is enough to persuade me that it is there for the taking because why else would it be cuddling up to the dustbin if it was not due to be thrown out with the rubbish? And even if this is a bit of a logical shortcut for theft, do they not say that alcohol is the cause of most crime? Who am I to dispute the statistics?

A tipsy inspection of the bicycle, involving much bell tinkling and tyre pinching, assures me that it is perfectly capable of getting me home so, with a push of the foot on the gravel and a wild swing of the leg over the saddle, I waver off on my trusty steed. Alan Ladd never did it better.

Not until I have cycled along Saratoga Avenue and turned down into Yorktown Grove does my brain bother to remind me that this is not the way home. Furthermore, it is only when I am winging down the deceptively steep gradient at a speed which no drunk should attempt, that I am rudely enlightened on the subject of Ronald's bicycle maintenance, i.e. the total bloody lack of it. There appear to be no brakes on this velocipede! The only response I get from my fiercest grip on the brake-handles is the squeal of metal to metal and the whiff of hot rubber. To add to my excitement, Ronny, for some reason known only to mad chemists and Satan, has applied a fixed wheel to this machine leaving me with two options: pedal like Buster Keaton in one of those speeded-up sequences in a silent movie, or stretch out my legs like aircraft wings and risk taking off. I opt for the latter and fly on.

But isn't it peculiar how booze dampens your fear and inflates your belief in your capabilities? Suddenly, I am indestructible, immortal, up there with Superman. And now, approaching on the starboard wing, I glimpse the Lucas sisters, heavily laden with shopping bags and labouring up the hill towards me. They stop to stare as I flash past them, my legs akimbo and a broad smile of pleasure on my face… an experience they will, doubtless, never enjoy.

All good things, of course, come to an end and now a tiny termite of doubt is gnawing away at the timbers of my euphoria. Adrenalin is putting up a stiff fight against the alcohol and my senses are finally beginning to face reality. My eyes and ears are doing their best to warn me that I'm on a short trip to catastrophe, but how curious that so many people seem to know me. They shout and wave as I career down the hill.

Dead ahead and crossing my path is the High Street and the 'Halt' sign which I should obey but, sadly, will ignore. Now I'm really worried. At this speed, veering to either side is suicide. Dead ahead, but slightly to the left, is Trotts the Butchers; to the right is Boots the Chemist. If I had the luxury of choice, I'd probably opt to crash through the plate-glass of Boots rather than complement the meats and offal in Bill Trott's window. At least Boots could patch me up a bit. But there is, fleetingly, one last hope open to me and I must act upon it instantly. Squeezed between these two shops is Nozzer Isaac's 'Secondhand Emporium', a labyrinth of shadowy corridors and dusty rooms filled to the gunwales with faded junk. Unbelievably, Nozzer makes a good living peddling all this well-worn tat. He will buy almost anything, at a price, and sell you anything too, at a much better price. You could walk in with a tired television set you want to sell for a fiver and Nozzer will do you a deal. Chances are you'll walk out five minutes later with a clapped-out hockey stick and a quid in your pocket, thinking you've done well; but you've overlooked the fact that you don't play hockey. But, hey, this is all by the by and, frankly, I don't have time for all this chit-chat when I'm hurtling to my doom.

My only chance is to aim this insane contraption straight at Nozzer's open double-door and pray that he still stacks all those old carpets and mattresses against the far end wall. And there is a trump card to my final hand: Nozzer recently persuaded the Council to remove the kerb-stones in front of his doors, creating a sloped ramp to enable him to reverse his van right into the building. Don't ask me how he enticed that bunch of tyrannical knobs to authorise it, but he did. Maybe he argued that it was a religious requirement, like circumcision. The good news is I now have a slope to hit instead of a solid kerb. The bad news is that, at this speed, I could well be propelled upwards and through the first-floor window. I have no way of telling.

I cross the High Street at full pelt, my legs bent up to avoid the whirling pedals. Only God and the Laws of Motion will get me safely to the other side. To my right I am briefly aware of a green bus; to my left a red sports car enters my vision and is gone instantly as I try to focus on the far side. The front wheel of the bike strikes the kerb ramp smack in the centre and I shoot across the pavement, scattering a family of dozy holidaymakers dawdling along licking ice creams. My bell takes the kid's cone with it and I hear a cry of anguish, but I have my life to save here and, besides, I don't much like raspberry ripple. I glimpse Nozzer's stunned expression as I enter his shop at the speed of light. He's perched up on his stool like some Dickensian bank clerk where he can keep an eye on his stock, just in case someone tries to do a runner with a wardrobe or something.

Fortunately, the central aisle of the shop is wide and, with the minor exception of the decapitation of a garden statue of Venus, I cause minimal damage as I head for the rear wall. To my enormous relief, the mattresses and carpets are in their appointed positions and I steer directly at them. As a piece of navigational mastery, my trip astride the bicycle from Hell should probably be up for an award, although my final impact with the mattresses did not account for a hidden set of bed springs sandwiched in their depths.

For the second time in the space of a few days I am lying on the ground temporarily unconscious and, when light eventually begins to filter through my eyelids, I lift them to find myself, once more, staring into the face of a gargoyle. Not our garden gnome this time, but something even more hideous. This, Colin Paddick, is it. You are dead, old mate, and this is definitely not Heaven. The face of the Devil himself fills my vision… and is it ever ugly! The enormous mouth quivers as a glossy black tongue darts out to wet the thick lips. The creature speaks in a harsh rasp.

"My life, you're in a lot of trabble, my boy," it whispers. And Nozzer draws back his face, slides a finger beneath that silly little skull-cap he wears, and gives his scalp an audible scratch. But wait, my wonky gaze is now drawn to another face peering down at me. The face of an angel... God has saved me, it's Wendy!

Pulling myself onto my elbows, I lose myself in Wendy's eyes... all eight of 'em. I blink a few times to clear my vision and, Allelujah, she's still there. But it's happening again, isn't it? She does it to me every time. Each time fate deals me a dastardly blow and I'm feeling vulnerable and humiliated, out she pops from the woodwork and turns me into jelly again.

"Colin," she says silkily, the ghost of a smile haunting her luscious lips, "whatever are you doing?"

I lean back against a mattress and sigh. I feel strangely light-headed and a trifle sick. Perhaps it has a lot to do with consuming raw moonshine and head-butting a bed spring, not forgetting that my forehead still bears the bruise from the incident in the woodshed. I drag myself into a kneeling position and, for some unaccountable reason, Nozzer offers me a Liquorice Allsort from a paper bag. I decline politely on the grounds that anything bearing the name 'Liquor' is not a good idea and, secondly, that Nozzer would certainly put it on the bill if I took one.

"Suit yourself, my boy," he says. "Now then, what about all this damage?" He gestures towards the head of Venus, smirking up at us from its position adjacent to a pile of Victorian chamber pots.

"'Fraid I'll have to owe you for the statue, Mr Isaac," I croak.

He shakes his head deliberately, picks a note-book from his shirt pocket and licks the end of a stubby pencil. He sucks air through the gaps in his broken teeth. "No can do, sonny," he sighs. "We gotta come to an arrangement. Broken stock is dead money."

What is this, the Jewish Mafia? Does he expect me to take out Hire Purchase on Venus's cement head? I could glue it back on for two bob for Christ's sake! But before I can protest or summon a lawyer, Wendy squeezes my hand and throws me a honeydew smile.

"Why don't you add the cost of the damage to my bill, Mr. Isaac?" she suggests. Suddenly, the soothing sound of celestial cellos fills my ears and the room takes on a rosy hue. Or am I passing out? Anyway,

Nozzer seems delighted and returns to his Bob Cratchit desk to make out her invoice. I climb shakily to my feet and we walk up the aisle together. Could this be a portent of what is to be?

"I've just bought a Dansette record player," she purrs in my ear, turning my already unsteady legs to jelly. "Perhaps you could lend me some forty-fives to listen to." Yes, yes, and maybe I could bring them round and deliver them to your bedroom. My imagination has gone into orbit and, long before we reach Nozzer's desk, we're snogging like crazy on her bed... and all to the strains of Conway Twitty crooning 'It's only make believe'.

"Right, young lady, that'll be three pounds eighteen and seven pence ha'penny," announces Nozzer, handing her the bill. The Dansette is marked up at three pounds five shillings, so, by some bizarre Old Testament accountancy, he's priced the head of Venus at thirteen shillings and seven pence halfpenny.

Once outside, we find ourselves walking in the direction of Wendy's hotel. This proves to be troublesome because, due to the now distorted shape of Ronny's bicycle, I am obliged to carry it. To add to my difficulties (and in spite of my elation at Wendy's revitalised interest in me) the bootleg booze is wearing off, leaving me with a nauseous hangover. Curiously, though, Wendy hasn't asked me exactly what I was doing riding a bike at high speed in Nozzer's emporium. Come to think of it, why was I heading down into town when I was supposed to be making my way home? I vow never to touch another drop of Ronald's moonshine.

We halt outside Woolworth's. "Mr. Isaac told me I need a new plug for this," says Wendy, holding up the record player. She places a hand on mine, sending a shiver down my spine and awakening Wee William from his slumber. "D'you think you've got time to come home with me and fit it for me?" she asks coyly. Adrenalin nearly explodes from my every orifice, and poor William writhes like a captured serpent down in his foul nest! I am temporarily incapable of speech but, despite the growing queasiness in my gut, I nod like a maniac.

Dumping the bike in the service alley that runs up the side of the building, we enter the wonderful world of Woolworth. Yes, we all love old F.W., don't we? And what a refreshing change he is from those idiots Hoover and Gaggia.

Wendy consults me on which plug to buy and my heart swells with pride as I advise her. The whole transaction is rounded off splendidly when she gives me a peck on the cheek over the thirteen-amp fuses. For a moment I expect to see all the display lamps lighting up spontaneously. But, as usual, Satan is lurking in the shadows. My stomach suddenly begins to churn like a cheese maker and I am obliged to steady myself against the counter to avoid swaying around drunkenly. I begin to wonder what Ronny has done to me. Let's face it, I don't have a clue what was brewing in that still. For all I know it might have contained fermenting hamster corpses.

When I walk into the alley to collect the bike, I find it missing (an expression I have always found confusing). What kind of twerp would steal a bicycle looking like it was designed by Picasso? I peer up the street expecting to see a bloke with a white stick making off with it, but all I catch sight of is the Council dust-cart disappearing into the traffic. Ah well, c'est la vie. Ronny's bike is on its way to the Great Tip in the Sky (actually it's at the back of Fayling Knoll). I have some explaining to do when next I meet Dr. Jekyll, but chances are he'll be too far gone to worry about his bicycle.

Fortunately, whilst in the alley, I had the considerable relief of breaking wind which has eased the pressure on my plumbing. I take the Dansette from Wendy and we walk hand in hand along the seafront and up the steps of the West Cliffs Hotel. To my surprise, her parents are busy in the terraced front garden laying out a massive floral message to the world. It reads:


'WELCOME TO THE WEST CLIFFS HOTEL... LET US BRIGHTEN UP YOUR STAY.'


Very clever I must confess, all spelt out with colourful bedding plants. It must have taken all spring to get it right. On the bottom level, below the flowers, Mr. Matthews has constructed a long, narrow fishpond which his wife is filling with a hose. They both wave cheerily as we climb the steps.

"Hi Mum and Dad," Wendy calls. "Got my record player. This is Colin."

We pass into the cool interior of the hotel reception area and on through the kitchen to the rear of the building. Wendy pushes open the door to her surprisingly small room and my heart sinks. All my salacious fantasies of snogging her in the privacy of her bedroom are snuffed out by the horrifying discovery that, not only does she share her room with her younger sister, but the little bugger is one half of the Burgess and Maclean spy duo! Here they are, in all their terrible Brownie splendour, sitting on the edge of the lower bunkbed reading Wendy's 'Boyfriend' magazine. They cease giggling instantly as our eyes meet and we stare at each other in contemptuous disbelief. Once more I have been outwitted by the forces of evil and the junior branch of the Guides Association (one and the same in my opinion).

"Janet, Olive, what are you doing here?" complains Wendy. "Why aren't you out Brownie-ing?"

"Brown Owl's got a cold," they chant in unison. "She fell in a rockpool," adds Janet/Burgess. She makes one of those exaggerated 'yah-boo' faces that little kids do so well and pokes her tongue out at me probably to remind me that she holds damaging information about me. I know in my heart of hearts that it's only a matter of moments before my cover is blown. And, sod me, Wendy inadvertently paves the way.

"Janet," she chides, "don't be rude to Colin. He's here to fix my record player so why don't you both scoot?"

"We know him," sneers Olive/Maclean, nodding at me with a triumphant gleam in her eyes.

"Oh, how?" says Wendy.

Here it comes, the hammer blow, the de-frocking, the exposure.

Burgess: "He was in the sand-dunes."

Maclean: "And Brown Owl said he was being disgusting."

What is the penalty for murder, provided you can claim provocation and you're ridding society of two dangerous psychotics? For example, are two Brownies equivalent only to one Girl Guide or, perhaps, half a Boy Scout? That sounds about right to me and I might get away with manslaughter. But what's the point? The damage is done. Wendy eyes me apprehensively.

"What d'you mean by 'disgusting'?"

The kid opens her mouth but I drown her out with an explosion of slightly hysterical laughter

"She probably caught me having a pee!" I chortle wildly, grasping the Dansette plug. "Got a screwdriver, Wendy? I'll get this going for you."

"Yes," she nods and thrusts a finger at the treacherous twosome. "Now you two can clear off."

Janet and Olive pout, mutter, and slouch away into the kitchen.

My nausea has now risen to new heights but I swallow hard, fix the plug, and switch on the record player. Wendy drops a Connie Francis LP on the deck and lies on the floor, swooning to 'Carolina Moon'. There seems little point in staying now so I make my excuses and she sees me out to the front entrance where she unexpectedly treats me to a farewell brush of her lips on mine. This has the effect of causing yet another tsunami in my stomach. To make matters worse and delaying my departure further, her mother comes trotting over carrying a galvanised bucket.

"Wendy," she trills, "look at our lovely new fish for the ornamental pond. They're called Japanese Koi and cost a fortune." She holds the bucket whilst Wendy inspects the contents.

"Wow, Mum, they're enormous. Look, Colin!"

I have a bad feeling about this; a premonition of imminent calamity flashes through my being. I lean cautiously forward and peep reluctantly into the bucket. My eyes are immediately assailed by a squirming, glassy maelstrom of giant goldfish, their mouths gaping and closing as they swirl around in a frenzied panic. One look is all it takes. Gripping the edge of the bucket with both hands, I vomit straight into it. Mrs. Matthews skips backwards with a terrible cry of horror, we all release our hold on the bucket, and it clatters to the floor, spilling its grotesque brew over the steps. Down at the pond, Mr. Matthews observes the unfolding catastrophe and scrambles up through the pristine floral extravaganza to help his wife who is now sliding down towards him on her backside.

To digress for a moment… One of life's little oddities (no, not Tulip) is the constant presence in a seaside town of *Larus argentatus*, the Herring-gull, a noisy, scavenging, incontinent bastard who is seldom more than ten feet from a free meal. He can be found in large numbers at any rubbish tip and can swoop from the sky, crapping at will (or anyone else) as soon as some gormless twit from the Midlands starts throwing bread crusts in the air....and right now, he and forty-five of his cousins have settled along the hotel roof, even before the bucket goes down. It's uncanny. With one united squawk of glee they dive amongst us, snatching up one flapping fish after another. But their gluttony has backfired because these fishies are not your average beak-full of sprat or mackerel. These boys are Sumo-size. In no time at all, fish are dropping from the skies like some curious Biblical pestilence.

Once, during an English language lesson, the Count used the word 'apoplectic' and, with his usual disregard for our advancement in the world, he omitted to explain its meaning. I looked it up at the first opportunity and wondered if the day would ever dawn when it would come in handy. Today is that day and Mr. Matthews is it... apoplectic, that is. He is, I firmly believe, temporarily deranged, because how else can you explain his behaviour? He is leaping recklessly from one terrace to the next, sliding carelessly through his flowery message with both heels, all in a madcap attempt to recapture the Koi carp. His wife is not helping matters with her rather silly efforts to rake them into a heap as though they were autumn leaves. As for the hotel guests, well, I'm sickened by their lack of compassion. I really think they are out of order to gather along the top patio with drinks in their hands whistling, clapping, and shouting hurtful remarks such as 'Oh, no, not fish again for lunch!' Wendy bursts into tears and runs back into the hotel, sobbing all the way.

As the last fish falls from the heavens, I turn and slope away, humiliated and heartbroken, wishing only to distance myself from the West Cliffs Hotel. I risk a swift glance back at the scene of havoc on the terraces and notice that, with a grim sort of poetic irony, the floral message has been reduced to something entirely out of keeping with a top-class hotel. It now reads: 'WELCOME TO...H..E..LL....UP YOUR..S'

All is lost. The Devil has had his day once more and there really seems little point in going on. Wendy will certainly never speak to me again and who could blame her? Yes, fate and Ronny Lee have dealt me a lethal blow today.

\*

Slouching morosely along the High Street and deep in thought, I collide with that ridiculous wooden, man-size effigy of a Red Indian that lurks outside Tucker's tobacconist. As I hop around rubbing my sore knee and cursing the Sioux Nation, Eric Tucker appears in the shop entrance, pipe gripped between his yellow false teeth and a face like thunder.

"Did you just kick my Indian?" he seethes.

I stand erect and stare resolutely into the lenses of his National Health spectacles. I am simply not in the mood for this kind of Third Reich belligerence and, to my satisfaction and with no encouragement from my brain, my top lip begins to curl into an epic Elvis sneer. I can only assume that Eric has never been confronted by anything quite like it. Perhaps he expects me to leap at him and savage his Meerschaum. Anyhow, the pipe slumps to the corner of his mouth shedding a storm of sparks onto his waistcoat, and he backs away into the fug of his shop. I poke my head around the door and notice that he has retreated behind his counter and is flapping at his waistcoat with his hand.

For some reason, Eric always puts me in mind of Ebenezer Scrooge so I take this rare opportunity to test him out. I jerk my thumb at the Indian.

"Are there no prisons? Are there no workhouses?" I call into the gloom of the shop. And adding for topical good measure. "Are there no reservations?"

Clearly rattled, Eric shuffles jars and cigarette packs on the counter. "We're closing soon," he says, pointing to the clock on the wall. But I'm not prepared to let him off the hook yet. Recent events have fired me up and someone is going to have to suffer. It might as well be Eric. I need a really pithy parting shot but, as expected, my brain is on a go-slow again. Meanwhile, gaining in courage, Eric has moved to the end of the counter beside a towering free-standing display of 'Navy Shag'. In a flash of inspiration, I call out to him from the pavement.

"There's a word for people like you, Eric."

"Oh, and what might that be, you cheeky little sod?" he answers pugnaciously.

I dart back into the shop and watch with glee as he jumps backwards with fright and disappears amidst the collapsing tobacco display.

"Tobacconist!" I bellow, and leave him floundering on his polished oak floor.

Although this successful skirmish with Eric and his tribesman raises my spirits, it's a temporary elevation and, by the time I lift the latch on our front gate, I am deep in despair again. To add insult to injury, who should I espy skulking on the doorstep in the company of my mother, but Lamont. He is clearly just leaving and seems to freeze as he turns from trying to furtively kiss her farewell and claps eyes on me.

His face has undergone yet another transformation. What is it exactly? I step closer and see that he has an Elastoplast stretched across his nose and is sporting a livid swollen cheek. This is most promising and, if I was myself in a better state of physical and mental health, I would hazard a grin. What the hell has he been up to this time? He certainly is a glutton for facial punishment.

"Colin," snaps my mother, "where have you been? Your father had to go round to Mrs. Lee's and fetch his tools!"

Bugger, I forgot the sander. Dad might be miffed.

Lamont is staring at me in a very disturbing manner and seems quite agitated. He growls something in my mother's ear and she addresses me in her finest SS tone.

"Were you riding a bicycle in the High Street today, my lad?" she crackles.

I adopt one of my best innocent victim expressions and then upgrade it to outrage. This usually works on mothers.

"Bicycle? What bicycle? You just saw me walk up the path," I protest, gesturing grandly at the crazy-paving with the sweep of my hand. "Anyway, is there a law against cycling in the High Street?"

"That's quite enough, Colin," flashes my mother. "As you can see, Quentin… Mr. Lamont has had another motor accident."

I glance at Lamont's battered features and permit the vaguest flicker of a smile to move across my lips. He pinks up with rage, but I know he's not about to upset his little apple cart of lust by blowing his ginger top in front of my mother. She, on the other hand, might be thinking that she's overstepped the mark a trifle with her thinly veiled accusations.

"I expect Quentin is wondering if you happened to see any... well... silly behaviour by boys on bikes," she says. I shake my head, mumble inarticulately, and squeeze past them into the house.

Safely locked in my room, I lie on the bed and consider the immediate future. My first conclusion is that there isn't one. But, dammit all to hell, there must be more to life than Fayling can offer! There's a big wide world out there full to the brim with other Wendys who have no connection whatsoever with Japanese carp or Polish lady-killers. There are plenty more fish in sea. The world is my oyster. I wish I could get off the subject of fish.

Outside, that pigeon has the bloody nerve to flutter onto my window-sill and look in at me. 'Yuh baas-tard,' he coos, and struts up and down the sill like a homosexual. I throw a maths text-book at him and miss by a mile. He dips his head in contempt and calls me a bastard again. Am I losing my touch with birds in general? I suppose it's possible. According to Tim Lewis, our biology teacher, it's all down to chemistry, which begs the question, why the hell is Tim teaching biology? But maybe Tim and the pigeon have a point: perhaps my internal chemistry is malfunctioning. I have no way of telling.

I pick up my guitar and strum a few random chords. Funny how they all turn out to be minor ones. I start to sing 'Think It Over' but the words make me feel worse. Next I try 'Tom Dooley' and it's a good choice. Here we have a bloke who murdered a girl and now he's gonna die for it, yes siree! And have I not just murdered my chances with Wendy? Yes I have. Guilty as charged, m'lud. Take him down for a long stretch. And talking of long stretches, perhaps I should exercise Wee William.

# CHAPTER 5

## *'Great Balls of Fire' (Jerry Lee Lewis...1958)*

We are gathered together at morning assembly and for we few, the small band of rebellious brothers strung out in a short line at the rear of the school hall next to the kitchen serving hatch, this will be one of our last. But this has more significance to us than just another assembly because it represents a small but meaningful victory over the Count and his minions. A war of attrition has been waged over the past year in this hall, a war of wills... and, if all remains unchanged for the next few days, we will emerge the winners. To elucidate (as our esteemed English master 'Soapy' Luxmoore might say): it was one wet, wintry Saturday afternoon at the Tarantella Coffee-bar when Tulip, Ronny, Jeff Atyeo, and myself set about composing an alternative version of 'The Lord's Prayer' as chanted by the entire school at morning assembly.

Having completed our masterpiece, in spite of an onslaught of shrewish remarks from Mama Bonetti about spending all-a day here and notta buyin' much, we each took a copy home with us to learn off by heart. In due course, we were able, daily, to hijack our corner of morning assembly by interjecting our anarchic 'magnum opus' into the mainstream doleful chorus of the prayer. From the first day, we observed the Count rotating his gaze around the hall like some grisly radar scanner. He knew something was up, but he couldn't quite pin it down. It took him weeks to finally locate the discordant phrasing to our location in the hall, but, so good are we by now at twisting and distorting the words, that he has been unable to categorically accuse us of any blasphemous outrages. This week is his last chance.

We watch with amusement as he furtively steps back from his prominent position up on the stage and slips away to the rear. The gap in the line is immediately filled by Taff Davis and the luscious Miss Julie Day (Domestic Science and Teasing) as they shuffle together. Aha, we smell a rat; there is a plan afoot up there. No doubt the Count has previously called a meeting to plot our downfall and each serf has his assigned task. We see him moving to the rear stage-door and disappear. His strategy is nothing short of pathetic. We know full well that he will now scurry down the side corridor to the kitchen, creep over to the serving hatch and attempt to listen in to our irreverent rendition. Some hopes! We saw this coming months ago and Jeff is on alert at our side of the hatch to pass the signal when he hears the kitchen door squeak open. Meanwhile we chant on thus:

(the school) 'Our Father which art in heaven, hallowed be thy name

*(us) Our Arthur Wishart in Devon, Harold be thy name*

Thy kingdom come, thy will be done

*Hiking to Brum, via Wimbledon*

On earth as it is in Heaven

*On surf he passes up the Severn*

Give us this day our daily bread

*Give us Miss Day on a naily bed*

And forgive us our trespasses as we forgive those who trespass against us

*And forbid us sour test-matches and we'll forgive those who test-match against us...*

Jeff suddenly makes the signal by scratching the top of his head in the manner of Stan Laurel. We all turn our heads to watch the Count's shadow falling across the serving hatch and immediately revert to the traditional version of the prayer, upping the volume with pious gusto. He hovers for a few moments then his shadow shrinks as he slopes away to lick his wounds. Seconds later he appears back on the stage and manoeuvres himself to the front where he stands staring icily in our direction.

"Amen," comes the final refrain from the ensemble. Amen indeed, mate.

The Count steps forward and grips the lectern with both hands. The room falls silent, people fidget, someone coughs. But the Count appears to be undergoing some kind of crisis. His gaze snaps round to our corner again but we meet it with a united show of defiance. He straightens his back, inhales deeply, and, curiously, grasps his gown on both sides and extends it as though about to curtsy. He has now taken on the appearance of a true vampire. There is a murmur of bewilderment from the assembled masses and the staff. Is he finally about to transform into a bat and do a circuit over our heads, I speculate? But, no, he merely gathers up the papers on the lectern, taps them into a neat pile and turns once more to eye our position.

"I will see those pupils who are leaving school this year in the chemistry lab in ten minutes," he announces, then turns and strides through the deferential space that opens before him in the staff ranks. Deputy Head, 'Soapy' Luxmoore (English Language, Latin and suspected Homosexuality) takes charge and issues the usual directions for exiting the hall in silence. We all immediately begin to chatter and Soapy gets very agitated. Nobody cares.

This summons for us to convene in the chemistry lab is a bit of a setback as we were hoping to spend the morning having a knock-about in the cricket nets with Taff Davis. No doubt he'll be peeved too. The Count is clearly hell-bent on a last-ditch attempt to 'save' any of us lost souls who have decided to enter the real world instead of his beloved sixth form. Although we are, as near as dammit, free-men and no longer part of his snivelling serfdom, we have no choice but to comply.

To add fuel to my own personal vexations, a letter appeared this morning inviting me to attend for an interview with Mr. J. Tottering of Tottering and Tripp, Quantity Surveyors. How the buggering hell did that happen, you are probably musing? Well, it would appear that, without my knowledge, my mother took it upon herself to type out a copy of my recent phoney job application, forge my signature, and send it off. Surely this contravenes the Geneva Convention? When I confronted her with my righteous indignation she merely huffed and puffed and told me I should be grateful and wouldn't I like to be a Quantity Surveyor anyway? My reply that I hadn't a clue what a Quantity Surveyor does with his time evidently fell on deaf ears and was drowned out by Housewive's Choice. Only when Dad popped in for a tea-break did I learn that it's something to do with pricing building developments. "There you are," intruded my mother, "you used to love your Meccano set." God help us.

So here we are, me, Tulip, Jeff, Billy Rice, and Clanger Bell, corralled in the chemistry lab with the Count, and Taff Davis umpiring. This is patently an exercise in terminal humiliation designed by the Count to send us out into the workplace with as large an inferiority complex as he can inflict. To snub his sixth form is tantamount to treason and to consider a life spent anywhere else than within the academic or military sphere is beyond his comprehension. It's equivalent to requesting David Whitfield to sing 'Long Tall Sally' or asking Hitler to host a bar mitzvah.

Taff is fidgeting nervously with a clipboard and crossing his legs at fifteen-second intervals. He knows full well that we won't budge and that the whole charade is purely a bit of theatre for the Count to indulge in. For a change, I feel sorry for the old Celt.

The chemistry lab is the only classroom in the school which has a raised platform at the front and where 'Jacko' Jackman performs his magical molecular show. Here we have all spent many a moment of stupefying indifference, crowded around his desk whilst he has regaled us with the mysteries of alchemy. Only once in our four years of attendance at his performances were we stirred from our collective coma of apathy to appreciate his bubbling wonders, and that was the morning his Bunsen-burner unexpectedly became a flamethrower and blew his apparatus to hell. But, alas, today the Count holds centre stage.

He begins his assault, not by berating us on our treacherous flight from his ghastly influence, but by reminding us of the impending 'staff versus first eleven' end-of-term cricket match due to take place this Friday. Having gloated on the certain outcome, based on the past records, he finally turns upon us individually and alphabetically to ridicule our career prospects. Jeff Atyeo, therefore, becomes his first target.

Holding up a copy of Jeff's last school report between thumb and forefinger, as though it was a confession to a mass murder or a piece of used toilet paper, he asks Jeff what he thinks he's going to do with his life. Jeff tells him he's joining the Navy. A surprisingly admirable choice, smiles the Count smarmily, and snaps his fingers in the general direction of Taff who fumbles with the papers on his lap and produces a 'Join the Navy' leaflet. The Count whisks it from his fingers and browses it for a few seconds before addressing Jeff once more.

"My own brother is a submarine commander, Atyeo," he continues smoothly. "Perhaps you, too, would feel comfortable serving beneath the waves?"

"Well, not really, sir, unless I'm wearing a life-belt," grins Jeff, "seeing as I'll be a steward on a cruise liner!"

The Count scowls at him over his spectacles. "You mean you're joining the merchant service, boy?" the corners of his mouth dropping as though he'd just smelt a particularly obnoxious fart. Jeff nods gleefully and it's one-nil to us. The Count stares for a while at Jeff's beaming face, sniffs, and moves on.

"Bell, I see from successive reports that you are one of the school's rare enthusiasts of the English language."

Clanger shifts nervously in his seat. "Well, yes, sir. Sort of," he concurs. The Count leans across and pulls a booklet from Taff's unruly heap of papers and brandishes it on high like the American Declaration of Independence.

"Then have you considered entering the teaching profession or the Civil Service?"

"No, sir," replies Clanger confidently, "I've got meself a job."

The Count sniffs sarcastically. "'Got meself a job'? What sort of good English is that, lad?" But Clanger chimes on regardless.

"The Fayling Gazette is taking me on as a trainee journalist, sir."

"Good God," declares the Count, sweeping his spectacles from his nose. "What am I up against here, Mr. Davis?" Taff shuffles his papers and crosses his legs again. The Count rants on. "So far, we've got a waiter and a newspaper hack!" Taff raises his eyebrows and shakes his head in mock empathy. The Count sighs wearily and turns his attention to Tulip. If we're lucky, this could be the straw that breaks the camel's back.

"So, de Groot, what are your own aspirations in life?"

Tulip has no idea what an 'aspiration' is so, in true Belch fashion, he waffles.

"Do you have the correct time, sir, by any chance?" he asks, shaking his wrist-watch energetically next to his ear.

Like a prat, Taff calls out "Nine-forty," and receives a withering stare from his headmaster. This gives time for Clanger to relay a whispered interpretation of the Count's question.

"Ah, well, yes," Tulip stumbles on, "I'm going into electronics and computers and stuff."

The Count raises one eyebrow in mild surprise. "And what precisely is 'computers and stuff' when it's at home?" he enquires tetchily.

"Oh, it's the future, sir," says Tulip, warming to his subject. "I've built one at home with my Dad. It could beat you at chess."

The Count peers down at him with a look that could kill a dog. "I'll have you know, laddie, that I am the Regional Chess champion, am I not, Mr. Davis?" Taff nods like a jack-hammer. "The very idea of my being beaten at chess by a pile of electrified scrap metal is ludicrous, boy."

"I'm sure it's the future, sir," insists our hero.

But the Count seems unimpressed with the future. In fact, I suspect he's already pissed off with the present. He folds his arms and regards us one by one. And it is during this short intermission, whilst we gaze around at one another in total bemusement, that an idea forms in my head. Call it a bolt from the blue, a revelation, inspiration... call it what you will, but it's filling my mind like an expanding balloon.

"Paddick."

The familiar sound of my name brings me out of my reverie and I look up to see the Count towering over me. He is standing now and, with the extra height of the platform, I have to force my neck right back to make contact with his dark, inhuman stare.

"Sir?" I croak.

"I said, boy, do you have one?"

God Almighty, what's he talking about? I've been in a daydream since Tulip's session and missed the Count's initial question. Do I have one? One bloody what? A pet boa constrictor; a pink shirt; an erection? To my relief he repeats his query.

"Do you have a career plan, Paddick?"

"Ah, well, yes and no, sir," I dither.

"I see," he nods sardonically. "'Yes' you have a plan, but 'no' it will amount to nothing."

I could hardly sum it up better myself, but I can't give him that satisfaction.

"Well, not exactly. I've got an interview with… with…"

Here we go again, complete breakdown of service between brain and vocal chords. For Christ sake, a brain is supposed to have a memory isn't it, otherwise what's the point in having one? Could I be getting senile at my age of fifteen and eleven twelfths? Ah, good, I know how old I am so I must be OK. And, lo and behold, here it comes:

"With Tottering and Tripp," I blurt.

The Count grimaces as though I'd just exposed one of his nastier fetishes. "Bernard Tripp the Quantity Surveyor?" he inquires. I nod cautiously. "Dear Lord, we were at the Normandy landings together," he mumbles, and gazes down at me as though I represent a bigger threat to Bernard's wellbeing than the combined might of the Wehrmacht.

The Count's interrogation of Billy is dispensed at breakneck speed. "Not much chance of the sixth form for you I imagine, Rice. No? Thought not. A life devoted to following the plough and squeezing the udder, no doubt." Billy opens his mouth, probably to point out that tractors have been invented and it's teats that get squeezed, not udders, but the Count silences him with a wave of his palm. He has suffered a major defeat here today, a five-nil whitewash, and we are happy to accept his offhand dismissal as he turns to confer with Taff.

Out in the corridor we all break into a sprint, yelping and hooting as we go and ignoring the high-pitched haranguing from Arthur Harold Wishart at the far end of the corridor. We gallop from the building, free as birds and laughing like lunatics.

Once we are out in the fresh air, I tell the others that I have a great idea to discuss but I can't divulge the details until I've talked to Ronny. Why don't we meet at the Tarantella in an hour, I suggest. Fine, so we part company and I hurry off in the direction of Chez Ronald.

*

Mrs. Lee opens the door with her repulsive Pekinese bitch tucked under her arm and wielding a chocolate covered wooden spoon. "Hello, dear," she smiles. "Do you like truffles?"

I glance at the dog's slobbering rich-brown tongue and decide that I don't. "Oh, well, never mind," she gushes. "Poochy-poo and I will have to eat them." She cackles with glee and offers the spoon to the snuffling canine mutant.

"Is Ronny in, Mrs. Lee?" I enquire, discreetly stroking the globules of choc-flavoured dog saliva from my face. She frowns briefly and then pokes me playfully in the chest with the spoon.

"Of course, you're young Paddick aren't you, dear."

She's chuckling again and Poochy-poo has turned his attentive little tongue to the chocolate around Mrs. Lee's mouth. "Oh, stop tickling me, Poochy-woochy-poo. Ronald's gone out, dear."

I don't think I can take much more of this.

"Do you know where he's gone?" I plead.

"Yes, dear, he's gone to that awful café with the loud music."

At last! I bow out and head for the Tarantella.

Ronny is standing at the juke-box, squinting at the titles and swigging on a Coke.

"Hey, man," he calls as I enter. "I can't find one Brubeck disc on here."

I grin understandingly and guide him away to our customary seat by the toilet door. Before I am able to sit him down and sound him out on the technical requirements of my project, Tulip turns up so we give Ronny a short recap of the morning's successful clash with the Count. I then get down to brass tacks. First, I remind them of the impending cricket match and the crushing defeat which awaits us. They nod resignedly and Tulip belches. I then hit them with my master plan.

"We need to terminate the match during the Count's innings. Get it called off and declared a draw." They gaze at me blankly so I try again. "We have to cause an uproar of some sort."

I flutter my hands in an attempt to create an impression of chaos. They both follow the movement of my hands as if I'm about to produce a white rabbit from thin air, but there is no response from either of them. OK, I'm going to have to let 'em have it. "Look, we need the ball to explode when the Count swipes it for one of his usual boundaries!"

They stare at me in obvious befuddlement, then at each other in disbelief, then back to me with mouths slightly open in shock. I lean forward, shield my mouth, and smile benevolently, as you might to an elderly person or a horse. "When I say 'explode'... I don't mean a fucking nuclear bomb!" They settle back into their seats with relief written across their faces. What a pair of prats.

"How we gonna do it, man?" asks Ronny, his eyes glistening with new found fervour.

I shake my head. "No, mate, how are *you* going to do it. You're the chemist."

"Yeah, Ron," nods Tulip grinning widely. "Surely you can come up with an exploding cricket ball."

Ronny taps his fingertips on the table surface in a Modern Jazz rhythm and whistles a barely audible melody. "Hot-diggety," he mutters. I can almost hear the cogs whirring in that dangerously outlandish brain of his. For a mini-second, the alarming thought crosses my mind that I may have unleashed terrible and unstoppable forces upon the universe. But it passes immediately as Ronny suddenly beams with satisfaction and gives us a thumbs-up.

"You know what, man? It's far out but I think I can come up with the merchandise."

Presumably, that's beatnik talk for 'Yes, I can do it.'

"By the way, Ron," pipes up Tulip, "how come you were in here today? Not your usual scene, is it?"

"Ah, yeah. I was gonna ask if you two cats will feed my animals for a coupla days, man."

What, enter his bedroom alone to face that man-eater Mr. Hyde? I agree strictly on the condition that Tulip comes armed with his diving harpoon and that leather gloves and a face mask are provided. Ronny concedes and explains that he has to travel to Exeter with his mother for consultations with a psychiatrist.

"Strewth, Ronny," I say, "I thought all that stuff was behind you."

"No, man," he smiles, "they want to talk to my old lady this time!"

Now that does make sense, which is more than Mrs. Lee does.

The meeting, I feel, has gone well and the plan is put into motion. Ronny will give the 'device' (our security name for the mini-bomb) some thought and is confident that such an ingenious contraption is well within his capabilities. The fortuitous trip to Exeter will, he assures us, also enable him to purchase 'certain ingredients'. Meanwhile, Tulip and I will visit the school cricket pitch and pavilion to work out a strategy at the scene of the proposed crime (for want of a better word). We will also purloin as many old cricket balls as we can in order to perform test explosions, something that Ronny insists will be necessary to avoid actually killing the Count on the day.

Tulip and I leave Ronny at the table, deep in thought and sucking on his Coke. The Gaggia hisses malevolently as we make our way out and Momma Bonetti twirls her tea-cloth at us in a Neapolitan farewell. Through the open side door Poppa can be seen polishing the chrome on his brand-new ice-a-cream van. He's singing some nutty Italian song at the top of his voice. I bet it's not a sea shanty.

As we step out onto the sunlit pavement, who should be waiting for us but Anthea. I scan the street and there is Wendy across the road talking to Danny, who sits astride his metal steed, looking for all the world like Marlon Brando. She looks absolutely gorgeous in a figure-hugging pale blue dress and pink high-heeled shoes. You would think some top model had just breezed into town to tease us red-blooded boys. Danny is grinning like a Cheshire cat and running his forefinger along her hand as it rests on his throttle. If that isn't suggestive then I'm a Welshman. She turns her head ever so slightly and catches sight of me. I notice her lips halt their movement in mid-conversation for a second, then she moves closer to Danny, edging her back towards me. That, Brillo, is the big snub, old pal. Shoulders do not come much colder than that. But, hey, can I blame her? Did I not puke upon her mother's expensive Japanese fishes and cause her father to wreak havoc among the floral terraces? I can only imagine the humiliation she must have faced as she went about her waitressing duties that evening. Isn't there always the spiteful, loud-mouthed wag amongst the guests who can't resist wisecracking throughout dinner? 'Eh-up, lass, no fish on t'menu? Oops, sorry to keep carping on!' No, I don't blame her for ignoring me. I just wish she hadn't thrown herself on Danny's mercy. There won't be any.

By now, Tulip and Anthea are at loggerheads. He forgot to meet her outside Woolworth's as arranged and she is having none of his ridiculous fabrication that a sudden attack of diarrhoea had forced him home. The glut of unnecessary bodily function details he's providing is all a bit much for Anthea and she cancels their date on the spot. She then turns her venom on me for some reason.

"I believe you owe Wendy some money," she says, giving me one of her special looks reserved for lower species.

"Did she tell you to ask me for it?" I ask.

"No, she just happened to mention it and I…"

"Then it's none of your business, is it, Anthea!" I explode. "I'll pay her as soon as I've got it."

Which could be some time as I need a full set of guitar strings and one of those Cliff Richard vertically-striped shirts.

Ronny reappears as I stand smarting from Anthea's onslaught. "You'll need our house key to feed the hamsters, man," he says. "I'll leave it under the dustbin by the bicycle." Do I notify him here and now that he no longer has a bike? No, I can't risk upsetting him when he's our Device Master. I'll have to sort out all these aggravations later. What's going on, anyway? Is the whole world and his wife ganging up on me? Am I such an undependable bugger? I strive to please and this is my reward. But it's impossible, I suppose, to please everyone at once, or in my case, anyone at all. It's certainly not easy being a teenager. Thank God it only lasts seven years.

*

To my delight there's a letter from my older cousin, conscript soldier Phil, waiting for me when I get home. I inspect the B.F.P.O. stamped envelope for any signs of steaming open by my mother but it seems untampered with. She is very suspicious of the letter content in these missives from West Germany. But Phil and I have devised a cunning 'wheeze', as he calls it. The envelope will, in fact, contain two letters; one full of army-life news and routine twaddle, and another 'special bulletin'. This second one is what my mother never gets to see and is replete with licentiousness and lewd detail; the harmless version is deliberately left on my bedside cupboard for her prying eyes. It works a treat.

I skip through the usual tosh about parades and army bull and unfold the solitary leaf of paper, my heart a-flutter. What naughtiness has he been engaged in this time? I read on.

*Hello again Col*

*I've got some news for you this time, old buddy. I'm seeing a thirty-three year old German woman. Don't have a bloody heart-attack! I can hear you saying, 'What the hell is he doing with an old lady like that? Well, I can tell you…EVERYTHING!! She's taught me stuff I never knew existed. I can't even put it in this letter. All I know is, when I get back those local birds are in for a treat. Whoopee!*

*Anyhow, that's about it for now. Oh, one useful bit of information when you're out with your bird… look for the clitoris. Find it, tweak it, and stand back for fireworks! Beware though, it can get out of control.*

*See you at Christmas*

*Phil*

*PS. Don't forget the usual procedure. Tear this into bits and bung it down the bog.*

*PPS. Now flush the bog!*

This is, indeed, important news from the front, and most likely from the back too. I can't wait to embark on my search for the elusive 'clitoris'. Of course, it would help a lot if I knew exactly what it is. I'd best look it up somewhere, perhaps a medical dictionary would list it. What a cunning little gadget it appears to be! I don't recall that sneaky sod, Tim Lewis, ever referring to it during our biology classes. He's probably hoping to keep it for his own personal use. Fortunately, when it comes to research of this nature, I am blessed with the co-operation of Caroline. She will, I'm sure, be more than happy to help me with my investigations. Things are definitely looking up. I now have two projects in process: 1. The cricket-match 'Device' and 2. The Quest for the Clitoris.

The unmistakable sound reaches my ears of an incompetent oaf trying to park a car in our back lane. I poke my head out of my bedroom window but see no sign of a vehicle, just a grating of gears and the over-revving of an engine, until the bonnet of an unfamiliar car jolts into view. I soon recognise the model to be one of those new Austin Minis. A door slams and, bugger my boots, it's Quentin Lamont! So the MG is clearly a write-off and the madman has gone out and bought a brand new Mini. I wonder how long this one will last?

I suppose he's here to try his luck with my mother again, the depraved scoundrel. I'm still determined to catch 'em at it and end his reign of lustful extravagances once and for all. In fact, today could be my best opportunity. If I'm quiet enough, I could creep downstairs, slip Dad's old Kodak camera out of the hat-stand drawer and, bingo, I'll have photographic evidence. The camera never lies. To capture them on film would give me undreamed-of power. I believe the Italians call it 'caught in flagrante delicto', but it's probably the same over here.

Making it soundlessly downstairs, I ease open the drawer in our hat-stand and, checking that the camera is loaded with film, I tip-toe like a sprite to the half-open kitchen door. From this vantage point I can hear every word they speak and occupy a perfect position from which to leap before them with my shutter clicking madly. I crane my neck forward to catch their conversation and am stunned to hear its content.

"Well, hold still, Marjorie," growls Lamont, "and I'll use my finger to get it in."

I bloody knew it… they're at it good and proper this time, and on the kitchen table too!

Have they no shame? I have to eat my tea off that table later. Besides, the legs are shaky enough as it is.

"Let me get a firmer grip," whispers my mother, "then you can slide the rubber thing on."

There is a grunt from Lamont. "That's it, now I can squeeze in my meat."

My god, this has gone far enough! I hurl myself into the kitchen with the camera viewfinder to my right eye and press the shutter. They stare at me in utter stupefaction, my mother with her hands clutched round her old cast-iron meat mincer on the table-top, Lamont poised to insert the rubber nozzle seal with a forefinger, a handful of cubed beef in the other palm.

"What in the name of God is he doing now?" he asks shakily, turning to my mother in bewilderment.

"I have no idea," she answers haughtily and nods towards the south-west. "There's a plate of salad in the fridge, Colin. Now for heaven's sake behave yourself. At this rate Quentin will think you're a little queer."

I don't see quite why he'd think that. Not all photographers are poofs, are they?

I slouch to the fridge and avail myself of the plate of dying vegetable leaves which are huddling for warmth around a shrivelled hunk of cheddar cheese. Pouring myself a glass of milk, I leave the kitchen in a silent sulk.

"Oh, come on, Quentin," I hear my mother say as I climb the stairs. "Let's have a quickie on the piano."

And why not?

Stone me, I've hardly reached the top of the stairs and the telephone rings in the hall.

"I'll get it," I bawl, not that those two will hear it above the din they're kicking out on the piano. I pick up the phone and wipe the milk from my lips. What a quirky coincidence, it's Caroline. Do I want to take her to the flicks today as it's her half-day off and there's a good film on at the Odeon? 'What, pray, might the film be?' I enquire.

"The Bridge on the River Wye," she replies. Hmmm, I don't recall the Japs pushing that far west, and if they had, they would have blown up the bridge themselves to keep the Taffs out.

"OK," I agree. "Wear a skirt."

"Why?"

"It's a project I'm working on."

"Oh, OK. What's a project?"

"Never mind. I'll meet you outside the Odeon at two-thirty."

This must be an omen; everything is falling into place for a change. With luck and a fair wind, the secrets of the clitoris will be revealed to me. I'll leave early and pop into the library to look it up.

Caroline is waiting patiently when I turn up at two forty-three. I got a bit delayed and ran out of Brylcreem trying to get my Elvis quiff to stay in one position. Well, you can't go out nowadays looking less than perfect and today I think I've cracked it. I'm wearing a black cut-away collar shirt with an electric blue tie, my charcoal-flecked one-button drape jacket, and black drainpipe trousers impeccably complemented with a pair of cobalt-blue suede shoes. Talk about sartorial flawlessness. I was also held up temporarily at the library due to their useless medical encyclopaedia giving me almost nothing on the clitoris. Luckily, I'm on nodding acquaintance with Barry the assistant librarian who was privy to a much more explicit version kept in a back room. Curiously, he insisted on providing me with a copy of a sketch he'd done for someone else. So, the news is out then.

"You look nice," mews Caroline generously. She looks pretty good herself and, bless her heart, she's worn a skirt.

To our joy, the corner seats at the very back of the circle are vacant and we settle down to watch a few minutes of the film. Alec Guinness is having a terrible time trying to get through the day with those wicked little Nips making life so awfully difficult for him. All the prisoners look bloody starving and now, lawks a-mussy, they have to build a bridge. It's all very depressing and enough to cause a tremor in the stiffest of upper lips. But to hell with Alec, I've got work to do.

I normally start Caroline off with a little light ear-nibbling followed, at my leisure, by some furtive breast fondling but today, in view of the urgent nature of my research, I am obliged to strike out immediately for the target. She registers a moment of surprise at my boldness but giggles nevertheless and responds by releasing Wee William from his lair. He springs forth like a Jack-in-the-box, eager as ever for a look around. To be honest, I could do without his intervention today as I need to concentrate on the main purpose of this exercise, but both he and Caroline are creatures of habit.

Can you believe it? A pair of dozy holidaymakers come stumbling along, calling to each-other in the semi-darkness and dump themselves down immediately in front of us. How am I supposed to apply myself to important exploration with some fidgeting foreigner rustling his toffee-papers just inches from my work area? They instantly strike up a conversation in their Midlands accents, poking fun at poor Alec Guinness and how small the cinema is.

"Yow couldn't swing a cat in 'ere, could yow, Oy-reen," titters the bloke.

"Not unless yow cut off its 'ead first, Broy-un," laughs his girlfriend.

Disapproving faces turn to scowl at their disruptive behaviour and the bloke waves a hand and apologises with a chuckle. Seething with anger, I proceed with my search, thrusting this way and that, probing the lush, warm rainforests of Caroline's intimate regions.

"What are you doing, Colin?" she whispers eventually.

"I'm looking for something," I hiss irritably. "Something that should be here but I can't find."

"Oh, God," she gasps, "it's not your lighter is it?"

Then, to my annoyance, Broy-un has the insolence to swivel his head round and tell us to shut up. That's when the unthinkable happens. From out of nowhere, Betty Tucker, the cinema's wizened usherette appears and swings the beam of her industrial-power torch upon us. All our enterprise is immediately revealed to Broy-un's inquisitive gaze.

"Bloimy, mite," he shouts. "You got a nerve, ain't ya?" and he struggles to his feet to get a better look at our activities. But Caroline and I have been here before. Wee William is popped back into his nest in a split second and Caroline can squeeze a loose breast out of sight in the wink of an eye. Before you can say 'Ship-shape and Bristol-fashion' we are both sitting back with hands neatly clasped in our laps and cherubic expressions of innocence on our faces.

Meanwhile, all Hell has broken loose. Betty comes tanking down the main aisle, flashing her searchlight around the auditorium and daring anyone to move. People call out requesting her to sort out Broy-un as he's ruining their enjoyment of the film. I'm sure one of the protesting voices was Alec Guiness himself.

"Shut yer traps, you lot," bawls the diplomatic Betty. "I'll deal with this. Just watch the picture!"

Row by row they obey and turn their eyes back to the screen where Alec is still struggling pluckily with the Nips.

Betty has wriggled her bulky frame between the seats to confront Broy-un and Oy-reen. "Right you two," she growls. "Out!" And out they flippin' well go. Betty bundles the pair of them over the seats and into the next row, then, with Broy-un protesting stridently, she prods them with her torch all the way out of the circle. She turns at the exit and wobbles the torch-beam over us as though daring us to get involved in any additional trouble. We smile politely.

Clearly, my investigations are over for today and the 'clitoris' temporarily remains on hold, so to speak. Caroline informs me that she's bored with the film because there are no love scenes in it, so we leave. To be honest, gawping at all those skinny, under-nourished POWs has made me hungry. A greasy bag of chips from the 'Cod Almighty' would go down very nicely but Caroline decides that an Espresso coffee and a slice of Momma Bonetti's cake is more to her liking. Quite where these sudden delusions of refinement have come from beats me, but I comply with her request.

To my surprise we bump into Ronny and Mrs. Lee exiting the bus depot. Ronny explains that the medical boffins in Exeter have no idea what is wrong with his mum so they've put her on some kind of medication. He looks tired but his face lights up when I enquire about the 'supplies' and he taps his holdall and grins. Mrs. Lee smiles wanly at me and turns her glazed eyes on Caroline.

"Hello, Patrick," she drones, apparently confusing me with someone else, "is this your new wife?"

"No, Mrs. Lee," I reply, "I've only just left school. This is

Caroline. She's just a good friend."

Mrs. Lee nods languidly and drops one eyelid in a listless wink. "Me too," she murmurs.

As Caroline struts away in a huff towards the coffee-bar, Ronny pulls me to one side and whispers in my ear. "Have you got the balls, man?" he asks.

"To do what?" I enquire with a frown.

"The old cricket balls, you nut… for the tests."

"Oh, yeah. Me and Tulip managed to find three. One's cork. We left 'em on your bed when we fed the man-eaters."

"Far out. OK man, they'll have to do." He scratches his ear lobe, a sure sign that he's on to something. He glances at his watch and tweaks the tip of his nose, a sure sign that he's done thinking and has made a decision. "Meet me at the Parish Church gate in two hours," he says enigmatically.

"Christ, Ron, you can't blow up the church!" I caution. "They still use it."

"Just meet me there," he says, and he's gone.

Caroline has chosen a seat by the front window and sits stirring her coffee with slow, precise rhythm. She's mad at me. How do I know? Because she hasn't bought me a drink. I sit down opposite her and smile. "What's up?" I ask.

"Two things," she snaps. "First, so I'm 'just a good friend' am I? And second…" She purses her lips meaningfully and points a finger over her shoulder. Leaning slightly to one side and peering into the dimness of the room my eyes immediately focus on Wendy. Well, the back of her head at least. She is sitting with Anthea who has spotted me and is in deep gossip, head pushed forward and tongue flapping like a flag in a gale. I glimpse Wendy's lovely shoulders rise in a shrug of disinterest and I guess that is for my benefit. To add further to my dismay, the door to the men's bog swings open and Danny emerges, running a comb through his immaculate hair. He catches sight of me, grins, and gives me a sarcastic little wave. Hey-ho, all's fair in love and war, as some insensitive bastard once said.

I wrench my attention back to Caroline and it occurs to me that I have well over an hour before meeting the mad scientist, time which could be spent pursuing that tricky little chap, the clitoris.

"Let's get out of here and take a stroll down to the Harbour View Gardens?"

Understandably, she agrees.

*

I know every inch of these municipal gardens, every hidey-hole and secret lair. Many an hour has been spent crawling on my hands and knees through the labyrinth of leafy tunnels that wind beneath the rhododendron shrubs. Here, in the company of my childhood companions, I have fought Red Indians, attacked pirates, slaughtered countless German infantry, coughed on my first cigarette, and fumbled with the clothing of various equally inquisitive females. Today, however, my visit is in the noble pursuit of science.

Caroline, as ever, questions our nesting place, not because of my obvious motives, but the fact that there are 'fag-packets, empty bottles and probably worse' scattered around. I point out to her that all explorers are faced with hardships and did she think that Christopher Columbus would have turned his ship for home if he'd spotted a French-letter floating in the Atlantic?

Anyhow, my renewed efforts to pinpoint the clitoris seem to be having a pleasing effect on my compliant partner. She begins to kiss my neck and pant in my ear. Maybe I'm closing in. And suddenly, bingo, I find the little bugger. Caroline is going nuts, just as Phil forecast.

"Eureka!" I cry triumphantly. "I've found my first clitoris!"

But I need further proof. Fumbling in my trouser pocket with my free hand I retrieve Barry the librarian's detailed sketch. It's asking a lot of Caroline but I must check the drawing against the real thing. This is science we're talking about, you know. So, manoeuvring myself on hands and knees within the confines of our den, I turn with Barry's sketch between my teeth, to crawl into an observing position. And what do I observe? Two tiny faces watching my every move from the end of the twiggy tunnel! Yes, the Devil has dispatched his newest recruits to thwart me again. Burgess and MacLean stare back at me, their grubby hands clutching jam-jars inside which I detect the fluttering movement of butterflies.

"Brown Owl," yowls MacLean. "That horrid boy is here again!"

From my limited vantage point I see only Hettie's large brogues looming into view behind the Brownies followed by a gloved hand swooping down to remove the innocents from any further glimpses of carnal behaviour.

"Well, are they making a baby this time?" enquires Burgess impatiently, reversing awkwardly from the bushy passage.

"No," cries her co-spy MacLean emphatically. "They're looking for butterflies too 'cos I heard the boy shout that he'd found a chrysalis."

There is no comment from Hettie.

*

Ronny is sitting on the bench inside the lych-gate when I arrive with Caroline still in tow. He eyes her with undisguised contempt and remarks on my lack of dedication to the project. Caroline, however, is oblivious to his scorn and seems to be still under the influence of my clitoral incursion. She keeps massaging my arm and gazing at me with a glazed expression in her eyes.

"What's with the chick?" asks Ronny in his curious Beatnik-talk.

"It's a long story," I say. I turn to her and give her a peck on the cheek. "Thanks for everything, kiddo. I'll see you around." To my surprise she kisses me back and wanders off into town.

"Why's she walking like that?" inquires the crazy chemist. I shrug and we make our way up the gravel path towards the church.

"I've got a bone to pick with you, man," announces Ronny as we stroll past the ancient gravestones. "Mr. Hyde was a mutilated mess when I got home. I had to put him down."

I halt in my tracks and register my astonishment.

"How the hell did that happen?" I ask.

"He tried to eat himself. Nearly succeeded too."

"Eat himself!" I echo, with just a hint of mirth in my voice. "How?"

"Through acute hunger, daddy-o, that's how," answers Ronald irritably. "Did you feed him last night?"

"Of course we did. We gave him and his mate the Weetabix as you instructed."

Ronny slides the duffle bag from his shoulder and lowers it gingerly to the flagstones inside the church porch.

"Is that all? What about the chopped earthworms and prunes I left?"

I shake my head. Ronny groans and pulls the bag back onto his shoulder. "Jesus, man, he must have been ravenous."

I stare at him in silence and I don't have the heart to ask exactly how Mr. Hyde managed to consume himself. Surely there comes a point where gnawing on one more vital organ would finish him off. Nope, I can't work it out. But, let's face it, Ronald had no right to create a monster like Mr. Hyde in the beginning. He should stick to distilling moonshine.

"How do we know Vicar Whicker isn't around?" I mention as we stand in the coolness of the porch.

"Well, I happen to know," says Ron, an air of mystery enveloping each word, "that old Whicker cycles round to visit a certain lady friend every Thursday afternoon."

"You're kidding!" I titter. "Who is it?"

"My old lady," he replies with a grin.

"Christ!"

"No, man, just his earthly representative," chuckles Ron.

Is the entire adult population of Fayling at it, I ponder?

I step outside to check that we are, indeed, unobserved and spot that Bill Potter, the sexton, has been digging a fresh grave no more than twenty yards from us. A bank of soil is neatly piled on the grass slope almost immediately beneath the tower but there is no sign of Bill. Glancing at my watch I deduce that he has gone home for an early tea. He will follow this with a visit to the 'White Hart' where he'll sit in the public bar all evening, fondling a pint of Guinness and boring the holiday-makers with his tales of derring-do in the trenches at Passchendale, where he served as a cook.

"Let's go," says Ron, much in the manner of a commando on a mission. And I guess that's what we're doing, risking body and soul for a few moments of glory. This is the stuff of life, creeping furtively around and hoping to experience a big bang. Ask my mother.

Ronny leads me into the church and closes the big oak door behind us. The 'clack' of the falling latch echoes around the building and the hairs rise on the back of my neck. Why are empty churches always so spooky? This is supposed to be a place of refuge from a hostile world, yet I always feel uneasy in here. Maybe this is the only place where God can actually see me, in which case I should expect a booming voice asking how I got these grass stains on my knees. On the other hand, wasn't He himself responsible for creating Caroline and all her attributes? Yep, so I need confess to no more than a healthy interest in his wondrous works.

Ronny appears to know his way around, including the hiding place of the key to the church-tower door, and we begin the long climb up to the sunlit parapets. Wow, it's tremendous up here! We can see right across the town and way out to sea. I point out my house and, bugger me, there's Lamont's Mini parked brazenly in the back lane again. What an insatiable goat he is. At least Vicar Whicker employs a little more discretion when he goes round to see to Mrs. Lee. But, hang on a sec, Brillo! A connection has suddenly clicked in my sluggish brain. That bicycle I 'borrowed' from Ronny... could it have been the vicar's? This might be the time to clear it all up. I turn from the parapet castellation, swallow hard, and put my theory to Ron.

"Oh, yeah, man," he laughs, "Old Whicker was pretty mad about having his bike nicked from our backyard. But, hey, you know what? One of his flock works up at the Council Tip and found another identical one for him. Crazy, eh?"

Crazy, indeed.

"What we need to do," whispers Ronny, slipping the duffle-bag cautiously to the floor and removing the primed cricket-balls one by one, "is to be bloody careful."

He lays the balls in a line and steps back a pace. He hands me a pair of Perspex goggles and pulls another pair over his own spectacles. "Leave everything to me, man," he warns, "'cos these cats are red hot." I'm not entirely sure what he's talking about, not being familiar with the Beat vocabulary, but I'm happy to play a very minor role in this part of the project, so I stand back as he bends and lifts the cork ball between thumb and forefinger. "Numero uno," he breathes dramatically.

He makes his way to the parapet edge, holds the ball over and beckons me to approach. "We both need to check out the actual magnitude of the explosion," he whispers. I nod and poke my head out over the edge. Below us, all is calm; Bill's precision-cut trench is off to the right and I notice he's left his old trilby hanging on the handle of his spade. I hold up my palm indicating to Ronny to wait whilst I scan the graveyard for any signs of human activity (surely a contradiction in terms). Nothing. OK, thumbs up and Ron releases the ball. We hold our breath, squint, and watch it descend. Thud! No explosion, just the dull bump of cork on granite flagstone.

"Bollocks!" barks the chemist, and strides away to pick up ball, numero two. Down it plummets and adds to Ron's irritation by having the audacity to bounce harmlessly and soundlessly into the long grass beneath a yew tree. "This is ridiculous," he snaps, and retreats to examine our final test ball. He pulls the two halves apart carefully and sniffs the contents. "If this doesn't work, man," he declares, "I'll take up midwifery," and with that, he walks to the wall and lobs the ball over.

I never previously believed those stories where people insist that some dramatic event they witnessed occurred in slow motion. I believe it now though because, as Ronny and I watch the ball dropping to the ground, Bill Potter's head and shoulders appear wraithlike from the depths of the new grave where he has obviously been taking a nap. In definitive slow motion the scene unfolds, and I swear if Isaac Newton was here he would amend his Law of Gravity because Bill even has time to hold his lighter to his pipe and draw on it before the ball detonates with a deafening bang, obliterating the whole area with dense brown smoke.

We lift ourselves from behind the low parapet wall and peer down into the haze. Fragments of red leather float to the ground amidst a squadron of startled jackdaws who are swirling inquisitively above the blackened flagstones. But there is no sign of Bill. This could be a bad sign. Without exchanging a word, we snatch up our equipment and thunder back down the tower stairs.

We creep to the graveside. "You look first," says Ron.

"Sod off!" I retort. "It was your bomb."

"Yeah? Well, it was your idea, man," he hisses, and I can't deny it.

I squat, placing my hands on the grass rim and pivot forward to look into the trench. Bill is lying motionless on his back, his pipe gripped between his teeth and a steady spiral of smoke drifting up from its bowl. His eyes are wide open but his face is ashen and I see no movement of his chest. Let's face it, he's stone dead! I pull back and sit on the grass, my head in my hands.

"Well?" enquires Ronny.

"We've killed him, Ron," I croak, feeling suddenly nauseous. Ronny stands, peers into the grave and snorts.

"He's had a heart attack, that's all," he announces cheerily, as though that makes Bill's demise more palatable for everyone, including Bill, and immediately absolves us from blame. I stare at him in disbelief.

"That's right, and we caused it. You could say we murdered him!"

"Are you nuts, man?" hoots Ron. "The bloke was a hundred and ninety. His time was up."

He stalks off down the path, calling to me over his shoulder. "C'mon, daddy-o, let's vamoose."

He's a one-off, is Ronald; mad, bad, and dangerous to know. A descendant, perhaps, of Lord Byron? Guy Fawkes, more likely.

For someone trying to give the impression that killing the local grave-digger is all in a day's work, Ronny is putting a surprisingly large distance between us and the scene of the crime. Before I quite realise it, we are walking to the very end of Fayling pier where the more energetic holidaymakers straggle to gawp into the ocean and marvel at the poisonous jellyfish and floating rubbish. Here, also, congregate the resident sea-anglers, one of whom today is my good mate Tulip. He's using his dad's excellent rod and has already landed a pile of twitching mackerel, a dog-fish, and a deformed umbrella. His grinning features are a real tonic in my current state of anxiety and I greet him with more than my usual geniality.

"Strewth, Brillo," he remarks, "you look a bit pale. You seen a ghost or something?"

Ronny draws him to one side and recounts our grave adventures in a straightforward, matter-of-fact narrative which, I feel, tends to gloss over Arthur's passing a little too light-heartedly. In fact, he's making it sound like the highlight of our day, whereas I know perfectly well that the guilt will follow me for years. I'm still terrified that we can, somehow, be linked to the crime scene and I begin to rack my brain for possible incriminating evidence we may have left there.

"My god!" I squeak in Ronny's ear. "The dud balls… we left 'em in the grass." I grab Ronny by the shoulders and shake him violently. "You stupid bugger," I splutter, "they'll have our fingerprints all over 'em."

Ronny wriggles from my grasp and waves the duffle-bag in my face. "They're in here, Sherlock," he says evenly. "Now get a grip. There's nothing, NOTHING, to connect us with the corpse… with Bill. You dig? Nothing."

"OK," I nod, "I dig."

Which is more than Bill will ever do again.

*

Friday morning arrives on schedule and with it the threat of thunderstorms and, God willing, the possible cancellation of the cricket match. The sky out over the bay is slate-grey topped with towering cumulus clouds and occasional lightning illuminates the dark line of the horizon.

I find myself grappling with my conscience again: should we proceed, as planned, with the exploding cricket ball and the ensuing glory of a drawn match? Or should we, following the disastrous repercussions of our experiments in the cemetery, abandon the whole idea? But after two days of argument, technical gobbledegook and waffle from Ronny, Tulip and I have finally agreed to go through with the project on the strict understanding that our deranged partner and armaments expert assures us of the Count's survival. Two murders in one week are more than my nerves could take.

I turn away from my bedroom window and sigh deeply. Perhaps, I ponder naively, the good Lord will send a great flood to drown out the match and save me from the gallows. My mother's voice calling me from the bottom of the stairs brings reality crashing in on me.

"Colin, someone called Clanger just rang to ask why you're not at the cricket pitch."

I lie on my bed for a few more minutes trying to compose my thoughts, then I pull my cricket shoes from the jumble of footwear at the bottom of my wardrobe and descend the stairs.

Dad has popped in for a tea-break so it must be around ten o'clock. He's sitting at the kitchen table reading the Fayling Gazette and smoking a fag.

"Hi, Col," he smiles cheerfully, folding the newspaper. "All ready for the big match?"

"Well, we're not going down without a fight," I grimace.

"That's the Dunkirk spirit!" says Dad, pushing back his chair and handing his mug to my mother at the sink. "Are you using your secret weapon?" Holy buggery, have we been rumbled? What made him ask me that?

"Secret weapon?" I query hoarsely. Dad pats my mother on the bum and she flicks soap bubbles playfully in his face. How odd, at times, is the behaviour of the adult *Homo sapiens*.

"Yes," continues Dad. "Your killing machine, Billy Rice. Hasn't he been signed with Fayling Town Cricket Club this season?" I nod with relief and Dad grabs his lunch-box. "I'll give you a lift to the pavilion if you take your finger out," he says. My mother tuts loudly and addresses the taps.

"I wish you wouldn't use that language to your son, Don," she chides. Dad just chortles. I push my feet into my cricket shoes and tie the laces. "Here," says my mother, "you can't swing a cricket club on an empty stomach," and rams a slice of burnt toast and margarine into my open mouth. "You look very smart in your white trousers," she adds, "so don't spoil them with nasty grass stains." I grind my teeth on the charcoaled toast and stare momentarily into her eyes seeking some sign of impish humour, but no, she's serious. Closing the back door behind me, I drop the toast into the dustbin and follow Dad to the gate.

When Dad's van has finished kangarooing down the rear lane and we are on a fairly even course down Bannockburn Grove, I decide to raise the delicate subject of Quentin Lamont's improper fascination with my mother. But, before I can string together a reasonably tactful opening sentence, Dad speaks.

"Did you hear about old Bill Potter?" he asks as we swing past the Parish Church and up the hill towards the school playing fields. Panic surges through my veins and clutches me round the throat, disabling my larynx. My brain, as usual, opts out of the proceedings leaving me to gawp through the windscreen like a moron. Eventually, I manage a sort of cawing sound, much in the manner of a garrotted crow, which prompts Dad to glance at me and ask if I'm OK. Nodding, I clear my throat and prepare myself for some damning evidence to be exposed, linking us to Arthur's premature bucket-kicking. Dad continues. "Yes, seems he keeled over and dropped neatly into a grave he'd just dug." He chuckles and shakes his head. "Fitting end, I suppose." Phew, as they say in comic-books.

Fortunately, the topic is dropped as we swerve to avoid a bunch of kids milling about in the road. They're on their way to the match and yell encouragement to me as we pass. I catch sight of Anthea towering amongst their ranks. She will be there to cheer on Tulip. If fate had been kinder, Wendy would be with her and rooting for me.

The match is well attended, despite the humidity and warnings of bad weather. So far the storm seems to be static out over the sea but, with luck, it might just move inland and scupper the game.

As expected we lose the toss and the Count puts us in to bat first hoping, no doubt, for a quick kill. He isn't disappointed by early events when one of our opening batsmen, the still injured but keen Jeff Atyeo, is out for a duck, clean bowled by the Count's nephew in the first over with a blatant no-ball. We protest to the so-called umpire, school caretaker and grovelling toadie, Jack Parsons, but to no avail. One withering glare from the Count is all it takes for Parsons to raise his finger and Jeff is pavilion bound. Parsons's finger points skywards again within minutes when our next batsman, Denny Beer, strolls out to join Clanger and smacks a brilliant six. The ball sails away and bounces on the pavilion roof, rebounding back into play and into the fumbling grasp of Arthur Harold Wishart. Once more we dispute the validity of the dismissal, claiming quite correctly that the ball was beyond the boundary when it hit the roof. No dice, announces ass-kisser Parsons and warns us that any further dissent will result in abandonment of the match and an automatic win for the

Count's eleven. This game is a total fix and a disgrace to the very spirit of cricket. W.G. must be revolving in his grave.

To our surprise and delight, Clanger and our number four batsman, Terry Mayne, an ambidextrous sixth-former with a bad squint, make a stand of forty-six runs, irritating the Count and his skinny nephew to the point of an open quarrel about the tactics of both teams. Why, seethes the Count, can't his nephew the supposed super-spinner, dismiss either of these two mediocre nonentities? And furthermore, he rants, where does it mention in the rules that a batsman may change his defence stance from left to right during an over entirely at his own whim? Nobody is able to answer either of the Count's queries so the match continues in an atmosphere of mutual rancour.

Meanwhile, Tulip and I sit on the pavilion steps, padded up and awaiting our call to perform a miracle. We don't have much to say to each other and even Anthea's appearance in a tight pair of shorts and unusually revealing sweater has little effect on Tulip. "I'm batting any minute," he explains. "This is serious stuff, Anthea." Well put, Tulip; you girls have to understand, there are times when a man has to do what a man has to do and a woman just has to go and re-apply her make-up.

A commotion on the pitch and the remarkable sight of Clanger hurling his bat at Parsons leads us to the conclusion that he has been dismissed on yet another flimsy decision. The Count accompanies Clanger from the field, lecturing him tersely on the importance of sportsmanship and if he had his way he would thrash him here and now with a wicket-stump in front of the whole assembly. Tulip sighs, rises from the step, and makes his way to the crease. Out over the bay, thunder growls ominously from within the dark and bulging clouds edging ever closer to the shore. There is hope for us yet. A prolonged thunderstorm during the enemy's innings would force even Jack Parsons to declare the match a draw.

Out of the corner of my eye I am aware of a figure approaching. Ronny sits down beside me, saying nothing. In spite of the oppressive heat, he's wearing a sort of long-sleeved zip-up knitted jumper. He turns to look at me with a silly grin on his face. His eyes look as though they've been gloss varnished and his pupils are huge.

"Hi, man," he murmurs. There's a curious odour on his breath.

He holds a wavering finger to his lips. "Been smoking a little grass," he whispers. What the hell is he talking about now? I'm really beginning to have my doubts about the sanity of the Lee family.

"Of course you have, Ron," I nod condescendingly. "You OK?"

"Never better, daddy-o," he drones. "Everything is cool."

He removes his hand from the pouch on the front of his jumper and holds up a cricket-ball bomb between thumb and forefinger.

"Christ, Ron, put that away!" I hiss. He grins, replaces it and comes out clutching a small screw-top bottle.

"Care for a shot of home brew?"

A cry of 'How was he?' focuses my mind back to the job in hand. The triumphant yell signals the end of Terry's lengthy and valiant stand against the tyranny of twelve umpires. I hear Tulip's voice protesting to Jack Parsons at yet another blatant miscarriage of justice. "The ball was rolling along the ground when he says he caught it, you short-sighted twerp!" The Count flounces across to stand between Tulip and the myopic brown-noser and bundles our furious batsman back to his crease.

"Wish me luck, Ronald," I say as I haul myself to my feet and head out.

"Stay cool, Brillo," he slurs. "Cometh the hour, cometh the man, man."

I assume he's wishing me luck. I have no way of telling.

With our total now at fifty-two for four and the middle order already on call, things don't look too good, but Tulip and I put up a solid performance and by eleven-thirty our partnership has extended our tally to seventy-one. Above our heads the storm clouds are gathering quite nicely and there still seems every prospect of a match abandonment. I swear I feel a raindrop on my face and, in a reckless moment glancing up at the sky, the ball rockets past me and takes out my off-stump. I have nothing to complain about. It was pure twattery on my part and I hear Tulip groaning his disappointment. I look over at him and we both shrug philosophically. A smattering of applause eases the humiliation a little and Ronny gives me a rousing cheer as I climb the pavilion steps. Well, at least he appears to be back with us again, a considerable relief as he is carrying an arsenal of unknown potential in his home-knitted pullover.

To Tulip's credit, he thwarts all efforts to dismiss him by the Count and his band of boot-lickers and he remains undefeated as our last wicket falls with the score at eighty-eight all out. His final partner is Billy Rice who, despite his recent signing with Fayling Cricket Club, is no batsman. No, Billy's talents are with the ball… or any other missile, to be honest. Quiet, unassuming, gentle even, that's Billy. But get him out on the sports field and something seems to take him over. He becomes a wild, prehistoric being with a deadly aim, and whether it's a ball, a javelin, or a discus, you need to get out of his way pronto. Tulip claims that Billy is possessed by Devils when he's on the sports field, but this could just be some old Belch superstition. Unfortunately, Billy's talents do not extend to fearsome skills with the bat. In fact, he uses a cricket bat as though it was a broadsword, flailing and chopping at every delivery in some misplaced belief that he can slice the ball in two. Consequently, Billy is bowled on his fourth ball.

The Count pronounces that this interval between innings shall be the lunch break so we all troop back to the pavilion. We, who are about to die (of humiliation) gather at the far end of the room to talk tactics but, as we don't actually have any that can be discussed openly, the conversation, for some reason, descends into a lament on the state of popular music. Tulip declares that it's all going down the pan now that Buddy Holly is dead and Elvis has been drafted into the army. Clanger and I argue that we've still got Jerry Lee and Eddie Cochran to carry the torch. Jeff sneers that Jerry Lee made a big mistake marrying his thirteen-year-old cousin. "What's he gonna play on his piano now, nursery rhymes?" he scoffs. We remind him that the marriage was legal in Jerry Lee's U.S. state. "So is owning a bazooka," he remarks.

A silence falls upon us and we tune in to the babble at the other end of the room where the Count is holding court with his attentive cohorts. Occasional laughter rings out from their ranks and eyes are turned our way as they munch on the goodies laid out on the pristine white tablecloths manned by various mothers and the delectable Miss Julie Day (Domestic Science and Teasing).

"Hardly surprising is it?" Jeff bemoans. "Eighty-eight all out! A bunch of one-legged dwarfs could do better."

"What we need is a stroke of good luck," says Clanger. "Something right out of the blue."

"And so shall it be," utters a sluggish voice from aside. We gaze around our little group, each of us seeking the fairy godfather who has spoken. And into our midst steps our very own Robin Goodfellow and demented chemist, Ronny.

Smiling rather vapidly and with a disturbingly odd look in his half-open eyes, he leads Tulip and I to one side to brief us on the proposed assault on the Count's person. I am, once more, feeling nervous about the whole plan. After all, in the space of a few days, I have, to all intents and purposes, murdered the town gravedigger and an experimental hamster. To add the Count to the count, if you get my drift, could be construed as excessive. Also, I suspect that Ronald has been quietly swigging on his bottle of moonshine and smoking his secret hay all morning which makes him nothing less than a human bomb. If he falls flat on his face there's a good chance he'll go off like a grenade. In contrast to myself, however, he seems calm and focussed.

"When the time is right, have a word with Billy," he instructs us, "and tell him to lob up a moderate paced full-toss to the Count. He won't be able to resist slamming it for six and then... pooof, it's lights out for the Beak!"

Tulip is nodding excitedly and chuckling like a gnome. Personally, I need a little more assurance.

"Yes, Ron, but can you guarantee that 'pooof, it's lights out for the Beak' doesn't turn out to be a permanent power failure?"

"Stop worrying, man," he grins, tapping the pouch rather recklessly. "This cat is cool."

As I have absolutely no idea what he's talking about yet again, I merely shrug and comment on my stupidity in ever suggesting the idea in the first place. Meanwhile, the thunder rumbles on, but the clouds just refuse to release any rain. I am beginning to suspect yet another conspiracy by the immortals to outwit me.

Tim Lewis (Biology and Lechery) and Jacko Jackman (Chemistry and Paranoia), open the batting for the Staff Eleven and make steady headway into the fifth over when our appeal for a glaringly obvious LBW is refused by Jack Parsons. The very next ball strikes Tim's pad in exactly the same place and Parsons shakes his head again. Now, Tim is one of the younger teachers and a pretty good bloke; he's even got a collection of Rock 'n Roll and Jazz records and plays double-bass in a local Trad Band. Holding up his palm to halt play, he walks over to Parsons and tells him that, in all fairness, he was out both times. This throws the lickspittle caretaker into a mild panic and his anxious stares towards the pavilion soon bring the Count storming over to investigate. An altercation then follows between the Count and squeaky-clean Tim, with agitated head-nodding to both parties from Parsons. Finally, with a raised hand of submission to us all, Tim tucks his bat under his arm and strides from the pitch. We break into spontaneous applause at his unshakeable honesty but fear for his career as the Count follows him at a short distance, his eyes on the ground and his lips mouthing silent oaths and threats. Parsons sniffs nervously and jangles the six pebbles in his pocket. My guess is he's forgotten how many balls remain in the over. I watch him squinting at the score-board which now reads thirty-four for one. They're pulling away from us already, with their best batsmen still to perform. Only an Act of God or some extreme secular violence will save us now. Either will be welcome.

The whole Tim Lewis affair has an unsettling effect on both teams but, fortunately, the other side seem more rattled than we are. Taff Davis takes the crease and parries the ball hither and thither with no sign of his usual Merthyr Tydfil aggressiveness. It takes him two complete overs to score four runs, whereas on a normal day he would belt us all over the place, laughing madly in Welsh. Perhaps he ate too many of those melon slices for lunch. I saw him slurping and licking his way through at least six of 'em, and all the while leering at Miss Day in a most lascivious manner. He really is a dirty old Celt.

In spite of Taff's uncharacteristic apathy, the score is creeping ominously upwards into the lower fifties when Jeff, our wicket-keeper, pulls off an amazing coup by sneezing like a Banshee just as Tulip sends down a rare, but accurate, leg-spinner. Taff is almost startled out of his pads and loses sufficient concentration to see his middle stump cartwheeling away. We all bawl with glee, drowning out Taff's protestations, and he eventually leaves his crease, casting a black look in the direction of Jack Parsons. Things are looking up.

Arthur Harold Wishart (Physics and Gluttony) waddles out to face the rejuvenated bowling of our Belch spinner and, bugger me, if he isn't clean bowled with the first ball! Tulip does a handstand and begins walking around on his hands, cackling insanely until Parsons bends to the ground to give him a warning about behaviour unbecoming to the spirit of the game and his bad back. In the meantime, A. H. Wishart wobbles off the field pondering, perhaps, on the vagaries of Kinetic energy. Or maybe he's just relieved to be able to remove that testicle-crushing 'box' stuffed down his trousers.

The Nephew takes the wind from our sails. From the moment he strides confidently to the wicket, a hush descends upon our ranks. This sod means business and, in no time at all, he's knocking Tulip's deliveries all over the field. It's clearly time to introduce the Nephew to the 'Beast', or Billy Rice as he is known on the school register. We brief Billy on the task in hand and suggest that his tactics should be focussed on pure terror. Forget the finer points of bowling and human compassion, we advise, just scare the shit out of him. This advice, of course, is superfluous to Billy. He nods cheerfully; savagery on the field of play is something Billy understands all too well.

To our bewilderment, Billy tosses up a simple ball which the Nephew strikes confidently through cover-point and out to the boundary for an easy four runs. He even has the arrogance to instruct Jacko not to bother to run from the other end as the ball sails away. Billy ignores our mutterings and Terry's terse reminder that their score is now at sixty-two. He turns to run in to bowl and I can sense that the Beast is stirring. He sprints to the crease and lets fly with one of his deadliest full-tosses, precision aimed at head height and designed to maim. The Nephew yelps and ducks in the nick of time. Billy receives the returned ball and strides back even further. He canters in and delivers another head-remover, producing an identical reaction from the batsman who complains to Jack Parsons. Parsons, who seems to have gained confidence with the Count now out of reach, shrugs and shakes his head. The Nephew is visibly shaken but digs the toe of his bat into his crease and awaits Billy's next assault. The Beast approaches the bowling crease at full pelt but, to our surprise, lobs down an accurate but perfectly harmless ball that even one of Jeff's one-legged dwarfs could swipe for six. However, the Nephew, who is now reduced to self-preservation at all cost, wanders blindly from his crease, crouching in terror and with his arms protecting his head. With a cry of triumph, Jeff swipes the bales off and does a little jig arm-in-arm with Tulip around the stumps. The Nephew has a brief but lively conversation with Parsons and leaves the pitch a chastened man.

Things have, indeed, taken a turn for the better but we are far from out of the woods yet; a couple of hefty overs from the opposition would seal our fate. It's decision time and, as the Count pulls on his batting gloves and struts towards us, I convene with Tulip to implement Plan A.

The secret sign is made to Ronny (i.e. Tulip bends and touches his toes five times) and we see our accomplice shuffling to the corner of the pavilion to await an opportune moment to execute the 'switch' of balls. The Count, as we know from experience, will always strike a ball in the direction of the pavilion hoping for maximum applause from the spectators as it crosses the boundary before their very eyes. Meanwhile, we pull Billy to one side and brief him as to his duty which England expects, and that is a complete over of full-tosses… no, not at head height, you idiot, we want him to be able to hit 'em towards the pavilion, and never mind why, just do it. Lightning flashes above the town and a crack of thunder startles us all. Do we really need the cricket-bomb after all, I wonder? But it's too late now. Events have overtaken us.

The Count is in his usual self-assured mood and smacks the first ball to the wrong part of the boundary for our purposes. He allows the shadow of a smile to toy momentarily at the edge of the vicious gash that serves as his mouth. Tulip homes in on Billy and mutters instructions. Billy licks his finger and massages the ball briskly as he listens, then nods, glances towards the pavilion and commences his run. The delivery is precise, the Count's swing is straight out of the manual, and the ball soars away in a perfect arc, trickling over the boundary and stopping inches from Ronny's size sixes. Our chemical genius bends nonchalantly and, as I arrive, hands me the exchange 'ball' with a wide grin. It's as though the whole thing was executed by the gods themselves. Plan A is running as smooth as one of Momma Bonetti's milk-a-shakes.

"Well, throw the ball back, Paddick!" the Count hollers impatiently. "I only need to hit another fifteen runs and we can call it a day."

Yes, my lad, we're going to call it a day alright… a day to

remember. I ignore his command and, instead, jog my way over to Billy and hand him the ball-bomb. "Whatever you do, mate," I say quietly, "do NOT pick at, massage, or bounce this ball in your palm like you normally do." He begins to examine it closely and I am forced to spin him round out of the Count's view. "Stop it, Billy!" I implore. "It's a special ball. It's very dangerous."

"Dangerous?" he says, his eyes lighting up like beacons and a beam of pleasure creasing his face.

"Yes, but I haven't got time to explain. Just bowl another one up as planned."

There is another clap of thunder and all eyes turn to the heavens, but still the rain holds off. It's as if old Thor and Mars are up there in the thunderheads rolling dice and wagering on the outcome of the match.

What occurs next will go down in the annals of Fayling cricketing history as an event of sensational drama. Elderly men will one day lean forward in their rocking chairs, wipe the Guinness froth from their moustaches, and recount to slack-jawed grandchildren the details of this day. Old boys of Fayling Grammar will gather at the bar and spill their gin and tonics down their 'Old Faylers' ties as they guffaw and reminisce on this momentous happening.

Intoxicated with self-confidence, the Count steps forward to punish yet another impeccable delivery from Billy. Slicing his bat at near shoulder height he makes contact, willow on leather. There is a flash of fire, an ear-splitting bang, and the Count is flung backwards onto the stumps, enveloped in a churning cloud of black smoke. Everyone within range drops to the grass and covers his head as hot particles of cork and leather rain upon us. What in the name of Alfred B. Nobel have we done? I can barely pluck up the courage to look, but look I must. I raise my head and peer at ground level into the swirling grey mist that was, but moments ago, Jeff Atyeo, the Count, and the wicket. I rub my eyes and refocus on the upturned soles of a large pair of shoes and what appears to be a fist grasping a smouldering stick. Clambering to my feet, I approach with thumping heart and dread gripping my stomach. Other figures sway through the fug to join me and we stare in silence at the scorched ground.

The Count is out for it... the count, that is. He lies across the flattened stumps, his arms outstretched like the crucified Christ, his face as black as a West Indian mid-fielder and devoid of eyebrows and lashes. In the charred fingers of his cricket glove he grips the shredded handle of his bat, now reduced to a mere glowing stump of timber.

"My god," someone whispers, "he's been struck by a thunder-bolt."

And, on hearing this, so have I!

Oh, sweet, smiling Jesus of Nazareth, you have seen fit to save me yet again. A thunder-bolt, what a brilliant theory! After all, here we are playing cricket high up on a hillside in close proximity to a thunderstorm. We're asking for trouble and now, by thunder, we've got it. You read about it every year: 'Golf player killed by lightning' or 'Entire football team knocked unconscious in electrical storm'. It's perfect in every respect and gets us off any hooks waiting to hoist us to perdition. I begin to grin and, before I know it, I'm chuckling hysterically with glee.

"Yes, that's it. A thunder-bolt," I cry joyously. Faces turn to stare at me, and Tulip is obliged to guide me aside to ask me what the bloody hell I'm doing. I can only gaze at him, my lips twisted in a half-crazed smile of utter relief. Even if the Count is dead, no-one will point the finger of suspicion our way because it was an act of God. Nobody is going to argue with him.

Taff Davis blusters through our ranks and kneels to attend to his headmaster. He pulls the victim's eyelids up to reveal the pinks of his eyes and moves an index finger across his line of vision. No response, apparently, so he fumbles for the Count's wrist (possibly a futile gesture as I understand the undead have no pulse).

"Come on now, 'eadmaster," prompts Taff and pats the Count's charcoaled cheeks briskly. To our surprise, the Count begins to mumble and move his limbs. "There's lov-elly," says Taff in daftest Welsh drivel. "Now, let's 'ave you sittin' up, look," and he grabs the Count by the remnants of his shirt collar with both fists and jerks him roughly into a sitting position. It occurs to me that old Taff is enjoying this! Is he taking revenge for years of humiliation at the hands of his superior? I believe he is. Well, bravo Taff, I say, and to my great satisfaction he fetches the Count a resounding slap across the face, leaving the shape of his hand like a negative on the headmaster's cheek.

"Steady on, Mr. Davis," booms the voice of 'Soapy' Luxmoore (Deputy Headmaster, English Lit, Latin and suspected Homosexuality). He leans to inspect the Count's condition for himself. "Ah, yes, concussion," he nods sagely. "Saw plenty of it during the blitz in London. My poor young boys at our school. All that bombing." 'Bumming' more likely, you sordid old bender.

Unexpectedly, the Count's eyes open slowly and his gaze drifts from one face to another. Finally, his eyes lock on Soapy.

"Ser-jeant," slurs the Count, "get on the blower and find out where the bloody air-cover is!"

"My god," breathes Taff, "he's back on Gold Beach with Forty-Seven Marine Commando!"

Soapy nods in agreement, placing a hand on Taff's shoulder and squeezing it with over-familiar warmth. "You're right, Owen. It's uncanny. Very, very queer." Much like yourself then, Soapy.

"Don't just stand there prattling," drones the Count, waving a tremulous hand randomly. "Get some bren-gun fire into that Jerry pill-box!"

"Shouldn't we call an ambulance?" suggests Jeff casually, scraping fragments of cork from the surface of his wicket-keeping pads. Thankfully, he appears unscathed, courtesy of the shelter provided by the Count. Tim Lewis presses forward, takes a gander at the woozy Count and says he will bring his Rover across and take the gibbering headmaster to hospital himself. There is an immediate sharp intake of breath from the entire ensemble, punctuated by an outburst from Taff.

"Oh, no, no, Timothy," he rebukes, "I can't 'ave tyre marks all over my strip!"

Heads nod amid a murmur of agreement and it is made abundantly clear that the welfare of the Count comes in at a miserable second to the preservation of the cricket-strip.

"OK," says Tim, "we'll just have to carry him to the car." And, in an instant, hands grasp the Count's anatomy at all available points and he is lifted bodily and trundled from the pitch. Throughout his short trip, he keeps up a barrage of abuse aimed at the absent RAF and their bloody nancy-boy pilots.

On reaching Tim's car we are gratified to observe the Count being thrown unceremoniously onto the rear seat and the door slamming on his whingeing blather. As the Rover pulls away, right on cue, large globules of rain begin to pat on the pavilion roof and, within seconds, the heavens open to a chorus of tumultuous thunder-claps. Jack Parsons scurries up the pavilion steps declaring the match a draw and our entire team performs a triumphal rain-dance with glee. History has been forged, the curse broken. We adjourn post haste to the grub table to sink our teeth into Miss Day's delicious buns. Yum-yum.

Thus it is, as I am engaged in mid-bun, that a voice straight from the end of a rainbow, flying to me on wings of sparkling gossamer, caresses my young eardrums.

"Hello Colin."

Yes, it is she… Wendy. Here she stands before me, in all her sumptuousness, breasts bristling and moist lips held apart just enough to reveal those beautiful pearly-white teeth. I am obliged to warn Wee William to restrain himself as he jerks with excitement down in his lair. To add to my difficulties, my mouth is bulging with Miss Day's artificial cream and I am unable to respond to Wendy's greeting other than with a grunt of animal-like pleasure followed by a grimace of pain as I swallow the contents of my overloaded mouth. Like a kindly nurse she hands me her glass of lukewarm orange squash and I down it gratefully. "You're soaking wet," she coos, running a dangerously electrically-charged hand down my arm. I nod like a buffoon, rendered speechless by her close presence.

Anthea breezes up, ignoring me totally, and asks Wendy if she's seen Tulip because he's done one of his vanishing acts. "He's in the bog," I report, a trifle crudely, and he reappears, walking towards us still grappling with the fly buttons on his cricket whites.

"The rain's eased off," he grins, placing a palm on Anthea's bum. "Shall we bugger off to the Tarantella?"

"I wish you wouldn't do that in public," snaps the snap-dragon.

"What, stroke your lovely bottom?" he leers.

"No, swear." Hmmm, interesting priorities, Anthea.

Before we can escape, Taff Davis and Jack Parsons corner us to confirm that, under the rules laid down by the Count himself, the match was indeed a draw and we are the first team to ever achieve it. The result will be engraved on the 'Darke Cup' and a team photograph must be taken immediately before some of us disperse into the wide world. We all tumble outside, where it is still raining, so troop back inside again and form two rows, one standing, one sitting, along the rear wall. The camera flashes, hands are shaken, backs slapped and off we go.

We set off as a foursome with Ronny, Billy, and Jeff tagging behind deep in animated conversation about the day's remarkable events. Ronny is busy perpetuating the 'thunder-bolt' myth and I hear him explaining at length how such a phenomenon comes about.

I am sure you will understand when I confess to being more than a trifle confused by Wendy's sudden re-interest in me. In fact, the more I learn about the opposite sex, the more bewildered I become. Is this due to some dimness of the brain on my part, or am I just destined, along with the majority of males, to live my life in a state of perplexed passion for them, never really knowing what they want? Come to that, do they know themselves what they want? I've frequently overheard my own parents arguing about some meaningless mole-hill my mother has converted into a mountain, and the conversation invariably ends with my mother contradicting herself and Dad making a cup of tea. One thing is certain where women are concerned: you never get to the bottom of 'em. Unless you're Tulip's right hand.

You see, here we go again… Wendy has just slipped her hand into mine. It's only a matter of days since the Great Koi Carp Debacle, after which I'm sure she was banned from coming within a hundred yards of me, and yet here we are walking down Yorktown Grove like Darby and Joan. I turn to her and she's smiling sweetly at me. Call me over-suspicious, but there's something a bit weird going on today. Where is Danny? I ask myself. Why the sudden interest in cricket? Why is my lip twitching into one of its strictly forbidden Elvis curls? My life is full of unanswered questions.

As we approach the Cottage Hospital, the long snout of Tim Lewis's Rover nudges out through the pillared entrance. He stops and winds his window down as we crowd at the car.

"How's the Count?" asks Tulip cheekily.

"I'll pretend I didn't hear that, Andrew," says Tim, frowning wryly.

I notice that Wendy has manoeuvred herself into a prominent position immediately by the driver's door and has rested her substantial knockers on the window frame so that, were Tim so inclined (and I suspect he might be) he need only to lower his head to nestle his face between them. He grins and answers Tulip's enquiry. "Yes, our headmaster is making good progress. When I left him he had already crossed the Rhine and was well on the way to Berlin!" We all laugh like bandits.

"Mr. Lewis," says Wendy coyly, as Tim slips the Rover into first gear and turns to stare straight into her cleavage. "Would you be able to drop me home? I'm running a little behind time for laying up tables for this evening."

Tim glances at his watch and shifts his bum squeakily in the leather seat. He's dying to say yes, I just know it. Keeping his eyes off Wendy's juicy attributes is killing him but he is, after all, in the company of innocent young children, as yet untainted by the world's wicked ways. On the other hand, of course, he's merely a red-blooded stud like the rest of us.

"OK, jump in, Wendy," he says, "but I must get right back to the pavilion to help Miss Day clear up."

This bloke's life is just one long totty-fest.

I watch the Rover drive off and observe Wendy through the retreating rear window as she smooches up to Tim on the big bench seat. I see her toss her head with laughter and I wonder what Tim has just said. I never, ever, make her laugh like that. What has Tim got that I haven't? Sophistication, experience, rugged good looks, a Rover 100 and a degree in biology. I have a way to go yet, then.

# CHAPTER 6

## *'Catch A Falling Star' (Perry Como...1958)*

The acrid smell of burning toast niggles at my nostrils and even follows me under the bedclothes. There's no escape, it's time to get up. I grope on my bedside cupboard for my trusty Timex, add ten minutes, and deduce that the time stands at the obscenely early hour of nine fifty-two, hardly a fit time for a young gentleman to be tipped from his mattress into the jaws of a hostile world. But my mother's entreaties warbling up the stairwell for me to attend downstairs to break my fast, and don't dare come down until you've washed your face, convince me that another five minutes won't hurt anyone. A loud grunt is sufficient to give me a short period of meditation.

Settling back with my hands behind my head, I contemplate the ceiling and its ever-changing topography (a word I recently picked up in a fleeting moment of attention during one of 'Gussy' Galway's geography lessons). I immediately observe that the ever-fascinating patterns in my cracked ceiling have now fashioned themselves into what appears to be a pod of dolphins assaulting a combine harvester. This is a considerable improvement on the previous dull map of Italy and I begin to wonder if the plaster is in the process of giving way altogether. Best let Dad know how bad it's getting. And the mention of Dad reminds me that I should be at Mrs Lee's house undercoating her back door as arranged. Sod it! Ah, well, I need that striped shirt and an Eddie Cochran LP (and don't forget the dosh you still owe to Wendy!) so I'd better get moving. Anyway, Dad always pays me over the odds.

The kitchen is in its usual state of post-breakfast shock. Nothing is spared the holocaust. Sausages lie charred in the frying pan next to hideously warped bacon rashers and fatally incinerated tomatoes. The stench of death hangs in the air.

"You're late again, Colin," chides my mother, removing her apron to reveal one of her slinkiest dresses. What is she up to today, I ponder? More shenanigans with the witless wonder, Lamont? Oh, let 'em get on with it! Why should I care if they wish to roll naked in the woods and frolic through the swaying barley stalks? Having said that, it's still my ambition to catch them at it. "Your breakfast is in the pan," she says, frowning as I slump into a chair. "Please don't make a mess." I gaze around the kitchen contemplating how anything I do could possibly make it worse.

Fortunately for both of us, the irritating beep of Lamont's car horn slices through the tense atmosphere and my mother whisks up her handbag, reminds me about my attendance at the House of Lee, and exits with a slamming of the door.

Maybe I've provoked her a bit too much this morning but, to be fair to myself, I am a teenager, a relatively new invention. It takes everyone time to get used to new-fangled things. Remember, kids quite like us never existed before; we have our own identity, our own music, clothes, and vocabulary. We are no longer smaller versions of our parents. I doubt that things will ever be the same again. But don't think I'm not grateful for what they did, kicking Hitler's ass, and all. That was really something. But life goes on, does it not? The war came and went, the music stopped, the parcel was passed, and we all found ourselves holding the bloody hydrogen bomb! Oh, what fun.

*

Happily, Ronny and his mother are not at home when I arrive at Chez Lee so the chances of being poisoned by either of them are nil. Mrs Lee has left a note pinned to the back door telling me that all the doors are locked but the back-door key is under the dustbin. Presumably only illiterate burglars will be calling today.

Before opening the pot of grey undercoat, I decide to take a look around the outside of the bungalow, primarily to peer through Ronny's window and check out any strange developments within. I should have guessed that the curtains would be drawn. Now my curiosity is aroused and, before I have time to argue with my brain, it guides me back to the dustbin and instructs me to take the key and enter the house. But surely there's no harm in taking a peek inside Ron's bedroom? Maybe I'll gain some clue as to how Mr. Hyde managed to consume himself, a marvel which has been puzzling me for some time.

I have underestimated Ronald's security arrangements: his room is locked. I place my eye over the keyhole and wait for my vision to adjust to the dimly lit interior. There's something moving in there, I swear I caught a glimpse of a large, bushy shape scurrying along the narrow strip of carpet between the bed and the cages. What in the name of Satan has Ronny created this time? There it goes again, scuttle, scuttle, hop... Hell's bells, it just leapt onto the bed with no effort at all! I can't make out exactly what shape it is. Is that a tail or a long snout; is it a gargantuan squirrel or a reduced aardvark? But before I can speculate further, the hideous thing flies towards the door with the speed of a cheetah, hit's the door with a crash, and begins clawing at the panel in a frenzy of rage.

I don't mind admitting, I am a mere buttock clench from fouling my Y-fronts. I fall backwards, scramble to my feet and sprint down the hall and into the back yard. Slamming the door shut, I grapple with the key until I manage to lock it.

I'm still trembling as I release the lid from the paint pot and commence with the first coat. Maybe if I lay it on really thick I can get away with just one coat. This added effort seems to settle me down a bit and soon, with the regular slap of brush on door, I am lulled into a minor trance. But not for long because there suddenly comes a wailing lament from inside the house, a pitiful, terrifying yowl that turns my blood to ice.

That's it, I've had enough. Shocking fantasies pour into my head as I quickly clean the paintbrush with turps: just suppose, yes, just suppose that creature from the bowels of Hell is Ronald himself? Jesus on a Lambretta, in this house, anything might be feasible! Supposing he's swallowed one of those concoctions he administers to the hamsters? How do we know what would happen? Look at what went wrong with Mr. Hyde, both Ronny's and Robert Louis Stevenson's. I leave in a hurry.

The Gaggia coffee machine hisses at me as I enter the Tarantella but, after what I've just been through, it's a pussy-cat. Momma Bonetti gives me a big-a smile and tells me that some of my friends is down-a the back. I scan the room and catch sight of Tulip in animated conversation with Ronny and Jeff. Wow, that's a relief! So Ronny is not the Beast of Fayling after all. I cheer up considerably.

"A-ha, the Three Musty Queers!" I say jovially as I join them, coffee in hand.

"Hey, Brillo," says Tulip, "take a look at this." He stabs his finger onto a sheet of paper laid out on the table. I lean across and see that it's some kind of roughly drawn map.

"What's it supposed to be?" I ask, sliding in next to Jeff and stirring my espresso indifferently.

What you have to understand is that this is not a unique event. On average, maybe five times a year, Tulip assails us with one mad-cap idea or another, most of which are laughed out of existence. Very occasionally, though, he comes up with a scheme which we find so outrageous that, out of sheer buggery, we agree to try it. Such an error of judgement was made last summer, when, in the half-light of a late August evening, we attempted to launch our fifteen-foot-long, home-made glider from the slopes of Fayling Knoll. Unfortunately, a sudden gust of in-shore wind caught us and, instead of carrying us a few yards and tipping the two of us into the bracken as expected, we flew a quarter of a mile and crash-landed in Fayling Municipal Rubbish Tip. That might have been the end of it except that some short-sighted nitwit out walking on the knoll rang the Fayling Gazette claiming to have seen a 'mysterious unidentified winged object'. The next day a journalist was up there looking for little green men and we were fearful of reprisals if he traced anything back to us. Luckily, two days later, a yacht went down off Fayling Head drowning half the crew, so the press forgot about our UFO.

"What it is," enthuses Tulip, bending his forefinger on the map and grinning like a pirate, "is a map showing an underground passage from the Parish Church all the way to the vicarage."

I snatch the map and scrutinise it sceptically.

"So?" I say.

"So let's find it and explore it, you raving nit!" rants the Belch Marco Polo. "Who's to say there's not treasure hidden there?"

Ronny leans forward in his seat and removes a small bottle from his pocket. "It's possible, man," he concedes, trickling moonshine into his coffee. "Those medieval monks had some far-out habits."

None of us is sure whether he's serious or making one of his bizarre jokes. We all look at him, smile and nod.

"Well you can count me out," says Jeff, waving his bandaged arm at us, "I'm not risking more damage to life and limb from you lot." He bids us adieu and says he's going fishing.

I have to confess to being mildly drawn to this latest escapade proposed by Tulip. I am, as you know, of an inquisitive nature and an adventurer at heart (you may recall my highly successful quest for the 'clitoris'), so when Tulip produces a photograph of the church interior with the passage entrance marked with a large 'X', my pulse quickens. The entrance to 'Ye Undergrownde Waye', as it is named on the copied map, turns out to be beneath a stone slab situated in front of the pulpit. It probably weighs half a ton, we point out. "Got that covered," Tulip assures us. "I'll bring my old man's crowbar."

"When's the best time to do it?" I query, quickly adding, "Assuming we're even vaguely interested."

"Saturday afternoon," grins Tulip. "Vicar Whicker will be busy with the Summer Fete at the vicarage."

We drink our coffee whilst Tulip regales us with information on medieval secret passages, priest-holes, and general cobblers he has gleaned from the library. Apparently, assistant librarian Barry was very helpful but kept bringing him obscure and unrelated data regarding the sexual deviations of monks and aristocrats. "There's something wrong with that Barry." says Tulip.

Momma Bonetti approaches our table and flicks her dish-cloth at us.

"You boys gotta no 'omes?" she admonishes. "Look, I got a line of customer lookin' for a seats!"

*

I arrive home to find Lamont's Mini parked impudently across our back gate and I pause and toy with the naughty idea of letting the air out of his rear tyres. It would give me enormous pleasure to observe his fury from the safety of my bedroom. No, I'll save it for another day. Besides, this could be an opportunity to catch them up to no good at last. My mother would be at my mercy if I was unexpectedly privy to their indiscretions. 'A little knowledge, particularly in your hands, Paddick, is a dangerous thing,' so the Count was in the habit of informing me. Maybe this is what he meant.

I creep soundlessly into the house and make my way up the hall. It's very quiet. I halt at the bottom of the stairs and strain my ears for sounds coming from any of the bedrooms. Nope, nary a grunt or a giggle. But, hang on, I do detect the murmur of Lamont's voice wafting from the front room and, treading cautiously to the door, I position myself in the standard eavesdropping stance. Squinting through the gap between the door and the frame, I can just make out their heads as they sit on the sofa. I am, once more, appalled at the content of their hushed tones.

"Let me stroke yours, Marjorie," I hear Lamont whisper, "it's so silky."

I am obliged to clamp my hand over my mouth to avoid crying out with wrath and disgust. But, before I can recover, my mother produces a further abomination.

"Oh, it likes that," she sighs. "Let me tickle yours now. Oh, look at its little head!"

I stick my fingers in my ears and step back from the door. This is beyond the pale; lines have been crossed here. Have we all sunk into an abyss of moral turpitude (a marvellous expression I once heard on the radio)? Well, some of us clearly have. But it's not over yet.

"Why don't you give it a kiss?" sniggers Lamont.

That's enough, I can't allow this depravity to continue under my own roof. (Fleetingly, my bold experiments with Caroline spring to mind. Am I displaying double standards? No, no, this is happening to my own mother and must be halted. And, anyway, I'm still learning.) I am compelled to take action.

I throw open the door and leap into the room, yelling 'Geronimo' so loudly that glass ornaments jingle on the mantle-piece and the window rattles. Lamont flies off the sofa screaming like a stuck pig and attempts to climb the bookcase in the alcove. Where does he think he's going? My mother springs to her feet facing me, her face white with shock. Cradled in her arms is a small, pale-grey rabbit. Its twin brother hops onto the arm of the sofa and begins to casually preen itself. In the background, books are falling to the floor as Lamont turns his harrowing gaze upon me from his perch on the second shelf, adjacent to Dad's volume of 'The Ascent of Everest' by John Hunt. How curious.

"Marjorie," he croaks, "I don't believe I can visit you here anymore. This boy is killing me."

The look on my mother's face could paralyse a snow leopard. She points to the door and we both exit, marching briskly to the kitchen where I don't think she is about to make me a cup of tea. She pulls out a chair and orders me to sit then stands, arms crossed, observing me from her favourite position by the sink. The rabbit has been dumped on the table and is examining the pepper pot.

"This can't go on, young man," she says rather wearily. "Since your exams finished you've been a complete thorn in my side."

The rabbit suddenly sneezes and sends the salt pot rolling, dribbling a trail of the contents. My mother darts forward to retrieve it. "Your father and I have almost lost patience with you, Colin." Strange, Dad hasn't mentioned a thing about my behaviour. I think this is all a ploy to divert attention from her own impropriety. I shall treat it with contempt. I nod at the table and ask why there are two rabbits running free in the house. "Don't change the subject," she snaps and snatches up the startled bunny. "And anyhow, Quentin breeds them. He brought these two babies round to show me." To my joy, the rabbit raises its rear end and lays a clutch of droppings in her hand. I rise from my seat and leave the room as Lamont enters, red-faced and adjusting his ridiculous cravat. We eyeball each other scornfully and, sensing a twitch of my upper lip, I allow it to blossom into a full-blown Elvis sneer.

*

Saturday is here and I meet Tulip and Ronny in the churchyard, averting my eyes from the open grave where Bill Potter met his demise. Tulip is leaning against the porch attempting to balance what looks like a burglar's jemmy vertically in his palm; Ronny is sitting with his back against an ancient gravestone smoking one of his curious, hand-made cigarettes and grinning foolishly.

"Ready?" Tulip says and leads the way into the church.

It is eerily silent in here. Why do I always expect to see the spectre of a monk kneeling at the altar? It beats me how Vicar Whicker can spend half his life in here. For a start, it's always cold, even now in mid-summer. In the winter months it's like a freezer. The only warmth in the building comes from three suspended electric heaters about twenty feet in the air, heating up the vaulted ceiling space nicely. Heat, of course, rises, it's a scientific fact. But we all know what the Church thinks of science.

Tulip is holding the photograph and checking that we are standing on the correct flagstone. He taps it cautiously with his jemmy and, sure enough, it gives a hollow ring. "Bingo!" he says and thrusts the bar into the floor join. The stone immediately lifts and I am able to slide my fingers under the edge, prise it up and lean it against the pulpit. A draught of cool, sour air floats up from the blackness we have exposed. Stone steps lead down and disappear into the darkness.

"I can hear rodents squeaking, man," says Ronny, on his knees and peering into the cavity.

"Well, you should feel right at home, then," I suggest.

He pulls himself up and draws on his ridiculous roll-up. "You don't think I'm going down there, do you?" he smiles. "I'm the 'lookout', remember?" And he settles himself horizontally on a pew, places a pile of prayer books under his head, and begins humming some strange Modern Jazz tune.

"Fine," says Tulip. "That's OK with me. Just don't expect a third share of any treasure we find."

A perfunctory wave of the hand followed by the emission of a perfect smoke ring sums up Ronald's judgement of our expedition into the unknown.

"Where's your torch?" he calls as we descend into the depths. We both reappear and sit despondently on the steps.

"Bollocks!" says Tulip. "What do we do now?"

"Look around you, daddy-o," advises the recumbent and

increasingly irritating chemist. "Candles galore."

He's right, there are numerous candles about the place. We choose a pair of stonking great white ones and set off once more, Tulip leading us down into the spooky passage like a pair of nineteenth-century tomb robbers.

In spite of Ronny's misgivings, we neither see nor hear any rats. I'm convinced those fags he smokes are giving him hallucinations. There are, though, plenty of cobwebs and some fearsome-looking spiders. What do they catch down here? Flies aren't known for their sense of adventure so they are unlikely to explore these regions. Unless there's something to attract them... like a maggoty monk. Don't be so stupid, Paddick, he'd be a pile of bones by now. Yes, insists my brain, but what about that bloke who went missing last November? All they found was a pile of clothing on the beach, they never found a body. Get a grip, brain, he walked into the sea and drowned.

Up to this point, the Great Undergrownde Waye expedition has been a miserable failure, even by Tulip's standards. There's nothing down here but slimy moss, spiders, smelly puddles and two brainless idiots carrying candles and a jemmy. We must have slithered and stumbled for about seventy-five yards so where does that locate us, I wonder.

"According to the map," announces Tulip, uncannily reading my thoughts, "we should be under the vicarage garden."

We stop to listen carefully for sounds filtering down from the Annual Fete commencing somewhere above us but we hear nothing and proceed. "This tunnel must end soon, at a door or something. Maybe in the vicarage cellar," he chuckles.

Actually, the prospect of making a dramatic appearance through some panelled wall in the vicarage, covered in cobwebs and carrying a candle (and preferably in the hall where Hettie and the Brownies have set up their annual jumble sale), appeals to me. What sweet revenge that would be for their relentless persecution of my investigations with Caroline.

Without warning, Tulip's candle is extinguished and I hear him scrabbling around on the ground cursing the Franciscan Order and their shoddy building practices. I move my candle from side to side in an effort to find him.

"I'm over here, you twat!" he calls, and my candle illuminates his mud-stained face staring at me from the other side of a pile of fallen masonry.

"I just tripped over the roof," he calls.

"How can you trip over the roof?" I enquire.

"Because it's on the bloody floor," he enlightens me, scrambling back over the pile. "All we've got above us," he snatches my candle and holds it aloft, "is this."

A tree root meanders along the earthen roof above our heads. This is, in fact, a worm's-eye view of a worm and I don't feel too easy about it. To compound my nervousness and in an act of pure Belchery, Tulip raises the jemmy and begins to poke and scrape at the soil roof.

"Are you nuts?" I yelp, restraining him with my free hand.

"I'm just seeing how deep it is," he shrugs, but steps back smartly as a large clod of earth falls at his feet, followed by a cascade of old mortar and soil lumps. "Christ, Brillo, don't just stand there... run for it!"

I have neither the time nor the breath, as we gallop back up Ye Undergrownde Waye, to remind Tulip that this brush with death is entirely his fault. If I had the option to halt for a second to kick myself, I might feel better, but the ominous rumble of collapsing roof is enough to propel me even faster.

Never have I been so glad to see the interior of a church and a reclining chemist wreathed in wispy smoke. Tulip and I throw ourselves to the flagstones and lie on our backs, gasping for breath.

"Everything cool?" asks Ronny, glancing at us with a sardonic, detached grin. Tulip struggles to his knees and levers the stone away from its leaning position against the pulpit. It falls back into place with a thud that echoes from every nook and cranny.

"Yep, we've seen all we want to see," he lies gallantly but accurately.

"So Ye Undergrownde Waye has lost its appeal," says Ronny. He makes no further enquiries regarding our explorations and seems perfectly content to lie on the pew smoking his stupid 'grass', as he calls it.

"Are we going to the Fete, then?" asks Tulip.

But before we can reach a consensus, the clack of the church door catch freezes my blood. Ronny, by contrast, merely arches his neck to take a look as the door creaks open.

"And now," mumbles Ron, "here be Ye Vicar."

Tulip and I rise slowly from the floor and attempt to look innocent by pretending to examine the wood carvings on the pulpit. This is a fruitless ploy as we have forgotten that Vicar Whicker has the poorest eyesight imaginable (borne out, I think you'll agree, by his attraction to Mrs Lee who has facial hair, poorly fitting dentures and, reputedly, one nipple. Lucky that Ronny wasn't a twin). To the vicar, therefore, we are merely distant moving forms. He removes his spectacles, polishes the thick lenses on his black cassock, and replaces them. He raises a hand.

"Ah, you must be the Boy Scouts," he calls. "More chairs required in front of the raised platform, boys, and a few on top for our V.I.P.s to sit. You'll find folding chairs down in the vestry. Quick as you can."

He lingers for a moment, staring our way with a puzzled expression on his face. The reason for his curiosity, I suspect, is that Ronny has blown a flawless smoke ring up from his hidden position and it has miraculously settled to hover just above Tulip's head. Saint Andrew of Fayling? Saint Tulip of Belch? No, I think not. The vicar draws a crooked forefinger slowly across his lips and scratches his head ponderously before leaving, deep in thought. Have we shaken his faith, I speculate?

So, the Scouts are organising the seating for the Summer Fete. That means cousin Adrian will be camping it up in his regulation issue shorts, trilling instructions to the younger boys, and breaking into a sweat whenever he sees one of 'em bending.

Ronny pulls himself from his pew, nips the end of his 'cigarette' and slides it behind his ear. "If you want to get into the Fete without paying the entrance fee, guys, follow me," he announces.

We exit the church and make our way to the rear of the graveyard where, to our surprise, Ronny opens a door in the stone wall and we step into the vicarage gardens. He leads us on a rather devious route which passes a long greenhouse and, for some reason, he spends some considerable time peering in through the dirty glass.

"What're you looking for, Ron?" asks Tulip.

"Just checking the crop, man," mutters the mad scientist. I can't imagine why Ronny finds the vicar's tomatoes so interesting.

We emerge from between two large chestnut trees into the full activity of the Fete, feeling pretty smart to have avoided the combined entrance fee of one and six. Ronny is keen to visit the Fortune Teller as he enjoys the guaranteed argument he will get with his contention that there is no such thing as the future.

"There can only be the 'past' and the 'present', man," he insists as we walk. "The 'future' is merely conjecture, speculation and guesswork based solely on past events." He may be right except that we haven't a clue what he's talking about.

We pause for a moment to read a poster detailing the wondrous content of the Fete. It tells us that the beneficiary of all the profits will be, as usual, the church tower which, according to the vicar, requires a great deal of remedial work. Well, it seemed pretty solid the other day when Ronald and I climbed its stone steps and detonated a bomb at its base. But, Ronald (being naturally suspicious of all ecclesiastical matters) points out that the vicar always takes a short holiday immediately after the Fete and accuses Whicker of creaming off some of the proceeds to finance an annual trip to France.

"Cheap booze and easy women, man," he sneers. "That's what old Whicker digs."

The poster also declares that the proceedings will be officially opened by Fayling's one and only local celebrity, Barnaby Small.

Let me tell you about Barnaby:

Now, Barnaby Small is a bit of a character and refers to himself as a minor 'star'. In fact, he's a complete prat with a seedy reputation and a very murky past. Nevertheless, he turned up one spring morning, found lodgings in the town, and took out a lease on the Pier Palace, Fayling's tumble-down Victorian music hall. He spent the first few weeks familiarising himself with the regulars at the local pubs and perpetuating the myth that he had hosted a TV show in

Canada. In no time at all, he had also ingratiated himself with the Town Council (not too difficult with all those palms thrusting forward to be greased) and announced that he would be running a summer 'Quiz and Talent Show' with 'grand prizes and first-class entertainment'. It was to be called "Smile... You're A Winner!" and he duly advertised in the local press and fly-posted every available space with stickers. Within hours, some resident wag had gone round and altered all the posters to "Small... You're A Wanker!" which amused many of us.

Nevertheless, Barnaby prevailed and his seasonal shows are now part of Fayling folklore. His 'grand prizes' are discount vouchers that can be exchanged for immovable stock at various retail outlets in the town or a half-price trip around the bay in Tom Berry's dangerous boat on a Sunday, weather permitting. Nobody has worked out what the 'first-class entertainment' is, although there are regular fire scares, the roof leaks onto the circle seats during downpours, and inebriated competitors occasionally fall off the stage into the empty orchestra pit.

Nowadays, Barnaby is escorted around town by two burly 'heavies' who are both, surprisingly, reputed to be queer. One of them doubles as a chauffeur, and our overweight quizmaster lounges in the back of his white Jaguar Mark One waving to the populace like the bloody great queen that he is. He lives in a large rented villa at the far end of the dunes where wild parties are allegedly held and from where seep strange tales of debauchery and orgies. Sounds like a lot of fun to me. But it's odd how the police frequently 'raid' the place but no-one ever gets arrested.

The Scouts are putting the finishing touches to the small stage they have erected and, as I predicted, cousin Adrian is overseeing the construction. We find him instructing two younger Scouts in the art of tying a bow in the red ribbon which Barnaby Small will shortly snip at the official opening. He catches sight of me and forces a wimpish smile. I wave to him with a limp wrist and he tosses his head and turns back to his boys.

To the side of the stage we discover a coconut shy manned by none other than Mad Farmer Wilkes, dressed up in his best checked shirt, tan corduroy trousers and gleaming Wellington boots. He greets us with his salesman's pitch, "Come on, lads... threepence for a quick toss!"

We thank him for his kind offer but inform him that we don't really need the money. He scratches his cheek with puzzlement but, as we move off, he grips my elbow and pulls me to one side.

"Have you seen your gorgeous mother here, young Paddick?"

I shake my head, more in wonder at his description of her than anything else. "Dammit!" he mumbles. "She promised to get here early and help me get me nuts up." I have no answer and he peers at me, anxiety etched into every crevice of his sun-tanned face. "I suppose she's alright?" he adds. I slide away cautiously, leaving him staring up at the church clock and stroking one of his coconuts fondly. The world of adults is, indeed, a curious place.

To Ronny's annoyance, the small tent which would normally house 'Madame Zonda… Palms Read and the Future Told' has a note pinned to it stating that the fortune teller will not be in attendance due to unforeseen circumstances.

We amble off into the marquee where the garden produce and home-baking exhibits are displayed, awaiting judging and prize awarding. What a cornucopia of tat! The tent is infested with daft old biddies fussing around, re-arranging plates of cup-cakes and precision-sliced wedges of Victoria-sandwich sponges. They jabber amongst themselves as they hover over the exhibits, titivating a cheese straw here, removing a crumb there. God, can they ever talk!

Further down the table, two potato-growing rivals are laying out their season's produce in an aura of mutual hatred. They beaver away in silence with their backs to one another. One of 'em even has a ruler in his hand.

To our mild surprise, we spot Flash Moule ambling towards us with the King Liddle Basta on a tight leash. They pause and Flash leans over a plate of miniature cocktail cases to examine them more closely, his damp cigarette butt sprinkling the fillings with ash. His deranged canine bares its teeth, blinks its one eye, and growls at the table leg. We move on, squeezing past a group of blue rinses sipping tea and stuffing their faces with carrot cake.

"I enjoy the Autumn Harvest Fete more," says one. "The fruit is such a lovely sight."

"Ummm," drones another. "Will the vicar be showing his plums this year, I wonder?"

Why wait until September, my dear? Flash will show you his right now.

The garden is beginning to fill up now as holidaymakers drag themselves away from the seafront and discover that Fayling has a little more to offer than a strip of gift shops, fourteen cafes, and a crazy-golf course. Even Papa Bonetti has arrived and is doing a brisk trade from his brand-new ice-a-cream van. He is wearing a peaked sea captain's hat, a curious choice for a man who very recently went down with his ship, but it does lend him a certain panache, atop his wide grin and swarthy Wopness.

The blast of a car horn announces the arrival of Barnaby Small, and his white Jag sweeps in through the vicarage gates like a presidential limousine. Who does he think he is, Dwight D. Eisenhower? He is accompanied, as usual, by his two burly poofters, one fitted out in grey chauffeur uniform, his colleague wearing sunglasses and a lot of finger and wrist gold. Barnaby waves regally from behind tinted glasses as the peasantry step aside, allowing the car to progress and pull up beside the makeshift stage. The Scouts scatter as our star emerges from his beige leather cocoon, and I swear I caught Adrian curtseying, but it could have been a trick of the light.

The vicar steps forward to welcome Barnaby, shakes him flaccidly by the hand, and introduces him to Alf Rendle, the Mayor of Fayling. All this false formality is, of course, nothing more than bullshit because Barnaby has had the Mayor in his pocket ever since His Worship was allegedly photographed in an embarrassing clinch with a floozy at one of Barnaby's parties. Alf swears to this day that he was merely helping the lady to her feet when his trouser-belt snapped, but he's never been able to explain to Mrs. Rendle why the lady in question had both her knockers exposed. Nobody I know has actually seen the photos, but I believe they exist and, nowadays, old Barnaby gets anything he applies for from the local Planning Department.

The attendant dignitaries follow Barnaby up on to the stage and they string out in a line behind him. Vicar Whicker taps the microphone and Ralph Ellis, our local electrician and sound wizard, gives the thumbs up. With a flourish of scissors and accompanied by the vicar's crackled announcement, Barnaby snips the red ribbon. There is a sprinkling of indifferent hand-clapping from the gathered ensemble and Barnaby launches into his nauseous spiel about supporting good causes, opening your heart to your fellow man, and what time his Quiz Show kicks off every night. His 'minder' with the sunglasses stands behind him and raises outstretched arms when he deems it appropriate for applause. Some sycophant in the audience yells "Smile, you're a winner!" and Barnaby beams with pleasure as other dimwits cheer and clap. He steps back from the microphone stand and allows the vicar to lead him to a seat at the head of an onstage trestle table heaving with sumptuous comestibles laid out on a sparkling white tablecloth. How the other half live! There's enough grub up there to pay for the church tower *and* several French tarts.

It is just then, as the great and not very good of Fayling pull their chairs in towards the feast, that Tulip declares that he has detected a weak, but discernible earth tremor. Ronny and I, as long-suffering victims of Tulip's ridiculous claims and fantasies, simply laugh and pat him vigorously on the head.

"I'm not kidding," he insists, "I definitely felt the earth tremble."

"Probably Barnaby Small's wallet falling out of his pocket," I suggest.

Ronny nods in agreement and starts a lecture on seismology which could take up the rest of the day were it not for the surprising sight of the stage suddenly tipping at a crazy angle, sliding the entire retinue of convivial worthies and racketeers out of view into a chasm which has opened in the ground! It is, indeed, a wondrous sight and the shrieks of terror from the erstwhile merry-makers can only be heard to be believed. Could this be Armageddon, I muse? Will there next be a plague of locusts or a host of asps let loose amongst us? I have no way of telling.

In the meantime, we three innocents stand in gleeful awe as the Fayling Scout Group, minus my craven cousin, clamber gallantly down upon the upturned timbers of the stage in search of the vanished tea-party.

Vicar Whicker is the first to appear above the ramparts, assisted by Alf Rendle's wife and two Scouts. Ashen-faced and jelly-legged, he is lowered to the grass and administered to by ladies from the W.I. who endeavour to pour hot tea down his throat.

Next to be lifted from the debris is Barnaby Small himself, who is manhandled across the jutting timbers by the Scoutmaster and the chauffeur. A gasp of horror emits from a throng of watchers as Barnaby reveals a crimson-soaked shirt front. My god, is our falling star mortally wounded? "Relax," bawls the chauffeur, "it's raspberry jam!"

Smile, you're a winner, Barny!

We decide to investigate the rear of the stage where everything seems to have been swallowed. Sure enough, the ground has sunk about four feet forming a long, narrow trench into which the banquet has collapsed. Mayhem has ensued down there as clod-footed Scouts claw through the wreckage searching for survivors.

"I've got a leg!" yells one.

"There's a head poking up over here," pipes another. "No, sorry... it's a coconut!"

We retire from the edge and sit down under a fig tree, where Tulip immediately pulls the map of 'Ye Undergrownde Waye' and begins to study it intently. He turns it this way and that and finally nods, chuckles, and stuffs the map back in his pocket.

"Yep," he declares proudly. "This is all entirely our fault."

He then explains how our earth-shattering experience beneath the vicarage lawn clearly weakened the roof of the tunnel and it has now completely collapsed. Ronny agrees and launches into a physics lesson on weight dynamics and stress points. We pull him to his feet and gag him as we move off towards the gate, barely able to conceal our glee at our day's work.

"This is a major coup, man!" admits Ronny.

"Coo!" chorus Tulip and I. "Cooo!"

My gaiety is brought to an abrupt halt at the appearance of Wendy and Danny swinging in through the gate hand in hand. Wow, she looks great in her skin-tight sweater and thigh-hugging jeans! Danny gives me a playful punch on the shoulder as they pass us. Wendy merely smiles at me and says, "Hi, boys," brightly. My heart is down in my socks. How much more can I take, I wonder?

On hearing the distant clanging of emergency vehicles, we opt to take one more turn round the stalls and attractions and check out the disaster zone again. Tulip insists on stopping to heckle the Punch and Judy show, much to the dismay of half a dozen little kids squatting beneath the red and white striped booth and cheering on the shocking violence displayed before them. Eventually, the puppet-master, a florid-faced bloke bearing a striking resemblance to his main character, sticks his head up behind Mrs. Punch and tells Tulip to bugger off or he'll come out and shove the crocodile where neither Tulip nor the croc will appreciate. The kids turn on us, jeering and hurling ice cream cartons at us. Honestly, kids today!

We drag Tulip away and almost collide with the St. John's ambulance as it arrives to cart off the casualties. Albert Tucker is at the wheel of the Bedford and leans out of the driver's window to hail us.

"Where's all these people trapped in a cage then?" he enquires. We gaze at each other blankly and shake our heads. Ronny then comes to the rescue.

"D'you mean 'a collapsed stage', daddy-o?"

"What?" yells Albert, twiddling the knob on his ancient hearing aid. His colleague appears from the rear of the ambulance clutching a rolled-up stretcher. He eyes us suspiciously.

"You lot don't look trapped," he sniffs.

We point across to the clamour around the wreck of the stage. Albert squints towards the milling crowd, rams the Bedford noisily into first gear, and the two Angels of Mercy grind over to the action. God help us if a meteor ever lands on Fayling.

To my deep distress I catch sight of Wendy and Danny snogging in the shade of the fig tree. I desperately want to turn my head, but my rebellious brain keeps my eyes locked on the gut-wrenching performance. If only the ground would open once more and swallow Danny. Finally, even my brain has had enough and I am able to lower my mournful gaze to the gravel path and move on.

Tulip and Ronny are standing at the entrance to the Produce marquee and beckoning me to hurry over.

"What's up?" I ask.

"Listen to it," urges Tulip. "There's one helluva row going on in there."

"Looks like Wilkes, your mum, and that twit of an actor," grins Ronny. Maybe he's relieved to see someone else's mother in the limelight for a change. Pity it has to be mine.

I step inside the tent and immediately see the three of them at the far end of the Home-baking table. They are, indeed, having a good set-to. My mother is standing between the two blokes and is obviously doing her best to prevent a fist-fight.

"I've been here all bloody morning waiting for Madge," Wilkes storms at Lamont, "and all the time YOU," poking Lamont heavily in the chest with a large, agricultural finger… "had her kidnapped in your daft little car!"

"What are you talking about?" retorts Lamont, the scars on his face glowing lividly. "I merely drove her into town to book a perm at the hairdresser's."

"Well, why didn't you drop her off here first and *then* go to book yer perm?"

"What the hell are you insinuating?" spits Lamont, his face aghast with umbrage. He steps forward and confronts Wilkes. There can only be seconds left before honour must be satisfied.

Suddenly, like something you might see in a film, my mother steps between them again.

"Hold it right there!" she shouts, and slaps a palm on the chest of each man. They both stare at her in amazement as she vents her wrath first on Wilkes.

"Now then, Norman. Firstly, had your harvesting machine not pulled down the telephone line in our back lane yesterday, I would have been able to get a message to you that I would be late today. Secondly, if you had not consequently been out at the vicarage gate looking for me just now, you'd now be floundering in that pit together with your nuts." She next turns her black look upon Lamont, and I must say I'm impressed so far. "And as for you, Quentin," she rails. "If you had brought me directly here instead of tearing along the Esplanade and round Fayling Knoll just to show me how fast your silly car could go, we would not have *been* late!"

The two protagonists open their mouths to protest but she holds a finger simultaneously to their lips. This really is quite a performance.

"And now," she says, catching sight of me, "I shall walk home in the company of my son." Out of the corner of my eye, I detect Tulip and Ronny sidling away. "Hello, dear," she smiles as she sweeps towards me. "Shall we go?"

I follow her obediently from the marquee but pause to observe Wilkes swinging a punch at Lamont. The ginger actor ducks agilely, throws himself at the farmer and they lock in a deadly foxtrot until finally lurching together with a mighty crash onto the 'Cupcake and Savouries' table. First prize, I think, for Footwork and Creativity.

My mother glances at me as we walk briskly up the tree-lined slope of Tobruk Avenue.

"Your Uncle Raymond has been asking about you," she remarks out of the blue.

This is mildly surprising as Uncle Ray, Dad's brother, runs a printing business miles away near Exeter. Our only contact with him, usually, is our annual pilgrimage to the big city at Christmas time when my mother spends a small fortune shopping whilst Dad and I visit the print shop. I really enjoy these outings because Uncle Ray lets me have a bash at making a printing plate or operating the giant industrial camera. Once he even let me loose on the litho-machine. Well, OK, under his instruction... but I printed a whole run of posters warning the clientele of gents' toilets on the dangers of venereal disease. It was one of my finest hours.

"Oh?" I prompt and she continues.

"Yes. He wants to know if you'd be interested in a printing apprenticeship, seeing that you've given up all aspiration to further your prospects at school."

This last bit is obviously a little addition of her own. Never would Uncle Ray have introduced a note of sarcasm; nor would he have belittled a career in the print trade. I am on the point of reminding her that Uncle Ray lives in a big detached house overlooking the sea and drives to work in a new Ford Zephyr, when she launches into an unprovoked outburst of venom against my choice of friends.

"Why are you always hanging around with that strange Ronald Lee and that scruffy Dutch boy, Andrew What's-his-name?"

"He's not Dutch, he's Belch," I mutter.

"I beg your pardon, my lad!"

"Well, what's wrong with them, anyway?"

We walk on in silence, each of us stuck fast in our own inflexible view of how the world should be. And thus, I imagine, has it always been. Only, nowadays, the gulf between our generations seems to have widened, and, like warring tribes, we each occupy our chosen side of the river and shout insults at one another. Who the hell is right? Maybe Ronny could explain it all to me. On second thoughts, I could be old and grey before he finished.

"I really must say," my mother sighs as we halt to check our crossing at the junction with Bannockburn Grove, "I've had quite enough of you men for one day!"

*

I close the door of my bedroom and flop back onto my bed and observe that the cracks in the ceiling have now formed themselves into an effigy of a leering dwarf. At least, that's how I read it but I may, of course, be losing my marbles. The dolphins and combine harvester which I clearly defined only a day or so ago have given way to this evil little bugger. And, talking of evil little buggers, here's that pigeon again. Worse still, he's brought his girlfriend along and he's trying to give her the business out on my window-sill. Is there no sense of propriety left in the world?

The pigeon's lustful exhibitionism sets me to wondering how different life would be if all sex drive was removed at birth. After some consideration, I conclude that it would be like one long, uneventful, mind-numbing Sunday. Although, we humans would still have alcohol so we'd all probably be permanently half-sozzled. I wonder if that's Ronny's problem?

Suddenly, I find myself siding with the pigeon and start calling out encouraging advice, but to no avail. His bit of stuff finally turns on him and flaps away with a scornful 'cooo'. I know exactly how you feel, mate; they're all the same, believe me. Get yourself a Norton motorcycle, a leather jacket, and a jar of Brylcreem… it's your only hope.

I close my eyes and ponder Uncle Ray's offer. I could do a lot worse than become a printer. As for Quantity Surveying, you can stick that where the sun never shines (Manchester, I believe). Yes,

I'm beginning to warm to the idea and, for some unaccountable reason, so is Wee William, who is demanding attention. He really is a greedy sod. I spoil him to death.

# CHAPTER 7

## *'Petite Fleur' (Chris Barber's Jazz Band...1959)*

'A promise is a promise, my lad, even if it does interfere with your social life'. Thus was the gist of the minor lecture from my mother half an hour ago, just prior to my theatrical sighs and stomping of stairs as I climbed to my room to change into work clothes. Well, OK, she's right I suppose. My summer work deal with Dad does involve turning up for work occasionally, and I still need some cash for that striped shirt. It'll be out of fashion by the time I've saved enough.

Anyhow, here I am outside Downs's Music Store, fully equipped with sandpaper, paint-scraper, blow-lamp, and step-ladders, all dropped off for me earlier. The job in hand? Rub down and prepare the entire shop window frame ready for undercoating.

I am surprised that Dad is content to let me loose with the blow-lamp, although he's given me plenty of training with it. 'Always treat it with respect, Col,' he advises, 'and keep the jet well away from glass and combustible material.'

Mr. Downs appears at the shop entrance and gives me a sceptical look. "Are you sure you know what you're doing, young man?" he asks. I nod enthusiastically and gesture with one hand at my array of tools.

"Everything's under control, Mr. Downs," and just to set his mind at ease, "Dad will be along in an hour or so." Relief spreads across his face and he melts away.

I pause before commencing my chores to drool with unabashed

desire at the Fender 'Telecaster' flaunting itself in the window display. I lust after it almost as much as I do for Wendy. In fact, in many ways, they are similar: pink, curvaceous, seductive, and with strings attached. Both are also out of reach for me. Ho hum, Brillo, pick up thy blow-lamp and blister!

The paint is stripping off the woodwork in gratifying sheaths of smoking, wrinkled skin and I soon find myself whistling contentedly above the roar of the blow-lamp. This activity must be what psychiatrists refer to as 'therapeutic'. And let's be fair, sometimes the world is not too bad a place. As my mood improves, I resolve to pop into Newman's on the way home to put a deposit on that elusive shirt. Before I know it, I have entered into a balmy reverie in which I see myself strutting along the Esplanade in my new shirt with Wendy on my arm and the Fender swinging at my side in its white leather case. Dreams are free, at least.

Talking of dreams, have you ever had one when you experience that terrible falling sensation? That's what I'm having right now because some insane idiot is shaking my step-ladder and I'm losing my balance. I manage to grip the top of the window frame and glare down at the assassin. To my astonishment, I am staring into the zealous eyes of Police Cadet Lipscombe. Who let him out on his own? I've heard he's a complete twit who needs constant supervision by a real copper.

"You're blocking the public right of way," he snaps. I gaze out at the vast expanse of pavement stretching to the kerb and at the pedestrians passing us with ease as they go about their business. I fail to see any of the public distressed in any way by my presence, or blocked in any shape or form. I open my mouth to point this out but he cuts me off. "You'll have to move these step-ladders into the rear alley," he commands haughtily.

I regard him with the steady eye of a citizen who has the weight of reason and justice on his side. It's an identical look to the one you might direct at a meddlesome half-wit.

"So how, then," I enquire evenly, "do I prepare this window frame. Hover like a kestrel?"

He seems to take this reply badly. "You're a bit of a cheeky monkey aren't you?" he says, and points at the blow-lamp. "Do you have a licence to operate that dangerous appliance?" he asks.

I lift it and turn it about, even upside-down, examining it closely. "It's a blow-lamp," I say, with just a hint of sarcasm seeping through. Cadet Lipscombe unbuttons the breast pocket on his tunic and removes a note-book and short pencil.

"What's your name?" he asks.

I do not believe this! What's he booking me for, being in the High Street wearing lime-green socks? I'm not having this. I turn back to my work and grunt my reply. "It's on the side of the step-ladder."

To my amazement he runs his eye down the edge of the step-ladder and intones the name stencilled there. "Arnold Hardware," I hear him mutter. That's right, the wholesale store where Dad bought the steps. He slides the note-book back into his pocket, adjusts his peaked cap, and addresses me. "Right, young Hardware, I shall continue my beat and when I return I shall expect to see you and your step-ladder off the pavement and up Mr Downs's rear passage." (Hmmm… sounds like another physical impossibility and on a par with Mr. Hyde's recent consumption of himself.)

Cadet Lipscombe turns on his highly polished heel, grips his hands behind his back, and saunters off down the street, nodding and smiling to members of the unblocked public as he goes. I sigh with frustration and turn back to the shopfront.

No sooner have I resumed my duties than some other mad sod is shaking my perch. I turn off the blow-lamp and twist round to give them a piece of my mind, but find myself looking down at the grinning face of human twerpery known as Tulip.

"They're here!" he says excitedly. "I've seen 'em."

Who, I ponder momentarily, are here? The Russians, an infestation of cockroaches, Dion and the Belmonts? I have no way of telling.

"The French birds," he chuckles, rubbing his hands together as though he'd just won a fortune on Vernon's Football Pools.

Ah, yes, of course, the long-awaited French crumpet. Since early spring, rumours have been circulating about the summer visit of a group of French kids. Hopes were further raised to fever pitch among us lads when it was whispered that they would all be female. I shall enquire of my informant.

"Are you sure they're *all* girls?"

Tulip nods like a deranged woodpecker and performs a compact Belchian jig on the pavement.

"Every last man of 'em," he assures me. I ignore the contradiction in terms and put it down to over-stimulation of hormones.

I must confess to a mild surge of adrenalin myself at the prospect of manhandling a bit of fresh totty. The fact that it might be 'foreign' is merely icing on the cake, and my recent successes on the clitoris front spring to mind. A momentary unease that the possession of a clitoris could be unique to English girls is instantly dispelled when I recall that my cousin Phil uncovered its existence beyond these shores in Germany.

Tulip has disappeared into the shop to buy a record so I pause for a moment from paint-stripping. Sitting on the top step, I gaze along the pavement at the hurly-burly of the mid-day crowd. Some are shopping, some are sight-seeing, most are just getting in each other's way, and from my elevated position, their heads bob and turn like so many corks on a rising tide. One of those cork-heads is wearing a black and white checked cap and is heading this way. Its Police Cadet Lipscombe on his return beat.

Tulip emerges from the shop and, to my surprise, hails Lipscombe as he approaches.

"Hi, Mervyn," he cries. "Out on your own?"

Lipscombe halts beneath my step-ladder and clasps his hands behind his back in an effort, I suspect, to appear relaxed and fully in charge.

"Hello, Andrew," he grimaces. He nods up at me. "So, you know young Hardware, do you?"

Tulip looks understandably bemused and glances up at me for guidance. I nod briskly and place a finger to my lips. He then demonstrates his unique Belch talent for instantly changing the subject.

"Yeah. Hey, Merv, will you be round tonight for your usual order?"

Aha, I get it! Lipscombe and his uniformed superiors are patrons of Rudi de Groot's fish and chip emporium. Yes, it would make sense for a canny Dutchman like Rudi to foster good relations with the local Ploddery. Discount for the boys in blue on night shift equals a blind eye turned, perhaps, for a minor parking offence. One good turn deserves another, etcetera.

"Perhaps," says the half-copper, and unbuttons his tunic pocket again. Is he going to continue with his harassment? Nope, surprisingly, he pulls out a packet of Refreshers and offers one to Tulip. He then turns his back on me and strikes up a conversation with Tulip. My suspicions are confirmed; the prospect of everlasting cheap fish suppers has triumphed. I snort with contempt, fire up the blow-lamp, and recommence my paint-stripping. Placing my blow-lamp on the top step, I set-to with my scraper in a particularly stubborn groove in the Victorian moulding of Mr. Downs's window frame.

I will happily swear on a stack of 'Melody Makers' that what happens next is entirely accidental. Fate deals out the cards and there are days when you just don't get a decent hand. Today is such a day for Cadet Lipscombe. Good fortune has deserted him and the ghost of Robert Peel has clearly abandoned him for the day. On the other hand, had Mervyn not been so bloody keen to see me incarcerated for a contrived misdemeanour, he would not now be standing so close to my fiery blow-lamp and about to demonstrate exactly how combustible is a police cadet's cap. I can testify, positioned as I am immediately above the aforesaid cap, that it takes but a few seconds of full-on jet to ignite it.

I doubt that Lipscombe will ever again spring into action at a faster rate. With a screech of terror and some astonishing footwork, he leaps towards the kerb, snatches the flaming cap from his head and hurls it to the ground. He then proceeds to pulverise it with his right foot whilst issuing profanities and threats which I doubt are in the Police Training Manual. To add to our hero's dismay, a black Wolseley police car draws up at the kerbside and a uniformed sergeant leans out of the window to ask what the hell he thinks he's doing.

"Get in this car!" bawls the sergeant. "And bring that smouldering headgear with you."

Lipscombe grabs the remains of his cap from the gutter and strides, red-faced to the police car. He pauses with a hand on the open door, smoke rising from his hair, and glares up at me, tapping his tunic breast pocket menacingly.

"Don't worry, Hardware," he hisses, "I've got your name." I salute him cheerily with my paint scraper as the car roars away.

Tulip hangs around until Dad turns up and hands me some very welcome cash. He commends me on my work but asks why there appears to be the remains of a small bonfire in the gutter. We shrug in ignorance and head off towards my house where I can change into more suitable apparel for investigating French crumpet. I don't possess a striped T-shirt, black beret, or a string of onions but I guess the French birds will expect us to be dressed in our own style. On the way home we slip into Newman's and I purchase the long-awaited shirt. Bingo!

It is with utter disgust that, upon turning into Bannockburn Grove, I see Lamont's Mini parked outside my gate. Is there no end to his relentless pursuit of my mother's paper-thin virtue? Has he no interests in life other than this shameless mania for seducing hapless housewives? Surely there must be a place where failed thespians can spend their twilight years safely hamming it up and forgetting their lines, far removed from normal society. Lunatics and criminals are locked up; why not actors?

"Why are we creeping in through the back door?" asks Tulip.

Oh, what the hell! I may as well fill him in on my mother's secret life. He nods sympathetically as I give a brief outline of the monkey business that I suspect is being perpetrated beneath this roof.

"I know just what you mean," he says gravely, "I've got a strong suspicion my old man is up to no good with our neighbour."

I halt in my tracks and look him in the eye. "What, Father Dooley, the Roman Catholic priest?"

"No, you prat," he giggles, "the unmarried mother the other side of us."

Well, thank God for that, on both counts.

I hold a finger to my lips. "I can hear voices upstairs." We climb up, one tread at a time to minimise squeaking boards. This time, I'm convinced, their infidelity will finally be unveiled and I shall be able to end their dreadful waywardness. Having a witness, albeit Tulip, will be a bonus.

Imagine, then my indignation when we make the top of the stairs and hear the murmur of voices coming from my very own bedroom! That my mother could have the brass neck to conduct her sordid shenanigans in her son's boudoir, quite frankly, takes the biscuit. In fact, the whole packet of ginger-nuts (and how appropriate is that!). To add insult to injury, they are discussing their lewd behaviour quite openly.

"Grip it more firmly, Marjorie, and jerk it up a few times," admonishes Lamont.

"Well, we can't just let it fly. Think of the mess," replies my mother brazenly.

"No, no, I'll catch it in the pillowcase," sighs Lamont.

The filthy swine, that's my bed they're cavorting on!

Tulip and I stare at one another open-mouthed, and then, galvanised into one avenging angel, we hurl ourselves together into my bedroom. Lamont jumps a foot into the air and falls across my bed clutching the aforementioned pillowcase. Curiously, he has his trousers on. My mother simply glowers at me and lowers the cricket bat she appears to be thrusting up towards the lampshade. I may have dropped another clanger here. Tulip discreetly moves behind me.

"I wish you would stop bursting into rooms like that, Colin," scalds my mother, redirecting her attention to the ceiling. "And how many more time do I have to tell you about leaving your window wide open?"

I gaze around the room in complete bewilderment. What are they up to? And I am swiftly led to the conclusion that the presence of the cricket bat is significant. I am reminded of one of Barry the librarian's furtive revelations on the existence of local circles of sadomasochists. So, that's it, is it? Lamont enjoys a good lathering, trousers on or off. What next, I wonder?

But then, "Yuh baas-tard," coos my mate, the pigeon, as he flutters down from the top of the wardrobe and coolly parades along the window-sill.

So, all is revealed, much to Tulip's amusement. Meanwhile, Lamont sits on the edge of the bed, his hands crossed on his chest and exhaling dramatically like the big ginger pansy he is.

"I can't take much more, Marjorie," he whispers. "He's brought on my palpitations again."

My mother ignores him and darts over to the window to shoo the pigeon away with my cricket bat. He squawks, craps on the sill in defiance, and flaps off. I wish I could do the same.

*

By good fortune, as Tulip and I make our way back into town, we espy Mike. He is window shopping outside the 'Bookworm', the used-book shop where he spends most of his spare time. He's very well-read is old Mike and it's an injustice that he failed to end up at Fayling Grammar. There's no doubt in our minds that, given the chance, he would have gone on to university and Christ knows what else. For the present though, he remains the brainiest milk-man in England. What he doesn't know about history, geography, art, and world affairs isn't worth knowing. Add to that his staggeringly outrageous good looks and a talent for lead guitar, and you have a bloke who commands an almost god-like eminence among his friends.

"Michael Peale," calls Tulip, "this is your lucky day!"

Mike spins round and beams at us. "Hearing that from you, Tulip, I can only assume that trouble is just around the corner."

"Au contraire," answers Tulip, surprising us briefly. "But what *is* around the corner, or more precisely, along the sea-front at the Half Moon Hotel, is crumpet a la Francais a la plenty."

Mike nods slowly and grins widely. "Best polish up my French, then, tout de suit."

"No need to call me 'sweet', there'll be plenty of totty to go round," says Tulip.

"Shall we check 'em out now?" I suggest, and we head off along the sea-front.

On approaching the hotel, to our surprise and delight, the entire French wench contingent have emerged from the dining room after tea and cakey-buns and spread themselves across the hotel steps in a variety of ostentatious Gallic poses. Some sport Continental sunglasses and loll back on their elbows absorbing the rays of the sun; others sit demurely, drawing on Disque Bleu cigarettes and chatting languidly together with half-turned faces; one or two are even laid out horizontally along the steps, causing British guests to stride over them with tuts of disapproval. It's a clash of cultures.

We home in on three bits of 'crumpette' who are sitting on the low wall at the bottom of the steps. Mike, naturally, makes a beeline for the tastiest one and there she sits, looking like she just fell out of Vogue magazine; tanned, raven-haired, and with a smile that could turn you to goo. Within seconds they are a perfect pair, and would blend in seamlessly if they were sipping cocktails on the sea-front at Cannes. Tulip and I turn our attention to what is left for us lesser mortals.

To be fair, the other two girls are reasonably attractive, in their own way. Tulip dumps himself down next to the tallish blonde with a marginally bent nose and long, shapely legs (which, as he points out later, is better than the other way round). Funny how he always gravitates towards gangly birds. He claims that tall women have long fingers. What can he mean?

I get the eye from the slightly chubby one. She pats the wall beside her and inflates her not unsubstantial chest in what I assume is some kind of Continental gesture of welcome. I saunter across and sit next to her, all the while warning my brain not to release an unwanted Elvis sneer at this early stage in proceedings.

With some degree of difficulty and amidst loud guffaws of laughter from the girls, we exchange names.

"What is 'Brillo'?" laughs Mike's beauty, Anne-Marie.

"And 'Tulip'?" titters the lanky blonde, Monique. "That is vegetable, non?"

"No," explains Mike. "He is a vegetable, but a tulip's a flower."

We laugh out loud but the girls just look at each other and shrug, so we attempt a translation which they seem to understand.

"Oh, mon dieu," cries my own, well-endowed plat du jour, "'e is 'fleur' and moi aussi... I am Fleur!"

Frankly, this is beginning to turn into a French farce, but as long as I don't end up rolling in the hay with Tulip by mistake, I can live with it.

Mike suggests a walk to show the girls the local places of interest, which I trust means the sand dunes, Farmer Wilkes's upper meadow, or the woods on Fayling Knoll. Les filles giggle and jabber together for what seems half an hour, then Anne-Marie nods and we all set off, the girls still chattering, we three boys coughing heroically on French fags. This really does appear to be a period of 'entente cordial'. Let's hope relations will become even more cordial shortly. I have no idea what 'entente' means.

The first sign of discord crops up as we draw level with a confectionery kiosk along the sea-front. Fleur hauls me to the counter squealing with joy and points excitedly to a variety of goodies on display. Before you can say 'sacre bleu', I'm three bob worse off and she's unwrapping Mars and Crunchie bars like it's Christmas morning. I've never seen anyone stuff so much in such a short time. Her jaws chomp like some hideous mulching machine and the slapping of her chops would put a Boxer dog to shame. Stone me, when we reach Papa Bonetti's ice cream van, she's off again! This time it's a double ninety-nine and a bottle of pop. Where the hell does she put it all? I can only assume it turns to breast-milk.

Tulip convinces us all that there is a panoramic view of the bay from Fayling Knoll and so we sally forth up the deep lane towards the lower slopes of the knoll. Here lie the ruined buildings and overgrown entrances to the horizontal mine-shafts of old iron ore workings. Naturally, we lads know every inch of this abandoned site, and the choice is a good one as the area is pockmarked with grassy hollows and mossy bumps of old slag. And, talking of overgrown bumps and old slags, Fleur has unsurprisingly developed severe hiccups!

My own particular choice of venue for an exploration of Gallic charms is the fern strewn entrance to one of the shafts. Here a young buck can romp and frisk to his heart's content, hidden from view by nature's greenery.

I press Fleur to the ground (actually, she pulls me down eagerly) and snuffle around her neck and ears for a while until she begins to breathe a little heavier, interspersed by loud and violent hiccups. My cousin Phil gave me this technique for warming up crumpet. He calls it his 'modus operandi', which is all Greek to me (well, Latin actually), but I can't accept some of the other stuff he recommends, like sticking my tongue in her ear. What a disgusting idea! I tried it only once on Caroline and she said it gave her butterflies. It gave *me* a bloody awful taste on my tongue.

Anyhow, to continue. No sooner have I succeeded in unbuttoning Fleur's blouse (to be honest, she did it for me) and prepare to place my hands where no Englishman has previously ventured, but she suddenly enters into what can only be described as a hiccupping frenzy. Gulps and yelps follow swiftly one upon the other, and the quivering of her breasts is a sight to behold. Were I not so focussed on the job in hand (so to speak), I would find the heaving and wobbling of her melons worth pausing to watch. But poor Fleur is now very distressed, and a dreadful vision enters my fertile imagination in which her limbs are literally shaken from their sockets in a violent combination of sexual excitement and diaphragm spasms. It's not a pretty sight, I can tell you, and I don't need yet another homicide on my conscience. I'm still having occasional nightmares about Bill Potter.

My first attempt at relieving her discomfort is the normally successful 'blocked ears, pinched nose, swig of liquid' trick. It's all to do with air pressure and bodily plumbing, according to Arthur Harold Wishart (Physics and Gluttony). Well, maybe the French have their own laws of physics because it doesn't work on Fleur. But I have another plan, a method I saw someone using at a party, years ago, when we had all drunk too much ginger beer. I instruct Fleur to get on to her hands and knees, and then explain in pidgin-French that I will kneel behind her, grasp her round the waist and squeeze her vigorously at regular intervals. To our mutual astonishment, after only a few jerks, the ghastly gulping and belching subsides to manageable proportions.

"Oh, Bippo," whispers a much-relieved Fleur. "C'est formidable. You are very good!"

I give her a few more contractions for good measure and she giggles with glee.

Now, I have always been a firm believer in the theory expressed by Tim Lewis (Biology and Lechery) that modern man is but a hair's-breadth removed from his primitive ancestry. Take away the trappings of our sophisticated twentieth-century society, says Timmo, and in the blink of an eye we'll be back whacking each other around the head with a stone-axe and devouring a warthog round a campfire in a cave at Cheddar. So, it comes as little surprise to me, as I pursue my public-spirited de-gassing of Fleur, when I get that old familiar

162

prickly feeling at the back of my neck. Someone, I just know it, is watching us.

I slide to my knees and lay a cheek on Fleur's buttocks (cheek to cheek, you might say) in order to get a clear view of the mine entrance. And, of course, there they are, Burgess and Maclean, daughters of Satan, standing in silent observation and both equipped with a torch.

Before I am able to extricate myself from my compromising position and employ basic semaphore to persuade Fleur to pull on her blouse, Burgess (alias Wendy's sister, Janet) blows my cover.

"Brown Owl," she bawls, "the horrid boy is here again and trying to make another baby, I'm sure of it!"

"Yes, Brown Owl," joins in Maclean (code-name, Olive), "I've seen cows doing it."

I recoil from Fleur's backside and leap to my feet, holding out my palms in supplication of my innocence. But my heart sinks at the sight of Hettie Trimble emerging wraith-like from the inky darkness of the mine. She swoops upon the Brownies and guides them to one side, her unblinking stare locked on me. I gesture inanely to Fleur who remains on all-fours, smiling warmly, and blithely unaware of my predicament.

"I'm trying to help her," I plead hopelessly. "Hiccups. Really bad hiccups." Then, desperate to find some common ground with Browniedom, "It's a sort of first-aid."

"Bippo," calls Fleur, "please, encore. Do it again!" Oh, Fleur, fermez la bouche!

Hettie sniffs disdainfully and ushers the girls up the grassy slope with her monster torch.

"Come along now, Brownies, we'll look for the bats another day," and they disappear over the crest. Maclean's voice floats back to me on the breeze:

"Brown Owl, how do bats make babies when they're hanging upside-down?"

Well now, Hettie, there's a tough question. Best get yourself down to the library; I bet Barry will know.

I look around and Fleur seems to have recovered. She sits cross-legged in the bracken, buttoning her blouse, with not a hiccup to be heard. She smiles and purses her lips in a mock kiss.

"You are wonderful boy, Bippo," she says.

Yes, I may be… but sadly underappreciated by the likes of Hettie Trimble, Wendy, my mother, and countless others. My infrequent good deeds seem doomed to everlasting dismissal. Is it even worth trying to be a Good Samaritan when you are portrayed, instead, as a depraved delinquent? And why does Fleur keep calling me 'Bippo'?

A hysterical giggle accompanied by a lewd cackle releases my mind from its grey mood, and I am privileged to observe a scantily clad Monique tripping lightly through the bracken pursued by a trouser-less Tulip. It is truly a sight of the utmost debauchery and I only hope that their paths and Hettie's don't cross. The Brownies might have questions for which she will have precious few answers.

We all regroup at the head of the lane and make our way back down into the town. Mike and Anne-Marie halt at frequent intervals for a long and passionate snog; Tulip and Monique (now fully clothed) skip and giggle hand-in-hand like a couple of nursery-rhyme characters; and Fleur links her arm in mine and hums Gallic-ly as she demolishes the remains of a Kit-Kat. Is this, perchance, the acceptable face of the Common Market?

We walk the girls back to the hotel where we give them the good news that we will be appearing tonight, in person, to entertain them with some Rock 'n' Roll. They are very excited at the prospect of hearing us perform and promise to jive to every number we play. This is the first time we've ever had a ready-made fan-club and a guarantee of some dancing from the kick-off. We explain that our fourth member, bass-guitarist Jeff, will require female company and 'Disque-Bleu' during the session breaks, and they agree to fix him up with a presentable example of smoking Frog crumpet (our description, not theirs). Thus, with further snogging and tomfoolery from one and all, we part company for the duration and bid each other adieu.

*

It's a speedy return to our respective homes for tea and a quick bath, and into our look-alike group outfits to transform ourselves into 'The Rock-its', our new name and Fayling's foremost (and only) rock group. Our 'uniform' is pretty basic, but stylish: white shirt with turned up collar, powder-blue trousers and matching crepe-soled suede shoes. Top off the image with slicked-up 'Trugel'-ed hair and fags drooping from our mouths and you've got a 'mean, keen, rockin' machine' as we bill ourselves.

Mike picks us up at our individual homes and we squeeze four bodies plus guitars, amps, and drum set into his Morry Minor pick-up van. Mike has now passed his test so we can tear around the town quite legally. As usual, we are running late, thanks to Tulip, who spends more time titivating his Eddie Cochran hairstyle than a room full of debutantes.

We park at the rear of the hotel and begin carting our gear in through the back door. 'Maurice and the Half-wits' are still banging away in the ballroom so we stash our equipment in the kiddies' playroom next to the bar and seek out Glyn, the drinks waiter. He gives us the thumbs up as we poke our heads around the double doors of the ballroom. This is the well-established signal for the imminent appearance of four halves of lager and the latest joke from Glyn's vast repertoire. Sure enough, within minutes we are spilling our drinks with laughter as he relates the one about the monks, the naked woman, the house-fly, and the strawberry jam.

There's a pretty good crowd in tonight, according to Glyn. All the French crumpet are in attendance, he confirms, and he's already got his eye on a couple of tasty 'fillets', as he calls them. We exchange glances, hoping that his choice has not overlapped with ours. Ah, well, there are plenty to go round and a bloke should not be greedy. After all, a chap can only attend to one at a time (although my cousin Phil claims otherwise and has promised to furnish me with full details at a later date).

Glyn offers one note of caution before we commence our act tonight. He warns us of a party of rowdies, led by a fat, loud-mouthed Australian pineapple-cannery owner over here for a wedding.

"Bunch of noisy wankers!" he declares in his strong Cardiff sing-song. "They've 'ad me runnin' round like a blue-ass fly. I never seen people drink so much beer."

We pull our seats into a circle and tune our unplugged guitars by ear. Mike is always spot-on so we tend to tune to his milk-white Hofner. Tulip, meanwhile, fiddles around with his drum kit and annoys us with the occasional paradiddle on his snare drum. Whilst we are thus engaged, Glyn ushers in our French mistresses and they drape themselves around our necks like we're real live Rock stars. Their compatriots press their noses up against the glazed door and gawp enviously. We're loving all this attention but, of course, they have yet to hear us play!

The girls sit on our laps and light up French fags for us. Tulip, who never does anything by halves, decides to pull Monique into the Wendy House and submit her to his advances. Being a high-calibre nitwit, he takes his lighted cigarette with him and, during his distasteful gropings, accidentally ignites a 'Beano' comic. Smoke immediately begins to billow from the chimney and the two lovers are coughing and thrashing about in their haste to escape. Mike casually pours the remains of Tulip's lager down the chimney and extinguishes both the fire and Tulip's ardour. (At times like this, I can't help but wonder if the Creator, infinitely wise as he is, ever had a bad day. Let's face it, we all have 'em and maybe, one grey morning when the universe just wasn't shaping up as he wished, he just felt like chucking the whole thing in. On such a day he might well have made some of his worst cock-ups, e.g. Brussel's sprouts, the duck-billed platypus, and Germany, to name but three. But creating the conditions which eventually gave rise to the emergence of the Belch population is certainly high on his list of travesties). However, I digress.

Tulip is dispatched to the bog to clean the sooty smears from across his face, and Glyn says he will lend him a pair of jeans whilst the wet patches on his powder-blue trousers are dried in front of an electric fire. In his absence, we set up our equipment on the tiny ballroom stage. The Half-wits have settled in the snug bar where they can drink themselves stupid (one pint each should do it). Oddly enough, they always play better after their break. When I say 'better', I mean in tune and at the same tempo as Maurice's erratic piano playing.

The Half-wits, naturally, resent our Saturday night intrusions and consider us nothing more than a bunch of degenerate teenage hooligans with no idea of how real music should sound. To them, Rock 'n roll is an abomination and all who indulge in it are sex-crazed delinquents with no dress sense, manners, or future. To us, Maurice represents everything boring, old-fashioned, and putrefying. Needless to say then, our every meeting is a stand-off steeped in mutual contempt. It's great fun.

Glyn scurries in to ask us a favour. "I can't stand no more of that bloody ozzy," he complains. "Keep an eye on the bar for a mo', lads. I got something up in my room that'll fix the sod!" He winks and hurries off.

Tulip wanders back looking considerably tidier so we make for the ballroom to get set up. Guitars are plugged in, amps are set to the correct level, microphones are switched on. Mike gives us the nod and we launch, full-blast, into 'Long Tall Sally', almost giving the Australian dingo-pack a synchronised heart attack. By contrast, the French birds clap and yell and storm the dance floor. Oh, vive la difference, cobber!

We notice Glyn returning to his duties behind the bar. He is immediately hailed by Chunky the Pineapple King from Cairns. His voice can even be heard above our instruments.

"Hey, Taff, ya half-pom, get us another round of beers, will ya?"

Unexpectedly, Glyn throws back his head in a false fit of laughter and gives old Big-gob the thumbs up. As he busies himself with pint-glasses and beer pumps, I notice him hovering over one glass in particular. Did he just drop something into it? He sets off on his circuitous trip, weaving between the dancers with his fully-laden tray held high. Meanwhile, Mike leans forward into the microphone to announce our next number.

"Thank you, ladies and gentlemen," says Mike. "We seem to have a cosmopolitan crowd in here tonight and…" But he's shouted down by Chunky.

"Cosmo-bloody-what?" he bawls. "Don-cha speak yer own lingo?"

Mike smiles diplomatically and waves a cheery palm at him. "Good evening, sir. I hope you're having a good time. I'm sorry I don't speak your language adequately but I'm sure you'll enjoy our next number." He glances at me and Jeff and we all increase the volume on our guitars. The opening chords to 'Jailhouse Rock' drown Chunky's riposte and the French girls obliterate him from view as they invade the floor again. But before the reverberation of the final chord has time to fade, he's at it again.

"Chroist!" he roars. "Ya can't ply cricket and ya can't ply propah music," and downs the contents of his pint glass. "Oi, Taff, get some more beers over here, pronto!" he yells.

Thumbs up again from Glyn and we watch impatiently as he grabs a fistful of tankards and fills them once more. Whatever he's spiking old Chunky's drink with is taking its time.

Our next number is our version of 'True Love Ways', in which I harmonise with Jeff's lead vocals. It's one of our personal favourites and usually goes down well at dances because the lights are lowered and the blokes get a chance for a bit of fumbling while they smooch. It normally fills the floor, which proves that the birds enjoy the fumbling too. Tonight though, it's a flop. I guess it's down to the diversity of the hotel guests; the French girls are unlikely to smooch with each other and the Aussie bunch are too drunk. But, there's always an exception to the rule. A solitary middle-aged couple have taken to the boards and proceed to give a display of that God-awful ballroom dancing, swishing and twirling around the floor with their heads turned askance like they've both farted. Ah, well, it gives us one up on the Half-wits... none of the French girls jived to his stuff.

Just as Jeff and I reach the final note, arching forward into the microphone to emphasise our vocal union, a ghastly noise offends our ears. Imagine, if you can, a geriatric pig with swollen adenoids trying to suck swill through its nose. Not an easy one to conjure up, I confess, but that's about as close as I can get. The disturbance is so gross that the two performing seals flounce off the dancefloor and back to their table, tutting loudly. All eyes are focussed on the Aussie contingent and a murmur of discord arises, interspersed with ribald comments and giggles from the French birds. To our immense delight, Chunky is face down on the table-top in a puddle of beer, snoring gloriously for Australia and the pineapple industry. One of his party, a skinny bloke with an oversized nicotine-stained moustache, is shaking the Cairns Canner by the shoulders, but he's dead to the world. Nothing his mates do can bring him round, and the booming, slavering grunts continue unabated. Mike steps up to the microphone.

"Perhaps you'd like to get the 'Thunder from Down-under' to bed, fellas," he grins.

There is much laughter and applause from one and all.

Our half-hour stint continues with uninterrupted success and we receive an enthusiastic ovation as we bow out and swagger off to the playroom to imbibe another round of lager and limes. Our privileged little quartet of totty Francais is steered in by a jubilant Glyn who enters the room doing some kind of Welsh bolero, rattling a bottle of pills above his head in imitation of castanets.

"Ole!" he calls, clattering his heels on the polished wooden floor and very nearly losing his grip on the tray of lagers. "Viva los sleeping pills!"

You know, for a Welshman, Glyn's a great bloke.

Les crumpettes leap upon us and smother us with adulation. Stone me, I've never seen anything quite like it! Don't they have Rock 'n' Roll groups in France? Maybe we should do a summer tour. On second thoughts, we might not survive.

Glyn suggests we all move outside into the tiny staff garden area as his boss is unlikely to appreciate the sight of a bunch of teenagers petting and smoking in his kiddies' playroom. We tumble out into the cool evening air and pair off on sun loungers to continue our conquest of French territory. Jeff has been furnished with a petite brunette called Nicole and appears to be making steady progress on the two-seater swing-bed. Judging from the hand-slapping coming from that corner, his injured arm seems to be much improved.

Should you ever find yourself, as I am now, splayed beneath the wobbly wonders of corpulent crumpet intent on sticking its tongue down your windpipe or chewing off one of your ears, you may be excused for failing to notice new developments taking place in the twilight, no more than a few feet from your creaking lounger. Thus, when Anthea's hysterical braying rends the cool night air, it's hardly surprising that we are all almost sent into cardiac arrest.

"Andrew de Groot!" shrieks Tulip's distraught girlfriend (winter use). "What on earth do you think you're doing?"

For reasons unknown, both Tulip and I scramble to our feet and stand to attention beside our sun-loungers like a pair of army recruits on kit inspection. To be frank, apart from the shock of Anthea's sudden appearance, I'm glad of the chance to breathe properly and dry my ears with my shirt sleeve. Tulip, of course, is in for an ear-bashing of a different sort.

Anthea approaches her errant boyfriend and stands before him, fists clenched with fury. She snaps a hand theatrically in the direction of Monique who sits on a step attending to her hair with an oversized pink comb. "And who," she demands, "is this?"

"Who is who?" replies Tulip in his finest Belch gobbledegook (or should that be 'gobble de Groot'?). I never cease to marvel at his ability to bamboozle his opponents by instantly adopting his own brand of conversational English. I've seen strong men, and Taff Davis, wilt and shrink before Tulip's onslaught of meaningless verbal garbage. I'm sure the world of politics awaits him.

"Well, who do you think I mean?" Anthea shrills, thrusting both arms in the direction of Monique. "Her, of course!"

"Ah, yes," nods Tulip, briefly acknowledging Monique's presence. "French, I believe. Can't make out a thing she says. Any idea what the cricket score is, my love?"

You have to admire his courage, or is it just insensitivity tinged with a death-wish? I have no way of telling. Nothing seems to faze Tulip when it comes to dealing with awkward situations. If Harald Hardrada came crashing into this garden right now with a dozen blood-crazed Viking warriors, I guarantee, within the hour, Tulip would have him drinking a horn of tea and promising to reduce the rape and pillage to a manageable level.

Anthea is now twitching with rage and raw emotion. Humiliation on this grand scale is not something she is accustomed to experiencing. As a self-appointed superior being, she is the one usually dishing out the put-downs. This is fresh ground for us, and for all we know, these may well be Tulip's final moments on Earth. And when Monique rises from the step and begins whispering in his ear, he must surely be as good as dead.

"Look at you!" Anthea screeches. "You're not even trying to hide it. Do you think I'm a complete fool, Andrew?"

This is, I believe, what Soapy Luxmoore would call 'a rhetorical question'. It doesn't actually require an answer, so there is little point in Tulip scratching the crown of his head and adopting a thoughtful expression as though debating the idea. But it's all too much for Anthea. We've seen it happen before and here we go again. Once superciliousness and sarcasm have failed, she will always resort to good old-fashioned drama. With a strangled cry, she launches herself at Tulip and Monique and the desperate trio fall back onto the sun-lounger which disintegrates with a tired creak. Unfortunately, the darkness obscures most of the action and we have to be content with sound effects. 'Cow!' yelps Anthea. 'Vache!' answers Monique, then 'Cochon!' followed by Anthea's 'Pig!' If nothing else, it's a French language lesson.

It seems an age before the grunting, writhing protagonists roll back towards us from the edge of the privet hedge, and we can see that the girls alone are locked together in combat. The glow of a lighted cigarette tells us that Tulip has left them to it and is sitting on the steps observing. What a sod he is! Or is he merely smarter than we think?

"Bippo," exclaims Fleur. "You must stop this."

She's right, it's gone too far now. It's time to break it up before it turns into an international incident and de Gaulle sticks his big Gallic nose in our affairs again. Mike and I manage to separate the two wrestling femmes fatales and they sit on the grass panting and spitting Anglo-Franco threats at one another.

It is at this stage in the proceedings that I am made aware of another figure in our midst. Just inside the back gate hovers a shadowy form, a form to which I have given much fantasising in my romantic and naughtier moments. Even in this poor light I can see it's my own true love and Wee William's dream-girl, Wendy. She moves into the garden and calls to Anthea.

"What's going on, Anthea? Are you alright?"

Yes, like an angel of mercy, Wendy is here to administer comfort and support to her impulsive friend. How lucky you are, Anthea, even if you do have a bruised face and a torn cardigan. Surely, Wendy must be the embodiment of Florence Nightingale herself, for here she is nursing casualties on both sides, dabbing Monique's bloodied nose with a hankie whilst gently fondling Anthea's shoulders as she begins to snivel.

Suddenly, the little garden is bathed in the harsh yellow light of the security lamp. Glyn appears in the doorway and comes over to tell us that Maurice and his mates have finished squeezing the life out of the hit songs of the forties and we are due on for our final session.

"What the 'ell's been goin' on yeuh?" he asks, gazing at the carnage. I shrug and turn away just in time to catch Wendy leaving the garden, her arm around Anthea's waist. All of a sudden, Fleur's attentions are getting on my nerves. Tulip, too, lapses into an uncharacteristic silence as we hear the back gate close with an emphatic click. Monique sits down beside him to indulge in a bit of sympathy fishing by sobbing quietly in his ear but he stands up and walks back into the playroom. I fear that our short dalliance with the Common Market has, just like a French film, come to a messy conclusion. Even Anne-Marie and Nicole have broken away to nurse Monique.

"Oh, don't let 'em get you down, boyos," heartens Glyn, throwing an arm around Tulip's shoulders as we enter the lounge. "Don't forget, the only good things to come out of France are brandy, Brigitte Bardot, and the ferry to Dover." He's OK, is Glyn, for a Welshman.

To our surprise, the remains of the Australian gang give us a warm reception as we traverse the dancefloor and even yell out a couple of Rock 'n' Roll requests. Maurice and the Half-wits eyeball us with silent contempt and slink off to guzzle a few more beers. We hop up onto the stage, plug in our instruments, and burst into 'Blue Suede Shoes'. The floor blossoms again with nubile French birds, plus a smattering of young blokes who have come out of the woodwork since old Chunky the Pineapple King was hauled away to bed.

To our enormous delight, a new foursome of perfectly acceptable 'crumpettes Francais' have manoeuvred themselves to a position immediately in front of the stage. (I'm beginning to appreciate why Vicar Whicker makes his annual trip to Calais.) They giggle and wiggle before us in that uniquely feminine way and I sense Wee William awakening down in his nest. It's uncanny how he can detect the presence of a tasty young bird from yards away. I understand some deadly snakes have the same ability.

By the time we have completed our final number and taken a bow, the new French night-shift have singled us out and introduced themselves. I believe mine is called Eloise but, curiously, my enthusiasm for more hanky-panky a la mademoiselle has waned. I just cannot get Wendy off my mind. Why did she have to turn up tonight in her waitress outfit and looking good enough to eat? Come to think of it, how did Anthea and Wendy know where we were and what we were up to? Aha, of course… Burgess and Maclean, the Brownie spy-ring! There is now no doubt in my mind that Tulip was, after all, espied romping through the bracken with an insufficiently clad Monique. I'd just love to know what question the Brownies addressed to Hettie.

Whilst we are busy humping our equipment off the stage, the French day-shift, led by a fully recovered and belligerent Monique, enter the room and begin a shouting match with the new girls. It's all getting a bit fraught now with very little evidence of any Gallic charm. We leave them all to argue it out and we regroup in the playroom to wait for Mike to bring the van to the back gate. With luck, we can beat a hasty retreat and live to fight another day.

Mike and Jeff both have early starts in the morning, Mike on his milk-round, Jeff out checking lobster pots in the bay with his old man. Tulip and I bid them adieu and decide to walk to his abode for a well-earned bag of chips and mushy peas. His dad usually waives my fee and sometimes even throws in a bottle of Tizer for us. We know how to live in Fayling!

So, with Senior Service glowing between our lips, we set off along the sea-front towards the town. We discuss the evening's events in detail and swiftly come to the conclusion that we are now both officially unattached. 'Dumped' might actually describe it more accurately. There is no way Anthea will come crawling back after her humiliation on the lawn. Pride and bloody-mindedness would stand in her way. And as for Wendy and me? Who am I kidding? We were hardly a couple anyway. I'm sure the sight of me floundering beneath the buxom Fleur was enough to turn her stomach. I seem destined to commit one 'faux pas' after another when it comes to winning her affection.

But, hey, the evening wasn't all bad. Our musical performance was received with great acclaim, even by the Aussies, and Glyn's elimination of Chunky was a master-stroke. No, there is light at the end of the tunnel and all is not dung. Given luck and a fair wind, Tulip and I will sail safely across these troubled waters and find welcoming arms awaiting us beyond the horizon. In the meantime, a bag of greasy chips will do nicely. Talking of 'a fair wind', those lagers have bloated me out something awful.

# CHAPTER 8

## *'The Happy Organ' (Dave 'Baby' Cortez...1959)*

Much as I hate Sundays, this one is a little special because today I have clocked up sixteen years on Earth. Yes, much in the manner of a good wine, I am maturing gradually. No doubt, were the Count in any fit state to express a lucid opinion these days, he might cynically sneer that I am a little 'corked' but, nevertheless, I am fit and sane with my life before me whereas he is banged up in a psychiatric sanatorium and, apparently, still fighting the Second World War.

Sunlight is seeping through the gap in the curtains and I can detect the shadow of that impudent pigeon as he marches up and down the window-sill. 'Ya-baas-tard,' he calls as he struts and bobs. Yes, so you say, mate, but at least I don't spend the morning tramping to and fro through my own droppings.

Ah, the all too familiar aroma of charred bread... or toast, as my mother glibly calls it! Why can't she master such a basic chore, I muse? Is it so taxing on her grey matter to be able to time the period it takes to turn fresh bread into crisp, golden toast? I've seen toasters with built-in timers so why doesn't she invest in one instead of wasting Dad's hard-earned cash on hair perms and dangerous shoes?

In a glow of expectancy, I link my hands behind my head, close my eyes and lie back to speculate on the gifts which surely will be showered upon me today. After all, sixteen is a bit of a milestone in a young buck's life. I can now legally smoke and ride a motorcycle on the Queen's highway... simultaneously, should I so desire. And, as I have mentioned before, in a mere two years, I will be old enough to be hanged. Talking of which, those cracks in my bedroom ceiling have worsened considerably since Lamont's recent clumsy attempts to remove the pigeon and have now formed themselves into a gallows, dangling from which is what appears to be a five-legged turkey. Such a freak could only exist, I suppose, in my imagination or Ronny's bedroom, but that's what it looks like anyway.

"Colin, breakfast is ready!"

My mother's voice trills up the stairwell, and I must say, her tone is almost civil. No unreasonable demands for my attendance 'this instant' or sarcastic references to noon. I slide from bed and pull on yesterday's clothes from various positions on the floor. A lightning visit to the bathroom to splash some lukewarm water on my face, and I'm thundering down the stairs in record time.

Dad is sitting at the kitchen table reading the 'News of the World'. My mother is busy persecuting an innocent group of sausages in the frying pan. She flips them deftly, one by one, onto a plate where they lie gasping in the company of a wizened egg and a brittle slice of fried bread. Incompetence has once more triumphed over hope and my deep sigh is drowned by the scraping of incinerated toast surfaces into the sink.

Ominously, there is no sign of the birthday-gift pile I was counting on. Maybe they are so numerous and bulky that they've been stashed in the front room. I put a sausage out of its misery with my fork and mumble my 'good mornings'. Dad drops the newspaper and grins broadly.

"Happy birthday, Col. Only forty-nine to go and you can retire!"

"For Heaven's sake, Don, he hasn't even started his working life yet," brays my mother as she fills our teacups with an insipid urine-coloured liquid from the pot. Is tea still rationed, I ponder, or have the green, rolling hills of Assam been decimated by a plague of locusts?

Dad's voice releases me from a flight of fancy in which I am hurtling through a tea plantation and gleefully swiping locusts from the air with Taff Davis's new cricket bat. Quite appropriate when you think about it!

"Well, are you going to open your present, son?"

I pull an entire, unchewable sausage skin through my lips and place it discreetly on the side of my plate. At the same time, I notice that a small, square, gift-wrapped package has materialised next to the tomato-sauce bottle. What can it be? Not a lighter, surely, even though they both know I am smoking regularly. Please Lord, don't let it be a cufflinks and tie-pin set! I slide it gingerly towards me and pick at the sticky tape. Glancing up, I see both my parents smiling, encouraging me to open it. I rip the paper away to reveal a pale blue gift-box and I lift the hinged lid slowly. It's a nice-looking watch, and Swiss-made to boot! Unbuckling my trusty Timex, I strap on the usurper and gaze in muted awe at the new whopper on my wrist. I have to admit, it looks pretty smart and gives my whole arm an aura of sophistication and maturity. Shame about the rest of me, I hear you mutter.

"Should last you a lifetime, son," Dad assures me, ruffling my hair affectionately.

"It's great. Thanks a lot," I grin.

"Don't wear it in the bath, Colin," advises my mother, standing with the teapot in one hand whilst resting the other hand on Dad's shoulder in a rare display of domesticity. "Or playing cricket," she adds. Even though I can see that the watch is marked 'waterproof and shockproof', I refrain from pointing this out. After all, this is a very nice gift and must have cost them a small fortune.

I sit admiring my new timepiece whilst simultaneously casting furtive glances around the kitchen for other bounty. I'm sure there must be a secret cache of parcels lurking somewhere in here. As if reading my avaricious thoughts, Dad stretches down behind his chair and surfaces with a neat pile of assorted packages, some wrapped brightly in tin-foil, others clad in brown paper. My mother takes charge and begins doling them out to me.

"There's one from your cousin, Philip; two from Gran and Gramps Paddick; one from your Auntie Gwen… and this one was popped through the letterbox this morning." She smooths out the paper and reads the inscription. "'Happy Birthday, Colin. From Wendy'. Who's Wendy, Colin?"

I stare at her in stupefied silence and extract the packet from her grasp. It's true, it's really, actually, completely bloody true! It's from my own sweet darling, the jewel of my existence, goddess of my dreams etcetera, etcetera ad nauseam. But what is she playing at? She gave me the snub of the year the other night in the garden at the Half Moon Bay. I can't understand it. This is a game of cat and mouse and it's me who's doing all the squeaking. I'm her poodle on a lead. One minute I'm cuddled in her lap with her soft hand stroking my head, the next moment I'm tied to a lamppost in the pouring rain outside the public toilets.

"She's just a girl I know," I answer to my mother's probing question. Dad grins and returns to his paper.

"I hope she's a nice girl," says my mother, turning to clatter some dishes in the sink. Nice? NICE? She's flaming gorgeous! But perhaps that's not quite what she meant.

I'm terrified to open the tube-shaped parcel from cousin Phil. Suppose it contains some outrageous literature or a pornographic photograph? Such naughtiness is not beyond his scope. I shuffle it to the bottom of the stack and pick up the one from my Aunt Gwen, Adrian's insufferable mumsy. God only knows what horrors could be contained beneath the colourful wrapping paper; as the mother of a raging homosexual, her taste could be very queer. As it turns out, I am presented with a half-decent tie and a record-token. Most surprising, as I fully expected a set of lavender doilies or a book on cake decoration.

My grandparents, bless 'em, have given me a really brilliant world atlas, something I've wanted for ages. Don't ask me why foreign shores beckon me so persuasively, maybe it's the adventurous west-country blood coursing through my veins. On the other hand, perhaps Gran and Gramps are telling me to get out of Fayling at the first opportunity.

To my sudden alarm, my mother swoops upon Phil's package and shakes it next to her ear. What does she expect to hear, sluttish giggling? She hands it back with a sardonic smile and I am compelled to open it. Thank the Good Lord and all his supporters, the parcel contains nothing worse than a pair of electric-blue socks and a German football magazine that I'm unable to read. What a relief!

Well, that appears to be that. All is revealed, except for the gift from Wendy which I have managed to shove down the back of my jeans. What can it be, so flat and gift-card size? You don't suppose it's a summons for the money I still owe her? No, no, she wouldn't do that, she's much too sweet.

In the privacy of my bedroom, I unwrap the mysterious Wendy-gift, and Lawdie, Lawdie Miss Claudie, it's a framed photo of the pair of us sitting on a park bench! Yes, I remember the day we persuaded Anthea to snap us with her new camera. I recall Anthea being her usual bolshie self as she considered it a waste of her precious film, even though she'd spent the morning taking shots of Fayling's historical buildings for some half-assed school project. I ask you, how can you compare a crumbling old edifice with the pristine beauty of my own true love?

I read, for the umpteenth time, the message written inside the birthday-card that fell out with the photo:

'To Colin, wishing you a very happy birthday.

May all your dreams come true

Love Wendy xxx'

What am I to make of it? 'May all your dreams come true'. Stone me, if she knew what my dreams about her give rise to, she'd change her tune pretty quick, I can tell you! For starters, she rarely appears in any of my fantasies fully clothed and some of the things she gets up to are, quite honestly, too scandalous to commit to print. If her parents could see her, they'd go mental! But this is my own dream-world so she is completely at liberty to let herself go, and I haven't heard one complaint from her so far.

As it is his big day also, I decide to give Wee William his birthday treat before venturing out in search of opportunities suitable for a newly graduated sixteen-year-old. The world, I am constantly informed, is my oyster... a curious metaphor, as the one and only time I tried an oyster, I was as sick as a dog. There is probably a warning for me there, but what it might be, I have no way of telling.

\*

Sunday is not the best day on which to become sixteen. However, a summer birthday in Fayling is much preferable to a winter one. At least the town has some semblance of civilization during the season, with the sea-front throbbing with life and colour. Take a walk through the High Street on a cold, wet Sunday in November and I defy you not to slit your wrists before you reach the last empty pub. With these thoughts in mind, and having attended to William, I set out from the house to see what further pleasures await me.

There is no point in calling for Tulip prior to mid-day as he is engaged in chip-making for his Dad. Mike is also a non-candidate due to his traditional Sunday lie-in after a week of early starts on his milk-round. Jeff will be out sailing the seven seas with his old man in their search for lobster. Thus, my previously jaunty progress is slowed somewhat as it dawns on me that my only hope of company at this hour might rest in the dubious hands of Ronald Lee, chemist, alcoholic and downright weirdo. The mere thought of paying a visit to the House of Lee sends a shudder down my back. After all, the potential hazards are numerous: food poisoning at the hands of his mother; alcohol poisoning from the illicit still; attack from one of the resident mutant animals. Not to mention being run down by a bicycle-riding vicar in rut. And yet, here I am walking down the driveway to Ronny's house. God, even the concrete is crazed!

Thankfully, cowardice overcomes me at the front door and I make my way around the side of the building in order to make a preliminary recce through Ronny's window. This seems to be the safest option. I know for a fact that his window is screwed shut so I won't need to face either of the Lees in the flesh, and glass will separate me from any newly formed furry atrocities. But I should have known better.

I rap on the window, the curtain flies back and Ronny's face appears at the glass. Cradled in his arms is some kind of misbegotten creature resembling a disfigured cat. I stare at it in horror and back away from the window as it widens its ghastly mouth and hisses.

"What's buggin' you, man?" shouts Ronny.

I gesture at the thing nestled in his arms. "What the hell is that, Ron? What have you done this time?"

He rocks the beast like a baby and it rests its swollen head on his arm and glares at me. "This?" he guffaws, tickling its ear. "This is Nemesis."

"Right," I call. "But what is it, mate?"

"Well, a bloody cat, of course," he bawls, and holds it out at arm's length to give me a good look.

Yes, OK, it might be construed as being cat-like, but why is it so long, why are its head and feet so large, and why are the hairs on the back of my neck standing on end? I know damn well that it's another of Ronny's home-made freaks.

"Why are you doing this, Ronald? You've got to get a grip, mate," I plead, "or they'll lock you up and throw away the key."

"No, no," protests the madman, stroking the malformed monster affectionately, "I'm helping him. He's cool."

I have no idea what he's up to but I'm getting that spooky feeling again. This is no place for a young man on his birthday. I begin to sidle away and raise a hand in a half-hearted farewell.

"Don't go, man," calls Ronny. "Hang on, I'll open the window and explain."

I let out a reflex yelp and press my palms on the bottom rail of the window. "No, please, Ron," I beg frantically. "Don't let it out! I'll listen I promise."

He vanishes for a few seconds and reappears holding a photograph which he tapes to the glass. I study it and can see that it's a snap of a very skinny, maltreated cat. Clearly, Ronny has rescued it from one of his neighbours and the creature has been liberated from a cruel home and welcomed into a mad one. I look up into Ronny's grinning face, hoping to find compassion and sanity shining there. I am sadly disappointed.

"Don't ya dig it, man?" he gloats. "I've transformed a starving, half-dead moggy into this." The cat spits spitefully as my eyes turn to it. "And when I turn him loose back in that house..." He throws back his head and hoots with laughter. "Revenge!"

I'm gone before Ronny finishes chuckling. I vow never to set foot in the House of Lee again as I slam the garden gate behind me and point my nose towards the quay. I desperately require the company of normal people and, today, holidaymakers will have to do.

The quayside is crowded already and every tourist-trap is open for business. The jangle of busy tills vies with the clink of teacups and the clamour of multiple voices, all pierced by the frequent cackle of gulls. Families of Brummies and Cockneys sit on the railings slurping ice cream or queuing at the seafood kiosk for shellfish snacks. Fat, scarlet-faced blokes loll at kerbside café tables sucking on fags and quaffing warm tea. It's a nightmare to behold, but it keeps the town ticking over year after year.

I sit myself down on a tarnished capstan beside the ridiculous bronze statue of Cornelius Blunt, a barmy sixteenth-century aristocrat who set sail from Fayling in search of Atlantis. Yes, I know that sounds barking mad but I can only assume that Cornelius was. However, not so the local dignitaries who, far from dragging him off to a madhouse, actively encouraged him in his enterprise. They saw his recruitment drive in the town as a heaven-sent opportunity to rid the streets of its drunks and wastrels in one fell swoop. And so it was, one balmy summer morn, that Cornelius sailed away with his crew of inebriated scoundrels and an inaccurate map of Ireland. Needless to say, they were never seen again and, after what was considered to be a decent period of celebration, the bronze statue was commissioned in his memory. The faded inscription at the base of the statue reads: 'Cornelius Blunt, Navigator. He hath sailed into ye armes of God. Praise be to God.'

Having come of age today, I feel justified in brazenly lighting up a Senior Service and blowing the smoke contemptuously up into the face of Cornelius. Maybe they'll erect a statue to me one day, I muse, and a vision swims into my head of a white marble effigy standing proudly atop Fayling Knoll. It depicts myself dressed in my best Friday night clobber, Framus guitar resting on my hip, my lips exhibiting a full Elvis sneer, and just the merest hint of Wee William's presence outlined in my jeans. But best of all, I see Wendy lounging back on the grass, gazing up adoringly at my wind-polished features. Then my fag burns down to my fingers and I drop it with a cry of, "Shit!" A middle-aged bloke with slicked-down greying hair and wearing blue braces over his shirtless torso removes his foot from the railings and glares at me. He mutters something to his lard-assed wife and they move further up the quayside. I slide off the capstan and descend the seaweed festooned steps to the little harbour beach, a patch of sand only accessible at low tide and shunned by most seasonal visitors wary of the sea.

As I saunter along the tide-line examining my blistered finger, I am startled to hear my name being called. Stone me, if it isn't

Caroline beckoning me enthusiastically from her beach towel! I have to confess, she looks very tasty in that bikini which, if I'm not mistaken, is a size too small to accommodate those lavish breasts. Never mind, let's not be picky.

I stroll over and dump myself down beside her.

"What are you doing on your own?" she enquires, running a hand through her hair and leaning back on her elbows in a most glamorous way. I cast my eyes down the length of her extremely attractive body and, as it's our special day, I treat them to a return trip, finally meeting her own hazel peepers.

"Nothing," I say. "It's my birthday."

She sits erect and slaps me playfully on the knee. "You naughty boy, you never told me!"

"Yeah, well, you'd only have gone out and bought me present," I grin.

"Course I would have," she squawks. "Now what can I do? It's too late now."

I lie back on her beach towel, cradling my head in my hands and closing my eyes. "It's OK," I sigh, "I intend to have more in the future, as long as the Russians don't blow us all to hell."

A period of silence ensues, interrupted only by the occasional chuckle of a gull and the creak of moored boats drowsily rising and falling at the water's edge. A pleasant tang tickles my nostrils, a captivating blend of ozone and Caroline's perfume. This must be heaven, or as close as I'll get.

To my surprise, Caroline moves closer to me and begins to nibble at my neck, something she has never previously bothered with. Could it be that my recent clitoral explorations with her are bearing fruit? She whispers something in my ear but, at such close quarters, it's more like an explosion. I pull my head away and look at her.

"What?"

"I said, why don't we go somewhere more private?" she drools, smiling oddly and raising her eyebrows. There's a look in her eye that I've never detected before. My stomach is suddenly invaded by a host of butterflies and Wee William has awoken from his slumber.

Something is up, and it's not just William. Caroline is acting differently today but I'm blowed if I can quite pin it down. If only I had a better insight into the female mind. However, the job immediately in hand is to come up with a suitable venue for some serious hanky-panky.

"Like where?" is my puerile response to her heavily weighted suggestion. My imagination is awash with possible hidey-holes. The Harbour Gardens once more? No, too many prickly leaves and idiots wandering through admiring the plants. The sand dunes? No, too far for Caroline to walk in those daft sandals she's wearing. What about Tom Berry's dinghy, then? My god, where did that idea come from? It was like the booming voice of God, a bolt from the blue! Yes, of course, Tom keeps his twelve-foot, clinker-built dinghy moored down here all summer. He does a few boat trips around the harbour for the summer visitors and, often at this time of the year, he'll get his coal-round done early, load his fishing gear and his old lady into the boat, and spend an afternoon out on the briny. The dinghy is covered over with a heavy tarpaulin but has been accessible as a 'secret camp' to us lads since we discovered it years ago.

Caroline slides into her shoes, throws her belongings into her wicker beach-bag, and entwines her fingers with mine as we set out towards Tom's boat. Some cheeky holidaymaker up on the quayside gives us a wolf-whistle and I grin to myself. Yes, my old mate, it's me down here with this delectable bit of crumpet heading off to unknown pleasures. And you? I'd hazard a guess that you're a middle-aged twerp with a lumpy wife, three tiresome kids, and a car that won't start on Monday mornings.

The tarpaulin on Tom's dinghy, much like his coal, contains a lot of slack, so there is no problem in finding a point of entry and we are soon inside the boat. Fortunately, there are numerous pin-holes and gashes in the canvas through which dusty spars of sunlight stab giving us enough vision to spread Caroline's beach towel on top of Tom's mackerel-net. It's as hot as hell in here so, when she suggests we strip, it seems like a good, all-round idea. She then produces her ace-card. Well, not so much a card as a packet of three!

"Put this on," she whispers and presses a Durex in my hand. Stone the crows, I'm about to lose my cherry! I can only surmise that she has been saving my de-flowering for this red-letter day in my life.

Being in the hairdressing trade I guess such accessories come her way. Not that I can imagine her enquiring of one of her blue-rinse clients, 'Something for the weekend, Mrs Harris?'

After a frustrating period of my fumbling with the Johnny, Caroline leans over to take charge.

"You silly boy," she chastises. "You've unrolled it!" And she snatches the rubber from my trembling hands, grips Wee William in a most business-like manner, and slides the sheath down his shaft. All a little too expert for my liking. Anyhow, William is ecstatic and stands proudly at full height, the little pocket at the end of the French-letter nodding excitedly like a rooster's coxcomb or a miniature hat. What a happy organ he is!

Caroline lies back on the towel and signals for my attendance. "Welcome aboard," she murmurs, maintaining our nautical theme. The next thing I know, she's pulled me down on top of her and William finds himself entering new territory. I must say, he is really going at it with the gusto you might associate with a steam-piston, and should be commended on his boldness. Caroline, too, has entered into the spirit of the moment and, apart from one breathless remark about the smell of mackerel and coal under here, she also seems to be enjoying my birthday treat.

But it would appear that the Devil never has a day off, and as I am entering the phase which I believe is known in the trade as the 'short strokes', the worst imaginable outrage is perpetrated. A hefty portion of tarpaulin is hoisted up, daylight pours in, and an angry male voice bellows at my buttocks.

"What the bloody hell is going on here!" roars Tom Berry.

Christ on a Vespa, I almost leap out of my pink and sweaty skin! Wee William, craven coward that he is, tries to escape by burrowing deeper into his play-pen, causing Caroline to squeal with pain or delight, I have no way of telling. Nevertheless, to her great credit, she cranes her neck over my shoulder to address Tom.

"Oh, hello Mr Berry," she chirps brightly, "I hope you don't mind but it's his birthday."

"I can see that," says Tom, the fury dissipating from his voice. My guess is that memories of his own misspent youth are flooding his old head. Perhaps, long ago, he pleasured Mrs Berry beneath this same canvas. Who knows, maybe a small army of mature Fayling ladies might smile nostalgically at the mention of Tom Berry's dinghy. At this particular moment, I suspect that the close proximity of my quivering rear quarters has renewed fond reminiscences and, perhaps, a stirring within his own loins.

"Alright then," he sighs. "Give the little bugger his birthday present," and down drops the tarpaulin only to be lifted immediately. "But make sure you don't leave no gift-wrappings in yer!" he adds.

We swiftly resume where we left off and, with one final burst of energy and a triumphant thrust, Wee William throws up in his hat. It's all over. I am deflowered. We lie back in the semi-darkness, panting and giggling and she tells me she feels better now that she's given me a birthday present. I thank her and declare it to be the best one I ever received, showing her my new Swiss watch at the same time.

Strangely enough, time itself seems to be standing still as we lie here. Adopting hushed voices, we start to chat and soon we are opening our souls to one another. She reveals that the world of hairdressing is boring her to death and she can't face a lifetime of snipping, blow-drying and listening to old dears wittering on about their useless husbands. She would dearly love to become a model but confesses to failing in the confidence department. Rubbish, I snort, you've got everything that it takes. She smiles and stretches across to peck me on the cheek. My own outpourings of doubt and insecurity are met with surprising sympathy and understanding. She advises me to wait for my exam results because I might change my mind and even decide to go on to university. That all seems highly unlikely, I chortle… but she does have a point. The big shock comes when I inadvertently slip Wendy's name into the conversation and Caroline turns to look at me, tenderness shining in her lovely eyes. "If you fancy her that much, Colin, let her know." I have a new respect for Caroline Dunn.

We vacate Tom's boat, leaving its interior in a neater state than we found it, thanks to Caroline's housekeeping skills. Unfortunately, the tide crept in a few yards whilst we were engaged in our carnal exploits and we both drop into knee-high water, submerging my suede shoes in the muddy brine. Nevertheless, we wade cheerfully ashore and, with a quick hug and another thank-you, I leave Caroline to her sunbathing. As I retrace my route back up the slippery steps, her two workmates smile and pass me on their way to join her. If only they knew how changed is this young buck who, a mere hour ago on his way down these same steps, was still a virgin. For some unaccountable reason, I feel much older, and a rather sweet feeling is permeating my body and soul. For the first time, I believe I'm beginning to understand the female mind. Or am I suffering mild heat exhaustion?

Tying my shoelaces together, I sling my ruined suedes around my neck and set off barefooted for the beach. Glancing at my whizzo watch I see that midday is approaching; maybe some of the local lads will be gathering along the sea-front, and lo and behold, there's Billy Rice astride a motorbike outside the gents' bogs. He's talking to a couple of kids who are clearly in awe of his new acquisition. He spots me, stamps on the kick-start, and careers towards me like a bat out of hell.

"Hi, Brillo," he says, switching off the ignition. "Waddya reckon to this little beauty, then?"

I give it the once over and nod my head in approval. It's a very tidy Triumph Tiger-cub T20-C, two years old, I'd guess.

"Very nice, Bill," I drool. "Cost much?"

"Nope. Two Large White piglets and a ton of turnips, mate."

I stare into his eyes seeking guidance and normality. He just grins and nods. Can it be true that such a bizarre deal could exist in 1959? Has the farming community developed a parallel universe with its own currency? If so, I'm all in favour of it. The thought of handing over three mangold-wurzels or half a sheep's head to get into the Odeon on a Sunday night is quite appealing.

"The lads are playing cricket on the beach," says Billy. "Jump on. We'll join 'em."

I make the stupid mistake of agreeing and soon find myself risking serious injury as Billy takes the shortest route to the beach down a flight of stone steps.

We slide to a halt way out on the hard sand to find Tulip, Clanger Bell and half a dozen younger lads knocking a tennis ball around with a cricket bat. No sooner have I slid from the seat of Billy's motorbike than I am assaulted by the whole gang, thrown to the sand, and subjected to sixteen ruthless birthday bumps. But, in spite of the jarring to my spine and the careless disregard for my best jeans, I just cannot help smiling to myself at the memory of my recent experience with Caroline.

"Look at him," bawls Tulip as they step back and grin down at me, "he thinks it's funny! Let's give him sixteen more."

I hold out an outstretched palm and beg for mercy. "No, no. Listen, let me live and I'll tell you something that will blow your socks off." Tulip snorts scornfully but steps back, bouncing the tennis ball in his hand.

"And what might that be, Paddick?" he asks, screwing his face into a ridiculous caricature of the Count.

From my horizontal position and propping myself upon my elbows on the damp sand, I give them a potted and slightly embellished version of my seduction. The main detail which I hide from them is the identity of the young lady, so I invent a gorgeous, almond-eyed holidaymaker from Nottingham called Bella. The younger boys accept my extravagant description of this fictitious nymphomaniac with the blind faith of the innocent. Tulip, on the other hand, gazes down at me with an expression which I would like to think is envy, but is more likely the scepticism generally associated with the Belch population.

Through half-closed eyes I observe my awe-struck audience. Soft whistles, sharp intakes of breath, and lewd chuckles greet my narrative. Naturally, I employ a modicum of story-teller's licence, jazzing up a few of the seamier details much to everyone's delight and, in due course, I settle back with my hands behind my head to answer questions. There are plenty forthcoming.

"Was Bella completely starkers?" asks a wide-eyed kid.

"Does she dye her pubic hair?" enquires a spotty twit with patched National Health spectacles.

"Did Tom Berry recognise your bum?" grins another.

"Where's Bella staying?" demands Clanger, his eyes shining with journalistic fervour. As if I would risk the chance of some seedy story appearing in the 'Fayling Gazette' about teenage promiscuity. I shake my head and smile at him, as though Bella really existed.

"Do you want to bat or bowl?" asks a clearly narked Tulip.

I climb to my feet feeling taller than when I fell to the sand. "Yeah, I'll bowl." I smile and take the ball from him.

"Oh, thought you might be feeling too tired after your fun and games with... Bella," he sneers. I guess he's seen through my little ruse and, yes, I owe him the truth. I slap an arm across his neck and lead him to one side.

"I'll tell you the real story later, mate." He jabs me in the side with his elbow and laughs. Well, thank God we're still buddies.

These informal knockabouts with bat and ball are a feature of our summer months. This stretch of sand is always flat and hard and usually sparsely populated, even at the height of the season. Today, for example, there is only one family of holidaymakers within fifty yards of us. They have laid out their blanket, erected a wind-break, and the mother is handing paper cups to husband and child who are both munching on pasties. The bloke is standing and eyeing us with obvious disdain. Hang on, I recognise those gargantuan shorts... sod me, it's the Nutter, Selwyn Boarhunt! And, as though eager to fulfil his destiny as the World's Biggest Prat, he swigs back his drink, tightens the belt on his shorts, and strides towards us. Something has definitely ruffled his feathers, but he really should be careful, it's merely a few days since he was warned to keep the peace by Judge Theodore Felch. Any transgressions now could land him in very hot water.

He approaches us holding a finger in the air, much in the manner of an umpire declaring a fallen wicket.

"Do you boys have hard balls?" he demands.

Tulip grips his nether regions, guffaws loudly, and holds up our spare tennis ball.

"Ours are white and covered in fluff," he shouts. "Why do you want to know?"

"My family are sitting over there," calls the Nutter, gesturing towards the mousewife and brat. "I don't want anything flying through the air and banging my wife."

The vision of a sex-crazed cormorant springs into my mind and I inadvertently laugh out loud. Selwyn's head snaps round and he glares at me. "I shall be informing the local authorities about this dangerous activity and leaving it for them to judge," he forewarns. It's too much for Tulip, he can't resist a final riposte.

"Would that be Judge Felch?" he calls.

The Nutter turns on his heels and heads back to his family where his wife is struggling to relocate the wind-break against the stiff breeze that has sprung up, sweeping miniature sandstorms along the beach. Selwyn takes charge, issuing orders to the brat who stamps his feet in indignation whilst his mother tries to placate him with jam tarts and pop. My own recommendation would be a whack around the ear.

But what's this? Just beyond the Boarhunt family, strolling towards us are two familiar figures... Anthea and Wendy! Well, well, what goes on here? Is Anthea thirsting for another confrontation with Tulip, or is there more devious female skulduggery afoot? Is Wendy here merely for her friend's moral support? My heart leaps at the other possibility: that she wants to see me. After all, did I not, this very morn, receive her birthday card?

The lads have abandoned the cricket due to the wind constantly flattening our makeshift driftwood wicket. Billy and Clanger have wandered off down to the water's edge to join the other boys who are observing something out in the bay. Tulip approaches me and nods in the direction of the girls.

"What do you reckon they're up to?" he asks, as though our ex-girlfriends were a couple of marauding Sioux warriors. I shrug and suggest we go and find out.

I greet Wendy with a friendly "Hi."

"Happy birthday, Colin," she smiles, causing my stomach to do a forward-roll. So, the old Wendy-magic is still there then, in spite of my recent confidence-boosting experiences with Caroline.

"Thanks for the card. It was a... surprise," I mumble. "How did you know we were down here?"

Anthea snorts like a pony. "We just followed the sound of Andrew's voice!" she says, kicking off her sandals. Tulip, of course, is not offended and beams from ear to ear.

"This is just like old times," he says sunnily.

Anthea has folded her arms and is doodling in the sand with her toes. We look down and notice that she has spelt out 'HORRIBLE PERVERTED BOY' in a precise line with an arrow pointing at Tulip. To her annoyance, Tulip bends down and replies with customary Belch jauntiness, scratching: 'NAUGHTY NAUGHTY ANDREW STILL WANTS TO KISS ANTHEA'S LOVELY BOTTOM'. Even Anthea is forced to giggle and Tulip runs off with his reconciled love chasing him with the cricket bat.

Wendy and I walk slowly down to the sea, exchanging small-talk, almost shy in each other's reunited company. She doesn't slip her fingers around mine like before, but she is keeping very close to me and our hands touch frequently as we move. We join the small crowd gathered at the water's edge and Billy explains that there is some reckless idiot out beyond the breakers in a tiny plastic dinghy. Immediately I hear the words 'reckless' and 'idiot' used in the same sentence my powers of deduction come up with only one contender… Selwyn Boarhunt. Sure enough, there he bobs out on the heaving deep water, clinging for dear life to the sides of a flimsy yellow plastic dinghy. He's lost the paddle and we watch his desperate attempts to control the little craft with his bare hands. It's a losing battle, of course, as the rip-tide across Fayling Bay is notorious along this coast. Combine that with a relentless cross-wind and I'm afraid the Nutter is doomed to end up on the rocks of Fayling Head. How ironic that the first ship that embarked from the town with the Pilgrim settlers met the same fate. Or maybe Selwyn is taking his research to suicidal lengths and tracing their original route. Nah, nobody could be that crazy. Could they?

The wife has thrust her way through our ranks, dragging the brat by the hand, and stands staring out at her floundering husband. The brat breaks away and runs into the ankle-deep shallows where he kicks savagely at the wavelets and screams to his father.

"Nasty, horrid Daddy," he howls. "It's my turn in the thingy!"

Suddenly, Clanger springs into action. No doubt he's spotted a journalistic coup to be extracted from Selwyn's plight. He seizes Mrs Boarhunt by the forearms and assures her that all will be well and he will summon help. Then, turning to Billy he reels off his plan.

"Bill, give me a lift to the Beach Café and I'll ring the coastguard. Then run me home to get my camera and we'll ride out on the cliff-road to get some shots of him being thrashed to pieces on the rocks." Billy's eyes light up like beacons.

"Yeah, great. Let's go," he grins.

"Oh, how cruel!" says Wendy and, to my joy, she buries her head in my chest. I slide my arms around her and pull her to me. As usual, Wee William, in spite of his earlier excesses, is without shame and raring to go and I am obliged to squirm him to one side to avoid embarrassment.

Selwyn is now a mere yellow speck out on the briny and is being swept ever closer to the 'Wrecker's Purse', an outcrop of jagged granite off Fayling Head where many a mariner has been consigned to Davey Jones's locker. I doubt that our hero has the navigational skills or the power in his paddling arms to avoid an encounter with that particular hazard.

Wendy and I holler goodbye to Tulip and Anthea and leave them bickering furiously 'like old times' as we stroll hand in hand up the beach. We choose to follow the sandy bank of the stream that spills out onto the beach in a wide, shallow delta, sucked away to a trickle before it reaches the sea. This is, in fact, the very same watercourse that meanders down through Mad Farmer Wilkes's lower meadow, scene of my previous camping adventures involving the rancid chicken, Wilkes's shot-gun, and the Bristol crumpet.

Bloated by the confidence gained from this morning's induction to manhood, I ask Wendy if the inclusion with her birthday card of the photograph means that we are together again.

"Perhaps," she frowns coyly. "If you can behave yourself this time." Is she referring to my naughtiness with Fleur at the Half Moon Hotel, or the goldfish debacle with her parents? Anyway, why should I be on the defensive after her frequent dumping of me for Danny? And whilst on that irritating subject, I ask her what went wrong between them.

"It was a mistake," is all she will divulge. You're not kidding.

We find ourselves leaning on Wilkes's five-bar gate sharing a few moments of contemplation. Actually, I'm planning my next move. Should we decide to open Wilkes's gate and make our way through the meadow (now devoid of hooligan heifers), I might be tempted to bring to Wendy's attention one of the interesting features concealed within. Just upstream of the little bridge and hidden from view by two gnarled and intertwining willow trees, is a riverside patch of grass known to courting couples as 'Lovers Ledge'.

When we reach the bridge, I pluck up the courage to point out the location of the secret dell and to my surprise she nods and says she knows it. To my further surprise and delight, she asks if I want to visit it!

"OK," I shrug, trying to control my glee. "If you want."

We part the leafy drapes of the willow-tree, scramble under the boughs and slide effortlessly to the grassy, sun-dappled shelf. It really is a perfect place; a poet might call it romantic, a heavenly hollow where the silence is broken only by the murmur of the brook. A place where more than trout can be tickled.

As soon as we make ourselves comfortable Wendy slips a hand around my neck and pulls me down to her, snogging me remorselessly. Wow, has she ever loosened up since our first dates! Before I know what I'm doing, my hands are all over the place and meeting very little resistance. This is a birthday and a half. Even Tim Lewis would be in awe of my boldness.

But, alas, the forces of Evil, which I sincerely believe abound in the universe, have clearly booked in for the season at Fayling. Far above our heads, in the clear morning sky, a puff of smoke heralds the loudest bang you can imagine, almost giving us a heart attack; the maroon has been fired off at the Lifeboat Station, summoning the volunteer crew to drop everything they are doing and hightail it to the harbour. Clanger's diabolical plan is obviously taking shape.

In the immediate wake of the explosion we detect a cry of anguish close by and I am instantly winded by something heavy landing on my back. I crawl to my knees, wheezing and hooping like a seal whilst Wendy leaps to her feet and stands trembling. I roll onto my back and manage to gulp in enough oxygen to carry on living. Through misted eyes, I'm suddenly aware of a familiar brown and distasteful form kneeling beside me.

"What in God's name do you think you're doing, Janet Matthews?" snaps Wendy, glaring down at her younger sister whilst swiftly re-buttoning her blouse. The Brownie-spy sits back, draws her knees towards herself and twiddles with a loose curl of hair by her ear.

"The rocket frightened me and I fell off the branch," she declares. The tree giggles and we all turn our heads upwards to glimpse the impish face of Olive peering through the leaves. Wendy continues.

"You stupid pair, look what you've done to poor Colin!" And she gestures to me as I sit hugging my ribs and breathing erratically. Janet scowls my way and changes her hair-tweaking to the other side of her head. "On his birthday too!" adds Wendy for dramatic emphasis. The sulky look on Janet's face melts away and her mouth drops open. Aha, the Devil's weak spot! Let's be honest, most kids revere a birthday, even if it's not theirs. I detect a welling of tears in her eyes and, for the first time, I realise that she does have a beating heart. She's only a little kid trying to have some fun. Hey, what am I thinking; am I turning soft in my old age?

Wendy, too, has mellowed her anger and leans to pull her sister to her feet.

"Sorry, Wend," says the mini-spy, and they hug. She then scrambles back up the bank and joins her partner-in-crime. Their faces appear briefly as they look down at us between the leafy fronds. "Wend," calls Janet, "why was what's-his-name rubbing your chest?" They disappear with shrieks of glee and Wendy can only stand and stare up at the willow, her hand over her mouth as she shakes with laughter. Ah, well, no harm done and a little progress made, I guess.

I am in complete awe of Wendy's handling of this tricky situation and, in spite of Janet's rebellious behaviour, it's quite clear who is the boss. I'm certain there will be no repercussions for her to contend with. I gaze up at her as she straightens her clothes and smiles down at me. She must surely be the most beautiful girl in England and, despite having only fondled one of her sumptuous breasts, I'm sure the other one is just as adorable. And, anyhow, we have the rest of our lives to find out. I walk her home with a grin on my face, and the glow in my chest is not just the aftermath of having a full-blown Brownie land on me.

As we walk along the sea-front towards the Westcliffs Hotel, my day is made complete by the sight of Danny chatting up a pair of holiday girls. We stroll past on the opposite side of the road and I wave cheerily as his eyes follow us. Birthdays don't come better than this.

# CHAPTER 9

## *'Smoke Gets In Your Eyes' (The Platters...1959)*

I am rudely awoken on this fair August morning by an unholy commotion on my window-sill.

Lifting my drowsy eyes from my pillow, I am greeted by the sight of that insane degenerate of a pigeon flapping about on top of his girlfriend in a blatant attempt to couple with her. What sort of behaviour is this? What, I ask, would be the reaction if I committed a similar outrage, for example, ravishing Caroline on the pavement outside Marks and Spencer on a sale day? Instant arrest, castration and deportation to the colonies, I shouldn't wonder.

I reach beneath my bed and seize one of my wrinkled, salt-encrusted suede shoes and hurl it towards the open window. It misses the amorous pigeons but sails on into the garden and a splash tells me that it scored a direct hit in the pond. It will now be totally unwearable and my only hope is that it took down that insolent bastard of a gnome on its flight.

Sighing resignedly, I bury my face in my pillow and turn my thoughts to reflect on the glorious events surrounding my birthday yesterday. What a day of triumphs it was! The loss of my cherry and the recapture of my honey. Yes, indeed, a sweet dessert of a day. And how my eyes have been prised open to the lusty nature of the opposite sex. Within the space of a couple of hours, I was invited to explore unchartered territories and experiences previously considered out of bounds to me. I'm beginning to wonder if general horniness is, perhaps, as rife amongst the females of Fayling as it undoubtedly is within the male ranks. What a bonus that would be!

Rolling over onto my back, I now contemplate the ever-expanding pattern of cracks in my ceiling and I notice that the five-legged turkey has transformed into a bulging pineapple. In fact, the whole caboodle looks on the verge of collapse. I should bring it to Dad's attention. Mind you, I don't suppose the thought of domestic decorating is very appealing to a decorator. After he's spent all day slaving away at the end of a four-inch paintbrush to keep my mother cosseted in luxury, I doubt if he wants to come home to more of it. Anyway, I'm feeling peckish so it's time to get up.

Downstairs is strangely quiet as I enter the kitchen in search of victuals. I thought I heard the faint murmur of voices as I passed the closed front-room door but it might have been next-door's radio. The Lucas sisters are a little hard of hearing and turn their radio up full blast which, when you think about it, is probably why they're both getting deaf.

A thin bluish pall of smoke taints the air, evidence of my mother's recent attempt at breakfast. The sink is liberally sprinkled with charcoaled toast crumbs and a blackened saucepan containing the debris from an exploded egg sits on the draining board. Everything, then, appears to be normal.

I find some cold baked beans sheltering in a dish in the fridge and set about preparing a baked-bean sandwich, a delicacy brought to my attention by Tulip (except that he adds treacle). A cup of warm tea to wash it all down and a young gentleman is ready to face his public. Furthermore, as I am now most assuredly a man of the world and about to make my way in it, I lean back in my chair, place my feet on the kitchen table and open the local newspaper.

Generally, the headlines in the Fayling Gazette would seldom urge you to cry out in startled amazement or glue your attention to anything in its uneven text, but today I am staggered to see Clanger's name (together with his mentor, Sid Platt) as reporter of the main story:

'WRITER SAVED FROM SEA IN DRAMATIC RESCUE' screams the headline, and continues...

*Historical writer, Selwyn Boarhunt, who was recently fined for causing an affray on Fayling sea-front, was in the spotlight again yesterday when he had to be rescued from certain death after drifting out to sea clinging to a leaking rubber-dinghy. An RAF Whirlwind helicopter, assisted by the Fayling lifeboat, plucked him from the swell just yards from the notorious Wrecker's Purse rocks off Fayling Head.*

*Mr. Boarhunt, a self-confessed poor swimmer, is a lucky man according to lifeboat coxswain Tom Berry.*

*"If it weren't for the vast pockets of air trapped in them there shorts of his," claimed Tom, "he'd be down with the fishes by now!"*

*Mr. Boarhunt was unavailable for comment following his dramatic deliverance, but his wife expressed her deep gratitude to the Emergency Services and to Millets of Leighton Buzzard where the shorts were purchased.*

Wow, Clanger is already an ace reporter! So much for the Count's predictions for his future as a worthless hack. I fold the newspaper and rock back in my chair with my hands clasped behind my head. This seems to be an opportune time to give Wendy a call and maybe fix a date for later today. My unopposed incursion yesterday into her upper-torso area has filled me with bravado. Who knows what further prizes await me?

I stroll down the hall towards the phone and it is whilst en route to whisper sweet nothings in my darling's ear that I am made aware of something amiss in the front room. A loud and bawdy cackle of unfamiliar female laughter, followed by my mother's exclamation of, "Oh Heavens, Quentin, it's rather small!" is not what I expect to hear at eleven-fifteen ante meridiem under my own roof. I halt beside the door to await developments and I don't have to wait long.

"Well, someone's got to have it," comes the nauseating bleat of the ginger thespian, "so make up your minds... who's going to be first?"

"It's terribly wrinkled," chortles the unknown female.

"Oh, what the heck, I'll try it first," sings my mother.

"Good decision, Marjorie. OK, tie her up good and tight, Doreen."

I step lightly from the door and lean against the wall in a state of shock. What in the name of the Marquis de Sade is going on in there? 'Tie her up good and tight'? Where was it that I heard mention recently of such references? Of course, now I recall! My last visit to the library resulted in Barry the librarian somehow manipulating my harmless enquiries about cricket manuals into the murky world of sexual perversions involving bondage and beatings. Evidently he has an uncle who regularly dresses up as W. G. Grace (minus trousers), and, whilst spread-eagled and roped face down on a billiard table, subjects himself to a thrashing with a cricket stump by his wife (dressed as a World War One nurse). Evidently it's called 'sadomasochism'. Good grief, something similar is happening on the other side of this door! But wait, Brillo old chap, you've been horribly wrong on each of your gung-ho raids so far. Not once have you caught them 'in flagrante delicto' or, indeed, enjoying anything 'delicto' at all. You need concrete evidence this time. You need visual proof.

I turn the front-door Yale lock soundlessly, creep outside, and sidle cautiously to the front-room bay window. The scene that greets me convinces me that I have finally hit the jackpot. Lamont has his back to the window and is standing behind an armchair, stripped to his underpants, his upper body garbed in some kind of leather singlet. Yes, I remember Barry pointing out the significance of leather equipment. Sure enough, he is also wearing a pair of knee-high leather boots. A tri-cornered hat is perched on his head and a scabbard is strapped around his waist. In his hand he grips a sabre which he slaps rhythmically against the side of his boot; probably some kind of ritual beat to get everyone excited. I am unable to see the two women but I can hear my mother grunting and sighing and pleading for mercy. "No tighter, Doreen, please!" she cries. So, the sex circus is about to commence.

I step backwards and squat to the floor to gather my thoughts. I need a plan, and bloody quick. And, as though by Divine Intervention, salvation materialises at our front gate. Glaring at me and already fumbling for his note-book is Police Cadet Lipscombe. My desperation and confusion melt away to a glowing sense of deliverance. Lipscombe is my scapegoat, my prat in shining armour.

"What the hell are you up to, Hardware?" he calls. I press a finger to my lips and beckon him down the path. He swings open the gate and strides towards me, notebook in hand and I guide him briskly into the privacy of our front porch.

"This is your lucky day, mate," I whisper. He raises his eyebrows and scans me suspiciously, proving, I suppose, that he's not entirely stupid. I continue. "Have you ever heard of 'sadomasochism'?" I ask. He looks blank for a moment, then frowns and screws up his lips.

"Is he a Japanese pop singer?" he says tentatively.

I shake my head wearily and grip his arm which causes him to flex his shoulders officiously.

"No, no, you twerp," I reply sternly. "It's not a person... it's an illegal practice, which at this very moment is being performed in that front room." I jerk my thumb at the wall. Lipscombe gazes at me with complete bewilderment written on his face. I try again. "Listen, there are adults in my front lounge performing a sexual perversion. You know, whips and leather underwear, all that kind of stuff." He frowns again but I think I've finally made a connection with the elusive grey matter beneath that new cap of his. Slowly and deliberately he removes his police issue 4B pencil from his breast pocket, licks the tip, and begins to write in his notebook.

"I there an 'H' in whip?" he enquires after some moments of intense scribbling.

"Yes, yes," I hiss irritably. God help us, if there was a murder in progress here we'd have accumulated a pile of corpses whilst Lipscombe was noting down the weather conditions and the colour of my mother's curtains. "Look, mate," I plead. "Get over to that window and take a peep."

He peers at me haughtily, sniffs and replaces his notebook. Have I persuaded him? "Take a look," I urge, stabbing a forefinger out the porch. He leans around the corner wall and peers out.

"I'm warning you, Hardware. If this is another of your little pranks, you're in for it," he says.

"It's true," I implore. "Take a look."

He removes his cap, exits the porch and creeps to the bay window. I hear him exhaling air through pursed lips and he returns with a look of stupefied disgust on his face.

"I've never seen anything like it, Hardware," he splutters. "There's three half-dressed people in there. The bloke is waving a sword around and the women are shrieking with excitement. What d'you reckon they're up to?"

"Well, it's flaming obvious," I laugh. "He's going to give 'em a thrashing with the sabre then they'll all have an illegal orgasm!"

Lipscombe stares at me in horror. "We can't allow that," he explodes, screwing his cap back onto his head. "We have to stop it."

"What d'you mean 'we'?" I smile, "You're the copper." I poke him in the chest with a forefinger. "This is your big chance, Merv. Just think how your career will take off if you single-handedly clear up an unlawful sex ring." He swallows hard and rolls his eyes with trepidation, but I think he's taken the bait. He removes his cap once more and begins to unbutton his tunic.

"What are you doing?" I ask.

"I'm going in through the window. Surprise is the best strategy for a swift arrest."

Things are working out beyond my wildest expectations. Today could mark the end of Lamont's shocking disrespect for common decency and his relentless pursuit of my mother's tainted honour. I take Lipscombe's tunic and cap and he unclips his police whistle and clenches it between his teeth.

"Right, I'm going in," he whistles tunefully. I give him the thumbs up and he moves off towards the hijinks issuing from the lounge window. I watch in awe as, with one bound, he jumps onto the window-sill. Pausing only to push up the window, he lets go an ear-splitting blast on his whistle and dives full-length into the room. The scream of terror from Lamont is a sound I shall cherish forever, and the crash of furniture as our hero fells him is just icing on the cake. Blood-curdling screeches from the women pulsate on the balmy suburban air bringing on a rash of curtain-twitching at neighbouring windows.

I indulge myself in one brief look inside the room before slinking away, unscathed and blameless. At first I can't spot Lamont and Lipscombe but suddenly an armchair tips backwards and there they are. Lipscombe is sitting on Lamont's chest with one hand over the fallen actor's mouth; his other hand has disappeared down the front of Quentin's underpants and, presumably, has his testicles in a vice-like grip. I have my doubts whether this technique is actually listed in any Police Manual; my suspicion is that it's a procedure developed by the local constabulary after countless summer seasons of dealing with pub brawls. Judging from Lamont's bulging eyes and muffled squealing, it appears to be very effective. My mother is garbed out in a very tight bodice which seems to squeeze her boobs almost up under her chin, and her half-dressed companion is attired in a bra and voluminous striped bloomers. They are both engaged in taking swipes at Police Cadet Lipscombe with a variety of bonnets and lace-up boots but, full credit to the lad, he's bearing up well. However, I believe the pea in his whistle has split. The whole scene resembles an eighteenth-century stage farce.

Not wishing to be noticed, I slope away grinning widely. This has been a major coup for me, a masterstroke of cunning and deception. Maybe I should take up politics.

As I pause to open the gate, I am confronted by a giant police sergeant leaping from his Wolseley squad-car and asking me if I have seen a police cadet in the vicinity because the silly little bugger should be waiting here on this corner. Curiously enough, I affirm, I did see such an item disappearing through that window but a few minutes ago. "Christ Almighty," he mutters and sprints up the path accompanied by a burly constable, and, to my astonishment, they too vanish through the open window. The noise level inside the room is a wonder to be heard, as screams and deep masculine bellows vie with police whistles and crashing furniture. The mayhem has, understandably, attracted the attention of the neighbourhood and quite a gathering of nosey parkers has accumulated at our gate.

I check the time on my glistening Swiss masterpiece and observe that I have plenty of morning remaining in which to call Wendy. In view of the furore at our house, I decide to make the call from a phone-box. In the meantime, I chat idly with one or two of the crowd, filling them in on the dastardly events which provoked this sudden police presence. Mindful, nevertheless, of the necessity for at least a smidgen of family honour, I exaggerate Lamont's part in it all and lay the blame firmly at his door. Heads nod and many agree that they always thought he was a sleazy character, poncing around in a cravat and changing his car every few weeks.

Our tittle-tattle is interrupted as an ambulance squeaks to a halt beside us and spews out Albert Tucker and his dozy colleague. He bursts through our ranks with a rolled-up stretcher over his shoulder.

"Injury to nose and genitals?" he asks, cupping a palm to his ear for my reply.

"No thanks," I beam. "Try up there." He dashes off up the Lucas sisters' path and they bundle him back and push him through our gate. Our front door is opened by a red-faced copper who beckons Albert into the hall.

Lamont is the first to emerge from the house, prostrate on Albert's stretcher, holding a bloodied wad of cotton wool to his nose and displaying a bag of frozen peas between his legs. This is not one of his finest appearances. Following on behind, a handcuffed Lipscombe steps blinking into the sunlight and is escorted to the car by the sergeant.

"Lipscombe," says the officer as he presses Mervyn into the rear seat, "you're a bigger danger to the public than the average criminal." Our dynamic law enforcer seems incapable of speech and sits staring straight ahead, slack-jawed and wide-eyed. I fear he may have temporarily lost his reason as well as his whistle.

As Albert and his mate manhandle Lamont up the rear steps of the ambulance, my mother materialises at the front door and waves a pair of long, calico drawers to attract his attention.

"Quentin," she trills, "don't forget it's a *full* dress rehearsal tomorrow!"

Lamont raises a limp forearm and passes out.

*

I enter the stifling heat of the phone-box at the bottom of Balaclava Road, push coins into the slot and dial my truelove's number. The phone rings at the other end and is almost instantly answered by Mrs Matthews. Why did I assume otherwise? She runs the place, doesn't she? Appalling visions of swirling koi carp and fountains of vomit immediately block my thought processes and all power of speech abandons me. This really is becoming a problem. I can't go through life seizing up at the drop of a carp... sorry, hat.

"Hello," repeats Mrs Matthews irritably, "is there anybody there?"

All I can manage is a pathetic, semi-choking gurgle which leaves me gasping for breath.

"Oh, I get it," she gibes. "You're one of those grubby little heavy-breathers are you? Well, let me…"

I cut her off with a muffled cry. "No, no," I pant, startled at the sudden return of my vocal chords. "I was hoping to speak to… uuhh… Miss Wendy Matthews. If it's convenient."

"I see. And who might you be, young man?" she enquires warily.

I can't tell her who I am. I just can't do it. I know she'll go crazy and slam down the phone. But, before I have time to slap my hand over my big gob, that treacherous swine of a brain tricks me into revealing my name. Fortunately, it's my nick-name so I'm briefly in the clear.

"Brillo," I blurt.

"Brillo?" she says lightly. "As in the soap-pad?" Did I detect a simper of mirth? But, incredibly, my mind has accelerated from standstill to breakneck speed. I just need one tiny connection to link Wendy to something perfectly innocent and feasible and I'm home and dry. To my surprise, my brain comes up trumps.

"Yes… uuhh… Mr Brillo from Woolworths."

"Oh, right!" she laughs. "That'll be about her sister's birthday present, won't it? Why didn't you say? I'll call her."

I hear her calling Wendy and here she is. "Colin, is that you?"

"Yes. Sorry, I wasn't sure if the thought of me would give your mum the heebie-jeebies."

"Oh, don't be silly. She's over all that."

That's good news. Let's have a stab at some more. "I was wondering if I could see you today… now… well, anytime?"

I hear her giggle at my jitters. "Well, as luck would have it, it's my afternoon off so why not come round now?"

My heart is bursting with joy and Wee William is trying to do cartwheels down in his nest.

"Yeah, right. I'll be there in about forty-five seconds."

Wendy meets me out on the pavement and we enter the hotel via the kitchen. Now this is what I call a proper kitchen, not your namby-pamby 'swing a very small cat' space. Everything in here is on a grand scale, the ovens, sinks, saucepans, everything. It's like stepping into the lair of a giant. She asks me if I'd like a glass of Corona and opens the door to a fridge the size of our hall. The shelves are packed with delights. She slides out a metal tray containing the remains of an enormous cherry pie and wiggles it temptingly under my nose. I nod enthusiastically and she cuts two slices and scoops a huge spoonful of thick Devon cream from a gallon tin onto each slice. Strewth, a month living here and they'd be pushing me around in a wheelbarrow! This is the way to live.

Picking up my plate and glass, I follow her shapely bottom out into the yard and up a flight of steps onto a sunny terrace tucked away out of sight of the guests' bedroom windows and looking out over Fayling Bay. It really is a very private little nook and ripe for some major hanky-panky. At least, it would be if not for the presence of a little old lady installed in a wicker chair and sipping sherry. Bugger my luck! It's the work of Satan again, I just know it. Every time I make any headway with Wendy, he pops up to thwart my plans. Maybe the archfiend fancies her himself.

"Hello, Gran," calls Wendy brightly, bending down towards the old dear. "This is my boyfriend, Colin."

Her words detonate in my head like Christmas crackers and honey seems to pour from my every orifice. She called me her 'boyfriend'! Can it be true? Well, she just said it, you dozy twerp!

Granny cranks her head round and gives me the once over. "Oh, my, he's a handsome devil isn't he dear?" she cackles. I'm beginning to warm to her after all.

Wendy sits on the padded swing-seat and pats the space next to her. I join her like an obedient pug. It's a wonder I'm not panting with my tongue lolling out. Well, metaphorically (as Soapy Luxmoore revels in saying) I am.

"I should warn you, Colin, Granny is a little eccentric," she says softly as we munch on our pie.

"Oh, yeah? How?"

As I finish my question, the longest, brassiest, trumpet-call of a fart suddenly shreds the tranquillity of our cosy little rendezvous. My teeth clamp tight on my pie in sheer astonishment and, for a second, I glance out to sea fully expecting to see a cruise-liner announcing its arrival in the bay.

"Like that," says Wendy.

"Whoops, the fleet's in!" cries Granny, chuckling into her sherry.

Frankly, I'm in awe of the old dear. And, as though reading my thoughts, she lets another one go.

"Hello sailor!" she guffaws as her uncontrollable flatulence tails off to a squeak.

"Granny, that's enough," scalds Wendy. "You're embarrassing Colin." On the contrary, I can't wait to inform Tulip that he has a rival who could, quite literally, blow him out of the water.

Granny laughs and begins to struggle to her feet. "I'll leave you two lovebirds to canoodle in peace," she says, waving away my attempts to help her up. But I insist and she leans on my arm until we reach the bottom of the steps. She turns to look up at me with a twinkle in her eye. "Thank you, sailor," she smiles. "Now you be good to that girl." I'm in love with the pair of them!

When I return, Wendy is outstretched on the swing-seat, one sun-tanned knee raised, her skirt slipping back down her thigh and an arm resting across her forehead causing her breasts to push skywards as two perfect peaks. Can there ever be a vision of beauty more alluring than this? I halt for a moment to implant the image in my memory. I doubt that I will ever witness a more desirable sight in my life. Wee William is wriggling for a chance to take a look too, but he must wait his turn. Maybe one day, if good fortune should shine upon me, I shall be able to introduce them to each other.

As I approach, she lifts herself off the seat, steps to meet me, and kisses me briefly on the lips.

"Let's go to the Tarantella and play the juke-box," she says. I'll do anything she asks.

\*

Momma Bonetti is polishing the glass door panel as we arrive and she swings the door wide for us. "Ciao, kids. You OK today?" I give her a hug and she giggles and slaps me with her chamois leather.

"You boys, you all-a the same, eh Wendy?"

The Gaggia roars at us as we pass with ice-cold Cokes in our fists, but I feel no rancour towards it today. After all, it's just a pretentious pile of chrome and hot air trying to impress the world. Much in the manner of Barnaby Small and his Jaguar.

The fuggy gloom at the rear of the coffee-bar gradually reveals some detail and, to our mixed pleasures, we see Tulip and Anthea installed in our usual bench-seats. Even at this time of day they are bickering over something. Probably Anthea resisting Tulip's constant groping and fumbling. Why does he bother? All she ever does is slap his hands and put him down. 'Yeah,' he pleads in his defence, 'but she's got great legs!' So has a Chippendale chair.

"Hallo, hallo. You two back together again?" Tulip remarks, offering the Senior Service around. Wendy and I glance at each other and grin sheepishly and, to my jubilation, she nods. Anthea rolls her eyes and I sense Wendy frowning at her, but Tulip pipes up before any hostilities can take hold. "We're going on an expedition. Want to come?"

Warning bells ring loud in my head. I still shudder when I consider the perils he subjected me to on his recent quest for treasure in 'Ye Undergrownde Wayes'. If there is merely the whiff of danger about this current enterprise, I'm backing off. Besides, I have the welfare of my sweetheart to bear in mind. "Let's hear it first," I insist.

"We're going up to the old burnt-down hotel on the American road," he announces, spreading his arms as though inviting everyone to a magnificent party at the Dorchester. We stare at him, but not in admiration.

"Pourquoi?" I ask, causing the visible raise of an eyebrow from Anthea.

"Because, you festering neddy," he grins, leaning forward. "It's there!" Who does he think he is, Sir Edmund Hillary?

The burnt-down hotel he refers to was, prior to the war, the 'Bay View Grand', an Edwardian pile sitting flamboyantly on the lower slopes of the downs, immediately above the sand dunes with an uninterrupted panorama of Fayling Bay. During the later stages of WW2 it was requisitioned by the American Forces and became the Officers' Mess for the troops training in the area in preparation for

D-Day. When the Yanks vacated the hotel in June 1944, they left behind in the grounds a malfunctioning howitzer, a damaged Jeep, and a stash of assorted live and dummy artillery shells. This entire bonanza came into the dubious possession of the Fayling Home Guard, a motley bunch of locals amongst whose ranks fatefully lurked a blacksmith, two motor mechanics, and a World War One ordnance expert. Before you could say 'Apocalypse', they had the Jeep stripped down and modified and the gun mounted on the back. This, they claimed with pride, would provide the town with a front-line mobile defence should Jerry attempt to invade at Fayling Beach. The fact that the Germans were on the retreat hundreds of miles away in France seems to have escaped them. Nevertheless, all might well have passed off harmlessly had not two of the younger members got tanked up on 'Fine Old Rat' cider one Sunday and decided to fire off a couple of dummy shells 'to wake the bloody town up'. The two inebriated errors they made were as follows: one… failing to aim the howitzer harmlessly out over the sands, and two… accidentally loading the breech with a live shell. Fortunately for the sole occupant of the hotel at the time, a Jewish refugee acting as caretaker, his sortie to the kitchen to prepare a forbidden non-Kosher ham sandwich certainly saved his life when the hotel lobby was blown to hell by a direct hit. The ensuing fire destroyed the whole building and, it is said, the caretaker converted to Christianity the next day.

"Actually," brays Our Lady Anthea, pulling a note-pad from her duffle bag, "I'm doing a project on the D-Day landings and Andrew has agreed to help."

Aha, now I get it! This little adventure is all for Miss Snooty's benefit. Tulip sits there grinning but I bet he's cringing with embarrassment inside. He must have cut a deal for some extra favours to agree to this.

"A project?" Wendy says. "But we're on holiday, Anth."

"Yeah, give it a rest," I add, seizing the rare opportunity to have a dig at her.

Tulip throws himself back in his seat and chortles falsely. "Aw. Come on, folks. Live dangerously."

Anywhere within five yards of you, Tulip, *is* dangerous.

*

Well, at least the deep lane that leads to Fayling Municipal rubbish tip is a cool haven on this scorching hot day. Just beyond the tip, we will leave the lane to make our way along the American road above the dunes. When this abandoned track fizzles out, we then have to negotiate the overgrown trail that once was the well-maintained metalled drive to the Bay View Hotel.

Meanwhile, as we amble slowly up the hill, we sing a selection of our favourite pop-songs and, I have to say, Wendy and Anthea are brilliant at the backing harmony vocals. We've done 'Only Sixteen' and 'It's only make believe' and we're half way through 'Peggy Sue' when Wendy stops singing and points up the bramble strewn bank and sighs, "Oh, look. It's Apple."

And so it is; a soppy-faced donkey, complete with old straw sun-hat through which its ears protrude, gazes down at us, chewing languidly and shuddering occasionally to dislodge the flies from his face. Apple is one of three working donkeys owned by Jack Butters who operates the Donkey Ride concession on the beach. For a 'tanner', parents can get their kids off their hands for ten minutes whilst Jack dumps them in the saddle and leads them out into an eye-stinging sandstorm like Lawrence of bloody Arabia. Jack rotates the beasts on a two-day work rota so the donkeys get a day off every third day. Today, then, is Apple's day of rest and very relaxed he looks too.

It takes us a good twenty minutes to traverse the difficult, pot-holed route that is the American road and then beat a path through to the site of the ex-hotel. The delay is partly due to Tulip and Anthea disappearing at intervals into the undergrowth where, I suspect, Tulip is collecting his reward for sponsoring the trip. My guess is that he's managing little more than a quick grope of some part of Anthea's anatomy and a vague promise of further foraging when he delivers on the hotel. Hardly the kind of deal I, myself, would be interested in nowadays.

Tulip and I wander the charred remains of the rambling ruin, kicking aimlessly at the blackened bricks, tiles and fallen timbers that are scattered among the heather and gorse that have claimed the site. There is no glamour here now, no sound of laughter and tinkling of champagne glasses. Just the relentless whinging from Anthea who has perched herself on a corroded bucket and is haranguing Tulip about the lack of wartime relics on display. It beats me why he puts up with her.

We leave the girls to chat about us and begin a more thorough search amongst the debris. What are we looking for? God knows, but Tulip is determined to find some memento of the hotel's glory days so he can scurry back with it to his tyrannical girlfriend in triumph.

"Anything connected with the Yanks," says Tulip. "You know, a cap-badge would be great, a dog-tag would be brilliant, and a silver dollar would be fantastic."

I snort with derision at his wildly optimistic expectations and, anyway, it's far too hot for all this bloody nonsense. I kick petulantly at a pile of broken roof-tiles and hurt my toe. "Oh, for Christ sake, Tulip!" I cry, hopping around clutching my foot. "There's nothing here worth the trip."

He is standing looking up at the remains of a chimney breast, a stack of bricks and carved stonework that soars about ten feet. It looks decidedly fragile to me and, as if reading my thoughts, Tulip reaches to the ground, grabs a sturdy looking spar of charred roof-beam and gives the whole structure a tremendous whack. Needless to say, the entire thing sways and collapses with a crash in a cloud of black dust. I get the feeling that Tulip is venting his frustration on the Yanks, the hotel, and his bitchy girlfriend, all in one fell swoop. The girls scream, leap to their feet and cover their mouths with their hands. But their fears are unfounded as Tulip emerges like a phantom from the dust cloud clutching a small box in his hand and grinning like a gibbon. You can't keep a Belch-man down.

He stumbles over to us and lays his trophy on the stone slab that once was the front door step of the hotel. Slapping dust from his shirt-sleeves he looks at us and beams with pride.

"See, I knew I'd find something interesting," he crows. Anthea stares down at Tulip's offering, ridicule written across her face.

"It's a box," she mocks. We all stand in a semi-circle and gaze down at the battered black metal box as though it was some mysterious, forbidding artefact that has just dropped from the sky.

"What d'you reckon is inside?" says Tulip, squatting to take a closer look.

"Well, why don't you open it and find out?" retorts Miss Snapdragon.

Tulip picks up the box and examines the faded brass escutcheon. He blows a 'raspberry' for no apparent reason, stands and shakes the box cautiously. There is no sound of loose objects such as coins despite its obvious past use as a cashbox. "We need the key," declares our treasure-seeker.

"Don't be daft," I laugh, pointing at the mound of rubble that was the chimney breast. "You'll never find it amongst that lot."

"And why would the owner hide a box with the key beside it?" asks Wendy. Hmmm, maybe the opposite sex does have a streak of logic after all. Meanwhile, Anthea is scrabbling inside her duffle bag and, to our astonishment, comes out with a hefty looking screwdriver. She hands it to Tulip, folds her arms and nods at the box with a look of lofty impatience.

It takes Tulip no time at all to open the box and, as I watch, I am reminded of his dexterity with the slot machine during the debacle at Christie's Cavern. He lifts the lid and lays the box back on the step for all to see. We bend expectantly to observe the hoard of jewellery or banknotes tucked within. What a flaming disappointment! The contents appear to be nothing more exciting than a pair of folded khaki socks. We straighten up, sighing as one and the girls begin to snigger.

"Hang on," says Tulip. "It was too heavy just to contain someone's laundry." He leans down and pulls the socks out revealing... another sock, but something is inside this one. Tulip lifts it out and peels it back. Jesus on a Thunderbird, it's a handgun! "Wow!" yells Tulip. "Wowzie-bloody-wow!" We all take a pace backwards as Tulip grips the stock and aims the gun out over the sea.

"Andrew!" barks Anthea. "Put it down at once. You have no idea what you're playing with."

Tulip grins but complies with her wishes and places the weapon gently down beside the metal box. He thrusts his hand inside and spills the remaining contents onto the step: a roll of oily lint, a full clip of bullets, and a grainy photograph showing a young G.I. aiming the gun at a line of tin cans in the sand dunes. Tulip grabs the gun again and, for some reason, weighs it in his palm. "What a beaut!" he drools. "Wonder what it is?" Instantly, Anthea loses her cool. She slaps his hand and physically wrests the weapon from him and lays it back in the box. Then, in her customary way, she astonishes us.

"It's an M1911," she states coolly. We gape at her in awe. "A U.S. Army Colt .45," she adds, shaking her head with a sort of inscrutable incredulity as though anyone should know this.

"How do you know that?" asks Wendy.

"My dad's got one," she says.

"What?" pipes Tulip. "Your old man works in the Housing Department at the Council."

"I bet he gets the council rents paid on time," I whisper to Wendy.

Anthea continues. "He's got a gun collection. He's got three Colts; one from the First World War even." She then picks up the gun and expertly removes a clip from the handle. She glances into it casually, mutters, "Empty," and slams it back into place. Who does she think she is, Ma Baker? We are all very impressed, but of course, Anthea knows that. "Don't mess with it, Andrew. We're not playing Cowboys and Indians," she commands. "And don't touch the full clip." Inexplicably, I get a feeling of foreboding at her words.

Wendy, meantime, is drooling over the photograph. "Gosh, isn't he handsome in his uniform." Tulip snatches the snapshot from her fingers and twists his lips cynically.

"Probably dead now, Wendy," he remarks. She retrieves the photo and I can detect tears welling in her lovely eyes as she stares at it.

"You're really horrible sometimes, Andy," she says softly. "He only looks a couple of years older than you." That shuts him up.

Anthea has clearly had enough and announces that we are leaving. Tulip says he is going to remove his shirt and jeans in order to give them a good thwacking to remove the brick dust. Not wishing to witness the grisly sight of Tulip in his underwear, we all opt to leave him to it and the three of us beat a hasty retreat. He catches up with us further along the trail and I notice that he now has the handgun tucked into his belt like Billy the Kid. Anthea goes nuts when she spots it but he insists on waving it around like a cowboy and, surprisingly, gets his own way when he promises to donate it to her dad's collection. Maybe that tells you a lot about Anthea.

The down side of Tulip having the pistol is that he launches into parodies of every Hollywood film star who ever carried a gun. Thus, throughout our journey along the American road to the lane, we are obliged to listen to impersonations of John Wayne, Kirk Douglas, James Stewart, and James Cagney. I have to confess, some of them are really good and the words he puts in their mouths are pretty funny, so it's not all bad. But, of course, when you are in the company of the Belch idiot, you can expect things to go downhill at any time. This time, however, even Tulip himself is taken by surprise at his own stupidity.

We have reached the place beneath the steep bank where we previously spotted Apple, and he is there again, only now he has strayed into the bracken right at the top of the slope and is clearly struggling to get back up. There is nothing much we can do to help him and I know from experience that he's a real awkward cuss at the best of times. This is knowledge gained from the mixed blessing of my three-week stint last summer as Jack Butters's chief donkey handler and charged with the saddle- safety of countless obnoxious little kids. God knows how many miles I covered trudging up and down that fifty-yard strip of sand in the company of a stubborn beast and a donkey. Don't get me wrong, I don't dislike animals, but donkeys...? Well, they're a bit on the boring side compared with, say, horses. For example, did you ever hear of a donkey winning the Grand National, leading a cavalry charge, or even making its way into a French meat-pie? No, on a scale of one to ten for being remotely interesting, to me, donkeys don't register at all. Not that they don't have a certain whimsical appeal and an undeniable cuteness but, then, so has a boiled egg. Having said all that, I concede that Apple could possibly be the only mildly intriguing animal in the whole of Donkeydom. And the reason for that is his deep hatred of children, many of whom he has bitten. Hmmm, a bit of a handicap on a kiddies' donkey ride, I hear you mutter, even if the little buggers deserved it. Well, yes, so Jack had to come up with a solution or he'd pretty soon run out of customers. The answer was a simple one: on duty days, Jack adds a half-bottle of cheap sherry to the donkey's breakfast and Apple spends the day in a sweet-natured stupor. Brilliant!

But, to return to our present dilemma.

As we stand gawping up at Apple who has stopped pawing at the bank and is now peering down at *us*, into our midst steps a gun-toting Humphrey Bogart.

"OK, big-ears," calls Tulip, waving the pistol up at the donkey. "This is where you get yours!"

But there is no dull click of the hammer and a wry chuckle from Humph. Instead, an explosion deafens our ears and we are all wreathed in acrid gun-smoke. The girls scream, I almost fill my Y-fronts, and cascading down through the bracken, sliding on his back like a demented equine tobogganist, comes Apple. His rear end hits the ditch in front of us and he lolls back into the undergrowth, hoofs lolling, eyes closed, for all the world looking like an old dear dozing in the sun.

"Jesus H. Christ, Tulip!" I cry. "You've shot him!"

Wendy is whimpering pitifully so I put a comforting arm around her which tends to settle me down too. Tulip's gaze is alternating between the pistol in his hand, blue smoke still drifting from its muzzle, and the prostrate daftness of Apple. Anthea is still coughing and rubbing her eyes from the effects of the gun smoke.

"It's not possible," croaks Tulip, sounding just like Bogart without trying. "Anthea told me the gun was empty."

"Well, she was wrong, mate," I assure him.

"What are we going to do?" sniffs Wendy, clearly distraught at the carnage.

"What's the penalty for shooting a donkey?" asks Tulip, looking genuinely shaken and uncharacteristically scared. I ponder this question for a moment and toy with the idea of suggesting horse-whipping or a kick up the 'ass', but I fear that any levity at this point might fall on stony ground.

Anthea suddenly springs into action and launches herself at the hapless gun-slinger, grabs the weapon from his trembling grasp and begins to pistol-whip his arms and shoulders. Boy, she's something else, is Anthea!

"You stupid, brainless boy!" she rasps. "I ought to reload this gun and shoot *you*."

"OK, OK!" I shout. "That's enough. We need to come up with a plan."

"A plan?" bawls Anthea. "This isn't a game of 'Cluedo', Colin. We have a murder on our hands."

"Aw, c'mon, Anth," snorts Tulip. "It's not that dramatic. And anyway…" He suddenly jumps down into the ditch and begins a thorough examination of Apple's head. "…See, not a bullet hole to be found. Maybe I missed altogether."

"So why is he dead, then?" taunts his girlfriend. Tulip shrugs and stretches forward to grip a dangling hoof. "What are you doing now?" she asks.

"Looking for a pulse. Does a donkey have a wrist?"

"Oh, get out of the ditch, Andrew," snaps Anthea. "You're acting like an idiot."

I sigh loudly. "He's not acting, Anthea."

But this is getting us nowhere and I am pleased and surprised when Wendy decides to intervene. "Look, here's my suggestion. We report to the police and tell them *some* of the truth. We were passing and saw Apple slide down the bank and hit the ditch."

"And just leave out the pistol bit?" I beseech. She nods, a little uncertainly, but it's a nod.

"That's brilliant, Wendy!" enthuses Tulip.

"It's a lie," adds Anthea.

"No, Anth, it's… well… just some of what actually happened. We saw Apple falling and we assume he's dead. Jack and the police will think he's broken his neck. There won't be a flipping post-mortem."

For a few moments, we stand in silence, reflecting on the substance of our proposed story and, as we are thus engaged, we hear the chatter of children's voices floating up from lower down the lane. The sound is unmistakeable and strikes fear into my very soul; the Brownies are approaching.

"Oh, no," wails Tulip. "Now what? That Hettie Trimble will drop us right in it if she spots a dead donkey near us."

Unlikely as it seems, my habitually cantankerous brain bounds forward with a quick suggestion and I bark orders. "OK, everyone, let's cover Apple with bracken. If we stand in a row to block their view, the Brownies will pass on by."

In no time at all, Apple becomes invisible to the casual observer and we stand at attention awaiting the arrival of the brown swarm. They spot us and, as we expected, Janet and Olive gallop towards us to commence interrogations. They halt and eye us suspiciously.

Janet speaks first.

"Hello, Wend. What are you doing up here?"

"Just walking, Janet. What are you lot collecting today?"

Janet holds out the bunch of wilting plants gripped in her tiny fist. "Oh, just poisonous plants. These are Deadly Nightshade," she beams proudly.

"Anyone particular in mind?" I ask, but she ignores me.

Olive pipes up, addressing her older cousin, Anthea. "Why are you with the fish and chip boy, Anthea?"

"That's very rude, Olive, and don't forget, you are my little cousin, not my mother."

"She wouldn't like it if she saw you with the fish and chip boy," says the cheeky spy-lette. Anthea makes a movement towards her, most probably to give her a clip around the ear, but she is restrained by Tulip. "Don't break the wall," he hisses to her.

The formidable figure of Hettie Trimble looms into view and her face darkens as she recognises us. She surveys us individually, her mouth twisting from a moderate smile for Wendy to a grimace of distaste as her gaze falls upon me. "Good morning, Wendy and Anthea," she says. "Are you on a Nature walk?" What does that mean, exactly? Is she implying that any female seen with me is automatically going to end up down in the grass? If so, I could either feel insulted or flattered. As it turns out, our interchange is brought to an abrupt end when, for some unaccountable reason, the Brownies begin shrieking and sobbing and rush to Hettie's side where they cling to her and form what resembles a twitching termite mound.

"It's a monster!" they scream, burying their heads in Hettie's skirt. "Don't let it eat us, Brown Owl," they implore, pointing our way.

Well, I don't mind confessing that we are startled and

dumbfounded by this outburst. But a hideous braying behind us persuades us to swivel round to witness the bizarre sight of Apple sitting in the ditch and baring his revolting teeth in a horsey grin. The daft bugger is very much alive and kicking. OK, he does appear a bit unusual with strands of bracken attached to his hairy face, but he's no monster. Looking at his bleary eyes, my guess is that he's been on the cooking sherry again.

"It's just a donkey!" laughs Hettie, wading her way out of the brown mound of snivelling girls, all wiping their noses on their ties. "Come along, then, ladies. Let's pull ourselves together," she shrills, striding purposefully towards Apple and removing her leather belt. "Now, here is our good deed for the day," and she slips the belt around Apple's neck, buckles it and begins to pull on it to encourage him up onto the roadside. "We will return this poor animal to Mr Butters. Follow me!" And the Brownie pack, chattering and giggling, fall in behind her as she sets off up the lane. To my astonishment, Apple complies with her, trotting complacently beside her as though they were old buddies. There's not a hint of aggression; not one child has been bitten. In fact, the whole occasion seems to have affected him in an entirely different way. We hear Olive's voice ringing from the throng.

"Brown Owl, what's this long thing dangling under his tummy?"

There is no explanation from Hettie.

Back at the Westcliffs Hotel, Wendy and I seat ourselves on the swing-seat for a short session of snogging and moderate fumbling. We soon give it up as we are subjected to some perverse law of physics invented, I am certain, by Satan. Ever tried maintaining leverage on the female torso when you are swinging backwards and forwards in ever increasing arcs? Don't bother.

We end up reflecting on the day's events. I recount my exciting adventures with Cadet Lipscombe and the naughtiness I assumed was occurring in our front room. Wendy is shocked but bursts into laughter when I describe the dramatic involvement of the local Ploddery and Lamont's curtain-call on the stretcher. Yes, all in all, it's been a day of minor triumphs over major adversities. Even the incident with Apple ended happily. As for Tulip and Anthea, well, when we parted company at the War Memorial, they were merrily quarrelling over the value of the Colt pistol with Tulip claiming favours which were quite clearly not up for grabs (if you'll excuse the pun!).

I leave with a glow in my heart and the smoulder of an earnest kiss on my lips. The world is back on its axis and the Devil has not, for once, had his day. Do you suppose he's easing up on me a bit?

*

My mother is alone in the house upon my arrival, although I am initially startled to find what appears to be an eighteenth-century strumpet peeling potatoes at the kitchen sink. For some odd reason she has chosen to wear her theatrical costume for the remainder of the day, 'to get the feel of it'. Words fail me.

I slump into a chair and pick at the Victoria-sandwich sponge cake on the Formica-top table.

"Don't do that, Colin," she says without looking round. "If you want a piece, get a plate."

As it's shop-bought, I feel safe in trying it and cut myself an enormous slice. "There's no need to be greedy," she remarks, once again seeming to observe me without turning. Is it possible she's a witch? She's always bragging that she's got eyes in the back of her head when I'm around.

I chomp noisily on the cake and notice her back heaving as she sighs with annoyance. I decide to take the initiative.

"Any news of Lamont?" I enquire casually. I see her bodice stiffen and she shifts her weight from one buckled shoe to the other.

"He's suffered another nose injury," she answers lightly, "and his brand-new tights are beyond repair." Hmmm, I wonder which the Fayling Light Opera and Pantomime Society (FLOPS) will consider to be the most serious? My money is on the tights. "What on earth that young police cadet thought he was doing, I'll never know," she continues. "It's a wonder poor Quentin wasn't run through with his own rapier. It's bent beyond repair as it is." Whoops, more damaged props.

I decide that this is the moment to strike.

"Perhaps he wondered what was going on when he saw a couple of women in their underwear and a bloke prancing around without his trousers. What will Dad think?"

My mother whips round and places a fist on one hip. Now she *does* look like a Georgian tart. Look at her breasts, they're almost popping out of her blouse!

"Colin," she snaps indignantly, "you know perfectly well that we were merely trying on our costumes. Your father will have nothing to get excited about when he gets home."

He will when he finds Nell Gwynne in the kitchen!

# CHAPTER 10

## *'Whole Lotta Woman' (Marvin Rainwater...1958)*

There is no justice in the world! I have been evicted from my room and billeted in the spare room, little more than a cupboard. Why, I hear you cry supportively, has a young man in the prime of puberty, been exiled thus? The answer is simple... my ceiling collapsed. Fortunately, I was about my ablutions at the time and suffered no physical injury but, on returning to my room after a luxuriant soaking 'en bain', I was enveloped in a cloud of plaster dust and was obliged to take another bath. Yes, the constantly changing graphics on my bedroom ceiling finally succumbed to gravity, indicating that all interior decorators should hone up on Isaac Newton early in their careers.

Under normal circumstances, I would probably be able to remain on site whilst the work is done, but there looms on the horizon a fearsome battleship for whom my room is being prepared. Aunt Dorothy is coming to stay.

Aunt Dorothy ('Dot' as she is imprecisely called, bearing in mind her vast girth) is my mother's older sister who, fortunately, lives in Texas. She had the only brief burst of inspiration in her life, one gin-sodden night in December 1943, when she became impregnated by an American Staff-Sergeant aptly named 'Buck'. Regretfully, Buck, being merely a store-man, was not required at Normandy the following June and missed the opportunity of getting blown to pieces on Omaha Beach and, thus, avoiding any paternal responsibilities. He was subsequently persuaded to marry the broad and take her back to

Houston. And there she thrived, growing bigger, her voice louder, and her brain smaller year by year. Her visits, accompanied by Uncle Buck, are mercifully limited to a three-year cycle.

By contrast, Uncle Buck is OK. He's a tall, slim, blue-eyed Texan with a weather-beaten face sporting a circular scar on his cheek that he claims was a bullet wound. If you saw him moseying down your High Street with his long Western stride and his big old Stetson pulled down over his eyes, you might be forgiven for thinking John Wayne had blown into town looking for a bar-fight. The thing I like best is his Texan drawl and the colourful language he uses. Until quite recently, I really believed he was a cowboy and spent his time out on the range branding 'dogies' and roping 'mavericks', whatever the hell *they* are. It turns out he owns a diner out on a freeway somewhere in Houston. Anyhow, he spins some great tales about his 'gran-paw' who actually was a cowboy. If it wasn't for Uncle Buck coming I'd be really mad about forfeiting my bedroom.

The Texans are due in on the morning train from Paddington and I have been hi-jacked into meeting them to assist with Aunt Dorothy's anticipated mountain of luggage. Last time they visited us it required two taxis to ferry them from the railway station, one for the luggage, the other for Aunt Dot. However, I have been allowed to rope in Tulip to give me a hand.

\*

The appointed day is here but, when I get to The Cod Almighty to collect Tulip, he is nowhere to be seen. He's hosing down the back yard according to his dad and there are certainly signs out there of an imbecile at work. The business end of the water-hose has been ingeniously propped into a vertical position with house-bricks and the fountain of water supports a large potato which bobs and turns at the top of the jet. It's clever but worryingly bonkers.

I hear the toilet flushing and the Belch sculptor emerges buttoning his fly.

"Hiya, mate. What's up?" he grins.

"I need some help."

"Yeah, you do. See a psychiatrist."

I explain my requirements and he immediately agrees to

accompany me. I give him a hand to finish his chores and we set off, ciggies glowing brightly between our lips.

One of Fayling's greatest failings is, in fact, its railway station. Obviously, when old Brunel sat down with a fat cigar and a map to plan the route of the Great Western Railway, he must have placed his brandy glass over Fayling Bay because the line eventually by-passed the town by miles. On the other hand, it may have had something to do with the fact that the only safe and feasible way to bring the railway here meant running a branch line up the steepest gradient in Britain and perching the station on a promontory five hundred feet above sea-level. Ultimately, this amazing feat of engineering was achieved when the local Chamber of Commerce, in an act of stupendous skulduggery, announced the discovery of gold nuggets in The Dribble, a small stream running near the old iron-ore workings on Fayling Knoll. Cunningly announcing their momentous godsend just a year after the Klondike goldrush, prospectors and investors flocked to the town and, before you could say 'fool's gold', the route had been surveyed, Irish 'navvies' had laid the sleepers and rails, and the first locomotive was chugging up the line. Sadly, nothing was discovered by the prospectors other than the enormous con-trick perpetuated upon them, and, after burning down the station and 'feather and tarring' the Mayor, they left. Fayling Bay then remained an unused branch-line off a branch-line for several years until a cult group of barmy artists and naturists rekindled its infamy by moving in and taking over some of the less accessible coves. Tourists began to flock in again and the Fayling Autonomous Rail and Road Transport Company was formed (FARRT Co. as it became affectionately known).

*

Have you ever heard the wail of a Banshee? Well, I suppose you probably never have, unless you live in Ireland but, I can tell you this much… it's a scary noise. It's this spine-tingling noise which stops me and Tulip in our tracks, halfway up the Railway Station steps. Rising and falling above the hiss of the steam-train, it's a howl from the very jaws of Hell. We stare at each other and climb the remaining steps, entering the deserted waiting room, past the unattended ticket office and out on to the platform.

Our first impression, as we peer up towards the stationary

locomotive, is one of confused activity. Steam issues from the engine, churning and eddying around a small group of men standing close to the first carriage. They seem to be involved in a heated argument, arms gesticulating and voices raised at frequent intervals. As we draw near, I recognise my Uncle Buck, towering head and shoulders above the station master, Bert Gaunt, and a blue-overalled engine driver. Uncle Buck suddenly whips the Stetson from his head and gestures towards the train. But, before we can get any closer, a blood-curdling howl assails our ears, an animal-like whine that rises to a crescendo and terminates in the screaming utterances of a very distraught female.

"Get me outta here, you bunch-a rat turds!"

I recognise that awful cry: it's Aunty Dot.

"Cool it, Dorothy, goddammit," bawls Uncle Buck. "I'm doin' my level best here!"

The engine driver removes his leather cap, scratches his head and addresses Uncle Buck. "All I'm saying, sir, is I'm responsible for this passenger while she's on my train."

"And I'm responsible for this passenger," insists Bert, "while she's on my platform."

Tulip and I creep in behind the men, itching to see what all the fuss is about and, as the steam momentarily wisps away from the side of the carriage, Aunty Dot is revealed… jammed tight in the open window of the carriage door. Like some ghastly Behemoth trying to squirm from its loathsome lair, she hangs half-in and half-out, her pendulous breasts wobbling furiously and her face purple with strain and anger. She catches sight of me and lets go a squawk of recognition.

"Colin," she cries, beckoning with both her blubbery arms. "Thank Christ for a friendly face. Get yer ass over here, son!"

Tulip and I approach her and she sweeps me in towards the gruesome, florid wetness of her face to smack an extravagant kiss on my forehead. It's like being assaulted by a gigantic and pitiless open oyster. She holds me in a vice-like grip and begins to sob and drool in my ear.

"Get me outta here, Colin. These brainless assholes ain't got a mite a' sense between 'em."

She releases me and I stumble backwards, wiping the dribble from my face. Tulip steadies me and then pipes up with a useful suggestion. "If we slapped some axle-grease around your shoulders," he grins, "I reckon we could pull you back into the carriage."

Aunty Dot stops snivelling and grunting and stares at Tulip, a huge smile spreading across the vastness of her face. "Well, slap my buttocks!" she explodes. "At last, a male with a brain! Hey, you dumb-asses over there," she yells at Uncle Buck's rescue team. "Take yer goddam orders from this young guy here!"

The men walk over and Uncle Buck shakes my hand and stares down at us, stroking his chin thoughtfully. Bert Gaunt gives a silly little false cough and fidgets with the pen-tops in his breast pocket. He glances up and down the platform and leans forward to Uncle Buck.

"I wonder, sir, if you could ask your wife to moderate her language. We're just not used to this kind of thing at this station."

Uncle Buck turns and gives him a look that could stun a longhorn steer. "Well, ain't that a tear-jerkin' shame," he rasps between clenched teeth. "And I gotta tell ya, buddy, I ain't accustomed to seein' my old lady jammed up tight in a goddam Mickey Mouse-size railroad-wagon door!" Bert clears his throat and says nothing. Uncle Buck turns his fierce glare to Tulip. "OK, son," he says evenly. "What's your bright idea?"

Tulip explains his grease theory and Uncle Buck nods sagely, pokes his Stetson back up his forehead and folds his arms as he studies Aunty Dot's predicament. The engine driver breaks the silence with the revelation that he has a tin of grease in his cab and whilst he goes to get it, Tulip utters one of his stupid remarks. "Yeah," he grins, "all she needs is a good yank!"

I close my eyes and pray to be transported to another place, even the dentist's. Does my Belch friend have a death-wish? Surely Uncle Buck will stretch down, grip him by the neck, lift him slowly into the air and shake the smirk off his silly face. But it looks as though it may be even worse. Uncle Buck slides a gnarled hand inside his embroidered jacket and I have a terrible vision of a shoulder-holstered handgun emerging and the barrel being stuck up Tulip's nose. Maybe I've been watching too many gangster films. But, to my relief, his hand slips back out holding an enormous cigar. He grins down at Tulip and chuckles, "Hell, son, you may be right!"

We are despatched into the carriage to take up 'yanking' positions to the rear of Aunty Dot whilst the engine driver applies liberal amounts of grease to her available flanks.

"Watch yer goddam hands!" she brays at him, her sagging, balloon-size breasts swinging gamely as he works around them.

"OK, fellas," yells Uncle Buck, "she's greased up. Take the strain and rope her in!"

Tulip and I grip loose clothing, place our feet against the wall and heave. The shrieks of indignation and threats to mankind issuing from Aunty Dot are a wonder to be heard but, with a sudden surge and pitch to fore and aft, accompanied by a loud slurping sound, the three of us fly backwards and she lands on top of us cackling with triumph.

"Glory be to Jesus!" she squawks as the door flies open and Uncle Buck fills the space with cigar smoke.

"You OK, honey?" he enquires, and he hauls her out on to the platform where she deposits her Texas-size backside heavily onto a luggage trolley. She whips the green railway flag from Bert Gaunt's hand and mops her florid features with it.

"Can I get you a cup of tea, madam?" wheezes Bert.

"No thanks, fella, but you can get me a goddam lawyer 'cos I'm gonna sue your ass!"

Bert looks a trifle taken aback by this transatlantic forthrightness; normally, I imagine, he would expect to quell any potential passenger rebellion with a tactful word and, perhaps, a cup of insipid British Railways brew. Having his ass sued would be a new and bewildering concept for him. Sadly, Uncle Buck's additional dollar's-worth is bound to confuse him even further.

"Too right, honey," drawls the big Texan. "We're gonna have to kick some limey butt over this."

Both Bert and the engine driver stare up and down the platform, presumably looking for the butt brimming with limes that Uncle Buck unaccountably needs to kick. Nothing seems to meet the bill so Bert jerks his thumb at the steaming engine and tells the driver to get moving and make up the lost time somehow.

Meanwhile, Tulip and I load up the trolley with Aunty Dot's assorted suitcases. You've never seen anything like it. I swear the Royal Family travel lighter than this!

Uncle Buck pulls a wad of banknotes from his pocket and peels off a couple of crisp pounds.

"OK, fellas," he says, handing me the dosh. "Get this baggage into a taxi and head for home. Me and the old lady will follow on toot sweet. And I ain't looking for change," he winks. Tulip and I can barely believe our luck. There's enough currency here to pay for the taxi, tip the driver, and still make a quid profit! I can see good times ahead with ol' Buck around.

*

We've finally got Aunty Dot back to our house. She's in the kitchen with my mother slurping coffee down by the mugful and her disposition oscillating back and forth between threats of terrible retribution to sobs of humiliation. What a din! Tulip and I high-tail it out the back with two tumblers and a bottle of Tizer.

We find Uncle Buck down by the pond lolling back in a folding chair and, to my delight, one snake-skin boot perched on the head of that pervert, the garden gnome. He holds up a big palm to greet us and we flop down on the grass, down-wind of his cigar smoke.

"Hi there, fellas," he says, removing his Stetson and placing it on his knee. "I wanna tell you what a swell job you boys did down at the railroad station. That was some trick you pulled with the goddam axle-grease. Tickled me pink, I gotta tell ya!" He tips back his head and guffaws hoarsely. "Kept visualising giving the old lady a bear-hug and seein' her pop upwards like a champagne cork!" We all have a good laugh and Uncle Buck offers us each a cigar, which we both decline.

"Any more stories about the Wild West, Uncle?" I ask, knowing full well that he will take the bait and spin a few yarns about his grandaddy, 'Polecat' Roberts. (What a great name, and given to him, not because he took to wearing a Davey Crockett-style polecat-skin hat, but, according to 'Granmaw' Roberts, primarily because he smelt like one each time he returned from one of his fruitless gold-prospecting trips.)

Uncle Buck leans forward in his chair, his hat dangling from his fingers, as he regales us with a multitude of incredible tales about his late grandaddy. From his arrival in the U.S.A. as a penniless boot-maker, through his adventures out on the plains with the U.S. Cavalry, and his remarkable presence in the same bar-room as Wild Bill Hickok when the great man was shot dead in Deadwood. Wow, this is all hair-raising stuff! And to think that I'm connected to it all (OK, very loosely) through Aunty Dot's father-in-law's father. My heart swells with pride at the very thought of it, whether it's true or not.

"So how did Polecat end up?" enquires a completely mesmerised Tulip. "Was he shot in a gun fight or anything like that?"

Uncle Buck sighs, draws long and hard on his cigar, and chuckles the smoke into the warm air.

"Nothing so sensational as that, kid," he grins. He pulls his chair closer, leans down to us and lowers his voice almost to a mutter. "You two boys ever hear of somethin' called a 'whorehouse'?" he asks. We look at one another, turn back and nod. "Well, that was the makin' and the undoin' of Granddaddy Roberts. And it ain't what you're most likely surmising. He didn't catch no nasty disease nor suchlike. No, siree, he was too smart for that." He leans back into his chair and allows a short period of silence to ratchet up our attention to fever pitch. "Nope, what ol' Polecat did was revolutionary. He created the West's first Travelling Tableaux Whorehouse!"

Our mouths fall open in surprise and puzzlement. 'Travelling Tableaux'? What the hell is that? Uncle Buck grins and nods at our frowning faces. "Well, he was a smart cookie, old Grandaddy Polecat. He got himself a coupla wagons and a bevy of loose women and headed out for all them wild frontier towns. He'd breeze into town, set up his makeshift stage, and get his girls up there in their goddam underwear posing like statues in what they call a 'tableau'. They had to keep as still as a rock, mind you. Any movin' and they broke the law. Some kinda European-style teasin' for the boys and, Jesus, they flocked to pay a dollar to see it! But here's the knockout: he'd have them same fired-up cow-pokes and prospectors coming back at night to pay again to get a bit more personal with the ladies!"

We rock with laughter and Uncle Buck beams with pleasure at our enjoyment. To my added delight, he lights a fresh cigar with the stub of the old one and then grinds out the stub on the gnome's hat.

"Anyways," he continues, "all good things come to an end, I guess, and I imagine Grandaddy finally ran out of towns where he was welcome. So one afternoon, during a tableau performance in some little one-horse town down in the Texas panhandle, the local sheriff fired his Navy Colt in the air and every half-dressed female on the stage dived for cover. Of course, all the girls was instantly arrested for indecency and Granddaddy was thrown in the calaboose."

We whistle with wonder and Tulip's eyes are bright with awe at the picture painted by Uncle Buck.

"I bet he had a hidden pistol and shot his way out of the jail," he suggests.

"Hell, no, son," chortles Uncle Buck. "He'd made enough dough by then to just buy his way out. He paid off the sheriff, settled up with the girls, and high-tailed it back to Granmaw. End of story."

He leans back into his seat with a broad grin on his face and jerks his big old Stetson down over his forehead. "Now, I'm gonna get me forty winks here in what you English folks call sunshine, so I'll see ya later fellas. And don't mention a damn word of what I just told you to yer maws!"

*

Tulip and I decide to take a trip down into town so we leave with our rich-pickings rustling and jingling gratifyingly in our pockets. Aunty Dot has recovered from her tussle with British Railways and is gassing away at full throttle about everything from the filthy state of our railway-carriage toilets to the wondrous attributes of her new king-size refrigerator. Uncle Buck waves a big hand as we exit the smoke-filled front room.

Our journey down the hill is interrupted by a surprise encounter with Ronny. Normally such a meeting would be an amicable affair involving a bit of teenage banter, a fag-break, and a mutual exchange of trivial news. On this occasion, however, things are a little less relaxed. Ronny has in tow his sedated mother and that abomination of nature that he glibly calls a 'cat'. Tugging at the end of a long piece of rope, the malformed beast is hissing and spitting at anything that moves. It is only the fact that it is wearing a muzzle (clearly hand-crafted by Ron from an old wire lamp-guard) that Tulip and I have the courage to cross the road to talk.

"I thought you were returning that thing to its owner," I say.

"Presume you mean the cat," he grins. "No, man. I decided to keep him." He jerks a thumb at his mum. "Besides, the old lady needs some company since Nemesis here accidently ate her dog!" I resist the mild temptation to request further details. Ronny turns to his mum and beams kindly into her glazed eyes. "Company for you, isn't that right, Mum?" She smiles wanly and brings her dilated pupils round to focus on me.

"Hello, Patrick. We've got fairies in the house," she says. "Do you have any, dear?"

I smile and nod kindly. "As a matter of fact my cousin Adrian is one," I offer. This seems to please her so I steer Ronny to one side. "What the hell sort of medicine is your mother on?" I ask.

"Medicine?" he giggles. "No, man, we've been smoking grass and listening to the MJQ. I've been reading her some Ginsberg and Kerouac." He winks theatrically at me as though I have even the vaguest idea what he's talking about. Meanwhile, Nemesis is circling us menacingly at the end of his tether, at which, metaphorically, I am too. Tulip and I move on with a wave and Ronny wishes us well in his inimitable style.

"Crazy, man, crazy!" he calls. You said it, Ron.

We swan into the Tarantella like a couple of Mafia bosses, waving a pound-note at Momma Bonetti and ordering two ice-a cream sundaes.

"And we don't care that it's Friday!" quips Tulip.

Momma Bonetti swipes him with her tea-towel and turns with a chuckle to prepare our luxurious indulgencies. We make our way to our usual seats by the toilet door. Funny how they are always vacant?

Before I even have time to light up a fag, Tulip comes out with his latest and most idiotic suggestion to date. "Let's open a summer whorehouse?" he declares, and I can see by the manic glint in his eyes that he's serious. Clearly, Uncle Buck's extravagant liberties with his family history have infected my Belch friend's imagination. I snort with derision and almost choke on my cigarette smoke.

"Have you finally lost the few remaining marbles rattling around in that tin-can skull of yours?" I ask. He grins on relentlessly, shaking his head resolutely. A bad sign.

"No, mate," he says. "Think about it. This town is crawling with blokes our age on holiday looking for a bit of fun. It's a potential goldmine."

"No, Tulip. It's a potential year in Borstal," I snap.

I'm already getting a queasy feeling about this, and it's the same feeling I get just before reluctantly agreeing to go along with it! What's the matter with me? Has my brain no mind of its own, or vice-versa? I really am beginning to wonder lately if I have the complete set. It's almost certainly my mother's fault. She was responsible for ensuring that I was a healthy foetus. And it's no good her complaining that she couldn't get hold of enough food coupons to feed me in the womb during the War because, from what I can gather, half the US Army was howling at our front gate. I've been told by reliable sources that she went without nothing whilst the Yanks were here. I don't mind admitting there have been times when I have questioned my own conception! In fact, I'm still in the process of checking back on dates when Dad was on leave. It's all a bit of a grey (or khaki) area. Could I possibly be half Yank? My mother is Cornish, so would that make me a Conk, or Yarnish? I have no way of telling.

But, back to my present dilemma. Where is my willpower when I need it? Ah, yes, there it is… hiding behind that sugar-coated turd called 'adventure'. With absolutely no encouragement from me, my brain manoeuvres my vocal chords into action. "And, anyhow," I blurt, "how many females do we know who would possibly be interested?"

Do you believe in Divine Intervention by the Almighty? Or, in this case, Infernal Interference by Satan? Either way, what is happening as I speak is not your everyday coincidence. Swaying down the aisle towards us, espresso coffee in hand, is none other than 'Two-hand Ruth', Fayling Grammar's fifth-form 'Relief-manager'. Her talent, as you may have deduced from her nickname, is ambidexterity and is practised in various hidey-holes around the buildings and grounds of the school. By some quirk of nature, Ruth is able to maintain perfect synchronisation whilst hand-servicing two young bucks at the same time. Not only that, she enjoys her work tremendously.

"It's an omen!" whispers Tulip as he gestures to the empty seat beside me. "Come and join us, Ruth," he calls. She halts and regards us with a look bordering on suspicion, but approaches us cautiously and sits down. Tulip beams amiably and taps his fingers rhythmically on the table in a business-like manner. Ruth eyes him as you might an inadequately restrained lunatic.

Let's get one thing straight: Ruth is no looker. Tall for a girl, spindly in stature and afflicted with acne of the chin; add in protruding teeth and poor eyesight which requires her to wear thick-lensed NHS spectacles, and she ain't Brigitte Bardot. Having said that, she is a generous soul, has a wicked sense of humour, and is popular with girls as well as horny boys. (She is also an accomplished virtuoso of the recorder, that pitifully crude musical instrument that would dearly love to be a flute but can't quite make it. At least Ruth can squeeze something resembling a tune from it which is more than can be said for the mangled cacophony wafting from the music room at school on Thursday afternoons. If you can imagine twenty castrated hoglets being mustard-gassed inside an empty oil drum, you've got an idea what it sounds like.)

Tulip offers her one of my cigarettes and lights it for her with my Zippo. "How would you like to earn some easy money, Ruth?" he asks. She stirs her coffee, pulls on her fag and exhales the blue smoke into her lap.

"I've already got a Saturday morning job," she answers.

"Oh," says the Belch entrepreneur. "What's that then?"

"I do two hours at Rudds Butchers. I operate the sausage machine. Mr Rudd reckons I make the best sausages he ever saw."

Why am I not surprised at that? Ruth seems to have cornered the market in finger dexterity. Tulip leans back in his seat and folds his arms, temporarily perplexed; but not for long. He taps the side of his nose and smiles at her.

"Yeah, but my offer will pay you for doing what you actually enjoy. You know… your other hobby."

Ruth allows herself a coy grin as she sips her coffee. "You mean, you'll pay me to play the recorder?" she frowns. Tulip laughs and shakes his head.

"No. Your *other* hobby," he announces. "And we'll pay you two bob per hand."

I feel a trifle neglected during this conversation and now Tulip is negotiating terms without prior discussion with me. But should I be involving myself with this? It's a bit outrageous, even by our usual standards. Nevertheless, my rebellious brain seems to have decided for me.

"Where does all this criminal activity take place then?" I blurt. "On a bench along the sea-front? Or how about the sausage-pulling room at Rudds Butchers? Sounds appropriate somehow."

Suddenly, the jovial wobbliness of Momma Bonetti appears beside us bearing two towering ice-a cream sundaes. She slides them onto the table and flounces off, chortling in Italian. Ruth stares at us and adjusts the specs on her nose.

"You two just robbed a bank or something?"

We laugh and Tulip says, "Close, Ruth. We just robbed a Yank!"

In between slurps and sighs of ecstasy as we devour our lavish concoctions, the dialogue turns to my earlier enquiry regarding a venue for the forthcoming naughtiness. Ruth has agreed to participate and comes up with a most surprising suggestion.

"My Aunt Mary will let us use her caravan if you slip her a packet of fags."

Tulip and I gawp at her in disbelief. To what sort of family does Ruth belong? She looks at us and giggles for a moment before explaining. "You all know her. Irish Mary who lives in the caravan by the old quarry? She's my dad's sister."

Tulip drops his spoon into his empty glass and lights up a Senior Service. "You mean, Irish Mary? The town drunk?" Ruth nods, and a beam of delight illuminates Tulip's face. He spreads his palms on the table. "Well, that's absolutely honky-dory!" he says.

I am beginning to get that gnawing feeling of doubt and impending disaster again. Or could it be the pint of ice cream and half-pound of raw fruit I've just consumed. Whatever it is, it feels familiar.

\*

So here I am on a warm summer afternoon, embroiled once again in one of Tulip's crazy adventures. I'm sitting at a small picnic-table immediately outside Irish Mary's decrepit caravan which nestles among a small grove of elder trees just off the track leading to the town tip. Ruth is busy in the caravan attending to two naïve young holidaymakers who have parted with five shillings each of their pocket-money for what my mad partner described to them as 'the experience of a lifetime'. The caravan is literally shuddering from the activity taking place within. These lads are the second pair to appear so far and Tulip has departed to the sea-front to harvest another brace. "I'm telling you, Brillo," he enthused earlier, "it's like shooting fish in a barrel. They can't wait to pay up and get here!"

My companion at the table is none other than Mary herself, well inebriated by now and coughing her lungs out on the packet of Players we gave her. She pours herself another shaky tumbler of whiskey, lights up a cigarette from the stub of the previous one and stares across at me. I have spent the past hour listening to her life story, from her roots in rural Ireland, born into a family of twelve, through her calamitous and chaotic childhood, at the mercy of her father, her brothers, the village priest and, eventually, a subhuman husband, and on to her employment in a fancy household in London where she was subjected to every degradation imaginable by the perverted politician who employed her. I'm not kidding, by the time she'd finished her tale, I was reaching for the whiskey myself.

"So then, young feller," she drawls. "What have you bin up to with moy niece... what's her name," she waves her hand vaguely in the air, clearly seeking inspiration.

"Ruth?" I ask.

"Dat's the one," she leers. "Now, have you bin seeing to her, or somet'ing?"

I can only guess at what she means but it's probably a good guess. "No, no. We're just school friends."

She nods sagely and almost slips out of her seat, spilling her drink on the table-top.

"Well, dat's a good t'ing, so it is. All de same, boyo, here's a sloice of advoice for preventin' unwanted pregnancies," she winks theatrically. "Always get off one stop before yer destination!" and she cackles into her tumbler like a witch. I imagine she's referring to some kind of Catholic birth control procedure.

Our disjointed tête-à-tête is interrupted by a sudden eruption of noise from the caravan and, to my dismay, Ruth steps out into the bright sunlight and heads off down the track. I jump up and call to her and she turns.

"I've had enough of those two cheeky twerps," she shouts. "They asked me to put a flippin' paper bag over my head or they couldn't finish. Bloody nerve!"

I'm totally lost for any kind of response and simply stand here like the prat I am. I shove my hands in my pockets and watch Ruth disappear round the corner. As a parting shot of consolation I yell to her. "Tell Tulip he owes you eight bob!" But she's gone.

The two unsatisfied customers emerge from the caravan buttoning their flies and with trouble written on their faces.

"We want our money back, mate," demands the short, stocky one.

"Yeah, it's a ruddy fiddle," grouses his spotty companion. "She was in too much of a rush. And, anyhow, we can get this done back home for nothing."

"That's right," nods his mate, "and by a much better looking bird too."

I have some quick thinking to do here, not a talent I can claim to have. But, to my astonishment, my usual sluggard of a brain comes up with a brilliant counter attack.

"OK, OK, lads," I say. "You deserve some compensation," and I gesture towards Mary, slouched at the table in a fog of cigarette smoke. "So, she'll carry on where Ruth left off."

Mary swivels slowly in her seat, salutes the boys with her wavering whiskey tumbler, and gives them a big, Irish grin. Admittedly, she would appear a little more alluring if she had her teeth in, but I think it's done the trick. The two disappointed punters back away from the hideous spectacle before them. I do believe I have the upper hand (if you'll excuse the expression) so I press on with the advantage.

"So, what do you say, boys? She's obviously up to the task... look, her wrists are shaking already!"

They turn and scurry away down the track and, just to turn the screw a bit tighter, I follow them for a few yards urging them to stay and get their money's worth. But they are not persuaded.

I return to the caravan to find that Mary has taken herself off to bed. Smoke drifts idly from the open door and the rattle of her cough startles the sparrows among the elder branches. I notice that she has taken the whiskey bottle with her so I'm unable to sneak a quick swig. Not that I like the stuff much but, until Tulip turns up, I'm here on my own.

I light up a fag and settle back into my rickety chair. Memories are flooding back to me of earlier days spent in this abandoned quarry when we would scour the lower slopes, kicking the scree around looking for fossils. Some interesting ones have been found here and we always hoped to discover something unknown. It never happened, but folks still come up here occasionally, searching for that elusive missing link. And, talking of missing links, where the hell has Tulip got to?

The smoke emerging from Mary's caravan is increasing by the minute. I can only imagine that she is taking a leaf from her niece's manual and holding a ciggy in each hand. No wonder she's got that hacking cough.

To my relief, Tulip appears on the track and jogs up towards me. He collapses into the adjacent chair and blows a large raspberry. "I just fired Ruth," he pants, "for gross misconduct and dereliction of duty."

"Did you pay her?" I enquire.

"I had to," he grunts. "You have no idea how strong her grip is when her hand is squeezing your nuts! They're still aching now."

I sigh deeply and throw him a Senior Service. "I gather, then, that the whorehouse has closed for the season." He shrugs philosophically and nods.

"We came out of it with a small profit."

"Of?"

"Four and six," he mumbles.

We have no need to discuss it; this has been an unmitigated flop.

Clearly, successful private enterprise is an art we have yet to learn. Perhaps the vice trade is beyond our scope at present.

"What's that crackling noise?" says Tulip, turning his head to look at the caravan. "Christ, Brillo... Mary's on fire!"

We leap from our chairs and dash to the doorway from where smoke is now billowing. From inside we can hear Mary's gagging cough and her feeble cries for help.

"Can you hold your breath for about thirty seconds?" says Tulip. I nod and we throw ourselves inside, dropping to our knees where the smoke is a little less dense. We immediately locate Mary who is on her hands and knees on the floor and obviously completely confused as to where the exit is. Feeling our way, Tulip and I grab a leg each and scramble backwards dragging a squawking, wheezing Mary with us. Tumbling out of the doorway, we manhandle her away from her little home in the woods just as the whole caboodle goes up in flames with a fearful roar. Boy, that was close! The elder trees that hug the old caravan are joining in the fun now and it sounds like a fireworks display as they pop and squeal in the heat. Lifting the smoke-blackened, whiskey-sodden Mary at all four corners we dump her down out on the quarry track and lie back in the grass rasping and coughing.

"On the whole," gasps my Belch friend, "this has not been a good day."

I sit up and look down at Mary. "No, mate, and it's not over yet. She's still on fire!"

And so she is. Her smut-encrusted cardigan is displaying a large smouldering hole which is growing like some brightly fringed amoeba as we watch. Let's face it, with all that alcohol inside her, Irish Mary could go up like an incendiary bomb. We tear at the cardigan buttons and they fly off like bullets, only to find that the grubby blouse beneath is already alight. We pull Mary into a sitting position and Tulip supports her whilst I remove the dangerous blouse.

But there is something amiss amongst all this feverish activity. Call me a Neanderthal if you wish, but, even as I am engaged in this act of human compassion, I am getting that old, ear-twitching, hair-raising feeling again. We are being watched. I snap my head round towards the quarry entrance and there they are... Burgess and Maclean, the terracotta troublemakers, demons in brown. They stand side by side, both with a pin-hammer in one hand and a lump of sandstone in the other. The fossil-hunters from Hell. God only knows how their despicable little minds will interpret what they are witnessing.

"Brown Owl," bawls Janet/Burgess over her shoulder, "that horrid boy is here again!"

"And he's taking off the lady's clothes, Brown Owl!" chirps Olive/Maclean.

"The fish and chip boy is here too, and the lady is smoking."

With this information floating back to Hettie, I can but only speculate as to the image forming in her head. 'Two sex-crazed teenagers having their way with some promiscuous, cigarette-puffing strumpet in broad daylight' springs to mind.

Hettie appears behind them, gaunt and menacing, and stares up at the smoke rising from the elder copse. She glances our way, says something to the girls, and, to our horror, approaches us. I clamber to my feet, still holding the smouldering blouse. Tulip stands too, callously releasing his grip on Mary's shoulders and she collapses back to the ground with a grunt and a cough.

"What's going on here?" enquires Hettie. "Did you start that fire?"

"No, no," counters Tulip. "We've just pulled this poor lady from her burning caravan."

"Yeah, we probably saved her life," I add, sensing an opportunity to ingratiate myself with Her Browness. I hold up the tattered blouse like a courtroom exhibit. "She was on fire, you know."

Hettie glares down at the prostrate Mary then turns to call to the girls. "Janet and Olive, run to the nearest house and ask them to call the fire brigade and the ambulance. Hurry now!" The spy-lettes scurry off with glee.

Mary, lying now in a state of partial undress, half opens her eyes and peers up at Hettie. A puzzled frown creases her blackened brow and she smiles wanly.

"Is that yerself there, Father Dooley?" she asks.

Hettie glares down at her with undisguised contempt and inhales indignantly. Tulip leans towards me and whispers in my ear. "She thinks Hettie is old Dooley the Catholic priest."

Mary winks a languid eye up at Hettie and mumbles on. "Help yerself to a drop of the Holy Fire-water, Father. T'is in the usual place." She struggles to lift her weight onto her elbows and takes a hard look at her own breasts, heaving like two quivering grain-sacks against the constraints of her grubby bra'. "Oi don't think oi'm up to any hanky-panky today, Father. Oi'm not feeling meself at all!" (So, debauchery amongst your flock is not restricted to the clergy of the C of E. Vicar Whicker has a rival right in his own backyard.)

But Hettie has seen and heard more than she can stomach. "How distasteful!" she mutters, and backs away, giving us all a final glower of utter disgust before turning and striding off. She summons her brown brood and they move down the track in single file, pausing briefly at the bottom to allow the fire-engine to lurch past, bell jangling loudly.

To our amazement, who should tumble from the fire-engine cab with the crew but ace reporter 'Clanger' Bell. He waves to us and hurries across, note-pad in hand and a wild look in his eye.

"Great fire, lads!" he exclaims and falls to one knee beside Mary who has opted to lie flat and close her eyes, much in the manner of an Irish corpse. Clanger scribbles in his pad as he inspects her. "OK, so it's 'Woman pulled from inferno by heroic local lads', is it?"

"Hang on a minute," cries Tulip. "We don't want our names all over the Fayling Gazette."

"Alright, alright," says the ever-resourceful Clanger. "'Mystery teenagers rescue frail woman from blazing caravan'."

How can you reason with a person who talks exclusively in newspaper headlines?

In no time at all, the firemen reduce the blackened skeleton of Mary's caravan to a pile of steaming ashes and begin packing their equipment away just as the ambulance judders to a halt amongst us. Albert Tucker hops out, readjusts his hearing aid, and strides over to the recumbent Mary. He stoops down and places a hand on one of her breasts. Is there a pulse here, I ask myself?

"So is this Iris Carey with thirty-three burns?" he snaps. His partner, Cyril, sighs and ambles over muttering to us over his shoulder.

"I've told him once already… it's 'Irish Mary with third-degree burns'."

One of the firemen wanders across and grins down at Mary. "Smoking in bed again, Mary?"

She opens her eyes and chuckles. "Is that you, Superintendent? Help yerself to a glass of the hard stuff, why don't yez?"

The fireman shakes his head and re-joins his mates. It seems that Mary has a soft spot for a man in a uniform, and, by the sound of it, there must be a queue forming outside her caravan on certain days.

Albert and Cyril are struggling to slide Mary's considerable bulk onto the grounded stretcher. She grunts and whimpers a bit, but eventually they heave her up and trundle towards the rear of the ambulance.

"Is that you there, Cyril?" I hear her ask as they slide her aboard. "Jaysus, is it Tuesday already?"

*

My luck is in when I return home to find the house empty. Dad will be working and my mother has probably driven Aunty Dot and Uncle Buck round to visit Aunt Gwen and Adrian. A brief glance in the downstairs hall mirror reveals my smoke-blackened face and I have no idea how I would have explained that to the household Gestapo. I make for the bathroom, taking the stairs two at a time, and run a hot bath.

Now, wriggling my toes in the bath-water, I observe how the ripples tend to break the film of filth on the surface into little islands. I wonder if each island has its own population of bacteria and, if so, will they fight for independence or try to form an alliance and maybe a federal state? On the other hand, who gives a tinker's toss?

My thoughts mull over the day's events: the railway station debacle with Aunty Dot; the creation of Fayling's first whorehouse, followed swiftly by its staff walk-out; and, of course, the roasting of Mary and the subsequent intervention by the emergency services. Tulip and I still have reservations about Clanger's promise to leave our names out of the grand scoop he thinks he has lined up for tomorrow's Gazette, but Tulip says he has some sordid information about Clanger's apparent lust for the chief editor's typist (something about a peep-hole in the ladies' toilet wall)... so we don't expect any trouble from him.

All in all, though, the day went quite well and I learned even more about the frail and peculiar nature of the human animal. I wonder how much weirder it can all get as I progress through my life? My suspicion is... heaps.

# CHAPTER 11

## *Wonderful Time Up There' (Pat Boone…1958)*

Bliss is getting your own bedroom back.

The Yanks have moseyed on down to the bus station and skedaddled out of town pronto. Aunty Dot insisted on travelling by bus as she now has a morbid fear of railway carriages. I have to say, I enjoyed the company of Uncle Buck although the house did reek of stale tobacco smoke when he left. My mother has spent the last twelve hours since their departure hoovering, polishing, and dusting anything that doesn't move. God, it's been a nightmare. Even the cat has moved into the shed to escape the holocaust.

But here I am once more lying on my own bed and gazing up at a smooth, freshly painted ceiling; not a crack in sight. Actually I quite miss them. I think my favourite was the dolphins and the combine harvester. But now, as I look up, there's nothing to stimulate my imagination. Plain, seamless white does very little to evoke bizarre images. It must be pretty boring to be an Eskimo. No wonder they go around beating the brains out of seals to relieve the monotony.

I reach across the bed and lift my trusty Framus guitar. What a glorious shape it is, all curvy and sensual, which instantly reminds me of the opposite sex and, specifically, my darling honey-hips, Wendy. Down in his lowly lair, Wee William twitches his approval and begs to be released. He's very much like a dog when you think about it: never happier than when he's being exercised and always glad to see you and wink his eye.

I resolve to give Wendy a call and see if she will be attending the Youth Club this evening. Oddly enough, Fayling's only regular meeting place for the younger generation is an old timber hut in the grounds of the Catholic church. Here, each Friday night, Father Tom Dooley (yes, same name as our hero in the song) presides over a motley assembly of local youth and endeavours to instil some Christian morality into us. Privately, I believe he is trying to indoctrinate us into the Catholic faith and worship the Pope but, to date, I know of no-one amongst us who can understand why anyone would want to revere someone who wears a frock and lives in a country the size of Paignton Zoo... other than Grace Kelly. As for his grovelling obsession with the woman claiming to be simultaneously a virgin *and* a mother, well, frankly I don't get it, although she undoubtedly did. Nevertheless, Father Tom does his best with the club and we get to listen to our own records, play snooker, and ogle birds.

It happens to be Friday today so I lie back and dream of the coming evening. It's Wendy's one night off from waitressing so I'm confident of a positive response when I ring her. What will she be wearing when I meet her, I ponder? Something tight-fitting I hope.

The next thing I know, I'm awaking from a shallow slumber during which I had an interesting dream. Wendy and I have arrived at the Youth Club hut to find it deserted but, mysteriously, with the record player churning out 'Blueberry Hill' by Fats Domino. Wendy hops onto the little stage and, to my immense joy, begins a striptease routine. It's all going well until, at the moment she begins to remove her panties, an acrid smell invades the room and she runs sobbing from the room. I awake with the noisome stench of charred toast in my nostrils. Bugger! It must be breakfast time.

"I was just about to call you, Colin," chastises my mother as I saunter into the crime scene, or kitchen, as she overconfidently calls it. I glance casually at my Swiss timepiece, grunt, and flick idly through the pages of the newspaper on the table. A plate of contorted sausages in the company of a badly savaged egg appears before me. Two slices of the infamous burnt toast are riding shotgun on the edge of the plate. I'm certain my mother, who claims to have an artistic bent, believes that this massacre is a minor culinary masterpiece, and I don't have the inclination to disillusion her at the moment. I merely tuck in with limited enthusiasm, avoiding the toast by slipping it beneath the Gazette for disposal later.

"I've got shopping to do," says my mother, "so lock the door when you leave." She removes her pinafore and hangs it behind the door. "Oh, and don't forget, my lad, you promised to go round and mow your gran's lawn."

So I did, and, had I remembered in time, I would have had breakfast at Gran's. How curious that my mother failed to inherit any of her own mother's talents in the kitchen. Too busy chasing blokes probably. Pity her tarting didn't include making some.

\*

Gran opens the cottage door and gives me a hug as I duck inside. I poke my head round the sitting-room door to shout hello to Gramps. He twists round to see who's disturbing his morning scrutiny of the Daily Sketch, tuts loudly, and turns back to his paper. "Beggaring boy!" he mutters.

In the tiny scullery-cum-kitchen Gran brews me a cup of tea and sits me down to a mammoth slice of her marvellous fruit cake, the world's best. She always does this, no matter what time of day I call. Tea and cake… the British Empire was built on it.

We chat for a while and then she accompanies me out to the garden shed where the old mower is kept. Gramps keeps it well-oiled so that it's permanently in tip-top condition for me to mow his postage-stamp sized lawn. He could do it himself, even at eighty, but he says he's only got time for his vegetable patch and, anyhow, grass is for sheep. Oh, and then there is his war wound that he got in 1917. Funny how that sharp pain in his buttock comes on at the exact moment the grass reaches two inches. I'm not sure Gran knows, but I once heard the late Bill Potter (you may recall Ronny and I accidentally murdering him a couple of weeks ago) claiming that Gramp's injury was received, not on the front line, but on the front porch. According to Bill, Gramps had one leg over the window-sill of the French madame's bedroom he was exiting one evening when monsieur returned home unexpectedly and emptied one barrel of his shotgun into the Tommy's rear end. I believe it.

When I've mown the grass, Gran lets me use their newly-installed phone to ring Wendy. Gran seems very pleased with the Bakelite wonder and says that it keeps her in touch with the big, wide world. Not that she's actually made a call herself yet, but she's received dozens! I laugh and spend a few minutes showing her how easy it is and she soon masters it. Don't you just love her?

Wendy says yes, come and meet her outside the hotel at seven but she has to hang up now because she's busy being a chambermaid. And that reminds me, I too should be at work; I promised to help Dad rub down some paintwork at the vicarage. Vicar Whicker wants his soffits touched up. I would have thought he gets enough of that round at Mrs Lee's.

*

Vicar Whicker almost runs me down as he hurtles out through the vicarage gate on, what appears to be, a brand-new bike. Maybe he missed his normal Thursday assignation yesterday with Mrs Lee and is desperate to make up for lost time. I hope that she's up to the task and not out of her head again on Ronny's mysterious 'grass'. Ho hum, the curious antics of our elders and betters! But no time to dwell on it because, like the good vicar, I must be about my father's business.

"Hello, son," calls Dad from the top of the ladder. "Will you carry on rubbing down here while I pop into town to price up another job?"

It seems he's getting really busy lately. I hope he doesn't have plans to make me the 'Son' in 'Paddick and Son'. Fortunately, my mother would kill any such notion as she still has ridiculous fantasies of me becoming a doctor or the Minister for Transport.

I scramble up the ladder and watch Dad's van lurching out into the road. He really should get that clutch fixed. From this lofty vantage point I can see right across the vicarage gardens and into the adjacent cemetery. There's a new grave being dug by some bloke I don't recognise and I shudder at the memory of poor old Bill, so cruelly cut down in his dotage by our explosive device. I can also see the Church Hall and a carnival float parked beside it. People are working on it, painting it up for the Fayling Festival next week.

Ah yes, the Fayling Festival; three days of unbridled mediocrity during which half the town population suddenly imagines it has a flair for something. We get a glut of pathetic Art Exhibitions (yes, my mother enters every year and consistently fails to receive even a 'Third'), Open Gardens, amateur dramatic events (usually a spectacularly awful outdoor production of Gilbert and Sullivan excerpts by FLOPS), talent shows and beach entertainments. The whole fiasco culminates in the Fayling Carnival, traditionally the only day of the month that we get a downpour. Of course, we local lads enjoy it if only because of its dreadfulness. There is also the opportunity of leering at scantily clad crumpet that often bedecks the carnival floats. Sadly, the theme this year is 'Space Travel', and the chances of sighting near naked female astronauts is as good as nil.

"Hey, Brillo! What are you doing here, man?"

Christ Almighty, I nearly fall from the ladder! It's Ronny hailing me from the drive and strolling along like it was his own. And, can you believe it? He's got that bloody monstrosity with him, prowling about on the end of a rope and hissing at the world in general. No, not Mrs Lee... Nemesis.

"Au contraire," I reply, gripping the ladder to steady myself and surprising myself on the residue of French conversational gems still lurking in my head. "What the hell are *you* doing here?"

"Everything and nothing, man," he smiles. Has he been consuming his moonshine or smoking that stuff again? But he continues. "I've got the freedom of Whicker's greenhouse, remember? Know what I mean?" He taps the side of his nose inscrutably.

"Not a flaming clue, mate," I answer. Ronny laughs and, thankfully, winds in Nemesis a couple of feet to prevent him attempting to climb my ladder. Ronny looks up at me.

"Me and the Vic, we've got an understanding, man," he says. "Each time he pays a visit to our house, I come over here to tend to... uhh... my plants in his greenhouse. Perfect conditions in the shade amongst his tomatoes. It's a hot-house. Cool, eh?" I don't see how it can be both but I nod anyway. "Wanna come and see them, daddy-o?" he asks.

"OK," I say. "But tie that freak up somewhere safe first."

When Ronny pulls open the rusting metal-framed door to the greenhouse, we are almost bowled over by the hot blast of sweet, humid air that hits us. Wow, it must be a hundred and ten degrees in here! As we amble down the baked earth aisle, I am astounded by the sight of enormous ripe tomatoes that dangle from the column of tall plants stretching away down the greenhouse. It's like a giant's larder in here. Every now and then, Ronny halts to stoop down and inspect some strange little bushes with long, slim, serrated-edged leaves. At each location, he carefully adjusts the tomato greenery around them to keep them almost hidden from the light and then moves on to the next one. Occasionally, he nips off a leaf and rubs it between his fingers, sniffing it with obvious satisfaction.

"Pretty much ready for harvest," he murmurs.

"So, what exactly is it then, Ron?" I enquire.

"Never you mind, daddy-o," he says with another wink. "The less you know, the less you tell. As far as the Vic is concerned, it's called 'Moroccan Mint' and keeps aphids at bay." He chuckles oddly and wanders on down the aisle, nodding and smiling to himself. He may be right, there isn't an aphid to be seen.

It's too hot in the greenhouse so I wait for Ronny outside in the shade beneath the vicar's fig tree where I enjoy a few moments of bland thought and a Senior Service. Before lighting up another fag, I conclude that Ronny's horticultural duties are going to be lengthy so I return to undercoating the woodwork. Half an hour or so later he's standing at the base of my ladder, gazing upwards with that far-away look in his eyes again.

"Hey, Brillo," he croons. "You wanna know what I'm doing for the Festival this year, man?"

In truth, I couldn't give a narwhal's nipple what he intends to contribute to the weekend's farce-tivities. As I recall, last year he tried to enter one of his grotesquely overweight guinea pigs in the Pets Corner feature but was expelled from the Church Hall and the contest when his exhibit broke loose and mauled some kid's rabbit to death. We should have guessed back then that he was breeding freaks.

"I'm sending Nemesis into space," he announces seriously, tweaking on the length of string that is attached to the neck of the mutant beast. I need to descend the ladder as quickly as I can because the convulsions of laughter I'm experiencing are putting me in peril of falling off.

Ronny squats to give his ghastly creation a tickle under its quivering chin and runs a loving hand along the deformed spine.

"Well, when I say 'space', I mean up in a rocket," he adds.

"Oh, well, why didn't you say?" I manage to splutter. "That's OK, then."

"You wanna see the rocket, man?" asks a deadly solemn Ronald. My attempts to answer him take some time as my ribs are aching with mirth, but I manage eventually.

"What, you've got a rocket-man too?"

I have to sit on the ground to catch my breath whilst Ronny smiles benignly down at me. He pulls me to my feet and we set off for his house as I briefly recall my vow never to enter his property again. But, hey-ho, life is an adventure.

*

You have to give Ronny credit... he always surprises you. If he says, 'Do you fancy a drink?' he's got a full-size 'still' dispensing raw alcohol; ask him to manufacture a harmless exploding cricket ball, and you get a cunningly disguised hand-grenade; he asks you to come and see his 'rocket', and your eyes pop out of their flippin' sockets! Let me fill in a few important details.

At the rear of the Lee's garage, and almost obscured by decades of ivy growth, is an old stone-built wash-house and ancient 'privvy'. Time and total neglect have reduced the building to four shaky walls, the roof having caved in years ago. But, when Ronny pulls open the rickety door, stands to one side to allow me to peer inside, and gestures triumphantly at his creation, I am lost for words. My jaw literally drops with utter astonishment. Supported by scaffolding, standing at least eight feet tall, and with dappled sunlight playing on the surface of its gleaming metallic sleekness, is a perfect replica of a space-rocket, complete with fins. Its nose pokes skywards beyond the roofline, as though trying to sniff the stratosphere. It even has a Perspex capsule at its point, large enough to hold, say... a freak cat! Christ on a Vespa, he's serious!

I turn to look, first at Ronny, then down at the tethered Nemesis, lying unusually quiet in the shade licking its paw. I turn my gaze slowly back into the dilated pupils of the mad genius.

"You're not?"

He grins and nods. "Oh, yes I am."

I step inside the shed, or launch-pad as he calls it, and walk around this incredible contraption, running my fingers admiringly over its smooth surface as I try to take in the wonder of it. Ronny appears, holding what looks at first glance like a black house-brick.

"Remote-control," he explains. "Watch this, man."

And, to my astonishment, the fins begin to waggle from side to side and, with a barely audible squeak, the nose-capsule opens on hinges, giving the rocket the appearance of a hungry shark opening its jaws. I slap a palm to my forehead in awe. "Wow!" is all I can come out with.

He assures me that it is perfectly capable of launching into the air and tells me how he built it with the help of his uncle who was an aircraft design engineer during the war.

"What fuel does it run on, then, Ron?" I ask.

"Can't you guess, man?" he chuckles. He nods towards the garage. I stare at him in disbelief.

"Are you telling me you got me sozzled on rocket-fuel?" I explode.

"Not entirely," he grins. "You had orange juice in yours."

No wonder I entered old Nozzer's shop at the speed of light!

"I need to give it an engine test," says Ronny as he flips open a panel on the flank and twiddles nobs and presses switches. "Pass me Nemesis will you, man?"

"You're joking!" I laugh. "I'm not touching that killer."

"No, he's fine. I've sedated him with some of Mum's pills. He's out until breakfast time."

Yes, as all normal cats should be, Ronald. He scrambles onto the lower scaffolding and holds out his hand. "C'mon, Brillo. Pass me the First Cat in Space."

To my relief, he takes the dozing monster from me and feeds it neatly into the capsule compartment. "First time he's been in here," he beams triumphantly, "and he fits like a glove."

Ronny steps back down to the ground and tells me to move up the yard a bit because when the engine fires up it could get very noisy and a little draughty. He closes the shed door and joins me at the opposite end of the yard where we slide the two dustbins out in order to crouch behind them. To my amusement, I notice that Vicar Whicker's bicycle is now exposed, leaning against the wall.

"Block your ears with your fingers, man," advises Ronny. "The rocket engine might be noisier than I anticipate. This is my first test ignition," and he pulls his ancient ear-muffs into position.

Suddenly, the engine fires with a deafening roar and, in no time at all, the whole launch pad/shed is shuddering as it struggles to contain the thunderous noise and vibration. Holy Buggery, this is dangerous! The back yard is a maelstrom of dust and leaves, and the fumes from the burning fuel are choking us.

Ronny raises a thumb and yells in my ear that he's going to the rear of the shed to turn off the fuel, but he finds that his progress is limited as he fights against the blast from under the shed door. Meanwhile, I squeeze myself up against the back door in an effort to escape the worst of the dust-storm and, as I am thus engaged in self-preservation, a curious event unfolds. The back door suddenly flies open and the vicar emerges, his high-powered spectacles askew on his face, his cassock slung over his shoulder, and one foot in his trousers. He hops around, frantically trying to manipulate his loose foot into the spare trouser leg and as he revolves amid the whirling dust-storm he catches sight of me. He lurches towards me and grasps my shoulders, shaking them vigorously, his podgy face contorted with terror.

"Save yourself, boy!" he yells, his voice breaking with emotion and his lower lip quivering. "This is Armageddon. Our sins have been revealed!"

Well, yours have, reverend, that's for sure. Your trousers are in a tangled heap attached to one shoe and your dog-collar is flapping in the wind.

The noise from the old wash-house is now rising to a deafening roar and I can only assume that Ronny has failed to switch off the fuel. Smoke and fumes are bursting from the gap at the bottom of the door, firing small stones around the yard like a Gatling gun. A sinister orange glow flickers high up among the few remaining rafter stumps, growing brighter as the vicar shields his ashen face from the onslaught. He seizes my arm once more and stabs a finger towards the driveway.

"The day of Judgement is upon us, my son," he screams. "Follow my example, run home and pray for your soul!" And with that, he grabs his bicycle, swings his free leg over the crossbar and cycles away like a mad-man, his trousers thrashing the ground with every revolution of the pedals. His hysterical entreaties continue as he flees. "Forgive me, Lord. I am a sinner. Accept my so…" But his voice is drowned by the next interesting episode.

Accompanied by an ear-splitting shriek from the rocket, the wash-house door crashes open on its hinges, the scaffolding collapses outwards and my smarting eyes are privileged to witness Ronald's masterpiece rise from its nest and storm away into the sky. Nemesis is airborne! Ronny appears with the radio-control in his hand and a look of pure bewilderment on his face.

"Jesus Christ, man. It's escaped!" he blurts as we both gaze skywards at the rapidly ascending tube. We dash out into the road to get an unrestricted view of the rocket's progress. It must be about three hundred feet above us now, glinting saucily in the sun as it banks slightly and begins to arc over the town. Ominously the engine seems to have cut out and, as it glides earthwards, I am instantly reminded of those film clips of 'doodle-bugs' in World War Two.

Meanwhile, the good vicar has come a bit of a cropper just down the road and is standing beside his fallen velocipede and pulling at his trousers which have become entangled with the chain. To add to his vexation, Albert Tucker, minus his hearing aid, is out walking his dog and stops to engage the vicar in a one-way conversation. Even from thirty yards away we can hear them.

"Hello, then, vicar," bawls Albert. "Bit of bicycle and trouser trouble?"

"Don't concern yourself with my tribulations," pipes the vicar, hysterically. "Our lives are ending and there is too much to lose. The Apocalypse is upon us!"

Albert throws back his head and laughs. "What? Our wives are spending too much on shoes? You're telling me, reverend!" and he pads away chuckling, oblivious to the falling rocket which has unaccountably burst into life again and has veered off on a horizontal

248

trajectory to the ground at about fifty feet above the road.

Ronny is having a fit with the radio-control. I am afraid his career as a space pioneer is going to be a short one, as is Nemesis's. In utter frustration he throws the control to the ground and covers his eyes, terrified, I guess, that his 'magnum opus' is about to destroy a large section of residential Fayling. But, as though touched by the hand of God or Wernher von Braun, the capricious craft zooms over the head of the fleeing vicar then loops sharply to approach us. We hit the deck as it thunders over our heads and watch as it roars vertically into the sky, levels out and disappears over the town and out towards the bay. We leap up onto a garden wall, just in time to catch sight of it plunging into the sea. What a relief for Ronny! All evidence destroyed and dead cats tell no tales. But his months of hard work and brilliant engineering have been wiped out in a matter of minutes.

Ronald, however, is ecstatic. "Holy shite, man," he crows. "Did you see old Nemesis in the capsule? I swear he was grinning from ear to ear!" He sits on the wall and gazes wistfully out over the roof-tops. "Well, amen, man," he murmurs. Do I detect a quaver in his voice? Did he really love that cat-freak? I have no way of telling.

Returning shakily to the vicarage to recommence my chores, I find an air of excitement is abroad. Two police cars are parked on the drive and Mrs Beer, the vicar's housekeeper is scurrying down the path towards the adjacent church in the company of three policemen. She is clearly in a state of extreme anxiety, talking non-stop and gesticulating wildly at the church, so, being of a somewhat curious nature, I tag along at a reasonable distance to eavesdrop on proceedings.

We are all startled when the church bells boom into life. It's definitely not the time of day for bell-ringing practice nor is there the vaguest hint of a wedding. Moreover, had there been a wedding party within earshot, they would immediately have demanded their money back because whoever is pulling those ropes hasn't got a clue. It's just an ear-bashing cacophony of clanging bells. And, incredibly, as though summoned by those very bells, here comes another one… Clanger rides up on his brand new Lambretta. Before he's even flipped the stand down and dismounted, the Fayling fire-engine arrives. How the hell does Clanger do it? It's like a sixth sense.

Fortunately, there are now enough people milling around for me to infiltrate surreptitiously and glean further information. There's nothing quite like a good glean. I position myself behind Mrs Beer as she gabbles her story to the police sergeant.

"He come 'ome half-naked on his bicycle, ran into the church, and locked 'imself in," she babbles, dabbing her eyes with a handkerchief. "I can't get no sense out of 'im, Sergeant. 'E's ravin' in there about the end of the world and 'is dinner is proper spoilt. Hearts with gravy. Stuffed."

I imagine they are by now. She blows her nose and sobs whilst the sergeant rubs his chin reflectively and peers up at the tower. In fact, all eyes are attracted to the tower because the bells have ceased ringing and, lo and behold, the vicar is now making a personal appearance up on the ramparts. There he is, arms outstretched and gazing at the heavens, trouser-less but undaunted.

Ace reporter, Clanger, moves in amongst us and slips a comforting arm around Mrs Beer's waist. "Tell me, Mrs Beer, is that the vicar's bike on the ground over there?" She nods tearfully and Clanger tightens the grip around her waist. "Why do you suppose the vicar's trousers are attached to one of the pedals?" he leers with arched eyebrows. The housekeeper slides her hanky over her mouth, as though attempting to stifle any words of betrayal. "I really have no idea," she whispers. But she has no need to cover for her eccentric employer's indiscretions because he is now confessing all.

"Lord!" he bellows from his lofty pulpit. "I have sinned. I have been a fornicator and I have led your lamb from the paths of righteousness and into temptation." A reference, I guess, to his unbridled naughtiness with Mrs Lee. "Strike me down, Lord, if it be your wish on this final day of judgement! I am not worthy." Worthy, though vicar, of an Oscar for a truly outstanding performance.

The police sergeant asks Mrs Beer if she is aware of any other way into the church.

"Yes," she answers, perking up and nodding. "I've got the key to the vestry side-door," and she scuttles away towards the house.

From the tower, Whicker continues his nauseating repentance, spreading his arms wide and lifting one oil-smeared, gartered foot onto the rampart. "Lord, I bow to your will and beg for your mercy. I have gazed this day upon the fearful countenance of the Devil himself as he roared above me in his chariot of fire." He removes his spectacles and polishes them briefly on his fluttering underpants before continuing. "He did covet my soul, Lord, but..." At this point his sack-cloth and ashes entreaties are interrupted by the sergeant's tinny appeal through a loud-hailer handed to him by a constable.

"Now come along, Reverend. Let's calm down and talk this through over a nice cup of tea, shall we?" he implores. The vicar places his hands on the battlements and stares down at us.

"Are you mad?" he laughs.

"No, but you bloody are," mutters a constable.

Whicker gushes on regardless. "The Day of Judgement is upon us and you offer me a cup of tea! Better to offer up your soul, my son, and pray that the doors of heaven will be open for you."

"Yes, and the doors of the loony-bin will be open for you, mate," snorts the police constable.

There is a lull in the proceedings whilst the police and firemen convene to discuss tactics and have a fag. Mrs Beer appears once more, trotting towards us bearing a dirty great iron key before her like an Olympic torch. Sergeant Hallet takes it and summons a constable and a burly fireman to follow him. Moments later, we spot their heads bobbing into view up on the ramparts. The vicar, clearly startled, turns to confront them brandishing a large wooden crucifix.

"Get thee hence, Satan," he cries, "I have gazed upon thy face once already today."

"Yes, yes, Reverend," soothes the sergeant, removing his cap. "See, it's me, Des Hallet, one of your parishioners."

"Ha!" explodes the vicar, backing up against the stone ramparts. "Satan has many guises," and he thrusts an accusing finger down at the fire-engine. "Is that not your fiery chariot below?"

Hallet nods reassuringly and gestures towards his companions. "Yes, and here is a fiery-man to help you down. Please, now let's descend."

"Descend thyself, Beelzebub, back to thy hellish kingdom!" yells Whicker, hopping agilely back up onto the parapet and standing defiantly, his bare white legs astride and his shirt-tail fluttering bravely in the breeze. But that's as far as it goes because the fireman has clearly had enough. He swoops upon him, slings him over one shoulder in the classic fireman's lift, and hauls him away out of sight.

The stand-off is over. The Devil has once again had his day and the rescue team very soon appear at the vestry doorway. The vicar, his mangled trousers, a distraught Mrs Beer and the entire entourage make their way back to the vicarage. I have no doubt that stuffed hearts and gravy will be shared out and enjoyed by all… with the exception of Whicker himself. Above the murmur of their fading voices, I hear Clanger's strident enquiry ringing out:

"Anyone know anything about a strange object falling into the sea today?"

Ah-ha, Clanger, you missed that one, old mate!

*

Having a full-length mirror in your bedroom could be construed as gross vanity, but I consider it a must for a young buck-about-town. How else can he check that his jeans are sitting correctly on his suede shoes, that his powder-blue jacket is hanging well below his rear, and that Wee William is making progress in the inch department? As it happens, everything looks more than adequate this evening and I close the bedroom door behind me with a glow of smug satisfaction. Should Wendy's eyes light up with admiration and desire when I call for her, I will know that my efforts have not been in vain.

My own peepers are certainly not disappointed when I arrive at the West Cliffs Hotel and Wendy appears, looking like a million dollars, to greet me at the side-door. But I have no feeling of inferiority being ushered in through the 'tradesman's entrance'. Am I not a sort of tradesman tonight? I have the tools of my trade with me: a pair of furtive hands, two eager lips and, should the job require a professional finish, a spruced up and raring to go Wee William.

Wendy is a picture of gorgeous perfection. I believe she has put on a modicum of weight and it really fills her out into every corner of her luscious curviness. I sit on the edge of her bed and watch her making her face up (not that it needs improvement but you know what girls are like). Unfortunately, her young sister Janet (Burgess) is lying on her own bed in the tiny bedroom reading 'Black Beauty', so there can be no early-evening hanky-panky. Well, at least the little sod is showing complete indifference to my presence and seems to be far more relaxed while she's wearing 'civvies'. I wonder if a brown uniform has the same effect on her as it did on Oswald Moseley?

As we walk up the narrow gravel path to the Youth Club hut, we see that Father Tom is in his usual position just inside the door and blessing everyone as they enter. Tonight he has to bless a little louder to compete with Little Richard extolling the attractions of 'Miss Molly', but old Tom smiles just the same.

It's hot inside the club and smells of that incense stuff that Father Tom waves around during his Mass. Why he brings it in here, I have no idea. Somebody once told me it's to erase the smell of Irish whiskey on Tom's breath, but that's a bit uncharitable. Maybe he's hoping it will tranquilise us all.

Anyhow, there's a decent crowd of local kids in here tonight, plus one or two young holidaymakers who have obviously honed in on the music. Billy Rice, Jeff, and Mike are lounging around sucking on bottles of Coke and watching Tulip teaching Anthea to play snooker. They are bickering, so I guess Anthea is winning.

Most of the other kids present are younger than us so we lord it over them a bit. Nothing nasty, you understand, just that age-old dog-pack thing. We also get a little more respect by being the only Rock 'n' Roll band in town.

I halt to inspect the goodies on sale at the 'Refreshment counter', a trestle-table manned by two grovelling girls from Fayling Grammar third-form. Strewth, they can't do enough for me. What the hell would they be like if a real rock star suddenly turned up? Wet their pants, I reckon. I manage to wrest a couple of glasses of orange cordial from their jittery hold, smile condescendingly, and join Wendy on one of the clapped-out sofas.

Mike reloads the record player and we sit around, tapping our feet to Bobby Darin singing 'Dream Lover'. Tulip and Anthea have embarked on a full-blown argument centred on Tulip's accusation that she nudged the cue-ball twice when lining up to pot the black, thus taking the game. It's entertaining at first but becomes boring after a few minutes, much like Father Tom's Sunday sermons. Oh, and here he comes.

He stands before us, legs apart and hands clasped behind his back in the standard stance of indulgent adults. "It's good to see youse all here tonight, kids," he says in his quaint Irish brogue, and whips a hand round to reveal fingers clicking erratically to the rhythm of the music. "I do like Buddy Darin," he fawns.

"He's not as good as Bobby Holly," smirks Jeff, a trifle cruelly. But Father Tom simply nods and beams amiably.

"We've organised a bit of extra entertainment for youse all tonoight," announces Father Tom, and, as though awaiting their cue, a minor commotion at the door heralds the entry of a group of adults, all clad in period costume. This looks very ominous to me, those costumes look familiar and, yes, my worst fears are realised: FLOPS have arrived, led in by that conceited fop, Quentin Lamont. Thankfully, my mother is not amongst them.

We rise from our seats and form a tight huddle behind the snooker table, where we can observe from a distance. Father Tom hauls his large frame up onto the little stage and instructs one of the refreshment girls to knock out the record player. A collective groan issues from our ranks as Bobby Darin is promptly throttled in mid-song. The ragbag assembly of pirates and tarts group themselves around the piano where Quentin has positioned himself on the stool and is flexing his ginger fingers as though he was about to perform Beethoven's Fifth. Father Tom continues.

"Thank you, boys and girls," he growls. "We are honoured dis evening wid the presence of a small section of our local loight opera society..." a murmur of dissent rises from various corners of the room, cut short as Tom raises his voice and sweeps an arm in the direction of the smiling performers, "...who have very koindly agreed to give us a selection of songs from their forthcoming production of 'De Poiritts of Penzance'." More muttering from the floor... "Now, please, a warm hand for Quentin and his troupe." I'd give him a warm hand alright, right across his arrogant chops! The refreshment girls clap wildly.

Lamont scrapes the stool closer to the piano, removes his three-cornered hat and adjusts his eye-patch (a convenient accessory since he is still sporting a black eye, courtesy of Police Cadet Lipscombe). The chorus members group themselves tighter around the piano, the ivories chime, and they burst into song. God, it's awful!

We turn to one another and grimace, giggle, or raise our eyebrows in disbelief. But all is not lost and, give Lamont his due, he usually provides good entertainment .. his piano playing excepted. And, as we all know from past experience, mayhem is his constant companion on his travels. In less time than it takes to keel-haul a cabin boy, someone has managed to irritate him. The unfortunate 'someone' today is Iris Trimble, sister to our celebrated Brown Owl, Hettie. Iris, though, could not be physically different in appearance from her gaunt and towering sister even if you made it up. Plump, purple-faced, and topping four feet eleven on tip-toe, she must by necessity, command a front row position in the chorus. Today, due to the limited floor space on the stage, her generous bosom is almost resting on the piano bass notes and her face is, consequently, but inches from Quentin's. Furthermore, and sadly for a would-be soprano, Iris is tone-deaf. Her vocal agility in veering a semi-tone either side of the required note is breath-taking.

Thus, a mere halfway through their second rendition, the pianist loses his rag altogether. Crashing both his forearms onto the ivories in a monumental jarring discord he leaps to his feet, eyes bulging with rage and sending his chair flying backwards.

"For Christ's sake, Iris," he bellows. "If you can't squeeze the right note out of your mouth, put a bloody sock in it!"

We all freeze with shock and astonishment at his outburst. Glancing swiftly at Father Tom, I see the rapturous smile shrink from his face and notice his casually clasped hands turn into scarlet fists behind his back. The colour runs up his bull-like neck like the rising tide and the veins expand into purple cables. This time Lamont has overstepped the Mark, Luke and John. 'What kind of blasphemous lunatic,' I sense Father Tom asking himself, 'have I invited in to charm my youthful flock?'

To our delight, pandemonium has broken out on stage as supporters of Iris seek to comfort her as she collapses into tearful distress. Two of the male members are remonstrating with Lamont who has removed his chair to centre stage and is sitting, puffing on his empty cigarette holder in a majestic sulk. Whether this is some form of method-acting or just a big fairy having a strop, I have no way of telling.

Needless to say, we plebs are enjoying this unexpected turn of events. Not only has Lamont's tantrum completely scuppered the pirates, but the drama taking place is worthy of several awards. And things are about to hot up as Father Tom takes it upon himself to enter the fray by hopping up onto the stage on a peace-making expedition. But, like all well-meaning missionaries, he goes blundering in and finds himself heading for the cook-pot. He's about to learn that you can't arbitrate between warring pirates but, being Gaelic, perhaps this fact has passed him by. (Although I'm sure there must have been Irish pirates because the life would have appealed to their inbuilt sense of lawlessness. After all, they certainly came into their own in the American West and produced a string of talented desperados. Maybe, when piracy was in its heyday, the Irish were too busy trying to invent a meal that didn't contain potatoes.)

But the other oversight that Father Tom has made when dealing with buccaneers is that they are armed to the bloody teeth! OK, this is a band of pitiful thespians whose most sadistic member is a dentist, but get 'em riled up, and they'll immediately reach for their weapons. In no time at all, steel cutlasses are flashing as the company disintegrates into scuffling factions supporting Iris, Lamont, or simply trying to bag a Roman Catholic priest. I bet this is the finest piece of theatre ever to have been seen on this modest stage and there is no doubt that many festering old scores are being settled here.

"Do you think we should call the police?" asks an anxious Wendy, squeezing my hand.

"Nah," says Jeff, "those sabres are all blunt. The only dangerous weapon up there is Lamont."

"Yeah, and what would they charge them with?" I add. "Impersonating an actor?"

"Ham-acting without due care and attention?" offers Billy.

On stage Father Tom is taking a beating but he's putting up a gallant defence. His main target, I'm certain, is Lamont, but he's finding it hard to get a sound purchase on him due to the general melee. Curiously, Iris herself has now turned upon him with Protestant venom and is making some extremely inflammatory remarks about the Vatican. Tom is doing his best to reason with her whilst fending off vicious swipes from a sea-boot wielded by Betsy Brown the local wool-shop proprietor.

"I'll fix this," mutters Mike, and ambles over to the electricity fuse-box and throws the main switch. The whole room is plunged into an eerie twilight and the kerfuffle on stage fades. The silence is broken, however, by one solitary thump followed by an almighty crash and a shriek from the refreshment girls. Mike re-illuminates the room and we gasp in awe as we observe Lamont spread-eagled on the collapsed trestle-table amid shattered glasses and packets of Smiths crisps.

A degree of calm returns as cutlasses are lowered, plastic daggers sheathed, and sea-boots pulled back on. People assist the superficially wounded to chairs and the dentist examines bleeding mouths for broken teeth. The only exception to the sudden outbreak of mutual compassion is Father Tom. With a youthful and purposeful agility, he vaults from the stage and, flexing his knuckles, he approaches the reclining Lamont who lies, dazed and prostrate, on the refreshment table. Kneeling down, Tom places his big hands around Lamont's scrawny neck and nonchalantly begins to throttle him. The felled actor gurgles and jerks hideously, his manicured fingernails tearing at Tom's grip in desperation.

"Oh God!" cries Wendy, jumping to her feet. "Shouldn't we help him?"

"Why?" says Tulip casually. "He's quite capable of strangling him on his own."

"I think we should do *something*. There'll be no Youth Club if Father Tom is de-frocked," points out Anthea the diplomat. Mike nods in agreement and strolls across to where the attempted homicide has now slid from the table to the floor. Father Tom glances up as Mike bends to whisper in his ear and, nodding pensively, his powerful hands spring away from the thespian throat. Lamont rolls to one side, gulping air like a large ginger trout. Tom then clambers to his feet and marches off to his little office, wiping his hands on his handkerchief as though he had just been handling something disgusting. The office door closes behind him and we hear the distinctive plop of a cork being released from a bottle. Holy water, no doubt.

We ask Mike what he said to Tom to bring him back from the brink. "Oh, I just reminded him that FLOPS were making a donation this year to the Youth Club indoor-toilet fund and that murder still carries the death penalty, even if the victim is an imbecile."

Finally, the procession of battered buccaneers exits stage left and files snootily past Lamont who is sitting on the floor kneading his throat with his fingertips. The refreshment girls offer him a glass of water from a dangerously cracked glass but he refuses with a wan smile. As she passes, Iris tosses the musical score at him and the sheets flutter down around his hunched figure like autumn leaves. How miserable he looks, slumped there in his dishevelled pirate outfit, his eye-patch covering one ear and beads of sweat vying for attention with the freckles on his brow. I believe this could be the crunch for Quentin, erstwhile darling and leading light of the Fayling Light Opera and Pantomime Society. His reputation is surely sullied beyond redemption, as are his new pantaloons. How the mighty are fallen!

But the evening is not without a final twist of fate for yours truly. Pushing his way forward, head and shoulders above the exiting chorus members, is the unmistakable figure of Danny Zawadski. And, lo and behold, he's in the company of Caroline. How bizarre is this? Danny tows Caroline by the hand and stands before us, his lips stretched in that dazzling Hollywood smile.

"Hey, kids," he chuckles, nodding at the disappearing column of bedraggled songsters. "What's all that about? I was up to my buccaneers in pirates!"

Tulip laughs and I glare at him. Meanwhile Danny is undressing Wendy with his Tony Curtis eyes. "Hi, Wendy," he grins. "Still waiting?"

Curiously she blushes and stares at her feet. If I was more of a man I would smack him in the mouth. What the hell is wrong with Wendy waitressing for her parents in their own hotel during her summer holidays? Better, surely, than *his* pathetic part-time barman duties and petty thieving. And, to her credit, Anthea springs to her friend's defence.

"As a matter of fact, Danny," she says, "Wendy does more work in a day than you do in a month!"

Danny merely grins all the wider and turns to Caroline with a sigh of mock resignation.

"Hey-ho, kiddo," he drawls. "Looks like we're not welcome here. Let's take a ride shall we?"

For some unknown reason, Caroline peers at me with a look of pure distress, almost a plea for help in her eyes. I give her a half-hearted smile and she turns to follow Danny as he makes his way past the recumbent Lamont who is being assisted to his feet and manoeuvred to the door by the refreshment girls.

The record player is fired up again and Jerry Lee Lewis bursts into 'Whole Lotta Shakin' Going On'. Jeff and Billy help the girls reassemble the refreshment table and Mike tidies up the scattered furniture on the stage. Tulip breaks the red-ball triangle in preparation for another thrashing from Anthea and, to my delight, Wendy pulls me down onto the rickety sofa and begins to snog me relentlessly. I am the King of Fayling.

# CHAPTER 12

## *'It Doesn't Matter Anymore' (Buddy Holly...1959)*

Something is up. No, I'm not referring to Wee William, Ronald's rocket, or the price of Senior Service. This is serious. I am unable to make any contact with my darling nectar-lips, Wendy. I've tried phoning, writing and, much against the grain, even asking Anthea to intervene. All to no avail; not a dickie-bird has been forthcoming. There's only one strategy left: a full-frontal assault. I will present myself at the West Cliffs Hotel.

I pull open the door on my dilapidated old wardrobe and whisk out my black suit. It needs a bit of brushing but, otherwise, seems fairly presentable considering that I now wear it every Saturday playing in the group. Apart from a small cigarette scorch on a lapel and a shiny area where my guitar rubs against the jacket, it's in reasonable nick. Good enough, I trust, to impress Wendy's parents and wheedle some information out of them.

Within minutes, I am spruced up to the nines, black leather slip-on shoes gleaming, and one of Dad's 'sensible' wide ties complementing a clean white shirt. All in all, a picture of sartorial elegance and polished gentility never before seen between these four walls. I even flatten my Elvis quiff in order to present a less cocky image. All that is now required is to jot a quick note to Wendy and seal it securely within an envelope, liberally inscribed with kisses on the back. Surely her parents will allow her to receive a personally delivered letter.

To my annoyance, my mother catches sight of me as I creep furtively down the hall. With my hand on the door handle and a mere two-inch thickness of stained wood separating me from liberty, her voice rings out from the kitchen.

"Oh, Colin, how smart you look! Are you going for an interview or something?"

"Sort of," I cry, clicking shut the door behind me and striding briskly down the path. This is not technically a lie. In my estimation, 'sort of' covers almost anything and everything. I do believe I'm getting the measure of my mother. Mind you, it's taken sixteen years.

Loosening my tie slightly, I set off confidently down the hill towards the sea-front. I get a few curious stares as I progress and the Lucas sisters lower their shopping bags to the ground to watch me pass.

"My, my, Colin," says one. "You do scrub up well."

"Going for a job interview?" asks her sister.

"Funeral!" I call cheerfully.

Their faces drop and they enter into an intense whispered exchange, racking their brains trying to recall who has kicked the bucket recently.

I make my way along the High Street, ducking and weaving through the hordes of seemingly semi-conscious holidaymakers who wander the town in gormless awe of the trashy delights on offer. They stand in untidy groups cackling at bawdy post-cards; they confront you, three abreast slurping on pink ice creams; they stray into the road and shout obscenities at vans that swerve and hoot their horns. If only they would just put their feet up at home for two weeks and send us their money and teenage daughters.

I slink guiltily past the revamped fish pond as I climb the front steps of the West Cliffs Hotel. Memories of that terrible day peck at my brain, but I cast them aside and clamber on. To my astonishment, I am confronted at the hotel entrance by the sight of a gleaming, newly installed revolving door. This must be a first for Fayling and even eclipses the extravagance of the art-deco front doors of the Half Moon Hotel. I push my way forward and jog into the reception area. A bold approach, you may think, but this is a mission requiring valour and testicles of steel. My love for Wendy drives me on. (Well, that and the edge of the bloody revolving door which slams into my backside on my entry.)

My first impression is that the reception desk is unattended until I hear a grunting sound coming from behind it. However, my jaunty approach and business-like rap on the counter produces the startled faces of Mr Matthews and his female receptionist rising from the floor. As you know, I am of a suspicious nature and cursed with a lurid imagination, but I sense an air of hanky-panky here.

Mr Matthews indulges in a short fit of theatrical coughing and waves a sheaf of A4 papers around as though offering this as a reason for being on the floor. The receptionist slips swiftly back into her chair and begins to type frenziedly. This unexpected sleaze is all very interesting and could serve me well as ammunition in my attempt to contact Wendy.

Standing here with my note in my hand, I am suddenly overwhelmed by a feeling of confidence. My brain, far from displaying its usual bout of rebellion at times of stress, remains crystal-clear and fully functional. I drop the envelope onto the Formica countertop and place my palms down each side of it. Mr Matthews backs away a few inches and begins to reshuffle papers that his glamorous receptionist has just neatly arranged in a tray.

"Can I help you, young man?" he enquires, his eyes narrowing as he gazes at me. Recognition is dawning, I fear. "Do I know you?"

"Carp," I utter abruptly.

"I beg your pardon?"

"Fish pond."

He inhales and draws himself up to his full height. "Ah, yes," he hisses through clenched and, apparently, unstable false teeth. "So, to what do we owe the pleasure of *this* particular visit then?"

I've no idea why he's being so sarcastic. I was led to believe that the debacle with the koi was long forgiven. From his attitude today, you'd think I was a hit-man from the Mafia or, even worse, an Inland Revenue inspector. Obviously he bears a grudge.

"I was hoping to see Wendy," I state. His jaw sags and a steel shutter seems to drop in his eyes. The colour rushes to his face and, for a moment, I half expect him to vault over the counter and kick me to death. He retreats to the receptionist's chair and grips the rear of it as though summoning up his resources for a counter attack. And here it comes. Striding forwards he leans across the counter and glares straight into my somewhat startled face.

"Are you one of the grubby little oiks that have been bothering her lately?" he snarls.

I grab the envelope and hold it up defensively but firmly. "No. I just wanted to speak to her. We've been seeing each other on and off all summer."

"Hah." he snorts, "'on and off' just about sums it up from what I can gather!"

What the hell has got into him? I notice the receptionist's shoulders heaving and this unnerves me even more. Is he having some kind of malicious fun with me? He certainly looks serious though. His eyes are almost popping out of his head. I wave the envelope forlornly. "Well, would you mind just giving her this?" I ask a little more contritely. He merely screws his nose as though I had offered him a fresh dog turd, snatches the note, tears it in half and makes an affected display of tossing it into the waste-paper bin.

"Look, kid," he says menacingly, "she doesn't want to see you or any other greasy little bugger who can't keep it in his trousers!"

The receptionist swivels in her chair with a look of astonishment on her face. I feel I may have an unexpected ally in her and, to my surprise, she suddenly leaves her chair and flounces off down the corridor. Mr Matthews stares after her in disbelief.

"Sandra," he whines, "what do you think you're doing?" But she walks on into the dining hall and slams the door behind her. He turns his attention back to me. "Now look what you've done. I may have to sack her after this," he snaps. I'm beginning to wonder if this bloke is the full shilling.

But I'm not caving in. Confidence is brimming in my breast. After all, has there been even one complaint from his daughter with regard to my behaviour with her? I think not. Am I requesting his permission to ravish her on top of one of his dining-tables? Certainly not. Then what, as they say in America, is his beef? And what's all this talk about greasy little buggers and trousers? I make one final appeal to his sense of common humanity.

"Look, Mr Matthews, I just want to talk to her. I'm very fond of her and…" But he cuts me off in mid plea.

"Just sling your hook, kid," he bawls, turning his back on me. It's perfectly clear that I'm getting nowhere so I head for the revolving door which, once more, catches me in the rear as I exit. Like its owner, maybe it needs looking at by an expert.

With my hook well and truly slung, I descend the hotel steps, each one taking me further down into an ocean of despair. Until, from somewhere behind me, I hear my name being called… well, whispered loudly actually. I turn and there she is, leaning from the balcony immediately over the main entrance, my own delicious honey-lips, Wendy. In a trice, I am transported back in my mind to an unusually pleasant English Literature lesson when we were studying 'Romeo and Juliet'. And now, in an instant, I know exactly what old Romeo was waffling on about: 'But soft! What light through yonder window breaks?' Could a part-time waitress ever look more alluring?

"Colin!" she trills. "I'm sorry."

I climb the steps and stand beneath her, gazing up like a lovelorn twerp. "Sorry for what?" I ask. She gestures with one sweep of an arm.

"For all this… mess. Sandra told me you were here. I just wanted to apologise for my dad and… well, everything."

I shake my head vigorously. "There's nothing to apologise for, but why can't I see you?"

She glances behind her and leans forward again. "Listen, I'm taking Granny to her Bingo session at two-thirty. Meet me outside on the pavement."

"OK," I nod, "I'll be there."

There is a metallic squeak and the revolving door propels a livid Mr Matthews out into the sunlight. "I thought I told you to clear off!" he seethes. "Who were you talking to?" he demands.

"Me," calls a voice from the balcony above and we both look up… to see Sandra peering down. Bloody hell, that was brilliant!

"Sandra, what are you doing in that de-luxe bedroom suite?" snaps Mr Matthews. "Get back down here at once or you can consider yourself sacked!"

Sandra tosses her head and gives a cynical laugh. "Yes, Horace, that's about the long and short of it in this establishment, isn't it: get groped or get sacked!" Mr Matthews steps back in astonishment and points an authoritative finger up at her, but she cuts him off before he speaks. "Oh, give it a rest, you bullying, hypocritical old goat! I *shall* be down in a minute but it'll be to type out my resignation." She then plants both hands on the balustrade, looks up, and a smile spreads across her face. "Hello there, Mrs Matthews," she calls and waves regally. Horace swivels on his heels and stares with horror at the sight of his wife slowly climbing the hotel steps in the company of Granny.

Horace's face has turned the same colour as the concrete terrace and his upper dentures have clearly parted company from his gum. "I'm warning you, Thandra," he hisses.

But Sandra is enjoying her moment of retribution and obviously could not give a tinker's toss for either his top-set or his marriage. She beams sunnily and addresses a stunned Mrs Matthews.

"I was just informing your husband that his summer-long imitation of a rutting octopus has finally worn too thin to endure. And, if you are prepared to accept the advice of a younger woman and ex-army nurse, I would recommend you get him on a course of bromide or, preferably, have him neutered." She then bows elegantly and vanishes from sight.

Mrs Matthews remains transfixed in silent shock, still gripping Granny's arm. Granny wriggles free and shuffles around to face me. "Hello, sailor," she smiles. "More shore-leave?"

I give her a grin as she is led away by Mrs Matthews and, as they disappear through the revolving door, I catch a glimpse of Mr Matthews sitting in Sandra's chair at the typewriter. I wonder if he's typing a suicide note?

\*

As I wend (oops, wrong word!) my way back through the town, I employ all my limited powers of deduction to solve the dual mysteries of my love's semi-incarceration in the hotel plus my sudden status as public enemy number one. But, of course, it isn't as straightforward as that, is it? It's not a case I can crack with forensic evidence like Sherlock Holmes. There's no body to examine (that was in my master-plan for the future). No, this is a complicated jigsaw and I can't find one corner piece to start me off. Why was Mr Matthews so angry with me? OK, he might still harbour a desire to throttle me after the fish pond affair, but for God's sake, I worship his daughter. Is that now a teenage crime, and are we to be pilloried for lusting after crumpet? I got the impression from Tim Lewis (biology and lechery) that it was the sole purpose for our existence.

What I need is some good counsel here, some sound advice from a staunch and reliable friend. Let's see now, who do I know who can give me guidance? Well, adults are out for a start. All I'd get from any of them is a knowing smile and a patronising pat on the head. 'You'll find out one day, son,' they would say. Well, I need to know now.

What about my circle of good friends? Of course, Tulip is a non-starter; his advice would probably involve tunnelling into the hotel from the cellar. Mike? Well, yes, he's older, wiser, and better looking than me, and that's the trouble: he's never been dumped by a female so he might be unable to help. Clanger is out of the running as his only interest would be to run my misfortunes as a weekly feature in the Fayling Gazette. And Ronny? Are you kidding! 'No problem, dadd-yo. Just slip her old man one of these smokes and he'll let you right into her bedroom'. No, this is a mystery for me to sort out myself.

At home I change out of my suit and, finding myself assailed by a sudden hunger, I saunter into the kitchen to forage for food. When I say 'food', I mean something which has escaped the calamitous hand of my mother. A tin of baked beans is discovered lurking in the pantry and an untainted loaf of bread is released from the bread-bin. I turn on the oven grill and slide a couple of thick slices beneath and within minutes I am tucking in to beans on golden toast. The whole culinary extravaganza is complemented by two large pickled onions. A glass of Tizer helps things down admirably and I ask myself, is this so difficult? So how come my mother finds it nigh on impossible to replicate this sumptuous feast? Is there, perchance, some defect in her brain preventing her from functioning properly in the kitchen? She seems to be up to speed in the other rooms.

I push the plate to one side, clasp my hands behind my neck, and raise my feet to rest them on the table-top. In this position (only excelled by moments of deep meditation sitting trouser-less in the company of my friend Armitage Shanks) I am able to do some of my finest thinking. Today, however, I find it difficult to relax. Gratifying as it was to get the better of Wendy's father and to see him squirming in the merciless hands of Sandra, there is still something unpalatable gnawing at my new-born, but fragile, self-confidence. Or could it be those bloody pickled onions? No, it's obvious that nothing will be made clear until I meet Wendy and hear her explanation for the curfew imposed on her.

*

Secreting myself cunningly beside the hexagonal Edwardian post-box that adorns the pavement outside the West Cliffs hotel, I await the arrival of my darling and her grandmother. And, sure enough, here they come, Wendy's hand supporting Granny's elbow as the old lady hobbles gainfully forward with the aid of her walking stick. The love of my life smiles serenely when she spots me and Granny waves her stick in greeting.

"Hello again, sailor," says Granny with a hoarse chuckle. "Jumped ship, have you?"

I beam and nod. "Nice to see you," I say, and give her a peck on the cheek.

Progress is understandably slow as we shuffle our way along the sea-front but the Bingo hall is, mercifully, only about eighty yards from the hotel. Wendy and I make small talk, remarking on the beautiful weather and how Fayling is transformed during the summer season from its dull winter character. Granny, meanwhile, grins and winks at any male she passes and breaks wind with enthusiasm whenever she comes across a particularly handsome specimen. I can only guess at what she was like as a young woman!

The Bingo parlour is more tin-shack than 'hall'. Set back from the road, as though attempting to hide its very existence, it is a wartime Nissen-hut constructed entirely of corrugated iron and painted dark green. Only the gaudily painted sign across its facia tells you that it is still in use. On Thursdays it acts as a venue for the local branch of Freemasons who have installed a bar, segregated toilets, and an emergency exit should an outbreak of fire oblige them to hop out on one leg during one of their ceremonies.

We guide Granny in through the entrance and find her a seat among her regular cronies, a group of dolled-up geriatric girls, some with their teeth in. Granny sinks into her easy-chair with a satisfied sigh and places her large handbag beside her. We hear the tell-tale chink of glass and Wendy pulls me to one side with a look of amusement on her face.

"She's brought her bottle of brandy with her again," she whispers. "There's no alcohol sold at this time of day but you can imagine what this lot get up to."

Granny looks up at us and asks me to get her a cup of coffee from the bar. "Black please, like I prefer my men," and the girls slap their knees and hoot with laughter.

"Now, Granny," chides Wendy affectionately, "please behave yourself while I'm gone. I'll pick you up at four o'clock."

"Don't you worry your pretty little head about me, dear," chuckles Granny. "You just take this handsome young matelot for a walk. But watch out… he can untie any knot!" And the coven shrieks with mirth again.

Wendy leads me by the hand across the road and down the beach steps where we drop into the soft, warm sand under the sea-wall. She leans back against the wave-smoothed stones, draws her legs up and hugs her knees. She stares out wistfully towards the water, saying nothing. I reach over and place a hand on hers.

"Are you still here with me, Wendy?" I ask gently. "You seem a million miles away."

She turns and gives me a melancholy smile. "I wish I was, Colin," she murmurs, and bows her head, eyes closed. "Colin," she whispers, "I'm pregnant."

Now, I've been kicked in the groin playing rugby; I've been publicly humiliated by the Count many times in class; I thought the world was ending when my closest cousin was drowned, but I would gladly suffer these combined hardships, threefold, if I could undo this catastrophic moment. A portcullis of unimaginable disappointment and dejection has come crashing down between us. In a flash, she becomes permanently out-of-bounds to the likes of me, and all my fanciful dreams and naïve plans have instantly been minced. But, simultaneously, lights are turning on in my puny brain, and, even though they offer no compensation, dark mysteries become brightly illuminated by answers: now I understand why Mr Matthews was so obnoxious, and what Danny meant the other evening when he asked Wendy if she was still 'waiting'. Of course, you nincompoop, waiting for her period! And how would Danny be privy to such intimate information unless… unless he is the father?

I am left speechless, not by my normally rebellious frontal lobes, but by the sheer magnitude of her news. But, hang on, let's get things into perspective here, Brillo! It's Wendy's life that's being turned upside-down. Your own life can stumble on more or less uninterrupted without her. It isn't you who will have to give birth to a new human being and suffer the stigma and shame that goes with being a pregnant school-girl.

She hides her face in her hands and lowers her head to her knees. "I don't have to tell you who the father is, do I?" she says, inclining her face to me and peering between her fingers. I shake my head and look away. "I'm so ashamed, Colin," she continues. "You might find it hard to believe now, but I had this dream that, maybe, one day… well… you and I would be together. But I've wrecked it all."

I can't respond; it's hard enough to listen to this, let alone offer her comfort. Let's not beat about the bush, this is adult stuff and we are just kids. Predicaments of this sort are for older people blessed with a bit of life experience, not unworldly children still wet behind the ears.

"There's something I have to ask you, Colin," Wendy says, dropping a warm hand softly onto mine. "I beg you not to tell anyone about Danny." I stare at her in disbelief. Is she going to just let him get away with it? "I know what you're thinking," she continues. "But I told my parents it was a terrible mistake I made with a holidaymaker. I made up a story about some boy I met in the summer. Someone I can't trace. Even Anthea believes it." She rolls her lovely eyes in despair and I see tears welling. "God, Colin, it's awful."

Finally, I am stirred out of my voiceless stupor by sheer compassion and affection for her. "Why can't you tell your parents that it's Danny?" I ask.

"My dad would kill him," she answers emphatically. Oh, would he? Who, Horace the Hypocritic Hero whom I watched crumbling to dust under the onslaught of Sandra this morning? Somehow I can only envisage him popping round to Anthea's house and borrowing one of her dad's Colt 45s if it was to blow out his *own* brains.

"I'm really sorry, Wendy." That's all I can manage. It's pathetic... but it's heartfelt.

"Me too," she whispers hoarsely, and tears begin to trickle down her gorgeous cheeks. "Dad's taking me to Plymouth tomorrow." She glances anxiously my way. "He knows someone down there who can... who can..."

"Get rid of it?" I interrupt a trifle harshly. She simply nods and stares out to sea, willing herself, no doubt, beyond the horizon.

I can sit and listen to no more. I clamber to my feet and offer my hand to pull her up. She accepts and we climb the steps back into the bustle of Fayling sea-front. Strangely, the familiarity of it all seems comforting to me. Outside the Bingo shack she kisses me briefly on the lips, slips her hand from mine, and leaves me to watch her disappear through the entrance.

'So, that, old mate,' says a tired voice from somewhere within my skull, 'appears to be that. You've both been shafted!'

Wandering like a lost soul along the High Street, deep in thought, I am accosted by a man in a white suit who spreads his arms to block my path.

"Hey, daydreamer, why the long face?" It's Dad in his decorator's overalls. I emerge from my cocoon of brooding despair and force a smile.

"Hi, Dad. You working here?"

"Just finished," he gestures at the bright blue paintwork enhancing the Victorian frontage of Down's Music shop. "What do you reckon, Col? We did a good job I'd say."

That's another thing I love about my dad, he's always ready with a word of praise or encouragement, even when it's only half-deserved. After all, my contribution here was a meagre two hours of preparation but Dad makes it as important as his own efforts.

"Don't, for heaven's sake, forget your mother's birthday tomorrow, Col," he reminds me. "At least get her a card," he grins. "Oh, and here's that one pound five shillings I owe you." He hands me the cash, gives me a wink and bends to lift a paint-pot. "See you later, son."

Bugger it all to hell! Yes, I had completely forgotten; but isn't that what males usually do, omit important dates in the female calendar? I know Dad does it at his peril. I recall he once forgot their wedding anniversary and my mother went nuts. She even hired a taxi to take her round to Aunt Gwen's for a monster whinge and Dad had to drive over there during a force nine gale to fetch her. I'd have left her to stew.

By chance, I find myself outside Nozzer Isaac's second-hand emporium, scene of my startling entry to his premises on the vicar's rogue bicycle and the subsequent decapitation of Venus. My heart aches when I remember how Wendy came to my rescue that day. Strewth, I still owe her thirteen shillings and seven-pence halfpenny! But I imagine that's the last thing on her mind right now.

Gawping aimlessly at the random display of used tat that fills Nozzer's window, my attention is drawn to a bright chrome-plated item sitting flamboyantly on its own cardboard box. As I move to one side to get a full look at it, a ray of sunlight catches it and dazzles me with its reflection. Surely this is an omen, a flash of Divine Intervention, because nothing more relevant could possibly materialise at this particular moment. It is an electric toaster! I will buy it.

I glance to the right and become aware of the substantial frame of the proprietor filling the doorway. He stands with his hands clasped behind his back and wishes me good-day accompanied by a broad, liquorice-stained grin.

"It's young Paddick, if I'm not mistaken," he says with a slapping of his oily lips. "My, my, it must be a day for the family. Your lovely mother was in here earlier. She bought a nice little folding stool to restore. Tells me she's taking up upholstery now. Oy vey." He grins gruesomely, sighs and spreads his palms theatrically.

Stone me, another hobby? Let's hope this one replaces oil painting... at least you can shove a stool under the table out of sight.

Nozzer's beady eyes focus on my area of interest in his window display and he shuffles nearer.

"Something catch your eye, my boy?" he asks, popping another Liquorice Allsort into his cavernous mouth. I point towards the toaster and enquire as to its history and price. He nods like an anxious horse and explains that it was an unwanted wedding present brought in by the bride. How sad to think that, like me, some poor bloke will probably spend the next few years attempting to spread margarine on charcoaled toast. The price, to me, bearing in mind my mother's earlier purchase, is a massively discounted one pound ten shillings. Pressing my nose to the window, I can just make out the price-tag of one pound twelve. Nozzer shrugs and raises his bushy eyebrows philosophically. "Business is business, my boy."

We adjourn inside to the shop counter where I pull my masterstroke. "'Fraid I've only got one pound five, Mr Isaacs," I announce, spilling the dosh onto his greasy counter-top. He stares down in horror at the money as though it was a pork chop I had presented, the tip of his tongue darting from one corner of his mouth to the other. This could be unknown territory for Nozzer: giving discount and then being faced with offering more. That or, Moses forbid, losing a sale! Finally, he turns to glare at me for a moment before his face creases into a grin.

"My life, sonny," he chuckles, "you're a sly one. You got a deal, but…" and he slides the toaster cable from the box and snips off the plug with a pair of tailoring scissors "…I'll keep this plug."

Strewth, what a tight-ass! But at least I've played him at his own game and come out with a little glory. I believe he acknowledges it, too, because he calls to me as I leave. "Any time you want a job, my boy, come and see me."

*

The house appears to be empty despite the front door being unlocked. I stand motionless inside the hall listening for sounds of occupation. My past experiences with Lamont and my mother have taught me to be wary of unexpected activity beneath this suburban roof. But there is only the ticking of the front-room clock and the faint humming of the fridge.

Dropping the toaster onto the kitchen table, I begin a search for wrapping paper and string. Ten minutes later I have found nothing better than a large sheet of greasy brown paper folded and shoved in a kitchen drawer. It'll have to do, but I still need some string. Luckily, I recall that Dad keeps a ball of it in the garage.

As I pass the wood-shed, I am aware of voices emanating from the garage, and, adopting my best commando stance, I creep forward to investigate. I slide soundlessly along the outside of the one closed twin door. From here, I am able to discern voices coming from inside the garage and, apparently, from the rear where Dad has his workbench. In no time at all, I recognise the lewd and despicable tones of Lamont in full throttle and clearly engaged in another attempt on my mother's moral downfall. But wait, Brillo, we must exercise caution; we have been here many times before and each time it has proved to be a total cock-up (or not, as things turned out!). Not once have you actually caught them even so much as canoodling. And yet... this little scenario has something different about it. Why are they hiding in the garage? Of course, less chance of discovery. Yes, they're getting crafty. Nevertheless, I have to be certain this time. I press my ear to the door and their conversation resonates through the woodwork. Lamont's voice assaults my eardrums with its shocking vileness.

"You'll have to open your legs wider than that, Marjorie," he grunts.

"Well, I'm doing my best," replies my shameless mother. "Anyway, how wide do you need them for such a short screw?"

Jesus Aaron Christ, this surely must be the jackpot! I risk a quick glimpse inside but I can see nothing from my position. OK, if I can't see them, they can't see me. So, with all the skill of an Amazonian forest Indian, I slip silently into the garage and melt into the shadows behind a set of scaffold-planks leaning against the inner wall. Hardly daring to breathe, I await their next depraved outburst... and I don't have to wait long.

"I really don't think I can get it in from this angle," says Lamont, sighing with frustration. "Lift your bottom up."

What a disgusting goat! But my mother seems to be a willing participant in their wanton abandonment. "Well, Quentin," she declares, "you'll never have much luck with that short little thing."

I can barely believe my ears. She's clearly an authority on the subject. How many has she tangled with in the past, I ponder? World War Two has much to answer for, I fear. But I have heard enough, and I steel myself for my customary shock tactics, safe in the knowledge that, on this occasion, there can be no doubt that illicit rumpy-pumpy is in progress. Steadying my shoulder against the scaffold-planks, I brace myself for the final plunge. And this is the point, of course, when Satan decides that my plans are going far too smoothly. Turning himself into the form of Archie, our cat, he suddenly leans into the calf of my leg and purrs like a Ferrari. Needless to say, I almost jump out of my skin, fall back against the scaffold-planks and watch in horror as the entire stack slides away from me and hits the garage floor with a mighty crash. Through the ensuing cloud of dust I catch sight of Lamont collapsing like a sack of spuds to the ground. My mother, her hands still gripping the legs of the stool they were repairing, stands transfixed with shock as she sees me framed in the daylight of the open garage door. This could be serious.

Archie pads over to inspect the prostrate Lamont, sniffs at the screwdriver he still holds and wanders out the door with his tail in the air. My mother drops the stool and falls to one knee to attend to Lamont who lies with his back propped against the work bench cupboard door and his legs splayed out. She begins to tap his face with both palms in the manner of a pastry cook shaping up a large doughnut. Sounds about right, actually.

"Come along, Quentin," she pleads. "It's all over now."

Lamont blubbers something incoherent and opens his eyes. He stares straight up at me, groans hoarsely, and closes his lids again. My mother turns her head to glare at me. "I don't know what you've done this time, Colin."

Well, if there's any justice in the world, I have rid society of an insatiable lecher, destroyer of theatre props and general bloody nuisance. But, no, Lamont lives to blight another day. Grunting like the foul swine that he is, his tongue lolling on his bloodless lips, he inclines his head to nuzzle into my mother's breast. Do I detect a smug leer on his face?

"He's barely conscious," frets my mother. Barely human, more like. "This... sudden shock you've given him," she rants, gesturing with one hand towards the fallen planks, "...is just too much after all he's endured this summer. What with car accidents and attacks from policemen and priests, it's no wonder he's passed out from exhaustion." Lamont shudders melodramatically and utters the most obscene snuffling noise. "Colin, fetch him a glass of water this minute!" snaps my mother.

"He's probably bluffing," I mumble.

"Quentin never bluffs," she barks. What? He's a flippin' actor!

My pride will not allow me to pander to this twerp so I make a compromise. I saunter over to the bench and reach for the bottle of distilled water Dad keeps to top up his van battery. Blowing the dust and two curled woodlouse corpses from a jam jar, I fill it with water and hand it down to my mother.

"For heaven's sake," she sighs, and grabs Lamont's chin in a steely grip, slopping the liquid into his quivering mouth. Well, that should get him started on cold mornings.

I slink silently from the scene and return to the house with the ball of string. Bugger the toaster, I'll wrap it later. Sweeping it up in the crook of my arm, I retire to my bedroom. To be honest, I'm now feeling thoroughly depressed. Nothing seems to be working out as planned and hoped. Wendy has let me and herself down; our GCE results are late arriving; Russ Conway is still in the Top Twenty; and Wee William remains at a lowly five and a half inches on a good day, in spite of rigorous training. All in all, I feel I have legitimate grievances but who will listen? I think you have to agree, a teenager's lot is not a happy one. Imagine being a teenage policeman!

I throw myself upon my bed and stare gloomily at the ceiling. It remains a pristine, unblemished white, much like my GCE Algebra paper when I handed it in. I certainly do miss those old familiar cracks.

Would you credit it? That insolent dope of a pigeon flutters to a halt on my window-sill and begins his ridiculous Groucho Marx strut along the ledge. Does he honestly expect any self-respecting female to find that sexy? No wonder he has to wear her down with unrelenting dimwittery before she gives in out of boredom. Having said that, Tulip's tactics are very similar.

To my annoyance, the toaster keeps floating into my line of vision and, finally, guilt inspires me to take action. There's no point in trying to ignore it, my mother's birthday is tomorrow. I need to pop down to Woolworth's and buy a plug. After all, it's to my own advantage to have it up and running for breakfast time in the morning.

I swing in through the main door of Woolworth's and, glancing at my watch, I notice that there are only five minutes left to closing time. I head for the electrical counter and my head swirls with fond memories of my exquisite moments with Wendy at this very spot. How bright and romantic these electrical accessories seemed then; now my world is illuminated by a lowly forty watts. But, to my astonishment, who saunters over to serve me but Caroline!

"What are you doing here?" I enquire amiably.

"Working. Isn't that obvious?" she scowls. Hmmm, no improvement in my popularity then.

"What happened to the hairdressing?"

"I fell out with the boss."

"Oh, sorry."

"No, it's better here," she smiles wanly. "More money too."

She takes the plug from my hand and drops it into a paper bag. When she hands me my change, she grips my fingers.

"Colin, can you meet me outside in a minute? I need to talk to you."

I shrug and nod, smiling apprehensively. What on earth could she want to talk about? Does she want to renew our casual relationship? Maybe my performance in Tom Berry's boat was better than I imagined.

I wait dutifully at the staff entrance where she appears with a group of giggling shop-girls and she breaks away to join me. "Let's go to the Tarantella," she says.

We make our way along the High Street and she entertains me with the sorry tale of her exit from the world of hairdressing. It appears that it was all the fault of the appointments book, or rather, whoever entered the booking for the mayor's new young wife in the wrong place. Apparently, her luscious chocolate-dark tresses were transformed to a ghastly streaky blonde when Caroline mistakenly treated her hair with the special bleach reserved for the Fayling

Carnival Queen. She was sacked on the spot.

"It was awful, Colin," she groans. "The poor girl came into the salon a lovely brunette and left as a dirty blonde." Well, from what I've heard about Alf Rendle, the mayor, nothing would excite him more.

We enter the coffee-bar to the sound of 'Livin' Doll' competing with the hissing of that ostentatious Latin twit the Gaggia. In the end, Cliff throws in the towel and hands over to Buddy Holly to try with 'Peggy Sue Got Married'.

Caroline orders espresso coffees and we find a two-seater table. "So what's new, kiddo?" I enquire amiably. She tips sugar into her coffee and stirs it pensively. Taking a sip, she places the cup down, leans forward and looks directly into my eyes.

"I'm pregnant," she says quietly.

Her words bounce around inside my skull like table-tennis balls. Am I having a waking nightmare or one of those déjà vu experiences you read about? Surely I heard these self-same words uttered earlier today by my ex-love Wendy? I slump back into my seat and stare at Caroline in disbelief and gathering terror. My magnificent defloration beneath Tom's tarpaulin... has it come back to haunt me for ever? Am I about to find infamy as Fayling's youngest father?

Caroline smiles thinly and shakes her head. "Don't worry, Colin. It's not you," she assures. "It's Danny."

A wave of deliverance rolls over me and the butterflies that invaded my stomach have mercifully been netted by her words. Of course, she's been seeing the Polish stud all summer. Her moments with me were probably just light relief from the bad treatment she almost certainly received from him. Ah, well, another lesson in life, Brillo!

"What's he going to do about it?" I ask, reminding myself not to mention his catastrophic recklessness with Wendy.

"Not much by the look of things," she sighs. "His dad tells me he's vanished, probably into the merchant navy."

Yes, that would be a fairly safe exit for him. He could sail the world, implanting offspring in every port with no responsibilities to hinder him. The bloke is a loose cannon... and he doesn't fire blanks!

Come to think of it, I bet that's how half the population of the world was created!

Without thinking, I ask her if she is planning to keep the baby or get rid of it. What an insensitive drip I am! But she takes it quite calmly.

"Dunno yet," she shrugs. "My mum wants me to terminate it by drinking gin in a hot bath… but gin always makes me ill."

Isn't that half the point?

"Put some lime juice in it," I suggest, but she just screws up her nose and sighs heavily.

"I think I'd rather have the baby."

Christ, she really must hate lime juice! Ah, well, I tried.

*

I awaken to the sound of rapping on my window and, turning lazily between the sheets, I squint and try to focus on the bright rectangle of sunlit world. Can you believe it, that deranged pigeon is tapping on the glass with his beak! I reach down to the floor for a suitable missile and hurl a slipper at the window. It hits the glass and drops to settle on the inside window-sill. The dopey bird cocks his head to inspect it and then starts his ridiculous courting routine, mincing up and down and cooing enticingly. Let's be honest, only an idiot would want to get intimate with an inanimate object. On the other hand, Tulip and Anthea's relationship springs to mind… and Anthea, I have to admit, is no idiot.

Sitting on the edge of my bed, I run my fingers through my hair and attempt to concentrate on the one hundred and one things I must do today. I rub my eyes and stare at the wardrobe, and soon realise that, in fact, there's nothing pressing at all. OK, it's my mother's birthday but I have seen to that. Her present awaits her on the kitchen table and, if I'm lucky, there might be an air of cheerfulness in her demeanour. In other words, perhaps there will be a temporary truce in our hostilities.

But what the hell is that smell? It's considerably more pleasant than the customary pong of my socks. In fact, it's an aroma never before sniffed beneath this roof during our occupancy. It is the scent of perfect toast!

I dress hastily and scramble downstairs to investigate this incredible phenomenon, all the while scarcely believing my nose. But it's true and the proof is here before me. As I burst into the kitchen, my eyes are immediately drawn to a plate brimming with everything a young gentleman should expect for his petit dejeuner. Well-tanned sausages snuggling up to a glistening fried egg; two healthy tomato halves sailing jauntily on a sea of baked beans; and, arranged in precise layers on a side plate, the world's first example of Number Three Bannockburn Grove Perfect Toast! The sight is eye-popping, the aroma mouth-watering, the architect beaming with pride as she stands still holding the frying-pan. It's a miracle, nothing less! We could have another Lourdes on our hands here. Pilgrims might gather at our gate to whisper in awe 'This is where it was first seen. It appeared from nowhere, so they say. The Blessed Toast'.

Dad greets me cheerily from his seat as he tucks in to his own breakfast. "Morning, son. Your mother couldn't wait so she opened her presents last night."

"Oh, Don," chides my mother, giggling like a naughty schoolgirl. "Now you've told him. Anyway, it's a lovely gift, Colin. It works beautifully." It works bloody miracles by the looks of things and, before I have time to sit, she sweeps across and gives me a kiss on the cheek.

"Letter for you," says Dad, waving a brown envelope.

A letter for me? Nobody writes to me, they telephone or yell from a distance. Please God, don't let it be an offer of employment from Tottering and Tripp. I take the envelope and stare dumbly at it, desperately attempting to make out the smudged post-mark.

"Well, open it then, Colin," urges my mother as she moves to stand behind Dad's chair. Oddly, she slides her hands down across his shoulders in a rare show of affection and, to my further puzzlement, he raises his own hands to fold around hers. What's going on here this morning? There seems to be an aura of fondness filling this kitchen, rather than the usual acrid smokiness of failed cuisine. I glance at them both and detect a curious softness in their gaze. My mother has almost a glow about her. It's very disturbing.

I tear open the envelope and out falls a folded square of thin, perforated paper displaying the heading 'University of London'. Oh, save me from perdition sweet Jesus… it's my GCE results! I pick up the paper and force my eyes to focus on the small pink area at the bottom where the subjects and grades are listed in harsh black type. This is, without any doubt, the pinnacle of fear in my short and lamentably insignificant existence so far, and the information on the page is burning a hole in my brain. Finally, my mother whisks the paper from my loose grip and reads the results aloud. "Biology, a two; Physics, a three; French, gosh, Colin, a two; and Geography… oh, my… a one!"

Dad removes the statement from her hand and passes it back to me as my mother lifts her eyes to gaze at me in wonder and pride. I gawp stupidly once more at the results, desperately trying to figure out how I have managed such an astonishing feat. Maybe this is a misprint, or more feasibly, someone else's results. I check the name on the page and on the envelope. Nope, no mistake there. The indisputable evidence staring me in the face is that I have passed six subjects, failing maths by a whisker. The truth is hard to swallow: I am clearly smarter than my vindictive brain gives me credit for. But, hang on, does this mean I may be cajoled into entering the sixth-form after all? It's still a possibility. And would that be so bad now that the Count is incarcerated (along with Vicar Whicker) in a psychiatric hospital, and Soapy Luxmore now holds sway at Fayling Grammar? Not at all, so long as you insist on receiving corporal punishment in some way that doesn't involve bending.

"Congratulations, son," says Dad, pushing back his chair and standing to tap me on the shoulder with his hand.

"Yes, well done, dear," mewls my mother, holding her hanky to her mouth and pulling my face to hers to slap a wet kiss on my cheek. Boy, have things ever changed in the space of a few minutes; suddenly I'm Mr Glitterballs! But, through all this golden air of goodwill and confidence aimed at me, there still lurks something they are sharing that I can't quite pin down. Has Dad won the Football Pools? Is my cousin Phil hiding in the front room, home on leave to surprise me? Am I still asleep and this is all a cruel dream? No, I just burnt my tongue on a hot tomato.

"Good grub, eh?" says Dad.

I glance up from my ravenous chomping and I am immediately stricken with apprehension. The two of them are, well, let's not beat about the bush… canoodling. Yes, there's no other way to describe it: fondling hands and snuggling up to one another. It's all a little distasteful when one is devouring one's nosh, but I lower my eyes, slice into an extremely tasty sausage, and hope they will have finished by the time I'm ready to butter my toast.

"Col," says Dad. I look up again and he's grinning. In fact, both their faces are wreathed in what can only be described as slightly insane smiles. "Son, your mother is going to have a baby!"

I'm sure I will never know quite how I manage to swallow the large section of pork sausage which has just begun its journey south. Dad's announcement seemingly has the effect of halting my entire bodily mechanism. Everything feels as though it has been put on hold, including the function of my oesophagus which, much like British Railways, seems to be on strike and refusing to move anything on its journey. In a state of panic, I take a couple of noisy gulps of tea and, to my relief, the rebellious sausage continues on its course. Meanwhile, the horror-stricken gape I direct at my parents has the effect of mellowing their beams of bliss to looks of benign puzzlement. My mouth falls open and a hoarse whisper rattles from my larynx.

"How did that happen?"

Dad bursts out laughing and stretches across to punch me playfully on the arm. "Oh, come on, Col, you've just passed biology, son!" My mother turns away with a coy giggle and clatters dishes in the sink.

Triggered by this earth-shattering news, my head is now awash with crazy theories and outlandish scenarios; and the possibilities seem as random as the sequences on the fruit-machines at 'Christie's Cavern'. Bearing in mind my mother's peculiar behaviour this summer, we could enter a variety of situations and personalities into Tulip's so-called 'computer' and come up with endless results for her current condition. For a start we have the ubiquitous Quentin Lamont, forever sniffing around and perfectly capable of a lightning sortie into mater's underwear; and let us not forget Mad Farmer Wilkes, admittedly busy with the harvest and the slaughter of wildlife, but, nevertheless, ever eager to introduce mother to the pleasures of the breeding process. Give the mixture another shake and up pops Uncle Buck who was ever forthcoming about his admiration for his sister-in-law. As for Danny on his Great Impregnation Tour… no, I don't wish to even countenance such an atrocity! But, all things considered, you have to admit, the list of suspects is impressive.

All this tripe is gushing through my mind like a sewer in full flood as I drain my teacup and push away the empty plate. I watch my parents as they deal with the dirty dishes. They look so happy and relaxed, Dad pecking her on the cheek and my mother pretending to swipe him with the dishcloth. So, tarry young Paddick, are you being entirely fair to them? Your father isn't exactly over the hill physically. Look at Charlie Chaplin, still knocking out offspring at his age. But why in the name of Lucifer would two ordinary and apparently sane people wish to produce another potential teenager? Surely it defies all logic and Durex advertising campaigns? Good grief, my mother is thirty-seven. Doesn't she know when to stop? Is it even legal?

"You don't seem too pleased, dear," calls my mother, a trifle peevishly, but still smiling dreamily.

"Yeah, 'course I'm pleased," I manage to blurt. "It's just a bit of a shock, that's all."

Dad throws back his head and laughs. "Don't worry, Col, we'll all get used to it in time. Just as long as it isn't triplets!"

Oh, please, spare me further dread. Sometimes your worst nightmares come true. It's bad enough contemplating that I shall be almost seventeen years *older* than the little bugger without joking that my troubles could be tripled!

I scrape back my chair and leave them to their billing and cooing. It's all too uncomfortable to watch, and somehow has the mark of a freak-show about it.

*

Well, here I am in my bedroom again, flat on my back and staring at the ceiling. What an eventful day it has been: three females knocked up; the 'Miracle of the Toast' event; and the even more astounding marvel of my GCE results! Truly a day to remember and enough excitement within twenty-four hours to fill an entire month of a young man's life.

What, I muse dreamily, does the future hold for me now? My options have surprisingly taken an upward swing. It would appear that I am not the incompetent, self-doubting twit that my brain led me to believe I was. From now on, I shall take command of my own destiny and my frontal lobes can bloody well do what they're told.

So, what are my immediate plans then? I suppose the two prominent choices I now have are, either, a career in the printing trade with an apprenticeship under Uncle Ray or joining the sixth-form back at Fayling Grammar with the aim of progressing to university. To study what, Brillo?

Oh, I don't know, what about geography? That seems to be my strongest subject. There's plenty of it out there to see and all I've done so far is read about it. OK, so be it. That's what I'll do. Well, that was flippin' easy.

I permit my eyes to take a languid trip around my bedroom. Suddenly, all these familiar objects have become captivating to me. Is nostalgia setting in earlier than anticipated? Good grief, that could be a sign of maturity; I'm far too young for that. Finally, my wandering gaze is arrested by the little framed photo sitting on my bedside cupboard; Wendy and I smile into Anthea's camera lens. It seems a hundred years since we posed together on that bench, but it was just a few weeks ago. And now that whole era has melted away into the past. The river of time has rolled on leaving these memories stranded upstream on the bank or twisting forever in some permanent little whirlpool in my head. Wendy will merely become a friendly face that smiles poignantly as I pass her in the school corridor or on the High Street. We will have no contact again thanks to that absent turd Danny. Maybe his ship will go down. Hey-ho, I guess it doesn't matter anymore. And with these words of Buddy Holly's ringing in my ears, I spring into action.

I leap from my bed, grab my guitar and plug the lead into my amplifier. Flipping up my shirt  collar and shaking my hair into a dishevelled mess, I turn the volume to full strength and strike the chord of E-major. The window vibrates like a machine-gun, the door handle rattles in protest, and an empty suitcase falls to the floor from the top of my wardrobe. Wow, what a bloody din! I bang out a whole series of introductory chords and begin a screaming version of 'Oh Boy'. The noise is colossal but my adrenaline is pumping and nothing is going to stop me now. The Lucas sisters next door are probably having a heart attack but I can't help that. This is my few moments of utter teenage delinquency and, by Holly, I'm going to enjoy it! With each full blasted syllable of the lyrics my frustrations are diminished and replaced with a sort of euphoria that I've never known before. It's absolutely fantastic!

As I crash the plectrum down across the vibrating strings of the final chord and throw back my head in ecstasy, the bedroom door is flung open and my parents step into the room. But there's something not right... they're beaming with admiration and clapping their hands like seals!

"That was really good, Col," says Dad.

"Yes, dear, quite exciting," enthuses my mother.

No, no, this is not what I wanted... is it? They don't appreciate this kind of stuff surely? If so, we've all been wasting our time trying to shock their generation with our Rock 'n' Roll, lime green socks, and mass destruction of cinema seats. They've just been humouring us on the assumption that we'll grow out of it in the fullness of time. Where have we failed?

I stand and stare at them as they slide their arms around each other's waist. I'm waiting for my mother to comment on my unruly hair or the state of the bedroom, but it doesn't come. Dad makes no reference to the open window and the tetchy neighbours. It's baffling and it doesn't bode well. I shrug, smile wanly and watch them leave hand in hand.

Feeling a trifle deflated, I drop my guitar on the bed, thrust my hands in my pockets and stare aimlessly out of the window. Bugger me if the two lovebirds don't appear below in the back garden and start smooching and giggling in full view of the neighbours. I close my eyes and turn away, totally confused by it all. Suddenly I feel very lonely. My only hope is that time will reveal answers to the growing list of questions I'm compiling in my young head. At this rate I shall need two lifetimes to deal with them all.

But am I being too harsh on my parents? Look at 'em down there; I've never seen them so happy. Dad is struggling with the cork on a cheap bottle of sparkling wine and it suddenly pops out and flies into next door's garden. My mother shrieks with laughter and holds out two wine goblets for Dad to fill. They chink their glasses, each takes a sip, and then they dip towards one another and kiss. Oh, come on, Brillo, be a little more charitable. Isn't this how you imagined you and

Wendy might one day be? Why shouldn't your mum and dad be over the moon and acting like newly-weds? Besides, doesn't this finally prove that she only has eyes for Dad? All those ridiculous theories you had about her infidelities with Lamont, Wilkes, and God knows who else have all been proved wrong. You should be relieved and pleased, you ungrateful twerp! On impulse I lean out of the window.

"Mum," I call.

She glances up and raises her glass to me. "Yes, dear?" she asks, smiling warmly.

"I'm really pleased for you both," I say. And, stone me, I believe I am!

"Thank you, dear," she answers, a note of mild surprise in her voice. "And congratulations to you, too."

Dad wobbles his glass at me. "Yes, well done, son. We'll make a brain surgeon of you yet!"

I collapse back onto my bed and consider the immediate future. (Not, of course, that it actually exists, according to Ronald Lee, mad scientist of this parish, but I'll contemplate it anyway.) And it can't be too awful, surely, in the sixth form. For a start the teaching staff will treat us, more or less, as human beings and potential equals. Many amongst our ranks will be elevated to the dizzy status of 'prefect'; and one will even be crowned 'head prefect' and wield unfathomable power over the plebs in the lower school. Christ, I'm beginning to sound like Flashman! Other perks might include a generous degree of free time and carte-blanche to move around the school uninhibited by many petty restrictions. Yes, I'm warming to the whole prospect now.

But even more appealing is something which has just occurred to me: the arrival last term of Lynne Spicer. Oh yes, how could I have overlooked that mind-blowing event? Lynne suddenly appeared from the Midlands last September and was placed in the 'A' stream of our fifth year in preparation for the GCE exams which we have all recently endured. The word soon galloped around the school that this rather dishy bird had dropped from heaven (Smethwick, actually) and, on clapping eyes on her, it was agreed that she was an example of exceedingly cracking crumpet. As members of the twin 'Z' class, we lads saw less of Lynne than we would have wished. The occasional glimpse of her in her gym kit or on the hockey field was all we could get. But, all in all, she caused quite a stir among the young bucks of the fifth form, and there is now every chance that I might be in a position to further my knowledge of her attributes as I understand from the jungle telegraph, by way of a quick telephone call to Tulip just now, that Lynne also did rather well in her Geography exam. There's always the chance that she has an enquiring mind similar to my own and will be keen on exploration into uncharted territories.

In the meantime, I have nothing to do but enjoy the remaining days of the summer holiday and give my overworked brain a rest. I am pleased to report that I have grown in height this summer by almost two inches. Sadly, the same cannot be said of Wee William who remains stubbornly at his previous stature. However, I've heard it whispered in darkened places (e.g. the back row of the Odeon on a Saturday evening) that girth is just as important as length for many items that we come across in life (pork sausages and marine rope immediately spring to mind). So, let's not feel downhearted, Brillo… there is much to discover in the years ahead! But will time alone answer all my questions? Unfortunately, I have no way of telling.

# THE END

22708225R00164

Printed in Great Britain
by Amazon